I.

HEART

OF THE

LINDEN

WOOD

Wishing you a
fairy tale adventure
of your own!
            —Ekta :♡

IN THE
HEART
OF THE
LINDEN
WOOD

EKTA R. GARG

atmosphere press

Dedication:
To all of the grownups
who still believe magic is real
and that fairy tales aren't just for kids.
This is for you.

THE KEEPER'S QUESTION

In our heart of hearts, where we let few people enter, at some point we've all wished someone dead.

Does it sound harsh to say this? I suppose some might consider it outrageous. Because to wish someone dead would mean we've gone past the point of revenge and simply want that person gone so our own pain can end. It also means we've lived through every level of that pain first, hoping things would change, wishing it away. Wishing someone dead means you have nothing left, that your soul is empty and your heart will never be the same.

I'm something of an expert on that.

All of us have experienced the searing pain of betrayal by someone we once trusted. A friend who knew our deepest secrets. A guardian who vowed to nurture us. A love who promised us the sky above the sun and the dust between the stars.

The betrayal I experienced was the last kind. Vincent, the prince of Linden, was impatient to take his throne. He believed the power I possessed would help him, so he leaned close and whispered promises in my ear. He told me I meant more to him than everything, including the kingdom. He lied.

When I discovered his dishonesty, the cut ran so deep I lost my heart and haven't regained it since.

But this story isn't just mine. This story belongs to all of us whom Vincent betrayed. Because he did go on to become king, and he ruled Linden with spite and distrust of anyone who questioned him. He married for political gain and had a child so Linden would stay within the family. Then he betrayed his son.

He belittled his son, Christopher, telling him he would never have the courage, the strength, the heart to rule Linden with any significance. He set himself on a pedestal so high that when the boy tilted his head back to look up, he fell and landed in a large hole of self-doubt.

When Christopher came of age, Vincent died in an accident. He should have had that accident much sooner. Not for my sake, you understand. I no longer had my heart; what did it matter to me what happened to Vincent? But I did wish that those under his rule would have gained their freedom from his tyranny sooner.

Christopher took the throne, and for the beginning of his reign the people of Linden held their breaths. Would the new king also work them beyond the state of exhaustion? Demand more in taxes than they could give? Would King Christopher taunt and disparage those under him as his father had done before?

He did not. Many Lindeners suspected he had suffered as they had, albeit as the heir to the throne. In quiet dinners together or crossing through the wood, when the people of the kingdom thought they were alone—even though I could hear them—they confessed how much they pitied Christopher. He must have endured worse than they did.

The new king didn't have much experience at court, but he knew how his father led. When the senior-most councilor placed the crown on his head, Christopher chose in that moment to lead his people in stark contrast. Where Vincent showed anger, Christopher showed kindness. Where Vincent extracted a person's life blood, Christopher requested his people's hard work. In every way, he endeavored to be nothing *like his father.*

This included the woman he married. When Christopher's mother was alive, she didn't voice her opinion about how the evil king ruled kingdom and castle. She wasted away, sick in heart and health, until she died.

Christopher treated his wife with a courtesy his father had not extended his mother, and the new queen became more than a figurehead to rule by his side. She became a trusted confidante. A friend. She gave back to Christopher every ounce of self-assurance the evil king had stripped from him.

She believed in him without any hesitation.

It took time for him to learn to trust, but Christopher returned the love tenfold, a hundredfold, to his new queen. People rarely saw one without the other. Under Vincent, he cowered like a plant left too long in the sun; with his wife, Christopher unfurled like a nourished tree to stand tall. I watched all of this from afar. It was too late for me to find my heart, but Christopher found the light of his and would do right by Linden and its people.

This is the power of love. It moves us to do things greater than we could imagine and redeems us. When Christopher needed someone, desperately, to believe he could rule a kingdom that had grown suspicious of its monarch, the new queen stood by his side to show the people—and him—that she supported him. The people regained their trust in the king and the queen, in the monarchy's ability to keep them safe and fed. The story seemed destined for a "happily ever after."

And yet...and yet.

Something has changed. I can sense it in the way the trees have slowed their growth. I am the Keeper of the Linden Wood, it is true, but my power will only last as long as I do.

This last fact—the revelation of it—makes me wonder whether I should have gone looking for my heart after all.

CHAPTER I

Once upon a time, in a kingdom far, far away, the queen screamed in pain and the king froze in fear.

She writhed on the birthing bed as another pain wracked her body. Her ladies-in-waiting scurried, some bringing warm towels, some lighting scented candles around the room to soothe the queen's anguish. Geraldine, the healer and lead midwife, wiped the sweat from the queen's forehead and neck with a clean cloth.

"Breathe, your majesty," she said, "just as we practiced."

King Christopher of Linden stood rooted to the floor not far from the bed. When he had walked Lily to the birthing chamber that morning, she only whimpered every ten or so steps. After each whimper, however, she squeezed his hand and smiled.

Nothing had prepared him for this sheer force that coursed through his wife as if it would rend her in two.

They had been working in the royal study on a trade treaty when a short exclaim dropped from Lily's lips in a rounded O. Christopher sent the queen's lady-in-waiting to find Geraldine, and he helped Lily stand. She rested a hand on her swollen belly, and her lower lip tremored.

"Lily?" Christopher asked, his hands fluttering close but not touching her.

She licked her lips, the apprehension in her eyes the only thing telling Christopher how she felt. "I believe the time has come to welcome the heir to your throne, your highness."

"Shall I call for a rolling chair?" Christopher asked. He searched her frame from head to foot as if the secret to relieving her discomfort hid in the locks of her hair or in a more comfortable shoe. She shook her head.

"I believe"—she swallowed hard—"I would like to walk, your majesty, if you will assist me."

To Christopher it seemed as though an age passed between the study and the birthing chamber where Geraldine had already assembled her team of assistants. A soldier darted into the chamber and did a quick circuit of the room to guarantee safety. As he pushed open the door for the king and queen, Lily sighed with relief at the sight of the bed. Geraldine acknowledged Christopher with a deep curtsy, imitated by every woman present. Then the healer went back to her tasks.

Now Christopher stood helplessly by the queen's side. In the seven years since his coronation, no one had ever ignored his presence in any space until now. He watched as the midwife made brisk trips to different parts of the room.

She stopped at a cart with steel instruments gleaming in the light of the large lamps and bobbed her head as though counting. Then she went to another cart holding an astonishing number of clean towels and thumbed through them. When Geraldine focused her attention on a knot of assistants in a third corner, a voice called Christopher's attention back.

"Go, your majesty," Lily said, the exhaustion in her voice belying the sparkle in her eyes. "The treaty remains unfinished. Please, finish your work."

Christopher squeezed her hand with gentleness. "Surely I can do some good here."

Her eyes screwed shut, and her face contracted as another birthing pain took her in its grip. Lily's grasp made

Christopher hiss, echoing the noises Lily made. Her own gasps punctuated her groans.

Geraldine appeared at Christopher's shoulder.

"There, there, your highness," she murmured, her full concentration on Lily, "not much longer now."

The healer uncurled Lily's fingers from Christopher's hand. She offered him a sympathetic grin, but her eyes conveyed a clear message. No, he would be of no help here. He turned his attention back to Lily, sure she would ask him to stay, but she had retreated into an unknown world where exhaling her pain seemed her only goal.

Christopher inclined his head to acknowledge Geraldine's help; in Lily's ear, he murmured a wish to be well. Then he left the birthing chamber. A soldier followed at a discreet distance as Christopher returned to the study and made an elaborate show of sitting at his desk. The gentleman-in-waiting standing by the door squared his shoulders, ready to fulfill even the smallest command.

The king frowned at the thick sheaf of papers on his desk, the latest draft of a treaty offering more reasonable trading terms to the compact kingdom of Fair Haven than his predecessor had extended. In the years since his crowning, he had begun making reparations on the trade treaties with all of the nearby kingdoms. He also took Lily's advice to reach farther than the borders of their current allies, and they had discussed, argued, written, and rewritten terms until every treaty was perfect.

"Kingdoms close to us will know of the wood," Lily said, referring to the famed primary export of Linden, "but others farther away will have only heard stories. They will want assurances. You cannot offer all of them the same terms you offered Wyndemere."

They exchanged a smile, and Christopher pulled her in

for a kiss. Nearly eight years earlier, after his father's death but before ascending the throne, he had traveled to Wyndemere to re-open a dialogue with King Malcolm. He came home with signed treaties and a promise to return to marry the princess.

Christopher glanced at the door to his study now. Should he return to the birthing chamber and ask after Lily's welfare? She had urged him back to their work, true, yet he was the king. More than that, he was a husband and soon to be a father. That last thought made him rise and take half a step toward the door of the study.

But it seemed as though only women are welcome during the birth. And what would Lily think if she discovered I had wiled away my time here? No, better to continue what we started.

With a conflicted heart, he settled himself in the chair and reread the opening paragraphs he and Lily wrote together.

Geraldine wiped perspiration from the queen's forehead yet again, demonstrating to Queen Lily how to breathe in even measures. The monarch followed her lead, mimicking the breathing. She scrunched her face in an effort not to scream again and let loose a final breath as the latest birthing pain released her from its vise.

"My courage seems to...have failed...me," Queen Lily said as she panted.

"You are about to become a mother, your majesty," Geraldine said with a smile. "You've already shown a world of courage."

She'd led many women through the birthing process. For almost two decades now, she'd delivered babies in and around her village of Ingleside. Never before, however, had the royal court summoned her. Out of the hundreds who answered the call to become the queen's personal healer and midwife, Queen Lily had chosen Geraldine. Others may have delivered more babies, but no one wanted the opportunity as much as Geraldine did.

The queen clasped her hand as she would a friend's, and Geraldine patted it.

"I'll check the baby one more time," she added, going to the end of the bed where two ladies-in-waiting held the queen's feet in the air.

Queen Lily exhaled a burst of air in exhaustion. "Thank you, Geraldine."

The midwife smiled in response and used her fingers to probe inside the queen. She moved with care and caution. As her fingers pressed against the queen's internal anatomy, however, her smile faded.

"What's wrong?" Queen Lily asked.

Geraldine shook her head. "Nothing. It's just—"

A torrent of blood and bodily fluids burst all over the bed, making Geraldine jump back, and the queen screamed again. The mouths of both ladies-in-waiting dropped open. After a moment, one of them closed her mouth and her face turned pale.

Geraldine's heart drummed. The queen screamed a third time. This time, the scream sounded different.

"Geraldine!"

The midwife saw the baby's head then, and another birthing pain began.

"Push, your majesty," Geraldine commanded, ignoring the unfamiliar panic making her chest tight.

The queen did as ordered. As the baby came out, Geraldine placed one hand under its head and another on its chest to help it. Her hands came across extra ridges just under the baby's chin, and the tightness in her chest threatened to cut off her breathing.

No, please, not the life cord, anything but the—

Geraldine guided the infant out of its mother's body, but by the time the legs came she knew what had happened.

"Is my baby all right? I cannot hear it crying. Why am I unable to hear my baby?"

"She is dead," the pale-faced lady-in-waiting blurted. "The life cord is around her neck."

The queen screamed again. And again.

Geraldine used a pair of scissors to snip the cord from the baby, but the woman was right. The baby's blue face and lack of movement told the tale. Still, she took a moment to wipe the little girl's face—*a princess*, Geraldine thought, the words dull in her brain—and handed her to Danielle, one of the assistants the castle had found for her from the healers in the capital city.

"Clean her body, and check her once more," Geraldine said in a low voice.

Danielle nodded and took the bundle as carefully as if accepting a blown-glass vase, but ridges of sorrow made her eyes narrow. This woman had worked long enough as a healer to know the truth. The baby would never draw a breath.

Another gush of blood brought Geraldine's attention back to the queen. She thrust her fingers back inside the queen's body, a gentle touch belying the need for speed. Her fingers searched inside the queen's anatomy for answers; when she got them, she sucked in a sharp breath.

She searched the room for another assistant; the fates

knew the king allowed her twice as many as she thought she needed, but now she thanked his generosity ten times over.

"You, girl," she said to a young woman in the corner transfixed by the episode. "The cart, now!"

The girl squeaked with a start then ran to the rolling cart of instruments Geraldine had set out the day before "just in case." She'd waved a hand in dramatic fashion over the cart and joked to Queen Lily about first babies testing their mothers' patience by taking their time.

"Good to teach them a little discipline early on," she said, and she and the queen laughed together.

Now no one was laughing. No one was smiling, and Geraldine kept wondering whether others in the room could hear how hard her heart banged inside her chest. It thudded in her ears too, and she had trouble hearing her own voice.

"Over here. Quickly, girl! Pass me the cotton wads."

The assistant grabbed two fistfuls of cotton and thrust them in Geraldine's direction. Just as she plucked a few, the assistant fumbled and dropped the rest.

"Foolish girl! Pick those up! They can't be allowed to get dirty, otherwise I can't use them."

The girl nodded, eyes wide in fear, and bobbed to the floor. She snatched up the wads and sorted through them. Geraldine waited for two or three precious moments to make sure the girl examined each one before setting it back on the cart then turned back to the bed. Queen Lily had begun perspiring even more now, and her own face had turned pale.

"Geraldine, my baby!"

"Your highness, we must take care of you first," Geraldine replied. "Can someone bring me a large candle?"

"But my baby. The heir to the throne!"

The midwife spared a glance for the queen between the woman's knees then turned back to saving her life.

"Your majesty, you must relax and let me focus on this first. Then we can talk about...other matters."

Another assistant appeared at Geraldine's side with an oversized candle, the four wicks already lit. She examined the queen and tried every method she'd ever learned to clot the blood. It refused to do so.

"Mistress Geraldine?"

She looked up at Danielle who carried the grief of an entire kingdom on her brow. Geraldine swallowed hard but fought to maintain her composure. She nodded.

"It's all right, Danielle; you did well," Geraldine said. "Prepare the child for..."

Tears welled in Danielle's eyes, but she nodded back and turned away. Geraldine could see the infant lying still on a table in the corner. Oh, how she'd wanted the child to live.

"Is that my baby?"

Geraldine whipped her head back toward the queen who tried to push herself to a sitting position. Her feet remained in the hands of her ladies-in-waiting, but Queen Lily tugged her right leg back. The ladies looked to Geraldine, panic on their faces.

"Your majesty, no," Geraldine said. "You can't move."

"But I must get to my baby; I must help her!" Queen Lily said in a wail.

Her dark hair, damp from the exertion of giving birth, lay in loose strands. The large brown eyes that had sparkled the day before at the joke they'd shared now filled with tears.

"I cannot let anything happen to my child, Geraldine!"

"Danielle," Geraldine said over her shoulder, "chloroform!"

Danielle dashed from the table with the infant to another table. She grabbed a clean cotton cloth and doused it in chloroform then came back. Geraldine jerked her chin in the queen's direction.

"Over her mouth and nose. If she keeps moving like this, she'll rip even more tissue."

"No," the queen begged, "please, no, I just want my baby. Please, Geraldine, my baby!"

The last came out in a sob that subsided as the chloroform took effect. As the queen lost consciousness bit by bit, Geraldine increased her speed. She barked at another assistant to thread a needle for her and whipped the stitches as fast as she could to stop the bleeding. Even so, her heart continued to pound. After losing this much blood—with the loss of her child adding more weight to her—the queen's chances of surviving also came into question.

The midwife gulped as she laced the last stitch in place. She'd never lost a patient in childbirth; never. She didn't intend to start today.

"Clean her legs and redress her," she said, "and change these linens. Burn them. She won't want anything to remind her of this day."

As the assistants burst into a flurry of activity, Geraldine turned away from the queen's bed and went to the oversized wash basin in the corner of the room.

We lost the child, she thought, the words burning into a ball of grief in her throat. *How did...? The king... How could I... What will I tell him? What did I do? What could have gone wrong? How do I—*

"Mistress Geraldine!" Danielle called.

Dread made Geraldine cough hard at her assistant's tone. She yanked a cloth to dry her hands, sparing only a glance for the drips of pale red fluttering to the floor.

Geraldine went to the head of the queen's bed and put two fingers to Queen Lily's throat. No beating; no movement. She checked the queen's wrist next then snatched her heart-hearing tool from the bedside table where she'd abandoned it earlier and stuck the earpieces into her ears. With quick movements, she placed the dial in different places on the queen's chest.

No beating; no movement.

Acid roiled in Geraldine's stomach as she climbed onto the queen's bed. Straddling the monarch and ignoring the gasps around the room, she grabbed the queen's palms and forced them to face up to place her own palms on top. Swallowing hard, she closed her eyes and tried to skirr the queen, willing that ancient power of the fates to work so she could use her energy to search the queen's body and find out what had gone wrong.

Despite every effort to stay calm, Geraldine didn't feel the telltale tingle between her hands and the queen's that told her the skirring was working. Instead of trying again, she placed her hands on top of one another and pumped the queen's chest as hard as she could. Several pumps later, she stopped and put two fingers to the queen's neck again.

No beating.

She tried pumping the queen's heart again, but nothing happened. Danielle rushed to the edge of the bed with smelling salts, but that didn't rouse the queen either. Geraldine pumped the queen's chest a third time, but she achieved nothing.

"Nooo!" Geraldine yelled, shocking even herself at the sound.

"Mistress Geraldine?" Danielle asked.

Geraldine hung her head, tears dripping. The pale face of the queen of Linden had become even more pale. The midwife clenched her fists to keep herself from beating on the queen's chest to make her heart start beating again.

She glanced at the oversized clock hanging on the wall to her right. Had the entire ordeal really taken only minutes?

She felt as if she'd lost an entire lifetime.

As sobs in the room reached her, Geraldine realized she had. The lifetime of a young princess who would never grow up to rule the kingdom. The lifetime of a king whose face burst into a sunbeam every time he saw his queen.

The king.

Geraldine climbed off the bed and straightened her healer's apron. She glanced at her hands and noticed that the queen's blood still stained them. With measured steps, she made her way back to the basin in the corner of the room.

"Danielle," she said, a tremor in her voice, "send a messenger to the king. He will want to bid his queen farewell."

Despite the severity of the situation—or perhaps because of it—Danielle bobbed in a quick curtsy and went to the door. Geraldine looked around at the hexagonal shape of the space as if seeing it for the first time. Tapestries lined the walls with scenes from famous stories. The queen had said she liked the room because it made her think of all the stories she wanted to tell her own child one day, real and fanciful, that would make the child a better ruler.

Geraldine's breath came in shallow spurts, but she didn't let her face betray what she knew. The queen had chosen her from all the midwives in the kingdom of Linden because of her ability to command a situation. Today, however...today, she needed more than her knowledge or her skills. She'd needed a dose of magic.

She scrubbed her arms and fingers. The blood swirled in the basin, taking all of the hopes of a kingdom with it. She didn't know when her salty tears joined the streaks of red.

She'd lost a child. She'd lost *the* child. She'd also lost the queen—her breath hitched—and now Geraldine had no doubt she would receive the stiffest of punishments.

Maybe I could have...I could have asked for the chloroform sooner, she thought as she continued to scrub hands and fingers that were now clean. *Did Danielle put the right dosage? I should have checked it myself. The queen... We just... Yesterday she and I... What will happen to me now? I couldn't have done anything, could I? Have I failed?*

The thought burned through her from head to toe. She had wanted, more than anything, for her care of the queen to be a new start. What she earned from the queen's delivery would have guaranteed a new life away from her husband, Sullivan. A fresh beginning for herself and her son, Alistair. The birth of the heir to Linden should have brought with it all the auspiciousness that new babies do, not just for the kingdom but especially for Geraldine.

Now, in this moment, fear gripped Geraldine's heart and squeezed all hope out of it.

"Mistress Geraldine," a voice murmured from behind her right shoulder. "Mistress Geraldine, the messenger should be back soon."

Geraldine nodded, turning her attention to everyone in the room. No matter what this day brought now, they would meet the king in a presentable state. She would not let the impending anguish of an entire kingdom show in their attire. As she returned to the cart of instruments to supervise their cleaning, however, she couldn't stop her grief from dribbling in streams down her face.

CHAPTER 2

Christopher stared at the third page of the treaty, making notes of paragraphs to discuss with Lily later.

Will she require a long time to recover from the birth? She may want some time with the baby in the first few days. But Lily has always returned to our work, no matter her health.

He remembered when, in their second year of marriage, Lily contracted a terrible cold that left her coughing as though her lungs were hollow drums. Even then, with chilled cloths pressed to her head to combat a fever, Lily had insisted on discussing state matters. Christopher instructed the ladies-in-waiting to remove all official papers from the room where Lily lay recovering, and they had fought bitterly about it once she returned to her full health.

Just as the king debated the possibility of another argument versus insisting Lily take care of herself after delivering the baby, a sharp rap sounded at the door. Before he could instruct his gentleman-in-waiting to see to it, the door burst open. Martin, the master of the royal Linden guard, rushed in. Christopher read the expression on the face of his oldest friend and rose to his feet.

"What is it, Martin?"

"A messenger has come, your highness, about the queen."

Christopher had already taken three strides toward the door in the time it took Martin to finish speaking.

"What news?" Christopher asked as he followed Martin

out and did his best to ignore the finger of apprehension that poked him. "Is her majesty all right?"

Martin moved down the main corridor that connected the private apartments of the royal family and gave a quick nod to two other guards. They fell in step behind the king. Christopher kept his attention forward, quickening his pace.

"I believe the midwife has summoned you," Martin said, his neutral tone at odds with his speed.

"Martin—"

The head guard shook his head. "I have no other information to provide, your highness."

The two guards trotted behind to keep up. Within minutes, Christopher stood outside the birthing chamber. He waited a moment then put his hand to the large circular handle with the carved wooden tree in its middle, a replica of the kingdom's seal to show its most prized possession and its greatest strength. During his childhood and his education in the ways of court, Christopher was taught to believe the wood of Linden comprised the kingdom's pride and joy.

His marriage to the queen transformed his opinion; to him, Lily was everything.

Martin gave a sharp rap at the door then glanced at the guards behind them and tilted his head toward the room. The men darted in to assess any potential threats. Seconds later, they rejoined Christopher and Martin in the corridor with drawn faces.

"Is it safe, Soldier John?" Martin asked.

John's gaze fell to the floor. "It is safe, Guardsmaster, but..."

Christopher charged ahead. He needed to see Lily. Now.

He shoved the doors open and walked into the chamber then stopped short. Geraldine stood on the near side of the bed and dropped into a deep curtsy. The other assistants in the room who saw him right away imitated her gesture and tugged on the skirts of the women whose attention was elsewhere.

Christopher's focus went straight to the bed and the pallid face of his wife.

"Lily?"

His voice must not have reached her, because she did not turn to him. He took two steps closer and stopped again. He wondered for a moment if she was asleep, if delivering their child had exhausted her so that she could not wait any longer to rest before he came to congratulate her on the royal birth. Surely it could not be anything else.

"The baby," he said, looking around the room at all the women still in a half-kneel. "Where is my child?"

The women rose, the rustling of their skirts breaking the eerie silence. Someone—he could not say who—made a strange sound. If he had been standing anywhere but a birthing chamber, he would have thought it sounded like a sob breaking lips and hearts. But that could not be the case. Not here, in a room designed for celebration and well-wishing and faces flushed with fatigue but also joy.

Christopher examined the faces before him. Many of them were flushed, yes, but not a single one contained happiness. He continued searching and found the crying sound. It came from a woman by the far wall next to a table. His eyes went to the table, and he saw a bundle of cloth. A bundle just large enough for a newborn infant.

He saw no face peeking out, however. No coos or soft cries. This figure was covered in white, the same way his people covered their loved ones when they—

He rushed to Lily's bedside and found he could not breathe; neither, it seemed, could she.

"Lily?" The word almost choked in the breath he fought to exhale.

She did not respond.

He caressed her cheek then sat on the bed and pulled her into a tight embrace, ignoring the way her head lolled out of control. His hand made it to the back of her head in the darkness of her gorgeous hair. In the last months of pregnancy her hair gained a glossy sheen, and he had spent several nights burying his face in it before he brought his lips to hers and—

"Lily, please," he blurted.

The sobbing in the room multiplied then, came from more souls, more hearts. Christopher squeezed her tight and drew back. His breathing came in shallow spurts as if the air in the room were diminishing.

"Geraldine, revive her," he called without looking away from Lily's face. "She is unable to breathe, and she needs your attention now."

"Your majesty, I can't—"

He glared over his shoulder.

"You will do as I say, Healer. Revive her. This is your vocation, is it not?"

Geraldine bowed her head but did not move.

Rage filled him. Why did the healer do nothing? He loosened his hold on Lily and jerked his head one way and the other, scanning the room for someone, *anyone*, who would step forward to help. No one did.

"Have you found the insolence to defy an order from your king? Assist the queen *now*."

"We've lost her, your majesty," Geraldine said. "She fought for herself and the baby, but in the end there was nothing any of us could have done."

His heart dropped into his feet, and his lower jaw trembled.

Christopher turned back to his wife. Laying her against

the oversized pillow at her back, he smoothed a few strands of hair. He picked up her hand, pressed his lips to her knuckles, and closed his eyes tight against the tears slipping down his face. One slid to the valley between her joints and touched his mouth. Its saltiness made him shudder.

No, Lily, he screamed inside his head, *I need you! How am I to rule Linden without you by my side?*

He coughed hard. When his tears slowed to a trickle and disappeared, he put her hand down. The heaviness in his feet made him turn around at a slow pace, and the healer moved back to a respectable distance.

"Who is responsible for this?"

Geraldine's eyes flicked to the queen and then to him. "Your highness, no one could have saved her. She'd lost so much blood that—"

Christopher took a step closer toward her, and she retreated. He sensed everyone in the room taking a step back, but they no longer mattered. What mattered was that Lily was... Lily was...and this woman was the last person to care for her.

"You were chosen, were you not, Healer, for your abilities?"

His tone lowered the temperature in the room. Geraldine clenched her apron so tight her hands turned white, but he did not take his eyes off her.

"Yes," she replied, her voice just above a whisper.

"Then why is my wife... Why is the queen..."

He wanted to hit the healer, and the realization stupefied him. He wanted to grab the fat candles lighting the room and throw them down, stamping out their light. How dare they brighten the chamber when his entire life had just plunged into darkness?

"Answer me, Healer. Why is the queen—"

"Because I couldn't save her."

The healer clamped her hands over her mouth, and her eyes screwed shut. Christopher clenched his fists to stop himself from harming anyone. He glanced around at the women again, enraged that not a single one had helped Lily.

"You will appear before myself and the royal councilors in two hours' time," he said, his voice still as cold as a sheet of ice encasing a pond in winter. "You will explain yourself, and you will accept the consequences of your ignorance and incompetence."

The healer's face crumpled.

"I will explain as best I can, your majesty," she said in a quiet voice, "but we all lost the queen today, and nothing we did could have prevented it. Her majesty's loss didn't come about because of ignorance or incompetence. The fates willed it so."

The fates? *How dare this woman lay her failure at the feet of the fates?*

"Two hours," he snapped, then charged back out of the room before anyone could see the anguish in his heart manifest itself on his face.

Christopher marched out of the room, the soldiers and Martin following close behind. He needed to keep moving. He knew if he slowed down, the reality of Lily's death would catch him.

Death; she is dead.

The thought brought him to a short stop, and the guards and Martin stumbled. He heard them collecting themselves behind him, heard Martin scolding the guards for not maintaining a respectful distance. Soldier John tried to argue that they were simply trying to keep apace with the king. As Martin reprimanded them, everyone's words seemed to zoom down a long tunnel away from him. His pulse picked up speed.

"Your highness? King Christopher?"

The edges of Christopher's vision darkened. Had evening fallen already? Why were the lamps in the hall still unlit? Everyone knew he liked the castle to be well lit in the evenings.

"...Sir Martin! ...his chambers... carry him if need be..."

More boots clattered against the floor. A strange moan filled his ears, and Christopher tried to find its source. His chest burned as if a corkscrew tightened the strings of his heart, twisting them, making it impossible to breathe. He opened his mouth to tell the guards, but the words did not come.

"Martin?" he mumbled.

"Have no fear, your majesty," a voice called. "You are safe. We are taking you to your apartments."

He tried to nod in response, but the world went black.

The king sat in the anteroom of his private apartments, his head in his hands.

A knock sounded at the door, but Christopher ignored it. His gentleman-in-waiting answered, and after a moment Christopher heard Martin's voice. The men at the door exchanged a few words, although Christopher hardly cared what they said. Nothing anyone said now would matter ever again.

The door to the room shut, and footsteps approached.

"Your highness, I have taken the liberty of asking the kitchen staff to send some tea and a light refreshment," Martin said.

His guardsmaster pushed forward the wheeled cart that

held a covered tray. Christopher did not acknowledge the food nor the man he had known since childhood. The man who became a surrogate brother when young Prince Christopher had no other companion. Despite the minimal gap in their ages Martin had taught him a great deal about the world, but Christopher doubted even Martin could give him a point of reference for how to deal with this.

"King Christopher," Martin said, his voice firmer this time, "you have set an audience with the midwife to begin an hour from now. You must, even in this darkest hour, care for yourself."

"She is gone, Martin," Christopher said, throwing his hands in the air. "Gone. The only woman I have ever loved. The only woman who knew my every wish, my every dream. I have no one left who will ever care for me that way."

Martin stood at attention as all the guards did, but his shoulders rounded just a bit.

"We all care for you, my king," he said. "You have an entire kingdom of residents who loved the queen as much as you did...do. Your loss is theirs as well."

"She was my wife, Martin! My wife! No one's loss is as great as mine!"

Martin bowed his head. "Yet we all share in it, and we will need your leadership on how to mourn her and how to honor her."

Christopher dropped his head in his hands again.

How could this be? How will I go on without her?

After regaining consciousness in his bed, he had bolted upright. Despite the protests of Martin and the soldiers and gentlemen-in-waiting who surrounded his bed, he scrambled out of the sheets, yanked off his royal outer robe off, and flung it across the room then stormed to the anteroom where he had dropped onto the chaise. For the last three-quarters of an hour, the same question rolled in his head until he felt dizzy.

How will I go on without her?

He stared now at the cool marble floor. His eyes had found a pattern in the stone that looked like a crocodile standing on its hind legs. He opened his mouth to call to Lily so he could show her the shape and ask her if she saw the same. Then he remembered he could no longer call to her.

How will I go on without her?

The question continued to circle in his head until he could not concentrate on anything else. Not on the crocodile, not on an audience with the healer, and certainly not on a ridiculous offering of tea and pastries. None of those things would bring her back.

Lily had known she was the love of his life. He never said it where others could hear, but their subjects knew it as truth. Their smiles as he and Lily greeted them on holidays or during festivals told the residents of Linden how its king and queen regarded one another, particularly because their relationship appeared nothing like that of the previous king and queen. Whenever Christopher and Lily stood side by side on those occasions, their hands remained clasped between them.

Whose hand would he hold now? Whose fingers would trace the diagonal scar on his forehead from the riding accident he had as a child? Who would clasp his shoulder during meetings with the royal council to let him know he had done well or needed to draw back from his ire?

"Your highness?"

"What is it, Martin?" Christopher asked, his head springing up.

Martin's jaw hardened. "Sire, you must prepare yourself for the audience with the healer. Please, eat something. At the least, you must drink something. And change your clothing. The eyes of the council and, by way of them, the entire kingdom, will be on you."

Christopher glanced around the room; under normal circumstances, an attendant would be called to help the king with his attire.

"I believe simple garments will suffice, your majesty. No need to worry about overly formal clothing at this time."

The turnscrew in his chest tightened another millimeter as Christopher rose to his feet. Martin gestured toward the bedchamber of the royal apartment, waited a moment to make sure he would follow, and then strode with purpose toward the room Christopher and Lily shared. After entering to assess the security of the space, Martin returned and held the door open.

Christopher entered and saw the room as if for the first time. Straight ahead sat the bed of the bedchamber itself, but he did not let his gaze linger there. To his left, another set of double doors led onto their private balcony. On the right, he looked at the oversized chest of drawers that held every-day items; undergarments and the like. Behind the bed, inside the wall, ran the long built-in wardrobe he and Lily had shared every day for the last seven years.

As Christopher crossed the room, flashes of the queen whipped through his memory. He saw her on their wedding day when he lifted the veil to greet her at the altar, a secret smile on her face. He remembered nights on the balcony when they discussed—and sometimes argued—the finer points of the law or trade negotiations. Lily had paved the way for so many of them. The fates knew how much Christopher depended on her; his father's reign had left so many relationships fractured.

His father. The former king, King Vincent. He, too, had

died, and with him Christopher lost the only family he had, such as it was.

Christopher shook his head hard as if he could knock loose the worst moments of his life from his mind.

He entered the wardrobe from the left-hand door and stopped. Rows of clothing on either side greeted him as if nothing had happened, as if nothing had changed since that morning. A quiet voice in the back of Christopher's head warned he should not linger, but he could not help himself. He walked the length of the narrow room, letting his hand run over the variety of fabrics and styles.

Lily took such pride in dressing herself and him as well. Within the first three years of their marriage, all the clothes he had previously owned disappeared. One robe at a time, one pair of pants at a time, Lily had enlisted tailors to source and stitch the finest garments for him. Not a single item in the wardrobe had appeared without her approval first.

Christopher found himself standing on her end now. Dozens of ballgowns, dresses for state dinners, divided skirts for riding—all these and more greeted him. The variety of fabrics flicked beneath his fingers rivaled only by the color choices.

As his eyes traveled down the rows, they fell upon a gown hanging from a rod facing him.

The simple pale green—*What had she called the color? Sage*—made Lily think of spring, she said. That morning as they made their way to the birthing chamber, he remembered now, Lily had taken a moment to ask a lady-in-waiting to take out the gown and prepare it to be worn.

"I hardly think you should concern yourself with your attire, your majesty," Christopher said as they continued down the corridor.

Lily's face screwed into a tight knot against another

round of pain, and when it ended she licked her lips then attempted a smile.

"I will wear it when I greet Lindeners for the first time after the baby has arrived," she said. She had spent the better part of the night pacing the floor in discomfort but still looked happy.

"Do you plan to ride in a carriage holding the child aloft for all to shower him with coins and flowers?"

She rolled her eyes affectionately.

"I thought it appropriate to wear for the season and that we might appear on the balcony, as we always do; our new little family."

Christopher's face twisted in a strange way. With horror, he realized he had been smiling. *Smiling.* At a memory.

Because that was all she would remain now: a memory. Lily would not wear that dress. She would not greet the kingdom as a new mother, would no longer spend her days designing ways to make life better for Linden. She would no longer stand before him with shining eyes and tell him she was proud of him.

His face contorted again, this time in anger. He whirled on his heel and went down to his side, yanking fresh clothes from their hangers so hard they swung on the rods. One hanger flipped in the air and landed on the floor behind him.

The healer will not do this to other people, other families, he thought. *She will not take anyone else's happiness. This I vow, for Lily's sake.*

Tears formed a knot in his throat, but he fought them as he dressed. With a long look at the gown on the hanger at the far end, he strode with purpose out of the wardrobe and his bedchamber. Martin trotted after him.

The time had come for justice.

CHAPTER 3

Geraldine paced in front of the entrance to the petitioners' courtroom, dry-washing her hands. She never imagined she would appear before the royal council about the death of a patient. The fact that the patient was the queen... She stopped, gulped a breath, and kept pacing.

"Mistress Geraldine, truly, you did all you could," Danielle murmured.

Her first assistant sat on a bench against the wall. Geraldine didn't know where she got the fortitude to stay still. Ever since the confrontation with the king, Geraldine hadn't stopped moving: cleaning instruments, changing into fresh clothing, unfolding and refolding clothes in the modest trunk she kept in her tiny room in the castle.

"The queen lost too much blood, and the agony from delivering a stillborn child..."

Geraldine stopped to stare at Danielle. The woman shrank; her eyes dropped to the floor. She folded her hands into tight loops of fingers and knuckles, and Geraldine went back to pacing.

None of this was Danielle's fault. In truth, as Danielle pointed out, none of it was Geraldine's fault either. Since retreating to her room, she'd gone over the entire matter in her mind a dozen times or more and came to the same conclusion every time.

I did everything I could. I worked as fast as possible,

made all the right decisions. Nothing could have changed the outcome.

She thought of Widow Hannity then, wondering whether her mentor would have made different decisions. Whether the widow would have saved the queen. Doubt made Geraldine's knees wobble.

Just then the tall doors to the courtroom opened, and a page exited. Thrusting out his chest, he lifted his chin with the importance of his station. His eyes flitted to Geraldine before looking straight ahead again.

"The royal court summons Geraldine of Ingleside," he intoned. "Present yourself for your case."

My case? she wondered, craning her neck to look into the hall. *Did the king reconsider? I could get the chance to explain what happened.*

It made sense. The king may have ruled Linden and its formidable economic trade, but he was a man after all. A man who'd just lost his wife. It was a given he'd speak in haste and anger.

The page looked at her for a moment with expectation.

"I...I am Geraldine of Ingleside," she replied.

He bowed.

"You will follow me," he said, his tone a little less official now.

Despite the wisp of hope, dread fluttered in her belly. She turned to Danielle who had already started crossing the space. When Danielle held out a hand, Geraldine squeezed it. Danielle squeezed back.

The page walked down the long aisle of the court, a rectangular space with pews for people to watch the proceedings. At the head of the room on a dais sat the king and his six royal councilors, three men and three women, all stony-faced. The king looked composed, yet he also appeared to have aged a decade in the two hours since she'd last seen him.

She pressed her hands to her stomach and followed the page to the podium at the side of the room. From here, she realized, she could see both the royal council and the constituents in attendance. A handful of people had come to court today, and Geraldine searched their faces for reactions to any pronouncements the king made before she entered. Most looked bored. One elderly gentleman in the back seemed to be nodding off.

"Geraldine of Ingleside," one of the councilors announced.

Her attention snapped to the front of the room.

"You are called to this court," the councilor continued, "because of your hand in the death of the queen and her unborn child."

Gasps raced across the aisles of audience members, and Geraldine looked at the floor.

"No!" exclaimed a woman in the front-most pew.

"It can't be!" another said.

"Not the queen!"

"The baby!"

Most of the people scuttled out of the courtroom, their footsteps slapping the floor like reprimands. Geraldine dared to look up. The few who stayed trained their eyes on her, and all of them shared the same stunned expression. Her cheeks burned. She couldn't untangle her fingers from their place at her waist.

"Geraldine of Ingleside."

She turned her attention back to her right. The king. His expression made Geraldine's mouth go dry, and she bit her lip.

"You were charged, Healer, with delivering my unborn child and helping her majesty, Queen Lily, through the birthing process, yet all did not go as planned, correct?"

"Correct."

"I cannot hear you, Geraldine of Ingleside. Is my statement correct?"

"Yes," she said, her voice louder.

The king narrowed his eyes. "Can you explain what went wrong?"

Geraldine blinked, unsure of where to start. "Your majesty, I am deeply sorry for your loss and the loss to the kingdom, but I don't think—"

"My wife entrusted you with her life!" the king roared, getting to his feet. "You betrayed that trust, Healer. Despite whatever training you might have received, it was not enough. What. Went. Wrong?"

Her breath caught then, and her lower lip quivered. She'd made mistakes in her early days as a healer, yes. Patients had undergone extra surgeries and longer recoveries. More than once, Widow Hannity stepped in at the last moment to help her with complications. Never, however, had anyone, patient or family, spoken to her this way.

"I beg your pardon, your highness—"

"No, you do not," he said. "You *can* not. I revoke your healer's badge, and you will not receive any remaining pay. You are to return to your village, and you will never hurt another person again. Dismissed, Geraldine of Ingleside."

His words echoed across the room; had the king just said what she thought he did?

"Your majesty, please, if I may explain—"

"Will your explanation change the fact that I have lost my wife and child?"

"We've all lost them, your highness," Geraldine said. "I did everything within my power, my skills, my knowledge to save her, but circumstances changed so rapidly that—"

The king's face contorted into an expression of anger Geraldine had never seen on anyone before.

"An entire delegation of healers and assistants stood at the ready, and yet you still managed to provide me with the greatest grief a man can know," he said, his voice wavering. "My decision is final. You will no longer practice as a healer. Gather your things and leave for Ingleside within the hour, or else I will find a more permanent solution."

The words pounded inside Geraldine's head, but she wasn't ready to let them become real yet.

"How much more permanent do you think you can make any of this?" she demanded. "You're taking away my livelihood. My source of income. The area where my greatest talents lie."

King Christopher rested his fists on the table and leaned on them. "Your greatest talent is in making excuses."

"I couldn't have done anything more," Geraldine exclaimed. "No one could. It's unfair that you would—"

"Guards," the king called.

Four burly men in uniforms stepped forward from the back of the room. One held a lance; a second had a quiver at his back with a few arrows and a bow in hand. The third shifted his mace from one hand to the other. The fourth fingered the sword at his belt.

"Escort this woman out of the castle. She has violated court decorum and will not be permitted to upset the councilors or myself any longer."

As the men marched down between the pews, Geraldine covered her mouth with her hand and couldn't stop blinking. She fought the tears that threatened to fall, but she couldn't hide the way her shoulders slumped as the soldiers approached the dais. None of them stepped forward to force her off it, but they looked ready to do so.

She climbed out of the petitioners' box and stopped to take one last look at the people who'd changed her life in an instant.

One of the women councilors kept her gaze down at her lap, and the other two stared at the king in shock. All three men looked angry, although one of them looked away when she met his gaze with her own. King Christopher she saved for last. His entire body shuddered with fury.

Willing her tears to stay inside until she could weep in peace, she nodded at the entire royal council. She took a step forward then back, confused about how to proceed with the guards. She'd never been escorted anywhere by royal soldiers before.

Two of them—Mace and Lance—moved apart. Lance gestured for her to come forward, and she understood they would form a square around her. The prisoner-like treatment made her duck her head, and her chin trembled.

She wished, more than anything, that she could run down the aisle. Get away from the humiliating episode and all the eyes following her. Instead, she decided to mimic someone she knew: the queen.

Gulping hard, Geraldine tried to pretend, for a moment, that she possessed the same grace and dignity. The same courage. Tears streamed down her cheeks—she couldn't hold them back any longer—but Geraldine held her head high.

Murmurs rippled through the courtroom.

"...not an ounce of shame..."

"...the queen! What will Linden do without her? What will the king do?"

"...kind of healer could not save at least one of them?"

Despite the measured steps of Sword and Bow-and-Arrow in front of her, Geraldine picked up her pace. Danielle met the group at the back of the room and opened her mouth.

The healer didn't know if she would be allowed to speak and shook her head; instead, Danielle fell in line with the group as Geraldine was escorted out.

The guards gave her a scant few minutes to gather her belongings from her room. Before she left, she took one long look around it. Seven paces would take her from the door to the opposite wall. The narrow bed to her right had fought her when she tried to turn sides in the night. A long, rectangular window to the left of the bed taunted her with its height; she had to stand on her toes to see out. Against the wall opposite the bed sat a desk just big enough for her elbows.

She would miss all of it. Every inch. Even the draftiness of the room had become her own.

A grunt from the hallway told her of the impatience of the guards, so she packed and followed them through the servants' quarters, the outer courtyard, the gardens, and the oversized stone arch gate leading to the castle. Danielle followed every step, hurrying at times to keep up. When the guards slowed at the carriage stand, the assistant came closer and threw her arms around Geraldine's neck.

"It was a privilege and an honor," she said in Geraldine's ear. "If I can ever do anything, Mistress Geraldine, please let me know."

She fought the urge to collapse in Danielle's arms; Geraldine didn't want the guards to report that she'd behaved like a coward. Instead, she returned Danielle's hug and whispered a goodbye. Mace hailed a carriage for her, hauled her luggage to the driver who secured it, and jerked his head toward the carriage door. Now, more than anything, Geraldine wanted to get away from the castle.

The enormity of what happened in the birthing chamber hadn't escaped her. Just before ducking into the carriage's main compartment, she turned to Danielle and the guards. The sticky tracks of her tears remained on her cheeks.

"I'm sorry for your loss," she said. "Linden is less of a kingdom after losing its queen and heir."

Danielle covered her mouth with her hands as if to press back her own crying. Two of the guards flinched. The third one narrowed his eyes. The fourth—Mace—studied her for a moment then gave a single nod.

Maybe I haven't lost all my dignity after all, she thought.

The scene replayed itself in her mind over and over as she bumped along inside the carriage. She refused to let her memory of the courtroom return. No, it would stay tucked in the same place where she'd stored the last visions of the queen and the birthing chamber. She forced her attention to the window of the carriage instead.

This would have been a perfect day for the birth of a new heir. Now, in the first full month of spring, the flowers sprayed the forest lanes with color. A soft breeze had twitched her hair just before she climbed into the carriage, and a few clouds lingered above as if basking in the soft warmth of the sun.

In the distance, even above the rumble of the carriage wheels on the hard-packed dirt path, Geraldine heard the rhythmic sawing of wood. Dozens of loggers would fell trees today. While Lindeners didn't let their bone-cracking winters keep them from cutting down trees, good weather conditions helped morale and the wood. More than one logger who came to her in Ingleside for a nicked thumb mentioned the trees seemed happier to grow in spring and summer.

Patrons in kingdoms near and far purchased the wood for its endurance and its fragrance. The aroma held the long days of summer, those perfect evenings when the temperature remained comfortable and stars twinkled in the twilight. Evenings when a person could believe magic winked from around the corner.

Where was that magic today? Geraldine thought, her fists balling in her lap. *Why didn't it come when I needed it most?*

The trees gave no answer, and exhaustion made her slump back and close her eyes.

The carriage jolted to a stop, and moments later a heavy banging sounded on the carriage door.

"Ingleside, mistress."

After a second, the carriage shifted weight from wheel to wheel. Geraldine knew the driver had climbed to the roof for her luggage. She stifled a yawn with the back of her hand and climbed out.

The carriage had brought her to the carriage stop at the edge of the town square, which was compact in design but busy nonetheless. The village of Ingleside bustled in its midday routine. Pedestrians hurried around one another on their way to their day's chores. Horses and other carriages traveled on the wide cobblestone path, and the jingling of harnesses and voices of Ingleside's residents made Geraldine tense.

"That'll be two silvers and two coppers," the carriage driver said, his hands shoved into his dingy pants, his face neutral.

Geraldine blinked twice. She hadn't even thought about the cost of the trip. Her gaze dropped to the cobblestones as if the money would materialize there.

"Mistress?"

She rummaged in her handbag and found the coppers. Rubbing her fingers over the coins, she made a decision. She handed the coppers to the driver.

"Take me to my home, and I'll give you the silvers. Otherwise I'll need to pay with a slip."

The driver took the coppers, rolled his eyes, and muttered under his breath. Geraldine waited, hoping the man would agree. As much as she didn't want to go home, she also didn't want the driver to come back in a day or a week demanding to collect on the promissory note.

With a dramatic sigh, the man grabbed the handle of her small wheeled trunk and struggled to pull it back up the ladder on the back of the carriage.

A victory. It surprised her how much the win cheered her up. She needed one, considering where she was coming from and where she was going.

After giving him directions to her home on the edge of town, she climbed back into the carriage. Despite the mild weather, a sheen of sweat made her face damp. She tried to tamp down her anxiety.

It's mid-day; Sullivan won't be home yet, she thought. *I might get a few minutes to myself.*

The possibility of returning to an empty house made her breathe with more ease. When the carriage pulled outside of her home, she sighed with relief. The driver hurried her trunk off the roof again and came back to the front of the carriage, crossing his arms.

"I'm not leaving until I get my silvers."

She nodded, trying to imitate Widow Hannity's serenity

and the queen's regality. "Just a moment."

Fishing for the key in her bag, she clutched it, took a deep breath, and unlocked the door.

"Hello?" she called inside her cottage.

No one answered, but the sound of movement from down the hall told her the house wasn't empty.

"Sullivan?" she called in a quieter voice. When she heard no response, her forehead relaxed.

She dropped her handbag on a chair and went back out for the trunk. With several tugs—including one that threatened to undo a muscle in her back—she managed to get the trunk inside the cottage. She dragged it down the hall and pushed it inside her bedroom then hurried to the box safe she kept in her closet and unlocked it with another key on her keyring. Extracting two silvers, she cursed the expenditure then forced her expression to appear more pleasant.

She made her way back down the hallway and reached for the front door when it flew open. Geraldine took a step back in surprise, and the silvers almost slipped from her hand.

Her husband, Sullivan, eyed her then glanced over his shoulder. "Who's the driver?"

Calm and steady, she coached herself.

"He's from the capital," she said. "He just brought me home, and I need to pay for my passage."

She took a step toward the door, and Sullivan grabbed her arm. The scent of roasted meat floated toward her, and her mouth watered. It reminded her that she'd eaten nothing since the breakfast she'd left half-finished that morning in the castle when Danielle had first called her that the queen's time had come.

"What happened with the queen?" Sullivan asked. "Why are you home all of a sudden like this? And why didn't the king pay for the carriage? This shouldn't be our responsibility."

She shook her arm loose from his hold and went outside and paid the driver. He inspected the coins for a moment then nodded in satisfaction. A tip of the hat later, he climbed back onto the driver's seat and drove away.

Geraldine came back inside and shut the door.

"Where's Alistair?"

"In his room, ill," Sullivan said, dropping into the chair with her handbag. He reached under him for the bag, glanced at it, then tossed it onto a nearby chair. "You didn't answer me. Why are you home?"

"Alistair's ill?" She turned toward the hallway, and Sullivan held up a hand to stop her.

"Don't bother; he's making it up."

Geraldine came back, one hand on her hip. "And how do you know that?"

"Because I've checked on him three times since this morning. He won't come to the inn, but he keeps saying he wants to go to the forest," Sullivan said, rolling his eyes. "What kind of illness makes you too sick to scrub kitchen floors but leaves you well enough to go running around trees?"

"You have workers. You don't need Alistair."

"Like a bloody axe I don't," Sullivan said, standing again, "and working at the inn teaches him responsibility. It'll give him skills to help him earn his way in the world."

"How does he learn that if you don't pay him wages like you do everyone else?" Geraldine said.

Sullivan squared his shoulders. "I'm the boy's father. I shouldn't have to pay him to learn things. Why are you home? Did the queen have her baby yet?"

Geraldine breathed hard through her nose, and Sullivan's

eyebrows turned down as he examined her face.

"What's wrong?"

"Why do you think something's wrong?"

"Because I can tell, Geraldine. We've been married for nearly twenty years. Give me that much credit. What happened?"

She crossed her arms but couldn't meet his eyes with her own. Despite the papers in her bag that stated her dismissal from the healers' guild and the queen's screams still ringing in her ears, Geraldine couldn't find the words to tell Sullivan about that morning. After a few moments of silence, Sullivan threw his hands in the air.

"Seven months away from your husband, and you're putting on airs like you're a member of the court. You probably think you're too good to come back to life in the little village now."

Oh, how she wanted to fire a response back at him. The spaces between the walls of their cottage contained the echoes of so many previous shouting matches. Today, though, she'd run out of energy to make her voice carry over his.

"I'm going to see to Alistair."

Without waiting for Sullivan's response, she turned on her heel and went down the hall.

CHAPTER 4

Word traveled of the queen's death throughout Linden and beyond. For the next five days, as Queen Lily and the baby lay in state in the funeral hall in the castle in Rosewood, no one in the capital city celebrated anything. The woodworking merchants only took on commissions for household items or those required in basic construction, refusing anything meant purely for pleasure. The bakeries stopped producing cakes or pastries, selling only bread and other necessary goods. The healers spoke in hushed whispers around those under their care.

The artisans stopped everything altogether—no painting; no sculpting; no music; no storytelling in any form. It had often been said that while the queen encouraged all of the guilds, as a painter herself she held a special place in her heart for the artisans. The entire city knew of the studio the king had gifted her in the castle, although she had allowed few to visit it. In truth, the queen herself had found free time scarce. The demands of her duties to the kingdom had kept her from painting as often as she liked. The artisans mourned her now.

Residents of the kingdom moved from one chore to the next, exchanging pertinent information with one another, avoiding the chatter that passed the time. Once, when a young child bounced a ball in the street and laughed in delight, everyone flinched. As if the sound could drive the queen from their memories.

On the sixth day, a proclamation found its way to the main announcement boards throughout the land. In one week, it read, the king would appear on the main balcony and address his people. The liveried workers moved in a businesslike manner, nailing the stiff pieces of parchment on one board and then another.

No one stopped them to ask questions, but everyone knew what they must do.

Often those living in the towns and cities farthest from the capital waited for the roamers to bring them news of their king and his activities. In the years he had reigned, he always treated them fairly. They had no reason to worry about information that would arrive a few weeks late.

This time, however, Linden's residents knew they must come to their king. To look to him for strength and understanding. To show him his grief did not belong only to him.

The residents in the nearest and farthest corners of Linden began packing and planning for their journeys.

On the day of the king's appearance, hundreds thronged the main roads of Rosewood. People spoke in soft murmurs, whether to their traveling companions or capital dwellers. For the first time since the queen's death, eating establishments opened their doors and merchants were busy once again with transactions for various foodstuffs.

People nodded to one another with a feeling bordering on relief. They had grieved for the queen in their individual cities and villages. Coming together reminded them they did not mourn her alone.

At the appointed time, they pressed en masse toward the castle. The previous king let minions deliver his words, not using the king's balcony affixed to the castle for its intended purpose. When Christopher came into power, he decided to use the balcony his ancestors used for addressing the kingdom.

The balcony stood tall on four columns made of only the strongest stone, connected to the castle by a narrow ramp. No other entrance point existed, and the columns themselves remained rough-hewn to discourage dissenters who would try to climb up and harm the king. Christopher was favored by many as a monarch, but dissenters still lived under his domain.

Even the dissenters seemed content to let their king have his say, however. The people waited at the foot of the balcony for the man they respected. For the queen they had loved.

Christopher looked at himself in the full-length mirror as his gentleman-in-waiting dressed him. He tugged on the lapel of the royal robe, ignoring the fine silk that edged it. The robe he had inherited from his father hung in the back of the wardrobe somewhere. Lily had had this one commissioned before the royal council formally crowned her queen.

He chuckled now as he remembered how he had moved about their private chambers that first morning after their wedding. Unable to sit still, he revisited a ledger that sat on his desk, then ducked his head out the door to ask Martin when the royal council would make its way to the ramp leading to the balcony. He wanted to make sure his entrance with the new queen would not get delayed by some miscommunication.

After he went back to the desk to check the ledger yet again, Lily came and stood in front of him. She put a hand to his arm, her touch light—they had not yet allowed one another familiarity as husband and wife—then brushed his lapel with the tips of her fingers. After a moment, she smiled.

"All will be well, your highness," she said. "They are your people."

He shook his head. "They do not know me. They only knew my father, and reports are conflicted on what Lindeners thought of him."

"You are here," she continued in that gentle, firm voice, "to build your own legacy, not continue your father's."

He gulped now. His father, Vincent, had possessed a brazen strength, but many also accused him of cruelty. Christopher knew from his own adolescence that he would not follow his father's example in the latter, but what of the former? How would he show his people his own strength?

A sharp rap came at the door, and Christopher sighed. How long had he stood here daydreaming? He looked back at the mirror, tugged on his lapel once more, then nodded for the gentleman-in-waiting to go to the door. The man opened it to Martin who saw the king well and then left. A page entered and offered Christopher a deep bow.

"The council awaits, your majesty," the boy said.

"I will be with them within minutes," Christopher replied.

"Yes, your majesty."

The boy bowed again and left. Christopher turned halfway back to the mirror when Martin entered. Surprised, Christopher turned back toward the door again.

"Yes, Martin?"

The guard bowed. "Your highness, I simply wanted to ascertain whether you were ready."

"I just informed the page I would join the council soon. Have you joined the pages, Martin? Decided to forego your post as leader of the guards?"

Martin's mouth twitched in amusement.

"No, your highness. But it is good to hear you making light of a situation again."

He bowed once more and left. Christopher turned back to the mirror. Perhaps, if he stood here long enough, Lily would appear behind his shoulder as she often did with a few last-minute words of encouragement. Since announcing the formal address, he had opened his mouth several times to call out for her—and twice actually did—to ask her opinion on one matter or the other. Each time, the realization came that she would never answer his call again.

Enough, he thought. *The people need you to be strong at this time. They have lost their queen. They need to know you will lead them, that you will stand with them.*

As he swept out of the room, he could not stop the voice inside his head asking, *But who will stand with you?*

Minutes later, the king surveyed the hundreds of people below the balcony then turned his attention to the large conical structure lying on its side before him. The inventors had sourced the unusual instrument from a neighboring kingdom. He simply needed to speak into the narrow end of the cone, and the wide end would project his voice. Oversized boards placed strategically on towers in the immediate vicinity of the balcony bounced the sound so those below could hear him without him shouting.

When the inventors first presented the concept, the queen had clapped her hands in delight. She always saw potential in the inventors to do great things and even made a private bet with him of her most beloved horse against his that the idea would work. He remained skeptical at first, but something about her optimism caught his fancy and—

He blinked, suddenly aware of the great expanse of silence and hundreds of pairs of eyes on him. His people. His alone, now.

How would he rule them without her?

"Your subjects await you, sire," a voice murmured.

He glanced over his shoulder at Martin whose counsel he had sought more than once in years past and gave his friend a single nod. Then Christopher stepped to the small end of the proclamation funnel and looked at those who needed just as much comforting as he did.

"My people," he said, trying to control his quavering voice, "I want to express to you my deepest gratitude. Your love for your queen has reassured me that her memory will live for years to come."

He swallowed the tears that threatened to burst and continued.

"Your queen was the epitome of grace, strength, beauty, and wisdom. I know you will all miss her. While it is difficult to move forward without her, I insist we end our grieving. Your queen would not have wanted us to spend our time in sorrow.

"So, after her burial in two days' time, I declare the end of the mourning period. You are all free to return to your responsibilities and duties, but I encourage you to speak about the queen, to remember her and share your stories and thoughts with the artisans. They have the full support of the royal family to memorialize her in any way they deem fit."

Several sighs floated up toward him, and it struck him then just how much the people had missed his wife.

"I thank you, my people, for the generosity of your support. With all of us working together, we can forge a future that would make your queen proud."

He raised his right hand in a blessing, indicating he had finished. Silence. The people continued staring at him in solemnity.

Normally when the king spoke, the people punctuated his words with cheers and whoops of delight. When he had made declarations of concern, people would shout questions. He always answered them, waiting on the balcony until the mood shifted from apprehension to confidence.

Now, however, no one uttered a word; Christopher was unsure of how to respond.

After several interminable minutes, a single voice called out. He could not understand the words—the voice was too far away—but then someone else repeated the cadence. Within seconds it got repeated again.

Movement caught Christopher's attention. A ripple began from a single point in the middle of the crowd. It looked like someone dropped an invisible stone there that pinned everyone in place.

The people were kneeling.

Their words came to him then, spoken in respectful tones that echoed the resilience of the people of Linden.

"For the queen," they said together. "For the queen. For the queen."

Christopher approached the entrance to the funeral hall, two soldiers following at a discreet distance. The reaction of the Lindeners outside the balcony that morning rang through his head. Their devotion to Lily had not surprised him in the least. Everything he had done since marrying Lily had been for her or for the kingdom. Half of his purpose no longer remained; how would he carry the weight of the other half?

He stopped at the oversized wooden doors and stared at the famed Linden trees carved into them. Christopher had not checked the lumber ledgers for days now. Every time he requested the information from the royal accountants, his eyes would slide over the numbers. Every time, he sent the ledgers to the council instead. Ross could review them or Duncan perhaps. As head councilor, Duncan had years of experience dealing with such matters.

Christopher, instead, found himself wandering through the castle, ignoring the way the pages and liveried workers avoided looking at him. At some point during his roaming, he made his way to this hall where Lily and the baby...

Today he came again. In all the days Lily lay in state, he had not summoned the courage to push the oversized handle and go in to view his queen. Seeing his people had bolstered him.

The funereal guild said she looked peaceful. As if she were sleeping. Perhaps...perhaps today I could...

He put a hand to the large seal of Linden, which bisected the door with a heavy seam, and bowed his head.

You would have been proud of me this morning, Lily. I did not once waver in my demeanor.

He thought yet again of the last time he saw her, of how heavy she lay in his arms in the birthing chamber and how he had done nothing to save her.

It is not your fault, he reminded himself weakly. *That ridiculous healer Geraldine is to blame.*

His heart refused to believe him.

A soft cough from behind reminded him that his soldiers waited with unending patience. Christopher raised his head, squared his shoulders, and pushed in the door. He took half a step inside and stopped.

Lily lay encased in fine-spun glass and did, indeed, look as though she simply slept, albeit in a gown. Sunlight streamed through the windows close to the ceiling; dust motes, disturbed by the opening of the door, floated down. The room seemed more suited to a quiet afternoon of reading, not mourning the death of a member of the royal family. Padded benches, one on each wall, invited visitors to sit for as long as they wished. The intricate tapestries on the walls showed images of generations of Linden's rulers, long deceased. Christopher ignored the blank space on the wall facing him that waited for the newest tapestry.

Instead, he turned back to Lily. For a moment, he had the urge to put his hand to her shoulder and give her a gentle shake. Why would she consent to lying still for so long? Had she forgotten all the work that awaited on her desk in their shared study?

Everyone is wrong, he thought. *She cannot be gone. She must awake and help me tend to this nonsense. They will all see what a silly mistake they have made and...*

A petite encasement lay near the queen. A tiny head covered in a bonnet. A white gown edged in the finest embroidery.

No fog on the glass in either coffin to indicate breaths taken.

Christopher's knees became soft, and he stepped back into the corridor. Without a look back, he walked as fast as his feet would carry him. After fifteen paces, he began running.

A clattering of footsteps told him the soldiers followed, and in a dim way the king saw from his peripheral vision the shocked faces of pages and castle staff as he dashed through the corridors and open spaces. He did not care. It did not matter. Nothing mattered anymore.

He reached the royal apartment, barged through the door, and fell to his knees with a loud scream of anguish.

Geraldine kneeled behind her house with her arms deep in a washing tub. Since coming home from the castle two weeks earlier, the clothes in her home had never been so clean. The countertops in the kitchen gleamed, and specks of dust didn't have the chance to settle before Geraldine swept them out again. Her excess energy made her skin tingle.

"Geraldine!"

She cringed at the sound of Sullivan's voice.

"Geraldine, where's Alistair?"

She took the last article of clothing, a pair of Alistair's pants, and rubbed it with extra vigor against the washboard. Water sloshed over the side of the tub, and a few bubbles floated in the air. She watched one as it rose higher before using a dripping finger to pop it.

The door to the kitchen banged open, and Sullivan came into the yard.

"Didn't you hear me call?"

As she dunked Alistair's pants into the clean water tub next to the one with the washboard, she could hear Sullivan's voice but couldn't make out the words. He tried again as she sent the pants through the laundry wringer to squeeze out the excess water. The grinding metal gears of the wringer, stuttering as the fabric worked through the rollers, kept Sullivan's reply from her. Without bothering to look at him, Geraldine made her way to the laundry line where she'd left enough space for the pants.

"I *said,* where's Alistair? I need him at the inn."

"He was tired after he came home from his lessons, so I sent him to rest."

She moved toward the house, but he grabbed her arm.

"Let go. I need to run an errand."

"What you need to do is return to the castle and demand the pay you're owed."

Geraldine jerked out of his grip. "The queen is *dead,* Sullivan, and so is the princess, and the king is mourning them both. You may not remember what it means to offer others your sympathy, but I do."

He flinched, and for a moment she regretted the dig. In the last several years, it had gotten easier to throw her words as darts. She tried to convince herself it didn't matter where they landed as long as they pricked Sullivan's conscience, but sometimes she saw the way she'd hurt him and wanted to apologize. If only she knew how to do so again.

Sullivan opened and closed his mouth. Embarrassment and anger flit across his face, reflecting her own feelings. Geraldine turned back to the laundry. She didn't want him to see what they shared in that moment.

"Matters of the heart may be important to you, Geraldine, but not all of us have the luxury of living in a dream world," he finally said. "I'm trying to run a home and the inn. If we cannot eat, we won't have hearts to consider."

Had he stood three feet taller and spoken in a booming voice, Geraldine may have taken his words more seriously. She found it difficult when faced with this soft-bellied man who stood with a slight stoop. Worse, he had come straight from the inn, stained apron and all.

Once—it felt like eons ago now—she looked at Sullivan and saw the love of her life. They stood at the same height; he didn't tower over her like some mythical fairy tale hero.

In the first few months after getting married, he joked that at least they would always see eye to eye.

His height had not changed, but his perspective had.

"I'll return to Rosewood when I deem it appropriate," she said, wiping her hands dry on her own apron. "I'm busy right now."

"With what? You haven't visited any of the sick in Ingleside recently, and I'm tired of making excuses for you at the inn. Why won't you go back to those who need you?"

Her heart tightened in anguish. Just before her departure from the castle, a page pressed a sheaf of papers in her hand. They outlined her dismissal; a note on top admonished her to file the papers with the head of the Ingleside healer's guild as soon as she returned. Geraldine arrived home, dropped the papers into a drawer in her bedroom, and had ignored them since.

Word of the queen's death had traveled to Ingleside, and now she spent her days avoiding almost everyone. She didn't want to face questions, implied or spoken, and so far everyone gave her a wide berth, looking at her with sympathy instead. Once or twice, she entered a shop to hear other residents express their concern for the king. She turned on her heel and left. Geraldine still awoke from nightmares where the queen screamed, and she didn't trust herself not to blurt out the truth.

"You don't need to make excuses for me, Sullivan. I can take care of myself."

"And what about our expenses? Who will take care of those?" Sullivan said. "The food at the inn can only sustain us for so long. It's still a ways out before the festival season, and we don't have as many lodgers these days. We need every copper we can muster, and the sick people here need to be tended to."

"I don't answer to you or anyone else," she snapped. "I'll do what I want when I want."

She stalked into the house and the extra bedroom she'd claimed as her own years earlier, slamming the door shut then leaning against it. Tears burned in her eyes, but she still tilted her head. Satisfied Sullivan hadn't followed her, she turned the heavy lock and went to the tall chest of drawers against the wall.

Geraldine retrieved the dismissal decree from the bottom drawer and sat on the bed, the sight of the ugly red stamp making her hand quiver as she reread it.

What are you doing? she asked herself for the hundredth time since coming home. *If anyone finds out you didn't file these with Master Thorne, losing your healer's badge will be the least of your problems. The king could have you thrown into prison for disobeying his order.*

She dropped the papers back into the drawer and pulled out the certificate, or badge, that named her a healer. As she traced the raised seal with her finger, a wave of pride made Geraldine's chest swell. The day of her induction ceremony all those years ago where she received the badge had been a day like today with a brilliant blue sky and a few puffy clouds. Except that day had brimmed with possibilities.

She shook her head and dropped the badge back into the drawer, shoving it closed with unnecessary force.

As a young couple with faces gleaming with the blush of new love, she and Sullivan had left home to forge a new path. Their families didn't approve of their marriage—some enmity that had lost the details to the decades but none of the sharpness of the hatred—so Geraldine and Sullivan came to Ingleside. He nurtured dreams of excelling in the kitchen; she wanted only to love and support him. In the beginning, it seemed entirely doable and completely romantic.

Sullivan found the job in the kitchen of the inn and cooked for her with love and eagerness, his flushed face full of hope in the evenings as he practiced his latest dishes. Geraldine would roll mounds of bandages for Widow Hannity or separate pills and herbs into individual sachets for patients, and Sullivan would urge her to stop and take a bite, practically pushing a fork or spoon into her hands.

As the years passed and the necessity of money became a reality, Sullivan stopped smiling so much. Life didn't seem quite as romantic with mounting responsibilities. Then Geraldine found herself expecting, and Sullivan found himself needing to support a family.

Being named a healer-midwife offered a new life, but Sullivan demanded Geraldine contribute to their household expenses. He counted every penny against the rate card she'd set for her services. It galled her that, like an uneducated, mousy homekeeper, she had to give her husband the money she earned.

When the burden of the growing distance between them became too much to bear, she made the decision to leave. Penny by penny, copper by copper, she built a nest egg by keeping part of her money and lying about the rest. Through the last ten years, she'd saved so she could move on. The final payment from caring for the queen would have given her enough to purchase a home for herself and Alistair away from Sullivan and the disappointment that formed the framework of their lives.

The king's dismissal threw a brick in her plan and knocked it down, letting the disappointment collapse on top of her.

The sobs came hard and fast this time, and she didn't stop them. The king kept more than just her money. He'd kept her from her freedom. When the queen died, so had

Geraldine's chance of getting away.

I took care of her; I did everything I could. I can't lose my healer's badge for doing my duty. Maybe I can go back to the castle and...

The thought of returning to Linden's capital made her tears stop. King Christopher had humiliated her. She would not go back for more of the same.

There must be a way around this. If Sullivan couldn't keep me from saving all these years, I'm not going to let the king of Linden keep me from getting away from this life. Alistair deserves more than that, and so do I.

Thinking of her beautiful son made her stand and scrub her cheeks with her hands. With a quick stop in the comfort room to splash water on her face at the sink, she took a moment to examine herself in the mirror and smoothed back a few of the wisps of gray. Had she really aged so much?

She cleared her throat a few times so she could talk without her voice catching on her pain. Then she practiced a smile or two. After a moment, she went down the hall and knocked on the half-open door.

"Alistair?"

"Come, Mother."

Geraldine fixed a smile on her face and pushed the door open. The room reminded her of the room she'd been assigned in the castle. Similar layout; similar lack of space.

Alistair lay on his bed, head propped in one hand as he leafed through a book. He'd grown again in the last year; now he looked as gangly as a new sapling in the forest. When she came home from the castle, she'd stared at him in astonishment for a full 30 seconds before he laughed at her expression and leaned down to hug her.

He looked up from his bed and grinned, but the expression seemed to take effort.

"How are you feeling?"

He shrugged with one shoulder and focused on the book again. "Tired."

"Are you in any pain?"

Her joy at seeing him when she came home became a knot of anxiety when she saw his pale face, and no amount of home-cooked food or sending him to bed early or anything else seemed to fix the problem. She put her hand above his brow now. No heat; no sweat. She cupped his chin with her hand. Bringing her face so close they almost touched noses, she stared into each of his eyes then asked him to open his mouth so she could examine his tongue.

"Did earlier," he said, irritated. "Fine."

"You're not fine if you keep complaining of being tired," she retorted. "Give me your hands."

She ignored the way he rolled his eyes and closed her own instead.

Please let the skirring work this time, she begged the fates. *I need to find out what's wrong with Alistair.*

His palms tingled under hers, and she almost dropped his hands in excitement. Healers were expected to know how to skirr, to use their healing energy to evaluate patients so they could decide how best to treat them. Not all could do it well or even at all. Widow Hannity could always skirr her patients. Geraldine's skirring skills worked some of the time, which meant she spent the rest of the time asking her patients questions about their health, researching old texts, and using her experience, and sometimes the widow's, to help her reach a diagnosis.

For a moment, an image flashed in Geraldine's mind of trying to skirr the queen in the birthing chamber. Of the paleness of her face when the skirring—and Geraldine—failed. She swallowed hard to distract herself and refocus her attention.

Today her energy rippled in tingles through Alistair un-interrupted, but that didn't make sense. If he had been ill, the rippling should have dropped into a black void. The skirring seemed to say Alistair was healthy, but one look at his face told her otherwise.

Geraldine drew her hands back.

"Done?"

She knew he was asking so much more in that one word; from his earliest days, Alistair spoke in fragments. Today she knew he wanted her to stop fussing over him so much. Geraldine ruffled his hair, which made him swat her hand away and scrunch his face in a frown.

"I'm going to visit Widow Hannity. I'll be back soon."

With a flop on the bed, Alistair nodded. She left the room and went down the hall, stopping long enough at her own bedroom to change out of her laundry clothes and grab her bag. She snatched the keys from their hook by the front door. If anyone could help her, Widow Hannity could.

A few minutes later, Geraldine sat in her mentor's kitchen at a tight table for four. As Widow Hannity hobbled with the aid of her walking staff to make tea, she kept up a string of small talk about the latest injuries and illnesses to make the rounds of the villagers. During Geraldine's time in the castle with the queen, the widow had resumed her role as Ingleside's healer. She seemed to enjoy it, despite her self-declared retirement years earlier.

The twinge of jealousy at her mentor taking her place, even on a temporary basis, still surprised Geraldine. The woman taught her everything she knew. Geraldine had served the villagers well for 19 years, but Widow Hannity lived there first. Why did she feel so possessive all of a sudden of the villagers?

"...a way to keep that boy from climbing trees," Widow Hannity said, breaking into Geraldine's thoughts. "It's the third time Simon's broken a bone in the last four years. If he's so eager to climb, he may want to join the artisans' guild as a circus performer."

Geraldine chuckled. "I've said the same to Julia."

"It didn't help that the Thorne boy was egging Simon on. They both need a firm hand or time in the castle's work program."

At the mention of Master Thorne's son, Geraldine's smile faded. She looked down at the table. Widow Hannity pulled out the chair across from Geraldine and sat.

"Out with it, girl."

Geraldine stared at her hands. Widow Hannity never held back the truth from any of her patients. Through the years, Geraldine came to emulate the woman's straightforward method of delivering bad news. Much easier to get it all out at once instead of using a slow-release approach.

"I didn't leave the castle of my own accord," Geraldine said in a flat voice. "The king threw me out. He holds me responsible for the deaths of the queen and the baby."

The former healer didn't respond. Geraldine braved a look at her. Widow Hannity's body curved inward, her face mirroring the shock Geraldine still felt.

"Well."

Geraldine nodded; what else was there to say?

"What happened?"

Geraldine exhaled all of the hours she'd spent reliving the delivery. "The labor was long, and the life cord wrapped around the baby's neck. We didn't know until the queen pushed her out. By then it was too late for the baby, and the queen lost a lot of blood. I tried to skirr her, but... Since then I've gone over it in my mind a thousand times, but I still haven't..."

Widow Hannity nodded with understanding.

"The fates know I've lost a few mothers and babies that way."

"But I haven't," Geraldine exclaimed. "I shouldn't have. Not with the queen. She and I... I'm not saying we could have been friends, not like I could with anyone else, but I would have never done anything to hurt her. But the king... He made it seem like I was some incompetent simpleton! I wasn't just her healer, Widow Hannity. We...we shared so much."

Geraldine breathed long and slow. Since coming home, she'd done everything she could to avoid the emotions that threatened to bury her. It had been easier that way, easier to stay mad at the king rather than remember everything else. All the times she and the queen discussed what motherhood meant. How a woman's body changed. She'd seen the queen in the most vulnerable state a woman could offer herself—unclothed—and never forgot how Queen Lily trusted her, a commoner.

No, easier to keep her fury front and center and ignore that bond she'd lost.

Widow Hannity patted her arm. "Did you plead your case with him?"

"He didn't let me say more than two words before declaring in open court that I was responsible. Then he stripped me of my badge and sent me back. The castle won't pay me the final amount owed. But, Widow Hannity, I did nothing wrong. The queen would have died no matter who was the healer."

Geraldine found her eyes burning with all the tears she'd already shed at those words. Maybe she wasn't as practical and clear-minded with her patients as Widow Hannity after all. The widow made it look so easy to stay engaged with everyone while still maintaining a respectful distance. She wanted to ask the widow's secret but distracted herself by pinching the fabric of her apron and twisting it first one way and then the other.

Widow Hannity exhaled a sigh of experience.

"People see the body as a great mystery. When we study healing, others often believe we've solved that mystery. What they don't know is the more we learn, the more we realize how much we have yet to find out. Have you gone to Master Thorne yet?"

Geraldine shook her head, and Widow Hannity raised an eyebrow. Not for the first time, Geraldine wished her mentor had accepted the nomination by the healers' guild as the head of its local chapter. At the time Widow Hannity had declined, saying she didn't want to spend her twilight years getting involved in squabbles about treatment methods. Master Thorne, Ingleside's mayor, stepped in when no one else received a nomination.

"Ever since you've come back, people have wondered when you'll resume your duties. And the castle will eventually send a representative to make sure you've followed the decree. Do you plan to ignore it?"

"It's not fair." Geraldine's voice shook. "The queen chose me from hundreds of other healers. I took care of her from her second month onwards. I followed all of the dictums set by the guild head in Rosewood that healers have followed for generations. Why should I get punished for doing what anyone else in my position would have done?"

Widow Hannity held up a hand to placate her. "I'm not

saying you did anything wrong or that I agree with the king's decision. I simply asked whether you plan to ignore his decree."

Geraldine's heart pounded when she heard her plan in actual words. The tea kettle whistled in a furious tone. Widow Hannity stood and hobbled toward it.

"Sullivan keeps demanding that I go back to the castle for the last payment," Geraldine said over the kettle's thin scream for attention. "I haven't told him the real reason I left."

"Given that you're planning to leave him at some point, I can see why."

For a moment, Geraldine's mind went blank. Bit by bit, her thoughts came back to her. Were her intentions so obvious?

She'd shared many personal details with her mentor through the years except this one. She told herself it was to keep the widow safe from any of Sullivan's verbal lashings, but she hadn't told anyone because she was scared. Scared she would fail and scared someone would try to talk her out of it.

"You...you know?" she asked.

Widow Hannity struggled with placing the tea kettle on a tray, and Geraldine jumped up to help her. She carried the tray with the kettle, two mugs, and a plate of cookies to the table. The widow hobbled back to the chair and sat, and as Geraldine served them both she reflected on how frail her dearest friend looked.

"I know your heart, Geraldine, and I know you have reason to do what you want to," Widow Hannity said after catching her breath. "I understand your situation, more than you might know."

Her limbs became loose as she sat down. "So you won't report me to the castle?"

The widow took a few more shallow breaths. "I won't report you to the castle."

Geraldine picked up her mug, fighting to steady her hand so she wouldn't slosh her tea. "If I'm caught and a castle representative finds out you helped me, you'll be punished too."

"Don't you worry about me," Widow Hannity said, waving away the thought. "I have my own ways of dealing with people in high places. I will say this, however. The king shouldn't have revoked your badge. You did what any healer would have done; what I myself would have done in the situation. Just like the king, as the ruler of the land, was within his right to exercise his judgment."

"But, Widow Hannity—"

The widow held up a hand to stop her. "I don't agree with his judgment, Geraldine. He was too harsh. Given the circumstances, however, his reaction makes sense. We all know how Vincent treated his son. Queen Lily was King Christopher's closest and strongest ally. For someone in his position to lose that...well, anger is warranted."

Geraldine's cheeks got warm, but she couldn't work through the tangle of emotions coursing through her. She didn't know if she wanted to. Instead, she picked at the thread easiest to snag.

"If I can't be a healer and earn a living, everything for me changes."

Widow Hannity tilted her head in sympathy. "I know things look dire now, but I have no doubt that you'll find a way to work through this and that everything will be all right in the end. Now, that's not the reason why you came to see me, is it?"

Geraldine's mouth dropped open. "Do you read minds as well?"

The widow raised her eyebrows in a mysterious fashion;

then a short laugh burst from her lips.

"Alistair hasn't come to see me in some time. Just before you returned, I visited your home to ask about him. He looked ill, not like himself."

"Ever since I've come home, he's been complaining of being tired, but I can't find a cause," Geraldine said. "I even tried skirring him this morning."

"And?"

"The skirring worked," Geraldine said, her cheeks flushing with her success, "but it didn't reveal anything. No infected areas; no illnesses."

Widow Hannity stared at the mug in her own hands for a few moments.

"I know he's missed you in the months you were away and hasn't slept well. I also know Sullivan has enlisted his help on more than one occasion—maybe too many of them—to work in the inn. It's possible he's just suffering from general fatigue."

Geraldine watched the steam rise from her cup. "Maybe you're right. Maybe he just needs rest."

Widow Hannity's face brightened with a smile, and she turned the conversation to other gossip from the village. As Geraldine laughed and nodded her way through the rest of the hour, a part of her wondered if, for once, her mentor was wrong. If Alistair really was ill.

Well, I'm home now, so I can keep an eye on him. On Sullivan too. No one is going to take advantage of Alistair and definitely not of me anymore.

CHAPTER 5

For perhaps the tenth time since leaving their castle in Wyndemere just as the sun rose that morning, King Malcolm found his fingers interlaced with those of his queen, Celia. As per Linden custom, now that Christopher had declared an end to the mourning period, Malcolm and Celia traveled to Linden to attend their daughter's burial. Since leaving that morning, they had spoken few words to one another. Yet Celia reached for his hand often. Now, as she rubbed his thumb with her own, Malcolm forced himself to remain calm. He did not want comfort. He wanted to lash out, to scream and rage at the sky.

He wanted to act as a mourning father, not as a responsible king.

Malcolm had lived in agony as a grieving father while still trying to rule his kingdom. When word came that Lily would no longer lie in state and would be prepared for a final farewell to her people, the monarchs of Wyndemere arranged for their royal advisors to act on their behalf for the coming fortnight. Malcolm anticipated returning to Wyndemere long before then, but the message from Linden about the burial came from Christopher's council and not the king. Malcolm wanted to arrive with enough time to help his son-in-law as needed.

Pulling his hand from Celia's, he flicked aside the curtain on the carriage window and recalled the first time he met

Christopher as an adult. The young man visited Wyndemere not long after losing his father and brought with him a more reasonable, if idealistic, trade treaty regarding Linden's wood compared to what Vincent had demanded years earlier. Christopher also walked in a cloud of confusion and loss after Vincent's sudden death. Assassination, some called it, although hunting accidents did happen. Even if the circumstances pointed to anything but an accident.

That trade treaty led to Christopher's marriage to Lily seven years ago. Seven years for Christopher to start believing in himself. In her letters, Lily wrote candidly about her husband's struggle with self-confidence; she detailed the slow, careful progress he made and how that affected their relationship. Although Malcolm and Celia had waited eagerly for news of an impending royal birth, they knew better than to push their bright, headstrong daughter in her marriage. What Linden relinquished in the early birth of an heir, it gained in a king with a fortified opinion of his ability to rule.

What state would he be in now, Malcolm wondered. Christopher's mother, Queen Dahlia, died right after her son's tenth birthday. Vincent met his end astride a horse with the arrow from a crossbow in his back. Now Lily. And the baby.

As if she heard the thought of their lost grandchild, Celia tugged on his arm. Malcolm turned from the window and saw tears cresting in her eyes. He pulled her toward him. They rode the rest of the way with her head on his shoulder, their lips pressed in straight lines. At least, Malcolm thought, he and Celia could mourn the loss of their child together. Christopher had no one now.

They reached Linden's capital city in the late afternoon. As their carriage rolled into the outer courtyard of the castle, the king and queen pulled apart. Despite his irritation earlier, Malcolm wanted to tighten his arm around Celia. This time she pulled away; she fussed with her skirts, black in color to represent the color of mourning worn in Wyndemere but with a wide white hem to honor the funereal customs of Linden. With a tug on the cuffs of her long sleeves, she pushed her feet back into her shoes. Taking them off during long rides was her one concession to comfort as they traveled. Behind him, he heard the rumble of more carriage wheels coming to a stop.

He looked through the window again. The group of ladies- and gentlemen-in-waiting moved with efficiency around the courtyard, organizing luggage. Since Christopher's coronation, diplomatic relations had been restored between Linden and Wyndemere. The people who traveled with Malcolm and Celia now knew where to go and what to do.

Malcolm let the carriage driver hand Celia down before climbing out of the carriage himself. A formal entourage of the Linden royal guard met them. At the front of the formation stood Martin, head of the royal guard and Christopher's oldest friend. His only friend, Malcolm knew, in so much as a young royal could become friends with a stable boy.

"Your majesties," the guardsmaster said with a deep bow. He straightened and put a fist to his chest over his heart. The king tilted his head to acknowledge Martin's gesture of condolences.

"Where is his highness?" Celia asked in a quiet voice.

Martin's gaze dropped for a moment.

"What is it, Guardsmaster?" Malcolm asked, wishing his voice did not sound so brusque. "Has anything befallen King Christopher?"

Martin shook his head. "No, your highness. Yet..."

Malcolm waited for the soldier to continue.

"Guardsmaster?" he asked.

"Perhaps you would like to retire to your apartment to refresh yourselves," Martin said. He turned around. "Soldier Devin, escort—"

Malcolm stepped forward. "Where is the king?"

The soldier looked back at him, his face unreadable. "He is in her majesty's studio making room for more canvases. He said it was high time he did so."

Malcolm stilled himself. He expected Christopher to be buried in reports at his desk or lamenting in the royal apartment. Why would he need to rearrange Lily's studio? She would not need it now that she...

"Take us to him at once," he said, blinking away the thought.

Martin bowed deeply. "As you wish. Soldiers, disperse."

The flurry in the courtyard increased as soldiers marched to their posts. The entourage from Wyndemere had long since followed their Linden counterparts. Malcolm turned and shared a long look with Celia before they followed Martin into the castle.

Christopher watched as two pages darted around the room at his direction.

"No, that canvas will go in the other corner. By the fates, have you two forgotten the order of things already? We have barely begun."

They stopped and offered apologies then continued their tasks. Christopher nodded to himself in satisfaction. Lily would be so pleased to see her work space cleared in this way. She had asked in all moods—with exasperation or affection, with melancholy or outright anger—for him to spare her time for the art studio. A few precious days she worked for hours; some days she snatched but a few minutes to walk among her works before he called her to draft another treaty or receive another ambassador. No matter how much time he gave her, it never seemed enough.

She displayed those swinging moods for him alone, however. With the castle staff, she remained warm and pleasant. Christopher's lips curled at the thought of Lily not needing to repeat herself with them. Everyone had been so taken with her from the first day. Not once did any of them look at her askance. Not once did they wonder in whispers about her ability to rule.

A clearing throat brought him back. How long had he stood perusing Lily's work? The pages bowed again, and he turned around.

"His majesty, King Malcolm, and her majesty, Queen Celia, of Wyndemere," Martin announced.

So they arrived at last. The previous evening, when the Linden messenger returned to say the king and queen would come as soon as possible, Christopher's imagination spun with wild possibilities. What if a horrible storm beset them or mercenaries hijacked their carriages? What if they were unable to arrive?

What if nothing horrible happened at all? What if nothing had happened to anyone? What if he awoke this moment to discover all this a nightmare?

"Dismissed," he called to the pages. As they trotted out of the studio, he bowed to Lily's parents. His shoulders became heavy as he straightened again.

"My apologies, your majesties. Had I known you would

arrive with such speed, I would have made sure the queen's studio looked more presentable and I..."

He looked down at the formal shirt he still wore from the previous day. Why had his gentleman-in-waiting not assisted him in changing his attire? Surely the staff would have known of the impending arrival of the king and queen.

And...yes, his stomach *had* rumbled just now. Had everyone in the castle forgotten their duties? Did they dare to forget to serve him his meals as well? How had Lily allowed this? He needed to speak to the queen.

"My son."

Before he could draw another breath, Christopher found himself grunting from the impact of a hard hug from his mother-in-law. The breach of decorum shocked him back into the present. To the reason for it.

Tears slipped down his cheeks faster than he thought possible, and an audible sob from Queen Celia released his own grief. After another moment or two, another pair of arms tightened around Christopher and the queen. Christopher's eyes widened as he heard King Malcolm weep aloud for his daughter. Within moments, Christopher found himself in tears as well.

"I could not keep her safe, your majesty," he said. "I broke my vow to you."

For a moment, the three forgot they were monarchs. They stood as a family mourning the loss of someone they loved more than any of them realized until this moment. As tears flowed and their cries wound their way around the room, the canvases echoed their grief back to them.

Christopher sat on the balcony adjacent to his private apartment, ignoring the white flags flying over the city. They flapped against a sky preparing to tuck itself into sunset, offering its final burst of blue before the day's end. He had last seen the white mourning flags after his father's death. The color showed the drabness of life when a loved one no longer lived. Christopher's soul mirrored the flags, a void of any meaningful expression.

The queen... Oh, Lily. The baby. Mother. Father.

He jerked away from the last thought. No; he would not link Lily's memory to the man who had made it clear Christopher fell short of all expectations. Lily's confidence, her belief in him, supplanted all of his father's disappointments. He would not dishonor Lily by remembering them together.

He turned to the pot of tea and reached for the cozy covering it but let it drop. The pot was full; despite his mother-in-law's encouragement to drink and eat, Christopher had not touched it. He flicked the covering on the tray aside just long enough to see what the kitchen had prepared: a light tomato soup with a cheese sandwich cut into four neat sections. Simple foods so mourners could spend their energy on the ones they lost.

As if he could forget that he sat and watched the sun set on another day without his wife.

A light tapping echoed through the bedchamber behind him. He heard the door open, a murmur of voices. Within moments, footsteps approached.

"Your majesty, the ambassador from Briarwood has arrived to convey the condolences of their court."

Christopher did not look at his guardsmaster. The fiery orange above the city resembled the burning in his heart, the embers of his anger still stoked. He liked it best when the sky faded to the coolness of twilight. So did—had—Lily.

"Send word to the councilors to receive the ambassador and inform the kitchen staff to offer her refreshment."

Silence. After a moment, Christopher realized Martin still stood in the room. He turned and glared at the soldier over his shoulder.

"Need I repeat myself, Martin?"

Martin bowed his head. "With deepest apologies for the overstep, your highness, the ambassador asked for you."

"Tell the councilors to receive her."

"She is the second ambassador to arrive. With their majesties of Wyndemere, Briarwood is the third delegation."

Christopher shot to his feet. "Do you presume to make a point, Martin?"

"I believe you understand what I mean, your highness."

Martin did not avert his gaze, the one soldier in the entire kingdom who looked the king in the eye without deference. At least, not the same deference the other soldiers gave. Martin always addressed him with a royal title, even when they were alone, but Christopher knew Martin remembered the hours they had spent climbing trees and practicing sword fighting and archery together.

Christopher certainly did. With a father bent on conquering the entire land and a mother who died early, the young prince found in the soldier's son a ready playmate. The young king found in him a loyal guard who always expressed himself honestly.

"I suppose you have become an expert on handling royal matters now. Perhaps, instead of the council, I should take advice from you."

Martin said nothing, yet he clenched his jaw.

Christopher hated every word coming out of his own mouth. Hated the anger. All of the people coming to pay their condolences and those who worked in the castle, they all wished him well. They had stood by him as he ascended the throne and fought his way out of his father's shadow. Yet ever since losing Lily, he found himself swinging from the depths of despair to a rage that made him use his words to strike people. As if striking them enough would lessen his own pain. It did not; instead, it confused him with its relentlessness. Which made him angrier.

"I am a soldier, your highness, not a councilor."

"Yet you instruct me on my responsibilities as king."

"It is not my place to do so, your majesty. I mention it because the ambassador asked to speak with King Malcolm and Queen Celia as well. They did not meet for long, yet they all seemed to find comfort for having spoken."

"If that is the case, then tell King Malcolm I grant him the task of meeting with any visitors to the castle who come bearing sympathies. I have more important matters to consider."

Martin's gaze pointed at the tea tray, but he said nothing. Instead he bowed long and deep. "As you wish, your majesty."

His gentle tone made Christopher reach for the chair back and squeeze until his knuckles turned white. Everyone had begun speaking in those soft voices. He wished he could order them to stop.

He closed his eyes, compressed his anger into a tight box, and stuffed it deep in the back of his mind.

"How goes the work with the Left Ones?" he asked as he opened his eyes.

Martin's lips parted in confusion at the change of topic, but he recovered in the next moment.

"It goes well, your majesty. The newest batch arrived four weeks ago. A few of them show quite a bit of promise with the sword in the practice yards, and one or two have already stated their desire to work with the artisans. Of course, all tasks were suspended because...due to...under the circumstances."

Christopher nodded, and the tension in Martin's stance eased. "The queen was so happy when you brought this idea to her. Make sure the work begins again as soon as possible. Her highness will be eager to welcome the newest Left Ones to—"

A wash of realization made Christopher's body go cold, and Martin looked away. Christopher let his limbs collapse as he sat again.

"You may go, Martin."

"Yes, your highness," Martin replied in a hoarse voice.

In the time they spoke, the sky had slipped from one shade to the next. The fiery orange had long since faded into a softer pink. The same pink of Lily's cheeks when he kissed her for the first time.

Christopher dropped his head in his hands as tears slipped from his eyes.

The next morning, the king stood at a vanity just outside the wardrobe and let his fingers trail over the mother-of-pearl combs Lily favored for her hair. The combs sat at odd angles to one another, her silver-backed hairbrush lying on its side as if she had only just dropped it and intended to return after a visit to the comfort room. Ribbons in horribly cheerful colors, the ones she liked to wear on feast days, strayed across the dark wood of the Linden forest that made the top of the table.

A blanket hung from his shoulders. It was Lily's favorite,

the one she kept close in a trunk at the end of the bed for those nights when the weather changed without warning and the grand fireplace on the opposite wall remained unlit. Christopher had taken to pulling the blanket around him when he first rose from bed.

He awoke late today. At least, he assumed so from the slant of the sunlight above his head when his eyes opened. Sleeping helped him, sometimes, to forget Lily; lately he had taken to rising later and later then ordering the council to oversee matters. It was not as though Linden were at war with anyone, and the trade treaties he and Lily had begun drafting in her final weeks could wait. More than anything he wanted to stay here, in their bedchamber, and just re-member her.

A tapping on the door irritated him, and he turned to his gentleman-in-waiting. The man gave a quick nod and an-swered.

"Your majesty, a page brings a message from King Mal-colm."

"The page may enter."

A few seconds later, the page came around the door, eyes wide with wonder. Or terror. Christopher could not decide which as the page bowed.

"His highness, King Malcolm, invites you to a late break-fast with his highness, her majesty Queen Celia, and Counci-lor Ariana for the ambassador of Briarwood."

Christopher attempted a smile. "Convey my apologies to the king and queen for not attending, but thank them for their generous invitation. Their leadership at this time will not be forgotten by the Linden crown."

The page bowed again and tried to hide how fast he wanted to hurry out of the bedchamber. Christopher turned away from the sympathy on the gentleman-in-waiting's face and looked back at Lily's vanity table. After examining every-thing one more time, he pulled out the bench underneath to rearrange the items there. Lily would not have liked her table in disarray, and he would not allow it to remain in such a state.

Councilor Ariana flicked her napkin open with a flourish at the breakfast for the Briarwood ambassador and slid it onto her lap.

"I am sorry the king could not join us," the ambassador said with a sad smile. "I had so hoped to deliver my condo-lences in person."

We would all like for the king's attention to return to Lin-den, Ariana thought.

In the next moment, her conscience chided her. Years earlier, when the king dismissed King Vincent's group of ad-visors and asked her to sit on the new council he formed, she took an oath to serve him in any capacity he commanded. Back then, her mind bright with confidence and excitement, she could not have imagined her oath would compel her to fill one of the duties reserved for the head councilor.

Why did Councilor Duncan choose today of all days to meet with the beekeepers of Oswego? she thought as Briar-wood's ambassador asked after her parents in Astoria. *Surely the records of honey would have looked the same tomorrow.*

Of course, when the head councilor had set the appoint-ment weeks earlier, no one knew Linden would lose its queen and the heir to the throne in a single day. After postponing the meeting twice, everyone on the council knew it was cru-cial for Head Councilor Duncan to keep the appointment with the beekeepers from the farthest village on the Linden border.

She forced her attention back to the breakfast, keeping the conversation on nonessential issues and promising to convey the ambassador's regards to her parents. As she smiled and nodded through the rest of the meal, Ariana fought the urge to ask everyone to hurry. She itched to get back to her desk and the pile of tasks that seemed to grow by the day.

Thank the fates the king and queen came, she thought.

She marveled at their composure. Growing up in the court of Astoria as the child of ambassadors, Ariana had witnessed royals staying calm in times of crisis, but King Malcolm and Queen Celia possessed a serenity granted by the fates alone.

"Please do wish his majesty the best from Briarwood," the ambassador said, standing at the end of the meal.

Ariana shot to her feet. "Of course."

King Malcolm stood and offered the ambassador a short bow. "The king of Linden and his people cherish the support of Briarwood in this time of darkness."

Queen Celia murmured a similar sentiment, and Ariana offered the ambassador a bow per Briarwood custom. After several more minutes of mundane conversation, the ambassador and the accompanying members of the Briarwood court bid everyone farewell and left. King Malcolm turned to Ariana.

"Is there a way to persuade his majesty to join us at these meetings?"

Ariana shook her head. "If any of the councilors have sway, it would be Councilor Duncan, your highness. The king values his opinion almost as much as the queen's…"

The rest of her words disappeared in the sunlight streaming

on the breakfast table. They floated above the empty dishes and the remnants of their meal. Color made King Malcolm's face red, and Queen Celia grimaced.

The fates help me, they have lost a daughter and I speak as if I have joined the council only last week.

"Forgive me, your highness," she said. "My mother is forever telling me to consider my words before they leave my tongue."

Queen Celia nodded, but her eyes narrowed as if in pain.

"I will seek out Councilor Duncan then," King Malcolm said. "Thank you, Ariana, for your representation of the court and the throne today."

Ariana curtsied and bid the king and queen a good day, eager to leave her embarrassment behind. Another emotion had crept upon her during breakfast: frustration.

I would not need to represent the court or the throne if the king did so himself, she thought, striding down the corridors toward her office. *How long will we continue to make excuses for him? Does he not know what even a small show of confidence could do for the castle staff and members? We all grieve for the queen and the baby.*

The hem of her long white gown swished with force as she entered her study. She went to her desk and sighed at the stack of messages on it. In the time she breakfasted with the ambassador, the stack had almost doubled in size.

Ariana sat and sorted through the notes. Most of them contained condolences from residents of the capital city. A few came from the members of royal courts close to Linden. In the years she sat on her throne, Queen Lily established a pristine reputation for kindness and concern for others. Message after message from commoner and royal alike expressed shock and deep agony that she had returned to the fates.

After the tenth such note, Ariana pushed the stack aside and rubbed her eyes. All six of the councilors should have shared duties in handling correspondence, but Ariana had spent more time learning about the ways of court life than the others. Many times they came to her with questions about the wording of a message. Before anyone knew it, Ariana found herself handling almost all of the highest-level communications that did not go to the king first. On most days the messages did not pose a problem, but this was the first time she sat on the council during a tragedy for the entire kingdom. The number of messages, even in their sincerity, had begun to irritate her.

If I sit here all afternoon replying to everyone, I will never get any of my own work done.

She pushed the messages aside and pulled out a report buried under them. Condolences could wait. The work of running the kingdom could not.

And if the king continues mourning in private, we may be running the kingdom for him longer than any of us anticipated.

The thought soured her mood, and she sat back in a huff. Her gaze wandered to her desk: the condolences, reports from various corners of the kingdom, her writing utensils, and a box of blank onion-skin paper ready for correspondence. She reached for the light paper and let her fingertips rest on it.

When King Christopher ascended the throne, he made clear he expected an open line of communication between the council and himself. In the first few months after his coronation, councilors hesitated to approach him. His affable nature convinced them he meant what he said, even if he let slip his uncertainty at the most inopportune times.

Queen Lily's self-assurance and calm demeanor changed

the king. When he hesitated, the queen spoke with confidence and clarity. At first, King Christopher side-eyed her. As the public's opinion of him became positive, he began watching with open admiration. By the end of their third year as married monarchs, everyone from one corner of the continent to the other knew of King Christopher's devout adoration of his wife.

Ariana sighed long and loud as she reached for the condolences again. The work of the kingdom waited, yes, but she knew her oaths bound her to serve the king in reality and the queen in memory. She shuffled through the messages and organized them in order of dates received. A knock sounded at her door.

"Come."

A page stuck her head around the door. "Councilor Ariana, I have the day's correspondence for you."

Without looking up from the stack in her lap, Ariana waved the page to come inside.

"Just leave them somewhere," she said, gesturing in a vague manner.

"Here, Councilor?"

Ariana looked up and caught the page suppressing a smile at the sight of her desk.

"Yes, well, I suppose I need a better system," Ariana muttered. She looked around her study and spotted an empty carton, shallow in depth. The sight of it made her sit up straighter.

"A more organized system," she said a little louder this time. "Roxanne, place the correspondence in that box and leave it here on the edge of my desk."

The page did as Ariana asked then stepped back and clasped her hands behind her back.

"May I carry any messages for you, Councilor?"

Ariana pulled out blank paper and a fountain pen. "Not at this time, Roxanne, thank you."

The page bobbed and breezed to the door. "There's an envelope on the top asking for your immediate attention, Councilor."

"Thank you." Ariana frowned at an inkblot that sat on the paper like a spider claiming residence. "The fates and all, I have lost all sense of speaking *and* writing today."

"I beg your pardon?"

"Nothing. You may go. Oh, and ask a kitchen page to bring me a tray for midday meal later."

The page bobbed again. "Yes, Councilor."

The door shut, but Ariana did not pay any attention. Instead, she dropped the ruined note into the box on her desk and pulled out a fresh sheet of paper. She bit the end of her pen to consider her words with care before committing them to the page.

The king may be shirking his duties at the moment, but I will not shirk mine, she thought.

CHAPTER 6

In the early morning hours of the next day, Lemuel straightened his most formal tunic, squared his shoulders, and headed to the petitioners' court.

Since the queen's return to the fates, castle representatives had stopped accepting new petitions until after the funeral. Ongoing petitions, however, could still be considered, and Lemuel's appeal fit the criteria. He'd been visiting the court for nearly two years, and he certainly wouldn't stop now.

Maybe the councilors will get back to my case now that things are quiet, he thought. *After all, there's nothing left to do for the queen but bury her.*

He glanced at the changing colors of the sky as he made his way to court. Lemuel liked coming early. The councilors often had more patience first thing in the morning. Of course, after a hearty breakfast, anyone would be in a good mood. Lemuel's stomach pulled into a tight fist as he remembered the days when he had the luxury of choices for food. Now he and his family bought what was most affordable, in the months they could afford it at all.

The council has to approve my petition. The court owes me that much after everything we've lost.

Nodding at the guard standing at the door, Lemuel entered the court and went down the long aisle to the front. He chose his favorite seat in the pews set aside for petitioners.

No one else came this morning, which made him feel better. He'd argued his case in front of every size of crowd, but he liked it best when he and the councilors assigned to court that day could discuss matters alone.

After several minutes, the guard by the entrance shut the main door and came down the aisle. He announced the formal opening of court and asked for all in attendance to stand in respect for the petitioners' court of Linden and the royal councilors. Lemuel jumped to his feet.

There's no one else here, he thought, a little sprig of hope blooming in his chest. *That has to be a good sign. Today I get justice for Fin and Father and the money the kingdom owes us.*

Three councilors filed onto the dais from a side door, and Lemuel recognized them right away: Councilor Caleb, Councilor Ross, and Councilor Beatrice. As they made their way to their seats, they made eye contact with him. He bowed then waited until all three sat before taking his own seat.

"Good morning, Lemuel," Councilor Caleb said. "First one into court, I see."

"Yes, Councilor," Lemuel replied with another bow from his seat. "I need to reach the guild offices early this morning, so I thought I would stop here first."

Councilor Beatrice tilted her head in sympathy. "Lemuel, you must know that even with your initiative in coming at this hour, we cannot offer you anything until the council rules on your case."

He could have recited her response himself; he'd heard it so many times before. Instead, he forced a smile. Clasped his hands in his lap. Tried to appear reasonable.

"Councilor, I'm sure you and the other councilors are busy with many important things, but this is my family's livelihood. We need what's owed to us."

Studying the document, Councilor Ross said, "And you are certain you are owed this many silvers?"

Lemuel clenched his teeth. Councilor Ross was the newest advisor to court, having just joined King Christopher's circle the previous year, and had only heard Lemuel's case once before. Still, it irritated Lemuel that he would need to repeat himself yet again.

Remember why you're here. Focus on that.

"I understand why it might be confusing," he said in his most contrite voice. "Both my brother and my father were members of the Linden lumber guild. Finley lost his life doing the kingdom's work under King Vincent. According to the former king's laws our family is owed two hundred and fifty silvers, but we didn't receive a single copper. Then, two years ago, my father became severely injured. I'm here to make sure King Christopher upholds the law for both my father and Finley; that's what my petition is about."

Councilor Ross shook his head. "The laws of the former king are changing, Lemuel."

"Not this one. I checked. In fact, I check with the official record keeper every month. King Christopher hasn't changed anything regarding what's owed to the lumber families."

"Be that as it may, there are certain forms to follow. Have you entered your name on the List of Grievances?"

Lemuel scoffed. The List of Grievances should have been named the Lifetime of Grievances. It felt that long anyway.

"You come to us in good faith, Lemuel," Councilor Caleb said in a gentle tone. "Keep that faith in the council and the king. You will have the opportunity to present your full case at the appropriate time."

"When?" Lemuel asked. "It's been years. Isn't the king duty-bound to protect us and make sure his people get their due? How long do we have to wait for him to rule on a matter?"

"The kingdom is experiencing a tragedy at this time," Councilor Beatrice said.

"My family was experiencing a tragedy long before the kingdom was," Lemuel said, his voice increasing in volume. "First King Vincent refused to grant payment, even though the law clearly dictates what we're owed. Then he returned to the fates, and I was told to wait for the transition of power. Now the queen. Can you actually tell me that in all this time the royal accountants haven't found what's rightfully ours? Does the king understand how it feels to wait for years to receive what's owed and then to be told to wait longer?"

The neutral looks on the councilors' faces made Lemuel bolt to his feet.

"I'm sick of waiting for the king to do what's right. Is this how he takes care of his people? Does he have any idea how wrong this is? Do any of you?"

His breath came shallow and fast, but the councilors still didn't respond. After a moment, he stomped out of the room. The guard on duty raised a hand to wave goodbye, but Lemuel ignored him as he made his way down the long lane back toward the heart of the city. He'd wasted enough time this morning.

King Christopher won't fulfill his promises unless someone makes him, Lemuel thought, his mood getting darker with every step. *I'll have to get his attention in a way he can't ignore.*

"He will not be the only one to argue a case," Ross said, sitting back in his chair. "With the queen gone, we must organize these petitions. When should we approach the king about them?"

Beatrice's grip on the papers in front of her made her skin taut across her hands. More than ever, she missed the queen's patience, her steady voice, and her reassurance that all would be well. Ross had proven a valuable addition to the council, but his lack of experience often exasperated Beatrice.

"We cannot intrude on the king's mourning, Ross," she said, trying to mimic the queen's composure. "Her majesty entrusted us to work with her on the petitions, and we must continue the work she is doing. Was doing. Did."

Grief overcame her, and she squeezed her eyes shut. How many times would she cry for the queen? How could a person contain so many tears?

"This is a difficult time for all," Caleb said as Beatrice opened her eyes again. "We must do what we are able and beg for patience from the petitioners. They will understand."

Beatrice's hand fluttered with anxiety as she retrieved one of the pages in front of her. She and the councilors had spent so many hours already dealing with the long lists of petitioners left wanting by King Vincent. When Queen Lily brought the council the task of untangling the mess Vincent left, Beatrice believed it would take only a year or two to straighten out.

She shook her head now at the naivete she and the councilors had possessed. No one knew until the royal accountants started pulling apart the ledgers one transaction at a time just how deeply King Vincent's betrayal of his own people went. How he had gouged them for what they had rightfully earned. Now, years after making the discovery, Beatrice had begun to see the positive outcomes of their days and nights cross-referencing and calculating and double-checking against the records of the lumber guild, but the list of petitioners was long.

Would they understand? Could they? She did not know, but she and the other councilors had to try to make it so.

A few hours later, the queen's funeral procession left the castle.

Christopher watched from a window as King Malcolm and Queen Celia rode in the open carriage following his wife's coffin. Reserve guards from the Linden force and the Wyndemere guards who came with the king and queen traveled on foot in tight formations around the carriage with more guards in front and behind on horseback.

Lily's parents sat with backs straightened by grief; Christopher's body curved inward as he trudged back to his apartments. Martin led the guard surrounding the royal carriage today, but he had posted two other guards for the king's protection and they followed Christopher now. He wished for a moment that his friend had stayed and then wondered why he would want to remain under the watchful gaze of a man who meant well but asked too many questions.

A day for contradictions then, Christopher thought, his words landing inside his head with dull thuds. *Lily here but not; the king of Linden fulfilling his duty but not; wanting a good friend for support but not.*

Castle staffers whispered about other contradictions too. The way King Malcolm attended council meetings while Christopher excused himself with a headache or an upset stomach. Christopher's irritability where he used to smile or offer a joke. His command to see reports only to turn them away again moments later. So many contradictions.

But life itself had become a contradiction for Christopher. In his childhood, he spent hours working on his lessons or practicing with a sword or a horse for a handful of words of praise from Vincent. When they did not come, he convinced himself he did not need them. After all, everyone in Linden spoke of his father's cruelty. Even he, as the crown prince, could not be immune to it.

Marrying Lily, at the time, had been a political obligation. He did so for the betterment of Linden and to regain Wyndemere's trust and its excellent trading posts. She, in turn, saw an opportunity to strengthen her father's alliances against any future skirmishes with other kingdoms. Their relationship, he had counseled himself at the time, could be nothing more. Any attempts to depend on Vincent had taught Christopher not to depend on anyone.

Then Lily came into his life and shattered that notion. From its shards, she fashioned a new looking glass for Christopher. She showed him that he possessed the potential to rule. She offered him loving parents who saw him as a son. She gave him a family.

She alone knew the stories of the loneliness in Christopher's childhood. She alone became their banishment. How could his people expect him to continue when the source of his strength no longer remained?

And what of the king and queen? Could you not remain strong for them?

He shook his head at his conscience as he arrived at his bedchamber. In time he would speak to them, offer them words of reassurance. Today, however...today he could not even reassure himself.

The familiar sense of inadequacy crawled up his spine like a line of stinging insects. To distract himself, he cast about in his mind for a way to stay busy. He crossed to the informal desk just to the left of the door. As protocol required, two royal councilors stayed in the castle during the funeral procession. That morning Christopher had sent a message to them to meet about the latest reports from

Linden's lumber trade as well as other matters. Today, he thought, would be a good day to honor his wife by continuing the work they had once done together.

As he reached for his formal robe, once again his eyes felt heavy. Since Lily's return to the fates, he found himself fighting this dragging feeling nearly every hour of the day. It drew him back to his bedchamber all the time. Martin had suggested sending for a healer, but Christopher refused. He did not need a healer. He would never employ the services of a healer again. Besides, he was not ill; he simply needed to rest.

"A short nap," he murmured as he settled into his bed, "then I will call for Ariana and Caleb…"

His eyes fluttered shut, and he fell asleep within minutes.

Ariana sat with her head in her hands, blinking at the reports on her desk. Maybe, if she blinked hard and fast enough, they would disappear. Maybe they would crumble into ashes.

Do not think of ashes. Do not think of destruction. The fates help us, what is happening to our trees?

She tried to ignore the pile of reports to her right, the ones dated the week before the queen's death. In that week, as the castle representative for matters of education, Ariana had visited seven schools upon their request. Two received funding for textbooks, and Ariana went as much as a royal guest attending a formal thank you event as to make sure the castle funds had been appropriately used.

Three schools asked to show Ariana the new tools they received from her home kingdom of Astoria for the study of chemistry. As the mediator for the procurement, Ariana considered it her duty to honor those requests. One school asked for her to listen to parents and administrators present their case for partial funding to renovate their higher-level institute.

The last school also invited her to thank her for the new desks it received. Built from Linden wood. Magic wood. Or it had been anyway. Until the reports made her reconsider.

She chided herself again for not paying closer attention to them. But how could she have done so? Between the school visits and then the queen's death and the visits by ambassadors from other kingdoms...

Your duty is to Linden first, a voice inside her reprimanded, *regardless of the goings-on of the castle or anywhere else. You missed an opportunity to address this earlier.*

I am human, she retorted in her mind, *only capable of handling so much and...the fates help me, am I actually arguing with* myself *now?*

She glanced at the report from a village in the far southeast corner of Linden. The missive arrived earlier but had been buried in the box on the edge of the desk. The box intended to help her stay organized.

And it has done just the opposite, she thought. She allowed herself the brief luxury of dropping her head in her hands again then looked up. *Will the king forgive me for this error?*

In a bid for industriousness, Ariana had decided just that morning to clean out the box. When she came upon the envelope marked "Urgent," she sat down with it during her breakfast. As she read the first five lines, she spat out her morning tea.

And stained my dress in the process, she thought, doing her best to distract herself. She looked at the blotch on her lap. Under normal circumstances, she would have taken the time to retire to her apartments inside the castle and change her clothes. The report forced her to stay in her seat, and she read it again to remind herself that some things counted for more than a ruined dress.

Three weeks earlier, a lumberjack in Severson Dells had set out early in the morning. The head of his team, he wanted to walk the area of the Linden forest to be felled that day to fulfill a large order from the village's furniture makers. A wealthy man wanted to present his new bride with an exceptional gift and requisitioned the craftsmen to create enough furniture to fill the house he had commissioned.

When the lumberjack reached the area he plotted on a map the previous evening, he came across a disturbing scene. A white moss-like plant had begun to creep up the trunks of many of the honey-colored trees. In his 20 years of the trade, the lumberjack had never encountered anything like this.

The lumberjacks' guild schooled all of its members on basic tree diseases, although the Linden forest never experienced them. The magic kept the wood strong and healthy and ensured that when the lumberjacks cut one tree, another one sprouted in its place overnight. Often, the lumberjacks were asked by guilds in other nations to help when large swathes of their non-magic trees needed cutting. They saw their share of tree disease in those trees.

Even with all his experience, however, the Severson Dells lumberjack had not seen this white moss. When he put his hand to it, he wrote, it became firm, as if refusing to loosen its grip on the tree. Unlike the varieties of moss on the ground resembling patches of fine grass, this moss looked like minuscule spiky plants. The poker-straight tentacles folded inward and formed a net when approached by human hands. As if wanting to keep the tree all to themselves.

The lumberjack contacted the head of his guild's chapter

in Severson Dells who, in turn, contacted the head of the kingdom guild in the capital city. Within two days of that first letter, however, the lumberjack witnessed an event that made him break into a cold sweat. When he returned to the forest to check on the trees, several had disappeared. In their places sat large mounds of white ash.

The trees had collapsed, leaving behind the dust of their former selves.

Ariana's hands became clammy, and she had already read the report twice. In her entire lifetime—even her parents' lifetimes, for she would have heard had it happened—the trees of Linden had never failed. Her parents had traveled leagues of miles and often spoken of the superiority of Linden wood. Its magic and reliability had endured through generations.

She got up from her desk and paced behind it, pressing her hands to her stomach.

As a student of history, Ariana had embraced the stories of her adopted kingdom. Tales of Linden wood went back to the kingdom's founding hundreds of years earlier. Lumberjacks would fell the trees, which would grow back to full height within a year. The speed of growth meant a dependable trade source for Linden, and the magic in the wood meant products made from Linden lumber would last decades.

The magic discerned a craftsman's intentions. If the craftsman handling the raw wood possessed any malice, any ill will in his heart, the wood refused to yield. Court jesters told tales of the countless villains who tried, by force, to shape the wood into weapons. Every single time, the wood's bark protected it from being carved. Often the tales ended with the ill doer dropping a heavy piece on a foot and fracturing ankles or toes, becoming maimed for life in the process.

Intentions of making items of beauty or practicality—beams for a house; a flute to play music; a toy cart for a child to pull behind her—brought about sturdy results. Some artisans who crafted wood sculptures swore the magic guided them as they carved flourishes and faces into their pieces. Ariana did not think that last bit true, but no one could doubt the solidity of a Linden wood item.

And now the wood had begun to fail.

She grabbed the back of her chair to steady herself but jerked her hands away. The chair, like her desk and so many other pieces of furniture, had been made of Linden wood. What if they, too, collapsed? How could they know what items were safe and what not?

A knock sounded at her door.

"Come," she said, wincing at how her voice wavered.

Her page, Eleanor, used her shoulder to open the door as she pushed into Ariana's study with a tray.

"I have your mid-morning coffee, Councilor," she said with a broad smile as she brought the tray to Ariana's desk. "I believe the cooks have made those light biscuits that you..."

Eleanor caught sight of Ariana's face, and her smile fell. She put down the tray on a narrow side table.

"What's wrong, Councilor?"

Ariana could tell the tray in Eleanor's hands was one made of Linden lumber, from the western end of the kingdom if she recognized the color of the wood correctly. She tried to picture the terrible disease bursting into existence on the tray. Her hands trembled.

Calm yourself, Ari, she thought. *You will do no one any good if you panic. But we cannot lose the trees. Our people will not be able to feed their families if we do.*

"Councilor, are you ill? Your face is so pale."

Ariana gulped. *The king must know. No one else can lead*

us through this. But how will he lead us if he is so mired in his grief?

"Go to the royal apartments with a request to see the king at once," she said, fighting to keep her voice steady.

"The royal apartments? Councilor, is everything—"

"Run, Eleanor," Ariana barked. "It is a matter of the kingdom's security."

The page offered Ariana a quick bob before leaving. Ariana gathered the reports and put them into a folder. Now more than ever, she could not lose heart.

Lily hurried down the corridor. Christopher called to her, but when she turned around her eyes tightened with anxiety. She resumed her pace, dashing down the hall. He called again, but she did not look back. Twenty paces ahead, she stopped at a door and knocked on it as hard as she could.

As the king reached her, the door swung open a few inches. Lily pushed it open with both hands, ran inside, and slammed the door shut. A moment later, the king heard a scream.

Christopher bolted upright in his bed, heart thundering. After a moment, he realized the knocking was not just in his dream. He ran a hand over his face and found it covered in sweat. Fumbling through the bedclothes, he pulled out a handkerchief. The knocking at the door became insistent.

"For fates' sake," Christopher called to his gentleman-in-waiting, "what do they want?"

The gentleman-in-waiting jumped and answered the door. He poked his head through, and Christopher could hear insistent tones. The king wiped his face again and tried to take deep breaths to calm his pulse.

The gentleman-in-waiting drew back into the room. "Councilor Ariana has sent a page to say she must meet with you on an urgent matter that is..."

The man opened his mouth, but no words followed; Christopher crossed his arms.

"Out with it, man."

"It is a matter of our kingdom's security," the man replied, his tone uncertain.

Christopher considered what might threaten Linden. "Is there news from their majesties of Wyndemere?"

"I do not believe so, sire. No runners have returned with word of ill will or harm come to the procession."

"Ariana may meet me in the councilors' study in ten minutes," Christopher said, "unless you believe it might take longer to make myself presentable."

Shaking his head, the gentleman-in-waiting leaned back through the door and relayed the message then hurried to the long wardrobe inside the wall. Within a few minutes, Christopher stood in a fresh shirt and a light robe. He affixed a royal circlet on his head then left his bedchamber with his two guards.

When he entered the councilors' study one corridor away from his private apartments, Ariana greeted him with a deep curtsy as did a page before she was dismissed by the councilor.

"What is the matter, Ariana?" Christopher asked as he made his way to the head of the table.

She reached into a large file folder and pulled out a sheaf of papers. "Sire, I have received reports of a disturbing trend. The trees are not well. There is some illness that has befallen them."

Christopher jerked back in surprise. "What do you mean?"

Ariana relayed the story of the lumberjack in Severson Dells and reports from other villages. The white moss seemed to inflict trees at random. One lumberjack in Rondout reported a whole line collapsing in ashes save for one tree at the end that stayed standing.

As she spoke, Christopher's back became rigid. He took a deep breath, which helped a little, but when he tried to swallow he found his mouth dry.

"While I waited for you to arrive, your highness," Ariana said, "I received another message."

"Another?" Christopher asked, cursing his croaking voice.

She nodded. The previous night a housewife in Rosewood reported that during a dinner gathering of friends, a chair fell out from beneath her husband. As the friends helped the man, the dining table, made from Linden wood and full of dishes, dropped to the floor.

"The message states it looked as if the legs simply gave way, and the table itself...disappeared in the ashes." Ariana averted her gaze, staring at an invisible spot instead.

Christopher fished for a handkerchief in his pocket and wiped his hands. He laid his palms flat on the top of the table. After a moment, he noticed no scribe had joined them; neither had the other councilor who elected to stay in the castle.

"Have you notified Caleb of this meeting?"

"He sent word he would join us as soon as he has finished filing his reports on dairy production for the month."

The king nodded, still unsure of how to react. He sat there and stared at the papers Ariana left on the table, considering what Lily would say when she heard. But she could not hear now. She would never hear again. The healer allowed Lily to die, and Lily had not fought hard enough to stay.

A block of anger hardened inside him. How dare Lily

leave him at a time like this? She knew he could not rule without her. What was he to do now?

And this foreign disease that attacked the trees of Linden. What right did it, or any invader, have to encroach on the livelihood of his people? Had they not already endured loss? His mother; his father. Lily. The baby. What more would be taken from them? From *him*?

Christopher stood and pushed back the chair. "Send word to Caleb that he will join us immediately. We must contact the Keeper of the Wood right away."

Ariana hurried out to find a page. Christopher pulled the reports toward him, shocked at how many he saw. At the dates and how far back the disease made itself known. Alone with his thoughts again, he knew Lily would not have left of her own accord. He lost her because he had allowed the wrong person to take care of her.

I failed you, Lily, he thought. *I failed to keep you safe. But I will find a solution to this problem. I* will *stop the destruction of the trees.*

I will not fail you in this.

CHAPTER 7

King Malcolm nodded at the mourners who lined the streets to attend his daughter's funeral procession.

He fought the urge to screw his eyes shut to the reality, wishing again he could make the entire tragedy disappear. By the order of the fates, of life, of parentage, he should not have lived long enough to fulfill this duty. Lily and Christopher should have been sitting in this carriage today during *his* funeral procession.

A hand slipped into his, and he laced his wife's fingers with his own. As a father, he felt as if he had failed his duty to protect his child. The fates only knew how Celia felt. Lily's older brother, in another kingdom by the sea, would have just received news of her death. He would feel the weight of this day in another way.

Thinking of his son brought Christopher to mind. His place was here in the carriage, not back at the castle. His son-in-law had plunged into his grief with abandon. Malcolm doubted even Vincent's death affected Christopher this much.

Then again, he was busy rescuing a kingdom from the possibility of chaos, Malcolm thought.

He surveyed the crowd. Lindeners stood with flowers in their hands, throwing them in the direction of the protected coffins of Lily and the baby as they passed. Many Lindeners cried, the women weeping without hiding it, the men hanging their heads and scuffing the ground or rubbing their eyes several times. Even as their presence reminded Malcolm of the awful reason why he sat in the carriage, the sight of all these people reassured him. They loved his daughter. Their cries of disbelief and the hands and handkerchiefs pressed to mouths told him they shared the depth of his anguish.

"Your majesty," Celia murmured from his right, "a messenger."

Malcolm scanned the crowd and saw the messenger's flag in the distance. This messenger, however, did not carry the standard of Linden. He wore the pastel tones representative of Wyndemere, and his speed told of his determination to reach the royal carriage.

"Do you suppose..." Celia said.

Malcolm leaned out of the carriage to the closest guard. "A Wyndemere messenger approaches, soldier."

The guard nodded and sent word to the front of the ring of soldiers surrounding the carriage. The carriage driver slowed the horses and stopped, letting the man approach. As he got closer, Malcolm saw a flurry of emotions cross his face: anxiety; trepidation. Impatience.

The messenger brought his horse next to the carriage and offered Malcolm and Celia a bow from the saddle.

"My deepest apologies, your majesties," he said, his breathing shallow, "for I know this is not a day to disturb you. The royal advisors deemed it necessary to notify you at once, however."

Malcolm shook his head. "No matter. What news do you bring from Wyndemere?"

The messenger opened one of his saddlebags and pulled out a letter. As Malcolm unrolled it, he could sense the agitation from his council in the writing. Inkblots dotted the page, and in three different places the writer had crossed out a word and rewritten it. Toward the end of the message, the script became looser as if the writer hurried to finish.

The ink stains receded as single phrases jumped out at Malcolm.

"...death of the child..."

"...stable collapsed..."

"...advisors cannot accept what happened..."

"How could Linden wood fail?"

For a moment, he forgot everything else—where he sat; the reason for the procession; why he came to Linden—as the news of more loss settled in his mind. Celia tugged on the note, and he let it slide from his fingers as he sat back, dazed. His wife's gasp startled him, and Malcolm blinked slowly as if waking from a long sleep.

The cheerful blue sky defied the message's harsh truth. Spring in Linden had always delighted him. Even when he would visit as a boy, he loved this season best. Gardens bloomed in rich abundance, and the city's gardeners showcased the best flowers in the beds dotting the capital. They had taken extra measures to prepare special flower displays in Lily's honor today.

Lily. She lost her life in an event out of everyone's control. Now this latest news. How many more would they lose before the fates restored the balance of the universe?

"Soldier, turn the procession around," Malcolm announced to the Linden guard nearest him. "We must return to the castle at once."

The soldier nodded and offered Malcolm a short bow from the saddle, although he could not suppress a flit of surprise. Malcolm instructed the messenger to follow the procession back to the castle. He wished he could mourn his sweet Lily, but it seemed as though the fates had decided otherwise.

"Poor Corin," Queen Celia murmured as the procession slowed. "And what Advisor Daniel must be enduring."

What we ourselves endure already, Malcolm thought with a grimace.

The caravan of foot soldiers flagged as word passed down the line that the king wished to return to the castle. Within minutes, Martin, using his knees to guide his horse through the crowds, approached the royal carriage. He offered Malcolm and Celia a short bow from the saddle.

"Is there any difficulty, your highnesses? One of my men informed me we are to turn around."

"We have received terrible news from Wyndemere," Malcolm said, "and we must prepare for an immediate departure."

Martin surveyed the people of the city and others pressing their way toward the carriage with the Wyndemere royals in it. The carriage with the coffins, not having received the command, continued on its way. After a moment, Martin turned his attention back and opened his mouth, but Malcolm stopped him with a raised hand.

"I realize the importance of this day, Martin. More than all the Lindeners gathered here, the queen and I understand how much it means to the people to express their sorrow. But we received word from Wyndemere that demands our attention. One of the royal stables collapsed two days ago just as the daughter of one of my advisors went to fetch her horse for her riding lesson. Her nursemaid and two stable hands accompanied her, and all of them—Adelaide, the maid, and the stable hands—were trapped inside."

Martin flinched then bowed his head. "My deepest regrets to you and young Adelaide's family. I will ask the procession to begin making its way back."

"Martin."

"Yes, sire?"

Malcolm knew he had yet to deliver the worst of the news but did not know how. Never in his decades as king had he heard of anything like this. It tied Linden and Wyndemere to one another in a way perhaps even Lily's death could not.

"The stable was made of Linden wood."

Martin's eyes became large.

"But...but, your majesty, how......"

Malcolm shook his head, as much in sorrow as bewilderment. "I do not know. But it is vital we speak to King Christopher and then return to Wyndemere."

Martin looked at the crowds again and, despite the hum of people, lowered his voice. "The residents of Linden have sustained a great shock in receiving news of the queen. This news would push them into pure panic."

"Let the procession continue with Lily for another hour," Celia said, leaning toward Martin to join the conversation. "The guards of both kingdoms may stay with her, but his majesty and I, as well as the Linden royal councilors, should return to the castle so we may address this matter with the king."

Martin nodded and bowed once again. He gave his horse a slight flick of the reins and maneuvered the mount to the head of the carriage procession. After a few words with the guard there, Malcolm watched as Martin continued to the procession around Lily's coffin and spoke to the Wyndemere guards around it. They stiffened at Martin's words but saluted him and raised their chins a little higher. The scene repeated itself when he went to the carriage in which Christopher's four councilors rode.

Malcolm's heart constricted as the driver received word to turn the carriage around. Saying so and accomplishing the task were two different matters, but after guiding the carriage around the large roundabout in the city center, the horses faced the way they came. With the carriage set on its return, Malcolm allowed himself the momentary luxury of letting his back round against the cushions. Next to him, Celia choked back a sob.

"How much sorrow can a heart bear, Malcolm? How much more can we lose? How will we help Daniel and Corin through the loss of their child when we still grieve the loss of our own?"

He did not answer. The part of his mind that always viewed matters as a king first wondered whether Christopher would have the fortitude to bear this news. Could he withstand the burden of what it meant? And what, in fact, did it mean?

How could the wood of Linden fail?

Lemuel followed the king and queen's carriage through the city, which wasn't easy considering the number of people who'd appeared to mourn in public. Fortunately, he wasn't alone. He knew if he lost sight of the carriage, even for a few minutes, someone else in the group would manage to keep it in their sights.

As he ducked under the arm of a towering man blowing his nose into a handkerchief, Lemuel thought again of what had happened at home that morning.

"You're foolish to think the king will stop everything and talk to you, Lemuel," his father said, readjusting the blanket that covered his severed leg.

Lemuel's mother brought a breakfast tray, and Lemuel took it. As she had every day, three times a day, for the past two years, his mother helped his father adjust the portable table he used for his meals before reclaiming the tray and setting it on the table.

"He's more than foolish," his mother said. "There's a reason why the court has a system, son."

"The system isn't working, Mother."

His mother sniffed in derision and went back to the kitchen.

"So you've decided a protest at the procession today is the way to handle this," his father said with a sideways glance at him. "Chelsea, where's my coffee?"

"I'm only one person, Harold!"

"Then make it first."

"If you have a problem with the way I run the kitchen, you can run it yourself."

His father's jaw went slack for a moment.

"If I could run at all, I wouldn't need your blasted mud in a cup," he muttered.

His mother bustled back in a few moments later, coffee pot and mug in hand.

"A protest will get people's attention," Lemuel said. "King Christopher won't have a choice. He'll have to listen to me with so many others watching."

His father shook his head and drank a large gulp of the coffee then scowled. "There you go again. You're not your brother, Lemuel. Just go to the procession, pay your regards like everyone else, and come home."

His mother patted him on the cheek with her free hand. "No one expects you to be a hero, Lemuel."

That was the problem. No one expected him to be anything. His brother had been the hero, the large strapping man who brought in significant wages. His father too.

Lemuel never had any interest in joining the lumber

guild. He preferred the world of numbers and books. Philosophy; art. Subjects no one at home understood.

His friends understood, or at least they knew how helplessness felt. Today's protest started as a joke in the common room of an inn, but the more Lemuel considered it the more it made sense. He needed to do something bold to catch the castle's attention. For two years, he'd followed the law to the letter by going to the petitioners' court to ask for what the kingdom owed his family, and what did he have to show for it? A pair of worn-out shoes and a pair of weary parents resigned to the pension the lumberjacks' guild sent every month. It covered basic expenses, but it didn't pay for the humiliation his father experienced because of his injury. It didn't pay for his mother's tears at night when she thought no one heard her weeping for her older son.

Enough was enough. Lemuel decided to try a different tactic. To force King Christopher to listen when the circumstances wouldn't allow for anything else.

It surprised him how many people agreed that day in the inn to the protest. They all had grievances against the crown. Against Vincent and the son who didn't seem confident enough to rule. With exchanges of slaps on the back and words of bravado, their protest became a reality.

Now, though, as he followed the carriage with King Malcolm and Queen Celia in it, his mind spun. The king of Linden, it seemed, had decided not to ride in the processional. Lemuel bowed to the queen's coffin as it rolled by and then stayed in place until the carriage of the Wyndemere royals came in sight. He'd followed it ever since it entered the city lanes. How could he protest when the person he needed to confront wasn't even here?

"Lemuel," a voice hissed.

He turned and watched his friend, Bailey, elbow his way

through the tight spaces between the crowd. A woman squawked at the way Bailey nudged her, and she glared at him. Lemuel made eye contact with her, and the glare settled in his direction. He shrugged, palms in the air.

"The carriages with the king and queen and the councilors are turning around," Bailey said in a whisper.

"What? Why?"

"No idea, but they went around the fountain. It looks like they're going back to the castle."

Back to the castle. Where King Christopher had, presumably, stayed behind. Lemuel's mind worked through a variety of scenarios, but only one made the most sense.

"Spread the word to head toward the castle, but stay out of sight. We'll regroup at the trees."

Bailey nodded with serious excitement and hurried back through the crowd as Lemuel crossed the street. He turned toward the castle, and after several moments he could spot its spires at the end of the long lane he'd chosen. Those spires seemed to point in arrogance over the regular people of Linden; people like him.

He was done being regular. Today King Christopher would hear his demands. Lemuel knew it.

Christopher entered his study, prepared to write an urgent message to the Keeper of the Linden Wood, and stopped just inside the door.

He had not returned to the room since the day of Lily's death. The mustiness in the air told him none of the castle staff had visited either. Papers remained strewn across his desk. Here in the study, time had paused.

He went to his desk and found the half-finished proposal he and Lily had started writing for the kingdom of Fair Haven. Rifling through the pages, he thought of the day three years earlier when he asked Lily whether it made sense to pursue a dialogue with his mother's former home. Lily's face lit up; true, Queen Dahlia no longer lived to see the efforts, but Lily supported Christopher's wish to try to mend the fraying bond.

During Vincent's rule, relations with Fair Haven had become strained at best. Christopher still recalled his mother's wistfulness when she spoke of her homeland. Fair Haven lay far to the east, close to the sea. She would tell him stories during his nursery days of fantastical creatures in the water and spending summers learning to swim and sail in addition to her other studies.

"Ridiculous, frivolous pursuits," Vincent declared once. "We have no need for sailing and swimming in Linden."

Landlocked Linden may not have needed swimming and sailing, but an ally on the coast could have improved the country's economic efforts to another scale. For unknown reasons, Vincent never saw Fair Haven as offering any sort of opportunity. Once, when an ambassador from another kingdom suggested it, Vincent said Fair Haven's distance from Linden and its small size did not offer him any significant strategic advantage.

Mother would have been so proud to know of Lily's solutions, Christopher thought now. *And it would benefit Linden so much. But how can we pursue a dialogue of export when the wood is...*

The wood. Vincent made it the focal point of his reign. Early on he convinced people he would fight for them. More aggressive trade agreements would increase Linden's riches beyond measure and scope. Instead, as the years passed,

Vincent pushed for higher prices and lower wages, more work for less benefit.

It is a wonder Father did not meet with a hunting accident sooner, Christopher thought, then glanced with guilt over his shoulder as if someone could hear his thoughts.

Pushing the proposal for Fair Haven aside, he retrieved fresh paper from a container at the corner of his desk and paused. He ran his fingers along the edges of the container, made of the honey-colored wood from the trees in the southern part of the kingdom. The dust could not dim the wood's gleam in the cheerful sunlight streaming through the windows, and the intricate decorative patterns showed no sign of breakage or failure. Would this, too, fall apart?

He pulled a pen from a ceramic cup and ran its nib across a scrap of parchment to test the amount of ink in the pen's reservoir. Satisfied he could finish without needing to refill the ink, Christopher commenced writing. He worked through the formal greeting and the first words of his knowledge of the trees when an insistent knocking made him stop.

Christopher turned and watched his gentleman-in-waiting consult with the person on the other side.

"When?" the man asked.

A murmur answered, and its pitch made Christopher drop the pen back into the cup.

"All right, I shall inform him," the gentleman-in-waiting said and closed the door.

Christopher stood. "What is it, Jeremy?"

Jeremy frowned. "Sire, a runner has returned from the procession. King Malcolm and Queen Celia have elected to return to the castle. I have no word as to why, but their speed suggests they will arrive within the hour."

Christopher nodded. "Prepare the minor dining hall to receive them. They may require refreshment."

Jeremy bowed and leaned out of the door again, this time to address a page with Christopher's instructions. The king sat again and continued with the short letter. After stopping and starting several times, he finished the document and tucked it into an envelope. He let a fat drop of wax plop onto the flap across the back and pressed the royal seal into it, then turned to Jeremy with the message.

"Ask for a runner to take this to the correspondents' guild with instructions to send it to the Keeper of the Wood. I will go and await the arrival of their majesties."

"With your leave, sire." Jeremy gave another bow.

Christopher waved him out of the room. He tugged on his light robe and made his way to the door of the study. At the last moment, he looked over his shoulder at the treaty due for Fair Haven and vowed to return to it soon.

Malcolm wished the carriage driver would push the horses harder. He leaned forward to ask the man yet again, but Celia tugged him back. He frowned at her, but she shook her head.

"He is doing all he can, your majesty."

The king resisted the urge to cross his arms like a child—his older sister always called it another form of pouting—and trained his gaze on the Lindeners lining the streets instead. The confusion on their faces as the carriage moved back toward the castle mirrored what he felt. For a moment he acknowledged, only to himself, his helplessness. How would they all find their way out of this impossible situation?

Soon enough the carriage turned down the long lane of trees leading to the outer courtyard of the castle. As the guards marched ahead, Malcolm saw several people step from behind the trees. The hair on the back of his neck rose.

"Who are these men?" Celia asked, her eyebrows pinching. "Has Christopher sent them to receive us?"

Malcolm examined them as the carriage rolled past. They did not smile or bow. A few of the men balled up their fists at their sides. None of them wore castle livery or uniforms.

"They are not a reception party, my dear," he said, offering a few of the men a genial nod. No one responded. "Not in the way to which we are accustomed."

The carriage slowed then, and more men stood in the lane.

"You there," the driver called. "Out of the way for the king and queen of Wyndemere! They must reach the castle at once."

"We're not moving until the king and queen hear us," a man at the front of the group answered in a raised voice. "We'll let them pass if they agree to take our demands to King Christopher himself!"

"Take our demands to the king!"

"My family hasn't had full bellies in years!"

"Does he know how his people have been suffering?"

"Take our demands!"

"Take our demands!"

"Take our demands!"

"Not a reception at all, Celia," Malcolm said, "a resistance."

On an ordinary day, Ariana maintained a regal posture when she walked inside the castle. The pages groaned when she admonished them for trotting during their errands. Some of them made a game of who could complete their tasks the fastest, using their pocket watches or counting seconds in their heads. She never understood the pleasure they received in such a frivolous undertaking.

She had maintained her measured pace when she left the king and went to speak to Caleb. Despite the urgency of the situation, Ariana followed her parents' principles: rushing often led to hasty decisions, they said, which could lead to disaster. Taking her time walking from Caleb's study back to her own had given her time to think about how to craft messages to the kingdoms that imported Linden's wood.

Ariana had only managed to spend a few minutes writing the first message, however, when her page, Eleanor, burst into her study. She looked as though she had bolted through the castle, and Ariana stood. She opened her mouth to reprimand the page when the girl delivered unthinkable news.

Now Ariana dashed to the private dining hall in the king's apartments and burst into the room, her breath short more from fear than running.

"Your majesty, insurgents! In the castle!"

If her willingness to race through the corridors shocked her before, she was flabbergasted now as the king jumped to his feet and did the same. She bolted to keep in step, as did his gentleman-in-waiting and two guards.

"They just arrived," Ariana said in short breaths. "King Malcolm brought them into the petitioners' hall, and they—"

The king stopped short, and Ariana almost lost her balance as her momentum threw her forward two more steps.

"The king *brought* them here?"

Ariana hesitated before nodding.

"The runner's message said there was no other way to deal with them, your highness," she said. "The king tried to convince them to leave some of their party outside the castle, but they would not consent to that either. They demanded an audience with you, and they said they would not leave until they obtained one. The king thought it better to bring them inside instead of forcing them to leave and creating an even bigger problem. Some of their members consented to wait in the corridor outside the court, however."

King Christopher's gaze dropped to the floor, searching, and then he looked back up at her. She thought he would say something; instead, he began running again. This time Ariana grabbed her skirts, hiked them almost to her knees, and ran after him.

Christopher slowed as he approached the last corridor before the petitioners' hall. Ariana had mentioned some of the insurgents waited outside, and he did not wish to arrive looking like a common innkeeper chasing a thief with a cudgel. As he stopped at the corner of the corridor, his pace slowed even if his breathing had not. He could hear murmurs that carried a timbre of unease.

Next to him, Ariana came to a stop and gulped large breaths. Councilor Caleb arrived moments later. He, too, looked as if he had run all the way from his study. The guards did not look winded in the least, appearing more ready than ever to assess what lay around the corner.

"Do we know any more about the situation?" Caleb asked.

Ariana held up a hand, then pressed both palms to her stomach. Christopher thought of the races he and Martin ran as teenagers, both bent at the waist afterward, hands on their knees, jesting about who had beaten whom. The mental image stirred an urge to laugh at himself and the others.

Instead, he closed his eyes to find his focus again.

Insurgents. In the castle. And King Malcolm brought *them here. I cannot let this situation escape our control.*

He opened his eyes.

"Jeremy," he said to his gentleman-in-waiting, "go and alert others in the castle of the potential for conflict. Ariana, what information do you have to share?"

She licked her lips, her breathing more even now, and nodded. "My apologies, your highness, for the unseemly haste, but I thought it necessary—"

"There is no need to apologize, Ariana. Urgent circumstances require unusual measures. What of this situation?"

Ariana heaved one more breath. "From what I can gather, the insurgents met the king and queen's carriage on the road to the outer courtyard. They charged to see you, to make their 'demands' known."

"And what are these demands?"

"I do not know, sire. They say they will only discuss the matter with you. But in addition to bringing fewer people into the petitioners' hall, King Malcolm convinced them to leave their arms in the courtyard before they entered. He stipulated he would not bring armed men into the home of the royal family."

Christopher checked to make sure his circlet sat straight on his head and squared his shoulders.

"Let us find out what they want so we may encourage them on their way."

Caleb offered him a bow, which bolstered his spirits, and Ariana dropped into a deep curtsy. Christopher nodded at the guards to move ahead, and he followed them at a measured pace around the corner to the petitioners' hall. Stony faces met his gaze. Christopher did his best to maintain a neutral expression, giving the dozen or so men a simple glance before proceeding. One of the guards, John, went to the door of the hall and waited for Christopher to nod his assent. The other, Steven, stationed himself to one side of the entrance.

John entered first. "His highness, King Christopher of Linden. Rise."

Christopher entered the hall. Footsteps behind told him of Ariana and Caleb's composed entrance, and after a moment he heard the guards shut the door and take their positions on either side of it inside the court. As he remembered their frenzied run through the castle, another knot of laughter threatened to untie the gravity from his face. He and the others must have looked quite the sight as they ran.

To fight the urge, he took a moment to survey those in attendance. The king and queen sat upon the low dais from where he offered judgments and decisions. His remaining four councilors sat, two on either side, next to their majesties. Linden guards flanked the dais with Martin standing in front of it. The soldier caught his eye and bowed.

Men filled the first pews on either side of the hall. All of them stood and watched him proceed down the aisle between them. Some bowed then elbowed others to do the same. Not everyone, Christopher noted, followed suit.

He considered ascending the dais with his father-in-law and mother-in-law, but the hardened looks of the men made Christopher reconsider. He could see determination in their faces to stand their ground until their complaints were addressed. Did he want to alienate them further by appearing as if he thought of himself of a higher station?

Instead, he stopped next to Martin and clasped his hands in front. Should he berate them, he wondered. Should he sentence them to some sort of disciplinary action? He wondered what his father would do and then realized he knew how he wanted to handle the situation.

"Welcome to the castle," he said.

CHAPTER 8

Lemuel blinked a few times. Welcome? Had the king just *welcomed* them?

He'd always imagined this day with raised voices and maybe raised fists. He never thought the king would be so polite. How was he supposed to answer a welcome?

"My councilors have informed me King Malcolm has brought you here, which makes you my guests." King Christopher spread his hands. "I understand you wish to discuss an important matter. How may I serve you today?"

Lemuel stepped forward. "Your highness, my brother and father both worked in the lumber guild. They served Linden and brought in an honest day's pay, but my brother died while working in Briarwood, and my father lost his leg in an accident and hasn't worked since."

King Christopher nodded for him to go on. Lemuel shifted his weight and exchanged glances with the other men. After a moment, he continued.

"Any man injured or killed while in the wood trade is supposed to receive financial compensation. When my brother died almost ten years ago, I went to the lumber guild to secure payment. The head of the guild said he couldn't give it to me until the castle sent him official notice. That notice never came. Then Father got injured two years ago. I came back hoping things were different, but nothing's changed. My family needs those funds for my father's treatments, for the bills we owe to the healer in our lane, and other expenses. But every time, I walk away empty-handed."

"Did you bring your case to the petitioners' court?"

Lemuel rolled his eyes. "Sire, I've been to this court so many times I've become friends with the guards. Who, by the way, are just as sympathetic to my plight."

The king turned to Councilor Ariana. "Why have I not seen a report on this matter?"

"Your highness, these reports are considered in turn by their submission dates, as the council has explained to Master Lemuel on many occasions. His petition has yet to be reviewed."

"I understand, Councilor, yet surely it would not take so long."

Councilor Ariana exchanged looks with Councilor Caleb who stepped forward.

"In truth, your majesty, there was a time when the petitions were not reviewed as regularly as they are now. Within the previous regime...that is..."

"Our efforts became organized after her majesty took it upon herself to head them," Councilor Ariana jumped in. "Now with...with recent events, the councilors and I are spending our time working through the reports for the day-to-day workings of Rosewood, which means those not necessary to the capital—"

"Not necessary?" Lemuel burst out. "Not necessary? My family has spent the last two years making every single copper last, and sometimes even that's not enough. We've relied on the kindness of friends who are struggling too, but they find a way to stretch a soup or make smaller loaves of bread so everyone gets something. If the people of Linden can make this work, why can't the castle?"

"Here, here!"

Lemuel glanced at everyone who came with him, glad they'd taken the day to do so. Their presence gave him the courage to take a step forward. The guardsmaster stiffened next to the king, but Lemuel didn't pay attention to him.

"The truth is, your majesty, many people, like my family, have lost their faith in the throne's willingness to do anything," he said. "That's why I'm here today. If the throne can't work for the people of Rosewood and the rest of Linden, *I* will."

"That's right, Lemuel!"

"We don't want a weak king!"

"If you can't take care of your responsibilities, find someone who can!"

Lemuel winced. He wanted to turn and find out who'd voiced the taunt, but he didn't want to lose his momentum. He also didn't want to waste time trying to find out whether it was one of his own men or one of those who joined the group on their way to the castle. During the processional, Lemuel welcomed their support. Now he wondered whether he should have kept it to the original dozen or so friends who committed to coming.

"I assure you," the king said, "your hardships are not lost in the eyes of the castle. As Councilor Ariana said, there is a matter of priority to consider. However—"

"If you can't make your people a priority," a voice came from Lemuel's right, "then you shouldn't be king."

Lemuel's eyes widened as he turned around.

"You are advised to watch yourself, sir," Guardsmaster Martin said in a raised voice. "If you continue to voice such opinions, you will be considered a threat to his majesty and may be taken into custody."

"Wait a minute," Lemuel said, holding up his hands, "no one's here to threaten the king. We're just trying to get what's owed to us. Linden law dictates—"

"Linden law dictates what the king states it does," the soldier growled. "You are fortunate his majesty has not dictated your arrest."

"Which he has every right to do," King Malcolm said, coming to stand next to King Christopher. "We all agree this is a matter of importance, but empty threats and angry voices will not resolve it."

"Then what will? I've visited the court every week these last two years, your majesty. Have you ever gone to the same place for that long and not gotten any results?"

"Your concern is well warranted," King Christopher said in a quiet voice, "but a new matter has arisen just today that requires my immediate attention. When it is resolved, I will personally consider your case."

Heat flushed Lemuel's body. What would it take for the castle to take him seriously? He'd behaved like a model citizen, followed the proper channels, filed all the right papers. After all that, he believed he'd get an answer. Now the king, the man supposedly responsible for the well-being of all Lindeners, was saying he'd have to wait some more.

Lemuel *had* waited. His entire life, he'd waited for his brother's shadow to stop hiding him. The girls all found Finley more attractive, more interesting, just more everything. Even his nickname, Fin, made them grin in anticipation. What kind of nickname could he make out of *Lemuel*, for fates' sake?

When Fin died, part of Lemuel broke away and disappeared into the blackness of grief he shared with his parents. But a tiny part of him, no bigger than the needle of jealousy that pricked him all his life, thought, *At least Mother and Father have me. I can take care of them*. Until they reassured him, with subtle taunts and admonitions, that he couldn't. So he waited some more for the wheels of the system to grind at their own pace.

Now the king, too, was telling him he'd have to wait his turn. That he wasn't important enough to be considered. Maybe another time, the king said. Maybe another day.

Well, Lemuel was done waiting.

"You can't take time for anything else, your majesty. I'll need an answer today. Now."

For the first time since entering the hall, the king frowned. "I am not able to give you an answer today, Lemuel."

"Then maybe we'll take our answer by force," one of the men behind Lemuel called.

"We *demand* justice."

"We've all been waiting way too long."

"Take care in your words, citizens," Guardsmaster Martin said, "or you may regret them."

All of the heat in Lemuel's body burned in his head. "Maybe the king needs to take a few minutes to consider our demands then. I don't think we're asking for too much."

"I am unable to do so," King Christopher said, exchanging glances with his two councilors. "As I explained—"

"You're lying. Enough is enough."

"There's no urgent matter," Bailey said, coming to stand at Lemuel's left. "He's making this up to get away from helping the common folk. He's as much of a coward as his father was."

Councilor Ariana and Queen Celia gasped. Lemuel saw a muscle twitch in King Christopher's cheek. Queen Celia and the other councilors came down from the dais to stand behind the king who set his jaw and opened his mouth to respond. Guardsmaster Martin motioned to the other guards to come forward.

"You are under arrest for deep insult to the crown," the soldier announced.

Within seconds Lemuel found himself surrounded by his men. "You can't arrest us."

"We haven't done anything wrong other than come to you for help," Bailey added.

"You have offended the sanctity of this court and the throne," King Christopher said, lifting his chin. "I will not stand for it."

"And we should?" a man to Lemuel's right asked with a sneer; he took a step forward.

"You *will* keep your distance, sir," Guardsmaster Martin declared.

"Or what?"

"Or you will find yourself beaten and then imprisoned."

A rasp of metal behind Lemuel made him jump, and he went wide-eyed at a man who came to stand next to him with a dagger in hand.

They said they'd leave their weapons outside.

"Try it," the man said with menace, "and you'll be sorry."

The royal guards drew their swords and held them ready.

"You cannot challenge the strength of this court, Lemuel," King Christopher said. "Tell your men to retreat. Otherwise, the throne and the castle claim no responsibility for what may come next."

"As if you've ever claimed responsibility for anything important."

The man with the dagger charged forward with a wordless cry. Lemuel blinked, and the room erupted in shouts and fighting. A loud banging somewhere behind him brought more yelling. Just as he opened his mouth to call for everyone to stop, a speeding fist knocked him back two steps.

"Bloody tree burner," he cursed and swung his own fists.

Men around him screamed. Weapon rang against weapon.

The temperature of the hall soared ten degrees.

"Stop the king!"

Lemuel didn't know what that meant; he was too busy kicking one of the guards in the shins. A burst of pain showered his foot, but the guard dropped to one knee to grab his leg. Lemuel kicked him in the stomach.

A roar filled Lemuel's ears, and it startled him enough to make him stop attacking the guard. All around him, his friends and compatriots stopped too. His attention went to the dais where one of the strangers from his group held King Malcolm around the neck with one arm. With the other hand, he pointed a dagger at the monarch's side.

"Enough," the man announced, his voice raw. "We've lost one king already; we're not going to lose this one."

Lost a king?

Lemuel realized King Christopher was missing. When had he slipped out? And where was the guardsmaster?

"You will regret this course of action," King Malcolm said, gripping the man's arm with both of his hands. "You are not mercenaries or revolutionaries. You are honorable men of Linden."

"And we deserve to be treated that way," Lemuel replied. He eyed the guard on the ground, then decided against a final kick. Instead, he sauntered to the dais and hopped up the steps.

"Men, prepare to stay. For now, *we're* going to rule the castle."

He pumped his fist in the air, and a raucous round of cheers answered him.

Christopher cradled his arm as he ran. Blood seeped through the cut in his shirt sleeve, and the sharpness of the pain made him suck in a breath. He pulled the sleeve back and nearly stopped short when he saw the severity of the cut. Beads of blood ran in tiny rivulets around the curve of his arm. The sight of them made him rush down the path into the wood.

He ran a dozen more paces then slowed and came to a stop, his face screwed tight. Here, where no one could see him, he knew he did not have to be brave. For the moment, he could just be a man injured and terrified about what to do next.

His mind raced faster than his feet as it retraced the frenzied route he and Martin had taken out of the castle. With knowledge of the royal residence's layout on their side, they ran from the petitioners' hall at the first opportunity and slipped through corridors. As they made their way into a quieter portion of the castle leading to the outside, Christopher stopped once and glanced over his shoulder, undecided on saving himself when so many others remained at risk. Without a word, Martin jutted his chin forward. The king understood the protocol for times of danger, Martin seemed to say with his gesture. He would do no one any good were he to fall to the mercenaries.

As if thinking of the man had summoned him, Martin appeared.

"Your majesty," he said, breathing heavily. "You have suffered an injury."

Christopher shook his head, the mask of king already slipping back on. "A superficial wound. Were you able to reach the king and queen?"

Regret filled Martin's face. "I was not, your highness. By the time I returned to the castle, that infidel, Lemuel, had stationed two of his men at the entrance to the outer courtyard."

"Where are our guards, Martin?"

"The majority of them are still with the Wyndemere guards and..."

He trailed off, and Christopher realized in shock he had forgotten the occasion: Lily's funeral.

"If I meet them on their way to the...the burial ground," Martin said, rushing over the last two words, "then I can send the Wyndemere guards back to their kingdom for reinforcements. And if we can find a way to alert the reserve guard—"

Christopher slumped against a tree. "I thought forming the reserves would allow the men to rebuild their normal lives, and the people would see I do not need a legion of soldiers to show strength as my father did. Now..."

Martin dipped his head to meet Christopher's gaze. "All is not lost, your highness. The fates will aid us, even with few numbers."

The king stared at the way the blood continued to bead on his arm.

"You must receive attention for your injury, highness," Martin said. "Ingleside is not far. If you are able, let us make our way to the healer there."

Christopher wanted to stay right there and wait for Martin to bring help back, but he knew he could not. Ignoring proper care for his arm would only allow for complications later. He did not want to create any more problems for himself, considering the ones already facing him.

"I am able, Martin."

He straightened and tried to breathe deep. Even after losing the circlet from his head in the fray of the fight, he fought to maintain his posture as king. The pain in his arm turned into a throb that extracted all the air from his lungs. With a hard swallow, he followed the path again.

CHAPTER 9

"On my honor, Mistress Geraldine, it wasn't my fault; Bryce made me."

Geraldine eyed the squirming ten-year-old boy as she prepared a poultice for his rash. His fingers, ready to scratch, drifted to his arm, and she cocked her head at him. The boy sat on his hand instead.

"He dragged you through the Dells creepers against your will?"

She put extra force into mixing the paste. The hard knock of the spoon against the bowl made the boy's eyes go wide for a moment. His knee bounced.

"Um, well... Is that going to hurt?"

She sighed in a dramatic fashion. "Well, if you follow my instructions, it won't hurt. Much. Might sting a little. But if you don't listen to me, the rash will be the least of your problems."

The boy's eyes got even wider, and he started shaking his head.

"I promise, Mistress Geraldine, I'll do everything you say. I won't scratch or anything."

Geraldine pulled his arm toward her. "Fates help me, Kirk, how many bushes did you run through?"

She applied the paste to his arm, and the boy tugged back on instinct.

"I don't know. I was too busy chasing the ball. But Bryce

was the one who threw it."

Using a clean cloth to wrap the first arm, she turned her attention to the other one and repeated the whole process. She rubbed some of the paste into his cheeks and forehead. Then she stood back and glanced at his legs.

"I was wearing pants, because my pa wanted me to help count logs later and I didn't want splinters," he explained, "so no rashes there."

Geraldine dug the paste out of the mixing bowl and put it in a jar. Screwing the lid tight, she carried the bowl and spoon to the basin in the corner and washed her hands. She ran a little water into the bowl and came back.

"Put this on once a day," she said, handing him the jar. When he forced it into his pants pocket, she put both hands on her hips. "The best time is in the morning after you bathe."

Kirk rolled his eyes.

"At least wash your arms so you can put the paste on. A little bit, just like I did. Using all of it on the first day won't work any faster."

"As if the fates haven't made my day bad enough," he said. "How long do I have to keep using it?"

"Until it's all gone. I'm going to write a note to your mother so she can help you."

Geraldine grabbed a sheaf of loose parchments she kept in the drawer of the table in the center of the room and scribbled quick instructions as well as the amount owed for her services. Her heart skipped once, then twice; writing the numbers made her think of the money the castle owed her. She dropped her pencil into her apron pocket, folded the note, and slipped it into an envelope. Then she handed it to Kirk with an admonition to remember it and the paste.

"I will, Mistress Geraldine. No more running through

Dells creepers for me."

He darted outside, and Geraldine followed him. She caught the door before it slammed shut and shaded her eyes against the midday sun. As she watched Kirk escape, she chuckled.

She turned to close the door, but movement toward the end of the street caught her attention. Shading her eyes again, she watched as two men came into town. One lagged behind the other and held his arm as if injured; she guessed they would come to her doorstep soon enough. After a moment, though, the two rushed past the clinic as if they had not even seen her sign.

The man in the front moved with an alertness she'd seen before, although she couldn't remember where. He scanned both sides of the street and turned once or twice to make sure the other man followed. Their behavior reminded her of the castle guards, how they always remained vigilant when they walked with the—

Geraldine clapped a hand to her mouth and slammed the door shut, the sound echoing like a scolding.

The fates help me, that's the king! *And his guardsmaster...oh, what was his name? Matthew? Miles? Mar...Martin!*

Her stomach screwed into a tight knot, and acid rushed up her throat. She ran to the wash basin just in time to vomit her breakfast and continued coughing for several minutes. Filling a glass with water, she swished the liquid and spit it out, then set the glass on the counter next to the basin and leaned hard against it.

How did they find out so soon? Are they going to put me in prison? Oh, Alistair, I'm so sorry.

She waited for the inevitable knocking on the door. Any minute now, they would come and find her still acting as healer of Ingleside. They would see her flamboyant disregard for a royal decree.

As a quarter of an hour passed, though, and no one came, her breathing became more normal. The stench of the mess in the wash basin caught her attention. She cleaned it, as well as the bowl and spoon she'd placed there earlier. After lighting a few scented candles to mask the odor, Geraldine shelved the ingredients for Kirk's poultice and reached for the bowl in the drying rack. She pulled a clean cloth out of a drawer and started to dry the bowl.

Just then it broke.

Geraldine watched as the bowl's two halves disintegrated. Within moments, they became an ashy white substance that hurried from her hands to the floor like impatient snow in the middle of winter. She stood there, cloth in hand, her mind blank.

"I will inquire at the inn, your majesty," Martin said, turning around again. He noticed how the king grimaced almost with every step now and debated between rushing ahead and keeping pace with the monarch. "Surely they will know where we may find the healer."

King Christopher nodded; his face paled a shade.

Martin made his choice and hurried ahead. In the main portion of the village, like so many other villages and cities in Linden, the businesses dominated the main square. Each village and city chose a Linden tree to grow at its center. Ingleside had chosen a darker tree with rich red-brown tones in the trunk. A sturdy bench squared the tree, and Martin could imagine residents taking a moment to enjoy the temperate days on the benches.

Buildings on either side of the street butted against one another like proud boys eager to show off, and each business displayed its wares and services with large wooden signs hanging from the eaves of the first floor. The cobblestone path made travel easy, although the village remained exceptionally quiet today. Few businesses were open, and no one dawdled in the streets or in front of the doors.

"Here, your highness," he said, gesturing to the benches. "I will return in a moment."

Martin went to the building with the large wooden sign displaying a stein of ale and a bed. Another sign hung below it, hooked onto the first, letting passers-by know the inn possessed room vacancies. He stepped through the door and waited a moment for his eyes to adjust to the indoor light.

"Is anyone here?" he called.

A portly man, half bald, came out of the kitchen. His clean apron struggled to cover his stomach. When the man caught sight of the knots on Martin's shoulder, his expression went from annoyed to astonished.

"Guardsmaster." The man half-bowed. "Welcome to Sullivan's Inn."

"I am looking for the healer of Ingleside. Do you know where I may find her? Or him?"

The man bowed again, and this time a glint appeared in his eye.

"The healer's my wife, Guardsmaster. You might have passed her clinic on your way into town. It's a small place, not much to look at, but she keeps it clean and does good work. Is this about the money?"

Martin frowned. *Money? The man does not even know why I seek the healer in the first place. How can we speak about payment?*

"Will the healer be in her clinic at this hour?" he asked aloud.

"Should be, unless she's running after our son," the man said, crossing his flabby arms. "Children just don't listen these days. Do you have children, Guardsmaster?"

"No."

"Oh. Well, um...in any case, I can find my wife for you. Is that all right, sir?"

Martin pursed his lips. "Make it quick, man. I have urgent business."

"Of course," he replied with another half bow. Without another word, he rushed out the door.

It is a wonder the man is able to move at that pace, Martin thought. He put his hands on his hips and surveyed the empty room then went back outside.

"Who was that round man running so fast?" King Christopher asked. He frowned as he stood. "I greeted him, yet he did not notice me for his speed."

"The innkeeper, your majesty," Martin replied, holding the door open for the monarch to enter the inn. "He has gone to find his wife who he says is the healer."

Geraldine finished sweeping the ashes into a trash pail and dumped them into the garden behind her clinic when the door in front slammed.

This is it, Geraldine, she thought. *The king's come for you. Now you need to decide how you'll handle yourself in front of him.*

She squared her shoulders, lifted her chin, and pressed her fingers to her lips to make them stop trembling. With another short pep talk to force her feet to move again, Geraldine walked into the clinic. Just inside the back door, though, she stopped.

"Sullivan?"

"The guardsmaster is here to see you."

"Did he say why? Or what brought him here?"

"No, but it must be something important for him to come today of all days."

Geraldine went still. The queen's funeral procession. Helping Kirk had driven the reminder from her mind, but now she wanted to sit down. The queen was really and truly gone. She'd returned to the fates and to the ground, and Geraldine would never see her again. No matter what the king said in court, Geraldine still mourned the fact that she'd lost a patient. Two, counting the baby.

"Well, what are you waiting for? Come talk to the man."

Shaking her head, she went to a shelf against the wall. She stared at the jars, all lined up in neat rows, with the labels she and Widow Hannity had lettered together. Why couldn't her life still be this well-ordered?

"I don't want to help him or anyone else related to the castle," she said with her back to her husband. "They can find someone else to do their bidding."

"Like a bloody axe, they can. You spent all of that time with the queen, giving her your time. You put everything on hold here in Ingleside, and you deserve to be compensated for that."

She whirled around, a fist on her hip. "Can't you think about anything else? I'm back in the clinic, aren't I?"

Sullivan took a step back, eyebrows pinching. "Are you actually suggesting you let your work go unpaid? You did what you could for the queen and her baby, and I know how much helping your patients means to you, but we also have to be practical. You're not asking for something you don't deserve. Why don't you see that?"

She planted her hands in the pockets of her apron and looked away from him. As much as she hated how Sullivan talked about the money, she hated something else even more: the fact that he was right. She deserved to be paid for her time in the castle, regardless of the outcome. If she wanted to make sure that happened, she had to go back to the king and demand what she'd earned.

"All right, I'll listen to what the guardsmaster has to say."

"And tell him we need our money."

She narrowed her eyes. "No matter what happens, Sullivan, you can be sure of one thing: that money is mine. I earned it, and I decide what happens to it."

With her stomach still fluttering, she marched out of the clinic.

Christopher watched Martin pace the floor of the Ingleside inn and tried to ignore the dizziness threatening to make the room spin out of control.

"You worry too much, old friend," he said, wishing his voice sounded more strident. "This injury will do nothing but slow me for a day. Two at the most."

Martin stopped moving and glanced at him, although Christopher knew his guardsmaster remained ready. Martin maintained a soldier's posture, gaze straight ahead, ears alert for any aberration of sound in the room, his stance poised to defend the king.

After a moment, he began pacing again.

Just as Christopher decided to ask his friend to stop, the door to the common room opened and the innkeeper swaggered across the threshold. When his gaze came to Christopher, his mouth dropped open in an O as round as his head. A woman followed him, her face as pale as Christopher imagined his own to be. His face would have been pale from pain, however; hers was pale from panic.

"Mistress Geraldine?" Martin exclaimed. "*You* are the healer?"

"By the fates, it's the king," the man murmured. "Your majesty."

The innkeeper dropped to one knee. After a moment, and an angry look from her husband, Geraldine offered a deep curtsy. They both stayed in their poses.

An urge came upon the king to push the innkeeper off balance; in his mind, he let the possibilities continue to play. Pushing the innkeeper and watching him roll over. Shoving Geraldine to the ground. Demanding to hear what she thought of herself, continuing her old life as if nothing had changed, when nothing remained the same for him.

So many fancies in just a few moments. Once again Christopher discovered a laugh bubbling in the back of his throat. Could he be going mad?

"Your highness?" Martin said.

"You may rise," Christopher said, standing. The pain in his arm had become dull. Or perhaps he had gotten used to it. "Healer, explain yourself."

Rubbing his chin, the innkeeper looked between him, Martin, and the healer. "Now, your majesty, Geraldine feels terrible about what happened, but she's served Ingleside well for more than nineteen years. She deserves—"

"The king has been injured and requires immediate attention," Martin interrupted.

Geraldine stepped forward and gestured toward his arm.

"Your highness, may I?"

"Can you?"

She stiffened and took half a step back, but Martin gestured for her to move forward again. After another moment, Christopher held his arm for her to see. She clasped his hand and leaned closer.

"How did this happen?"

"I believe the more important thing is to treat the wound, yes?" Martin said.

Geraldine spared an irritated glance for the soldier before turning back to Christopher.

"Knowing what type of instrument struck you and how long ago will offer me valuable information," she explained in a semi-patient tone. "It's to your benefit, your highness."

Christopher looked at the cut. The blood had begun to dry, forming a hideous ridge along the four inches of the line. He twisted his arm back and forth to make the muscles twinge, and the cut broke open once again.

"Your majesty," Geraldine admonished. "Guardsmaster, my clinic isn't far from here. Just out the door and to the left. You'll see the sign with the healer's cross. The door is unlocked, so just go inside."

Squelching a moment of satisfaction at his childish gesture, Christopher nodded to Martin. The soldier went to the door and exited first; after a moment, he returned and announced it was safe to go. He went back to the door and held it open.

As Christopher moved toward it, furious whispers erupted behind him. When he turned around to face the innkeeper and Geraldine, they stopped talking and offered him strained smiles. The innkeeper bowed.

"My Geraldine's the best healer in the kingdom, your majesty, but I'm sure you already know that," he said, putting his hands on his hips with pride. "You're in capable hands with her."

The king crossed the threshold. Before the door shut behind him, the whispers resumed. Their intensity made Christopher uncomfortable.

He and Martin walked in a silence charged with their discovery. The king knew it was just a matter of time before his friend expressed his opinion. Several minutes later, Martin obliged.

"She ignored a direct royal edict."

"It certainly seems so. I did not see any notices on the board outside the inn announcing the dismissal of any guild members in Ingleside."

"She does not strike me as a simpleton. How, then, could she show such blatant disregard for authority?"

"The same way Lemuel did," Christopher replied.

"This requires disciplinary action, your highness. Geraldine's insolence cannot be tolerated."

Christopher stopped in the middle of the street. "And what action would you suggest? The woman received a direct order from the court to relinquish her badge and she ignored it, yet I am in no position at the moment to enforce any additional commands."

Martin faced the king with hooded eyes. "Blatant insubordination demands greater consequences, your majesty."

"Oh? And here I believed it to be rewarded. I am sure Lemuel would agree, considering he now holds the fate of two kingdoms in his hands. Perhaps Geraldine can join her defiance to his."

Without waiting for a response, Christopher stalked the rest of the way.

Geraldine returned to her clinic vibrating with exasperation at her husband and trepidation at seeing the king again.

How could he have found out about my returning to practice? she thought. *Did someone tell him? But who? And he didn't need to come himself. And with an injury to boot. How did he get injured anyway? And why would he come all the way to Ingleside for help? Is this some sort of new way to humiliate me?*

The words rang through her mind but didn't feel right. After making her fate known in open court, the king wouldn't have wasted time on traveling to her village to continue badgering her. What brought him here then?

Just as the clinic came within sight, she spotted Alistair on the bench next to the front door. She slowed for several steps before resuming her pace. Had the guardsmaster summoned him?

Forcing a smile, she put a hand to Alistair's cheek. He ducked his face away from her palm, but she held it there long enough to feel the coolness of his skin. His strange condition had continued, but he still didn't exhibit any outward signs of illness.

"Hello, darling. I'm happy to see you up and about."

"Bored," he said. "Help?"

She hesitated. As much as she enjoyed Alistair's company in the clinic, how would she explain the presence of the soldier and the monarch waiting for her? Worse, how would she look Alistair in the eye when he discovered why they were there?

"Quiet," he reassured her. "No trouble."

"No, of course not; I know you won't bother me at all. I only have one patient waiting, though, and there isn't much work to do today."

"'S okay," he said with a one-shoulder shrug. "Help."

"All right, but you have to promise to stay quiet."

A grin crossed his face, and her heart faltered again. If the king ordered her to the dungeons, she would have to stay away from her sweet son. How would she figure out what ailed him? How would she explain to Alistair that the king saw her as a criminal?

But you're not a criminal. You're not. You did nothing wrong. Don't act like it.

She opened the clinic door before her courage could fail her again.

The king and the soldier sat on opposite sides of the receiving area. Neither looked at the other, and both spared just a glance for her. Geraldine could sense the tension between them.

"This is my son, Alistair. Alistair, sweetheart, the king and his guardsmaster, Sir Martin."

Alistair's mouth dropped open the same way Sullivan's had earlier, but still he bowed. Straightening his lean frame, he gave her a questioning look. She shook her head. No, she didn't know why the two men were mad at each other.

The king stood. "Spare me any more formalities, Healer. I must undertake a journey soon."

"I'll do my best to go as fast as possible."

And the faster I help you, the faster you'll leave me alone.

"Would you be so kind, your highness, as to inform me of your intended destination?" Sir Martin asked.

"I will do so when I deem it the proper time. Healer?"

She looked at both men askance and gestured to a chair with an empty table on one side and a table of clean instruments on the other. "Please sit, your highness. Alistair, can you hold a candle for me, please?"

Her son, goggle-eyed at the monarch and the soldier, trotted to a cabinet on the far side of the room. He retrieved a fat candle and put it on a holder, then lit it and came back to stand next to Geraldine. She let the king get comfortable, took his arm with as much gentleness as she could muster, and placed it palm side up on the empty table. Sir Martin bolted to his feet to stand next to the king.

"Now, what kind of blade did this, and how long ago did it happen?"

The king's expression remained stony. Geraldine turned to Sir Martin. They'd come to her for help; she had no trouble waiting until they would answer her questions.

"He was attacked," Sir Martin said, relenting. "In the castle. An infidel used a dagger on his arm."

She looked back at the king. "You were attacked?"

King Christopher bowed his head a moment, and Geraldine wondered why he looked distressed. For anyone else, she would have said they looked embarrassed. But what would embarrass the king to this degree *and* leave him injured?

"Do you know anything about the dagger?" she asked. "How long it was, whether it might have been clean?"

The guardsmaster shook his head. "I did not see the actual encounter. I was fighting off another man."

She put her hand to the king's forehead.

"You're not feverish, a good sign." She retrieved a bottle and a clean cloth from the table on the other side of the king. "I'll just need to clean the cut and then—"

"You were to relinquish your badge and refrain from practicing again," the king said, "and yet you stand before me without remorse for ignoring a royal edict."

Out of the corner of her eye she saw Alistair's mouth drop open again, but she put all of her attention on the stopper of the bottle. For a moment, she considered telling the king she would leave it all behind if he promised not to imprison her and take her away from her boy. The nagging sensation that she would get caught had finally settled now that it had happened, but her stomach still fluttered.

She thought again of the queen, as she often did now. Of the queen's regality. Of how she behaved those days when her feet swelled and her chest burned from the food that disagreed with her. Even then, the queen lifted her head, squared her shoulders, and faced her duties.

Maybe I can be as confident as Queen Lily.

"Yes, your highness," she said, "I ignored a royal edict. Given your current state, you should be grateful I did."

"Grateful," the king scoffed. "You are not indispensable. The healers' guild would have appointed a replacement."

"You need to take your arm out of your shirt, please."

He glared at her, which made her grab the bottle and cloth tight enough to make her knuckles burn. She matched him stare for stare. After another moment, he focused on his arm.

"Why can I not just roll up my sleeve?"

She suppressed a sigh; patients always looked for the easy way out.

"Rolling it up will prevent you from moving freely, your highness."

"I do not think it right to destroy a shirt because—"

"The shirt's ruined anyway, and if I don't stitch up your arm soon it could prevent proper muscle realignment. Please take your arm out of your sleeve."

He muttered under his breath for a moment then unbuttoned. "Let us get on with this then, so I may be on my way."

Despite his own exasperation, the soldier helped the king maneuver his arm out of his sleeve then moved his tunic so it hung off his left shoulder. The gash had clotted somewhat, the blood dried and matted in places. The attacker had missed major veins, which was good, but the injury would still cause the king pain for a long time even after it healed.

Geraldine tried to tamp down her smugness.

"All right, sire, I'll clean the wound first, and then I'll stitch it and apply an ointment to prevent infection. Do you have any questions?"

He said nothing. She applied the cleansing solution to the cloth and pressed it to his arm, bracing herself for a jolt. The king jerked his arm and yelped but didn't tell her to stop.

Put him on a throne, and he's a king with the power to change lives, she thought. *Bring him to a healer, and he becomes human like everyone else.*

A human who has lost someone dear to him, her conscience reminded her in a voice that sounded suspiciously like Widow Hannity. *A man who is in mourning and deserves compassion, just like everyone else.*

She pursed her lips at the reminder and worked fast to clean the wound.

"That was just the beginning, your majesty," she said as she finished, an apology creeping into her tone. "I'm afraid this next portion will hurt even more."

He nodded, his anger less prominent now. "I understand. May I have some water, please?"

Taken aback at his even tone—at least the condescension had disappeared—she directed Alistair to bring the king a glass of water. While he drank, she went to a drawer in the center table and retrieved her surgery needle, a threading tool, and a long wire made of steel beaten as fine as a single hair. She threaded the needle as the king finished his water.

"Now, the cleansing solution included something to numb the pain, so you won't feel the full effect of the stitching. I'll need you to sit as still as possible, however. The more you move around, the longer it'll take and could even cause greater damage."

He nodded and ran his tongue over his lips. "Just get on with it."

Geraldine leaned into her work. She thrust the needle just below the skin at the bottom of the gash closest to his wrist. The king exclaimed in shock, but she ignored it. One careful stitch at a time, she worked the needle into his arm. She had lost two members of the royal family already; she couldn't afford to make any mistakes with the only royal left.

The king continued his wordless protests, but the noise faded as she bent close to his arm. Now, as every time, everything else in the room fell away as she heard Widow Hannity's instructions in her mind. The woman had taught Geraldine well. Every patient came back and thanked her for her fine work. They marveled at the minimal scars, telling tales of a cousin or an aunt who lived in another village and had undergone stitching from other healers. The ugly scars they bore meant an inexperienced hand or an unrefined one.

"There," she said as she put the last stitch in place and knotted it off. "The worst is done, your majesty."

He stared at his arm.

"It is one of the ugliest things I have ever seen."

"Well, that can't be helped. Now for the ointment."

She put the needle and the spool of wire away and applied the ointment, rubbing it on his arm with a clean cloth. Alistair went to the drawer where she kept the dressing cloths and brought one to her. Within minutes, she'd finished taking care of the king's arm and turned to Sir Martin.

"The wound should stay covered for a week," she instructed. "Be sure to open the dressing once a day for about five minutes to let air flow to it. Do not, under any circumstances, allow that arm to get wet, otherwise infection could set in. I can provide you with more dressing cloths."

"And how do you propose I bathe?" the king said with a scowl.

She continued talking to Sir Martin. "A cloth or sponge can be used for necessary areas, but that's all for the next week. After that, any healer can cut the wire and the skin should hold."

Sir Martin gave her a grim nod. "I will do what I can."

"I am not a child and do not appreciate being treated as one," the king snapped. He pushed himself out of the chair but swayed. Martin steadied him, and the king sat down hard.

Geraldine shook her head. "Your majesty, I think it might be best for you to rest for a little while. In all honesty, you're not in a condition to go anywhere."

"You are responsible for my condition, *Healer*."

"I'm not responsible for this," she said, splaying a hand toward his arm, "and I'm not responsible for those men getting into the castle in the first place. Where were the guards?"

The king narrowed his eyes. "You have no right to question my soldiers or anyone else. Considering the circumstances, they behaved admirably."

"What circumstances?"

Soldier and monarch exchanged a look.

"A man came to the castle with several others," Sir Martin began. He relayed the story of the men who stormed the castle. When he mentioned King Malcolm and Queen Celia taken hostage, Geraldine squeezed her eyes shut.

She'd met Queen Lily's parents on a few occasions. Queen Celia had visited monthly since the announcement of the impending royal birth, and King Malcolm joined her on three of those visits. While she didn't spend long talking to either of them, their joy for Lily radiated around the room. Everyone always smiled for days after they came.

And now a common man with revenge on his mind held their lives in his hands.

"I'm so sorry," she said as she opened her eyes. "If I can help in any way—"

He lifted his head, and his watery eyes shocked her.

"You took away the most important person in my life, Healer," he said, his words cracking. "Lily trusted herself, our *baby*, to you, and you failed both of them. You failed *me*. How can you possibly help me with this? How can you understand what I feel?"

"I do understand, sire. You've suffered a loss that cuts you deeper than that dagger did. It makes you wonder why every ounce of your heart and soul haven't bled onto the floor. That's how it feels, right? When something so precious is taken from you?"

His astonishment gave her the tiniest bit of satisfaction, but it didn't last. She sighed long and deep, surprised to find tears pricking her own eyes. Geraldine turned to the tools she'd used to stitch the king's arm but didn't move.

"You've lost a child, your highness," she said, "and with your edict I'm supposed to give up this calling that I've nurtured as a child of my own. My life's purpose has always been twofold: to care for Alistair and the people of Ingleside. And now you've snatched away half of the reason for my existence."

The king's head jerked back as if she'd struck him with her words. The look on his face changed too. Geraldine might have called it understanding. But could she expect anything like that from the king?

It doesn't matter, she thought. *You need to set the right example for Alistair and keep any other feelings to yourself.*

She and the king stared at one another for several moments. Alistair coughed behind Geraldine, and she inhaled a deep breath and let it out. Then she lowered her gaze and decided to take a chance—the one she'd desperately wanted in court—to speak from the heart.

"I am truly, deeply sorry for the loss of the queen and the princess. You have no idea how many hours I've spent agonizing over what happened. I even consulted with my mentor here in Ingleside. No one could have saved them, your highness. That's the truth. But it's also the truth that, of the two of us, I'm the only one who lost the only real dignity I've ever known."

After a moment, the king nodded. "We have both spent equal measures of time in suffering, Healer. Perhaps...perhaps that might be punishment enough."

Her heart flipped, but she held it in check. "Does that mean I won't have to relinquish my badge?"

"Your highness," Sir Martin admonished.

The king pushed himself to a standing position again. "No, Martin, I must consider the greater danger in this case. None of us can change the fact that Lily and the baby...that they no longer... I must do what I can for King Malcolm and Queen Celia, not to mention everyone else in the castle and beyond Rosewood. We have not considered how far or wide Lemuel's men have influence."

The lines on his face and the hollows in his cheeks told Geraldine how little he'd eaten and slept.

"Martin, you must return to the castle and intercept the Wyndemere guards at the burial ground. Send them back to their kingdom, and tell them to go with full speed and stealth. I will take Mistress Geraldine's advice and rest. When you return, we will devise our next course of action."

The soldier offered the king a stiff bow.

"At once, your highness," Sir Martin said and left without another word.

"Do you know of a quiet place where I may lie down?" the king asked.

She nodded. "There's a small room in the back. It's not fancy, I'm afraid. Nothing like in the castle. But it's clean and ready."

The king gestured for her to lead, and he took a few steps then lost the balance of his pace. Alistair reached forward to steady the king.

"Thank you, my boy."

Alistair beamed at Geraldine, and she smiled back. Her smile faded as she watched them go to the quiet room at the back of the clinic. The king seemed ready to rescind his order to take her badge from her, but he hadn't mentioned the money still owed. Would he find a way to hold it back?

He gave me back my badge, Geraldine thought. *That's a start. Now I just have to make sure he returns the rest.*

CHAPTER 10

Ariana paced in the entry area just inside the door of her castle apartment. She could not sit still. After several trips across the same small patch of hard floor, she went to the door and tried to turn the knob.

It still refused.

As it had ever since this wretched business began.

The bloody tree burners, she thought, fighting tears.

"Ariana?"

She went to Queen Celia who was just waking up from a short nap on the compact settee. The queen pushed herself into a sitting position and ran her fingers through her light blonde hair. Without the monarch's circlet on her head, she looked more like an everyday woman.

"Yes, your highness?"

"May I have a glass of water?"

"Of course. My home is your home."

The queen smiled. "If this was to be my fate today, I am so glad I am not alone."

Ariana went to the kitchen off the sitting room. She filled a glass from a pitcher and took two steps toward the queen but turned back. Fetching a decorative tray, she placed the glass on it and brought it back to Queen Celia.

A short laugh escaped the queen's lips as she took the glass. "What is all this?"

The councilor sank into the comfortable chair facing her.

"Our circumstances aside, your majesty, you are still a queen. Formalities must not be forgotten."

Queen Celia's smile faded, and she placed her glass on the table between them.

"I am afraid Lemuel and his men have already forgotten them," she said, "else they would not have trapped us."

Ariana laced her fingers. "We must find a way out of this, your majesty. We must."

She looked with longing at the one large window behind the settee. In the months following King Vincent's death, agitated threats came to the castle from people unwilling to accept the regime change. After Councilor Duncan spotted shadows outside his apartment one night, the king ordered bars put on the windows to prevent intruders. How were any of them to know they would need those very windows as an exit one day?

A heavy scraping noise sounded from the other side of the door. Queen Celia rose and brushed her skirts. With a toss of her head, she faced the door. Ariana rose just in time to see it open.

"Are you enjoying your respite from the day?" sneered one of Lemuel's men.

Ariana balled her fists at her sides. "We demand to be released. Now."

"All in good time, dear councilor." The guard came inside and leered at Ariana from head to toe.

"I order you to take me to Lemuel this instant. He cannot hold us here forever."

"You should be grateful he didn't send you straight to the dungeons." The man continued to caress Ariana with his gaze. "Of course, if you prefer the dungeons to your own apartment, I'm happy to stand guard—"

"What do you want?" Queen Celia asked.

The man broke eye contact with Ariana and glowered at the queen. "Lemuel's asking for this one." He jutted his chin at Ariana.

"I will come if you let the queen return to her homeland," Ariana said.

The man laughed, his contempt filling the entire room.

"You're hostages. Hostages don't get a say in their treatment. We can choose to be kind"—he stepped as close as a breath to Ariana—"or cruel."

Her hand itched to slap him, but she knew he spoke the truth. She and everyone else captured held no favorable position to bargain for their freedom. Perhaps meeting Lemuel would change that.

"I will come with you on the condition the queen will not be harmed. King Christopher will not stand for it."

"The king's not here," the man said with a chortle, "but you have my word no harm'll come to the queen."

"Go, Ariana," Queen Celia said. "I am capable of defending myself."

The man laughed again and offered Ariana a mock bow. "After you, Councilor."

She resisted the urge once again to strike him. Instead, she walked through the door. The guard locked it from the outside, and Ariana wondered whether he had stolen the keys from the headmaster who oversaw the castle's living quarters. She hoped Master Michael had not been hurt in the process, shuddering as she considered the possible ways Lemuel's men could have wounded the man with hair as white as winter's first snow and stooped almost in half. He had served as the head of the staff of the castle living quarters for three generations now and would not have had the capacity to fight back.

The guard dragged a chair to the door and wedged it

under the doorknob then gestured for Ariana to walk.

"Where do we go?"

"The main kitchen."

She turned on her heel and continued to the kitchen without looking back. As she walked, an eerie stillness covered the castle. Despite the day's horrific start, it actually had the gall to change from late morning to mid-afternoon.

They crossed through the outer courtyard to the inner courtyard, and shafts of sunlight dappled the smooth cobblestones. Unlike normal days, no castle staff with arms full of linens and mouths full of gossip crossed the courtyard. No pages carried messages with self-importance. No ambassadors traversed the cobblestones.

The entire castle, it seemed, held its breath for whatever might come next.

Ariana pushed through the double doors of the kitchen and let them swing behind her. A howl made her smile. Did the fool of a guard believe she would hold a door for him?

I hope the tree killer took it straight in the face.

Several steps into the kitchen, however, she slowed and then stopped. Bonnie, the head chef, stood next to one of the two main kitchen counters with her apron strings twisted in knots around her fingers. Her helpers formed a long line next to her. Some of the young men and women stared straight ahead. Two stood with rounded shoulders. One young girl wept without bothering to hide her tears.

Lemuel strolled back and forth before them. As Ariana came closer, Bonnie broke formation and rushed to her. Before the councilor could utter a word, Bonnie threw her arms around her with a sob.

"Mistress Bonnie, are you all right?" Ariana asked, her stomach quivering. She put her arms around the woman's well-padded frame and squeezed. "Have these men hurt you?"

Bonnie continued crying but shook her head. Ariana let loose a short breath and patted the chef on the back. She encouraged her to calm herself, and after a few minutes Bonnie did.

The chef pulled away, her breath still hitching. "I'm so sorry, Councilor. Please...please forgive my impertinence, but we've had...had no word of any...of the councilors or anyone since...since..."

Her eyes welled up again, and Ariana rounded on Lemuel.

"What have you done to these fine people?" she asked, hands on hips. "Is it not enough you have taken everyone hostage?"

Lemuel rubbed the back of his neck. "I've done nothing to them, Councilor Ariana, and I've made it clear to my men not to do anything either. This woman just went all mute the minute she saw me. All I did was ask for the staff to make us some food. My men and I are hungry. It's been a busy morning, what with taking over the castle and all."

Ariana fought the urge to scream. "Is it impossible for you to discern just why she and the others may be averse to helping you?"

"I don't care. We haven't had anything since our breakfast. I promise, all I want is a meal. Nothing else."

An idea fluttered through Ariana's mind, and her gaze fell to the ground. After a moment, she looked at Lemuel. She would not respect the man, but perhaps all he needed was the illusion of it.

"If you allow me to speak to Mistress Bonnie and the others in private, I will ask them to cook for you."

Lemuel crossed his arms. "And how can I trust you?"

"Leave the doors to the kitchen open. One guard already stands there, yes? He may stay at the door, but he is not allowed to enter nor interfere with what I say to the staff. Will that suffice?"

The man stepped closer and examined her face as if searching for a lie. Ariana forced herself to keep a neutral expression, almost bored in fact, as if she and the entire castle were held hostage almost every day. After several tense moments, Lemuel nodded.

"I'll give you five minutes to talk to them, Councilor. My men and I should have a meal within the hour."

"You have my word."

He left, and Ariana motioned Mistress Bonnie and the staff into a tight circle around her.

"Is everyone all right?"

They offered words of reassurance, and Ariana sighed with relief. Bonnie's breathing became more even. The chef closed her eyes and bowed her head for a moment then opened her eyes again.

"Councilor Ariana, what do we do?"

"For now," Ariana said, "you all should prepare a meal for these...these..."

"Tree killers," one boy exclaimed.

"Donovan," Bonnie chided, although she could not keep from smiling.

"They are horrible people," Ariana agreed. "If we are to defeat them, we will need to make them believe they have us cowed."

Bonnie glanced over Ariana's shoulder and lowered her voice. "How?"

"We need to call for help. The only way we may do so is if someone escapes. I do not have a plan yet, but I will work with Queen Celia to devise one. In the meantime, prepare their meals and take care not to be noticed. Mistress Bonnie, do not let the girls serve any of these men by themselves. Send them in pairs."

Bonnie nodded, her eyes filling with apprehension.

"Is the queen all right?" another kitchen helper asked.

Ariana nodded. "Lemuel has allowed her to stay in my apartment with me. One way or the other, we will fight our way out of this. For Queen Celia and King Malcolm."

"And King Christopher," someone murmured.

The mention of the absentee king made Ariana wonder yet again where he had gone.

"And Queen Lily," Bonnie said.

Ariana risked a look at the guard before turning back to the group. "For Queen Lily. For all of them."

She murmured a few more words of encouragement then stepped away from the group and followed the guard out of the kitchen. The sounds of pots and pans clattering, of Bonnie's instructions in a confident voice, gave Ariana courage. As she walked ahead of the guard back to her own apartment, her thoughts returned to the king.

Your majesty, where are you when we need you most?

Christopher's eyes fluttered open. The mattress beneath him poked his back in strange places. Since when did his bed contain so many lumps? And why did his shirt scratch so?

After several seconds, the king turned on his left side. A stripe of pain made him howl and sit up. He sucked his breath through his teeth for several minutes.

Not...a...nightmare, he thought between pulses of pain. *Lily...gone... King Malcolm... Queen Celia... If Lemuel has...hurt anyone...in the castle...*

Somewhere a door opened and closed, interrupting his thoughts. Footsteps approached the sick room where Geraldine's son had led him...when? Earlier that day? The day before?

The fates help me, how much time has passed? Where is Martin? I must return to the castle or...or travel to Wyndemere. Yes! I wonder if the healer will allow me to borrow a horse—

The door to the room opened, and Geraldine greeted him with a tentative smile.

"How are you feeling, your majesty?"

He used his right hand to push himself to his feet. "I must leave at once, Mistress Geraldine. Martin—"

"Sir Martin has returned," Geraldine said, coming closer. "He's waiting for you outside. I offered him a room as well, but he refuses to rest until he sees you."

"Thank you," he said, trying to step past her. Instead, the woman held up a hand.

"Your majesty, may I skirr you? Your arm should be all right, and Sir Martin didn't mention any other injuries, but I want to make sure I didn't miss anything."

Christopher moved back. Once, as a child, when he fell off his horse during a riding lesson, his castle guardian had called for a healer. The man skirred the young prince, which angered the king.

"You are not so fragile," Vincent roared as he strode *through his study with big arm gestures. "A simple toss off a horse should not require a healer. Do not let the staff coddle you."*

"Yes, your highness," Christopher said in a dull voice. *"May I go now, your majesty? My shoulder pains me."*

"Go."

To this day, when the memory returned to him, Christopher could not say whether his father had whispered "weakling" to his back or if he had imagined it.

"It's not painful," Geraldine assured him now. "In fact, I skirr Alistair whenever he falls ill. I've been skirred myself many times."

He nodded and sat back down on the bed, trying to ignore his defiance toward the memory.

"Palms up, please," Geraldine said. "Thank you. Now, close your eyes and sit still. This will only take a few minutes."

Christopher obeyed her instructions, shifting to get more comfortable. After several seconds, Geraldine's hands became warm on his and then transferred the warmth to his hands. It spread through his forearms, went up to his shoulders, then continued throughout the rest of his body. Within moments, his muscles relaxed from the blanket-like effect.

"All done," Geraldine announced. She pulled her hands away from his, her eyes bright. "Nothing other than the arm, and that should heal nicely."

He stood, grateful the wound would not maim him for life. "Thank you, Mistress Geraldine. Now, I need to see Martin."

Without waiting for her reply, he left the room. Geraldine followed, as did an air of expectation. She wanted something; Christopher could sense it. He crossed the clinic space and met Martin in the sitting area. The guardsmaster stood and bowed.

"Did you reach the guards in time?"

Martin nodded, relief in his face. "I did, your highness. They were on their way back from the royal burying ground."

Christopher became still for a moment. Lily and their baby were now relinquished to the earth and the fates. That part of his life had truly come to an end.

"We discussed breaching the castle, but the guards thought the venture might put the king and queen at greater risk," Martin went on. "They agreed that returning to Wyndemere and then coming back with additional forces would be a better course of action."

"Were you able to ascertain anything further about King Malcolm and Queen Celia?" Christopher asked.

This time Martin shook his head, his face troubled. "Nothing. I believe we must trust his majesty and her majesty will take any steps within their power to thwart Lemuel's plans."

The door to the clinic opened, and Alistair entered carrying a wicker basket. Christopher watched the boy, his sluggish steps a direct contrast to the animation on his face when their eyes met. The boy bowed, and Christopher inclined his head to acknowledge him.

"Your majesty," Geraldine said, stepping forward to take the basket from Alistair, "I've prepared a meal for you and Sir Martin. Maybe, as you eat, we could discuss—"

"What now, Martin?" Christopher said. "I cannot sit idle and wait for events to fall where and when they may."

He tried to fold his arms and gave up, as much for the pain in his left arm as for the scratchy fabric of the borrowed shirt rubbing against his skin.

"Maybe a good meal would help," Geraldine said, thrusting the basket toward him. "Sometimes, when I'm stuck for an idea, I find it's because I'm hungry."

Christopher's stomach growled then, loud enough for everyone to hear; they all exchanged looks.

"Yes, perhaps a meal is in order. Mistress Geraldine, would you mind laying it out?"

"Of course, your majesty." She knelt in front of the low table in the waiting area, but Christopher caught her snickering. He spared a glance for Martin who fought a smile at the sounds that continued to rumble from his midsection.

"I am a king, not a divine being," Christopher said.

The others laughed, and Alistair nodded in amusement.

"Majesty? Sit?"

Christopher sat and gestured for Martin to join him as Geraldine took items out of the basket. He stretched his hand toward the hardboiled eggs, but before he could take one the table collapsed. A cloud of milk-white dust burst into the air above the table and permeated the room with a moldy odor.

The king sprang to his feet. Martin grabbed the basket before it fell sideways. Alistair's eyes went wide, but he hurried to the far side of the clinic and came back with a broom and dustpan.

Geraldine seemed in shock.

"It seems as if the basket held too many treats, Mistress Geraldine," Christopher said, trying to keep his voice light.

She pressed her hands to her mouth. "No, your highness. I... Earlier today I was cleaning a wooden bowl, and it crumbled. Just...came apart into white ash. Like...like the table just now."

Christopher's mouth went dry.

"The wood," Martin said. "Your majesty—"

"The Keeper of the Wood," Christopher said. "He holds the key. By the time the Keeper replies to my letter, there will be no one at the castle to take the proper course of action."

Geraldine blanched. "The Keeper? Your majesty, what do you mean? What does this have to do with the Keeper of the Wood?"

Despite the few hours of respite, a dragging sensation overcame Christopher. He lowered himself to the chair and relayed the story of the letter from the lumberjack in Severson Dells. The housewife in Rosewood whose dinner crashed to the ground. The royal advisor in Wyndemere now mourning the loss of a child.

At least he has the luxury to do so, Christopher thought with bitterness.

"And you think the Keeper of the Wood can help?"

"I have no other course of action. I wrote a letter for the Keeper, but Lemuel's men stormed the castle and I do not know if the correspondence guild collected it. In truth, I have never needed to communicate with the Keeper until now and would not know where to start."

"Meet Keeper," Alistair said, patting his chest. "Help."

"What?"

"Meet Keeper. Help."

Christopher looked at Geraldine. "Is he asking for help or..."

Geraldine took Alistair by the shoulders. "Sweetheart, are you saying you know the Keeper of the Wood?"

Alistair rolled his eyes. "Meet. Help."

"He's telling us he meets the Keeper of the Wood," she explained. "He can take us to where he—"

"She."

"*She* resides."

Alistair shook his head. "Meet."

"Well, all right, where they meet."

Despite his stomach rumbling again, Christopher stood once more. A spark of purpose flickered inside him. He did not want to douse it while it smoldered into something larger.

"We must leave now. Alistair, is this meeting place far? Martin, maybe we should procure horses."

"No, sire," Geraldine said. "Alistair won't help you until you agree to a condition."

That air of expectation had returned.

"I will not entertain lengthy requests, Healer. Name your condition. My kingdom needs me."

"And my son needs *me*. If you want Alistair to help, you must agree right now to pay me what I'm owed for Queen Lily's care."

A short laugh escaped his lips. "You surely cannot believe I am in any position—"

"Not at this moment, no, but at some point you'll return to the castle. When you do, your first official act must be to give me the funds I rightfully earned."

He narrowed his eyes. "Are you blackmailing me, Healer? Will you hold the fate of an entire kingdom in your hands for a principle?"

Some of the tension eased from the healer's shoulders. "Not blackmail, your highness. I wouldn't dishonor the queen's memory that way. I just want to be reassured that I get what I rightfully deserve at the first chance it's available. All I'm asking is that you pledge in front of Sir Martin and my son that you'll pay me the balance due."

Christopher clenched his jaw.

Everyone has chosen this day to demand their right. Lemuel and now the healer. Do all Lindeners believe I am their personal treasury? Am I king only to solve their life problems?

For a moment, he thought about conjuring other means. If Alistair, a mere boy, could find and converse with the Keeper of the Wood, he could as well. He was the king, after all, and Alistair possessed no proof he knew the Keeper.

And if he does know her? Without help, I might spend weeks searching for her.

Agreeing to Geraldine's terms meant betraying Lily. How could he collaborate with the woman responsible for her death? What did that say about his loyalty?

"Your Highness?"

Just when I find one solution, another problem confounds me. Why could Father not have paid Lemuel and his family what was owed them? I could have dealt with the wood from the castle with the force of the royal guard behind me.

"I'm asking for what's mine, Your Highness. I don't expect—"

"All right. If all goes well and I do not encounter any undue hardships in returning to my throne, you will receive your payment. But hear me well: after that moment, we owe one another nothing."

Her self-satisfied nod made his anger flare.

CHAPTER 11

Alistair had never understood adults.

His father, for one. It was clear to Alistair his father loved to cook. Planning and preparing meals for the inn always made him the happiest. Father's face relaxed when he stood at the stove in the lodge's kitchen, the steam and aromas from his latest dishes making Alistair's mouth water. Maybe, though, his father was just as much to blame for the way people saw him. The minute he left the kitchen, he let all of his worries push his mouth down into what seemed like a permanent scowl.

The way the king scowled now as they left the clinic made Alistair think of his father. Mother's disagreement with the king—the king!—reminded him of all the fights tucked away in his house between her and Father. Their shouts became so loud that they didn't notice when Alistair slipped out the door. Sometimes he went to help Widow Hannity. She was getting older, and Alistair worried about her.

Widow Hannity wasn't always home, though, and Alistair didn't feel comfortable anywhere else, so he often walked the woods. Many times he watched as the lumberjacks felled trees. After they hauled away the logs, Alistair visited the tree stumps. He sat next to them and placed a hand on the stumps, the scent of sawdust still fresh. The rings of the tree pressed into his palm, as if in a greeting. His own special handshake. Like him, the woods could feel and think the words they needed. It made saying them aloud almost unnecessary.

Almost.

The woods provided him with refuge, a word he'd learned in his lessons not too long ago. They offered him a safe place, away from the adults who didn't listen and the boys who bullied him for the way he talked and how he couldn't catch a ball no matter how many times he tried. But the woods had begun to change.

The day Mother came home from the castle, he'd been so happy. *Now I can tell her something is wrong with the trees*, he thought. But Father had been working on the accounts earlier that day, and the accounts always turned Father's mouth into an upside-down U. When Mother came home, they began screaming about money. They always screamed about money.

Now, once again, his mother made a case for the funds she said were hers. Didn't the adults understand? The trees were in pain. All of them pleaded for help. Maybe that's why he understood them; he and the trees didn't need all the words others seemed to need.

Every time he visited them, even though he couldn't stay away, his body dragged more and more, like someone had tied stones to his ankles; that scared him the most.

Alistair wished he could explain all these things, but words only flowed inside his head. Every time he opened his mouth, most of them skittered away like the squirrels that used the trees for their games. Besides, the adults didn't listen.

He hoped with all his heart he never became one.

Geraldine allowed herself a sigh of relief as they followed Alistair to the edge of the village.

You've done it, Geraldine, she thought. *The king can't back away from his word now.*

She tried to ignore the nagging feeling that her victory seemed insignificant compared to the king's problems. Losing the queen and the princess. The wood failing. A man holding King Malcolm and Queen Celia hostage in the castle. Did she have a right to demand her pay when bigger challenges lay before King Christopher?

My challenges are no less real. I deserve what the king owes me.

Alistair kept to the main path for ten minutes then turned right onto another path that had no stones to mark it. The hard-packed dirt spoke of frequent travel, however, and after taking the path he turned around to make sure they still followed. Geraldine gave him an encouraging smile.

"Your son does not speak," King Christopher said, appearing at her side.

She flinched but kept walking. "No, he doesn't."

"Does some condition prevent it?"

"He's very smart," she said. "His teachers have always said so. He just... I don't know if it's because of Sullivan or something else, but... He's fit otherwise."

The king fell silent, although she saw him considering her from time to time. Her memory burned with the number of healers she'd consulted, the letters she'd sent, about Alistair's lack of verbal responses. In the end, they'd all agreed on the same thing: as long as the boy was developing in other ways, ate and played and studied like the other children, there was nothing to worry about.

She'd read the letters, and her professional mind agreed; her mother's heart worried.

After almost an hour, Alistair turned to the right yet again. Rays of light slanted toward the path as the sun sat in its late-afternoon position. Geraldine's stomach growled, and for a moment she grinned as she remembered the king's own belly making the same noise earlier.

The adults followed Alistair toward a massive tree in the center of the path. Geraldine guessed that if an arch were carved through its middle, two horses could ride through side by side and still leave one another room. The trunk glowed in an ashy color even though the surrounding trees featured much darker bark.

The branches of many of the darker trees drooped as if tired. Narrow dirt paths, hardpacked from generations traveling them, crisscrossed between some of the trees, but at the moment the wood was empty. Neat mounds of crushed leaves harvested from the cut logs sat in rings around the trees. Birds chirped in the distance somewhere, and she heard the chatter of a woodland creature.

How is it possible that such a place—this place of magic— is failing? Geraldine thought.

Alistair put his hand on the trunk of the tree. After a moment, he rubbed the wood and Geraldine heard him murmur. She couldn't make out his words, but hope filled her. Maybe Alistair could speak after all.

The ground began to vibrate, and Geraldine's balance tilted. Sir Martin held her arm. She steadied herself as he and the king readjusted their standing positions, then watched in awe as the vibrations traveled away from the ground beneath them and up the trunk of the tree.

For the first time, Geraldine wondered whether their decision to arrive unannounced was the soundest one. Leaves rained on them, drenching them in the scent of the Linden wood. The scent contained something else, Geraldine noticed now; the possibility of spoilage to come but not yet happening. The ground shook even harder, but the trees with darker bark stood still. She exchanged worried looks with both the king and Sir Martin.

Just then an orb the size of an apple, lilac in color and hazy, appeared in the center of the trunk. Before anyone could blink a half-dozen times, the orb grew to the size of a large melon. Minutes later it expanded to the width of the trunk, detached from the wood, and took on the vague shape of a person.

"King Christopher, welcome. Welcome to the heart of the Linden Wood."

The voice came from the shape, feminine in nature, and it terrified and soothed Geraldine by turns. She gulped. The king looked as if he wanted to leave; instead, he moved forward a few steps.

"I thank you for your welcome," he said; Geraldine was impressed at the steadiness of his voice. "May I ask with whom I am conversing?"

"I am the Keeper of the Linden Wood."

For the first time since Queen Lily's death, the king's shoulders dropped with relief.

"Keeper, we bring you a grave problem," he said. "I have received several reports of furniture, structures, even kitchen utensils made from Linden wood collapsing into white ash, and my councilors and I decided our best course of action lay in coming to you. For generations, the wood of the Linden forests has held firm. Why is it failing now?"

The Keeper did not respond for a minute, and Geraldine couldn't help looking from the person-shaped orb to the others and back again.

"I suspected this would happen," the Keeper said as if speaking to herself.

"You knew this calamity could befall us?" King Christopher asked. "Did you not think it your duty to send word of this possibility?"

"In all honesty, your highness, I always assumed the wood's magic ran deep enough to sustain the lumber. It has, in fact, for many years. Since well before your time. But now..."

A sigh made the orb shimmer a little brighter for a few moments.

"What is causing the wood to fail, Keeper? And how do we stop it?"

Once again the Keeper went silent. A fluttering nearby alerted everyone to a bird resting on a tree branch. It paused then took off again and landed on another branch.

"The wood is failing, your highness, because I'm...ill."

No one spoke; the bird continued to twitter.

"What ails you?" Geraldine asked. "I might be able to help."

A chuckle rippled toward them from the orb. "I have a broken heart, Healer."

"Well, heartache can be hard to endure, but with enough time and distance a broken heart can heal."

"Mine can't."

"What do you mean? Why not?"

"I mean my heart is broken. At one point in time, my heart shattered into four pieces. I kept one and disposed of the others."

Geraldine did a double-take. "That's not possible. The heart can't break like that."

"Oh, I assure you, Healer, it is. I live the reality every single day."

"How did this come about?" the king asked.

"It happened because of your father, your highness. I

knew him long before he met your mother and before he ascended the throne. He was determined to control the magic of the wood and tried to use me to do so."

The king shifted his weight. "Can the magic be harnessed?"

"Not the way Vincent wanted, but he refused to accept that. I was an apprentice to my father, the Keeper at the time, but I was also young and naive. A fact Vincent exploited."

"How?" Geraldine asked.

"He made promises of love and a life together. He wooed me with flowers and expensive gifts, and he kept saying I should share the secrets of the wood's magic. What I explained to him over and over, what he never understood, is that those secrets aren't mine to reveal. They're burned into the skin and memories of the Keepers just as breathing and living are; we're aware of them, but we can't fully explain their nuances.

"He refused to believe me and said he would make me suffer for the rest of my life for it. In those days, my father mingled with the royal court, and Vincent designed a trap showing my father as treasonous against the throne. He sentenced my father to be hanged. After the sentencing, I appealed to what I thought was Vincent's humanity and he laughed in my face. He *laughed*, your majesty. I can... Sometimes, in my quieter moments, I can still hear it."

The Keeper paused. After a few moments, Geraldine could hear the king's breathing become shallower. His nostrils flared.

"You have no right to malign my father's name, Keeper," he said. "I know he made mistakes during his reign—"

"You know nothing of those mistakes, your highness. You weren't there."

"You are purporting that the failing of the wood is my

father's fault, and I will not tolerate it."

He cradled his arm and walked a few paces into the woods. Even as he faced away from all of them, Geraldine could see the angry breaths making his body pulse. She turned back to the orb.

"If we accept what you're saying as the truth—"

"It is *not* the truth!" King Christopher yelled into the forest.

Geraldine blew out an exasperated breath. "If what you're saying is the truth, that still doesn't explain what you call your broken heart."

"Believe me, Healer, had I not held the pieces in my own hands, I would not have believed it either."

"How did it break?"

"After my father's body was taken down from the gallows, the guards led me to a room in the back of the castle. There was one little window, and the room was just large enough for the table where my father lay. I was permitted to gather any personal effects from his body before they took it to the graveyard of criminals.

"I stood there, looking at my father, in that room full of the stench from all the deaths that had come before, and I finally realized the depth of Vincent's betrayal against me. I screamed loud and long and fell to my knees, and then I experienced a searing pain such as I've never felt before or since. It was as if someone had stabbed me in my breast with a dagger and jerked the blade down my body in one fierce stroke.

"I cried and felt everything a person could feel in that moment. Fear; grief; anger; despair. All of these emotions for all of those moments in my life that caused them. The death of my mother in childbirth and never knowing her. The death of my father, the kindest, dearest man, even if he had trouble showing me his love. And Vincent. Yes, even for Vincent. For the loss of him. For the loss of love. I gave Vincent everything of myself, and he took it with abandon. My pain became unbearable. I would have welcomed death to end it."

The Keeper fell silent once more. Geraldine bowed her head out of respect for the woman's suffering and noticed the king returning to the group. She couldn't read his expression, but she hoped he wouldn't lose his temper again.

"I thought I lived an entire generation in those moments, but the pain finally lessened. When I sat up from the floor, no more than an hour had passed. Then I saw it beside me. My heart."

Geraldine huffed with frustration. "You keep saying this, Keeper, but I don't understand. What do you mean?"

"Exactly what I said. When I sat up, I felt this dull ache and saw an angry scar burned down the center of my body. My heart lay on the floor next to me, turned into stone and broken into four pieces."

Alistair moved back two steps, and Sir Martin's eyes got wide. The king rubbed his forehead with his fingertips, shaking his head after a few moments. Geraldine's own shock made her blink at a fast rate.

Questions zipped through her mind.

Were the stones hot to the touch? Did they fit back together? Did it pulse with a beat?

"When I saw my heart in pieces on the floor, I realized I no longer felt the betrayal inside of me. I felt no sorrow. I felt nothing. I no longer had to deal with the pain of losing my love. In all honesty, it would have been a relief to feel anything at all. When I looked at my father's body again, I felt nothing. Just a calmness that remains with me to this day."

The king clasped his hands in thought.

"While I am sorry for the loss of your father, I do not

know what your tale has to do with the wood. Why has it begun to fail?"

"The wood's power is tied to the strength of the Keeper, and the Keeper's strength comes from purity of heart and soul. I have my soul, your majesty, but my heart...well, I no longer have that."

"You no longer have your heart," the king repeated. "Whatever does that mean?"

Another sigh emanated from the orb. "When I discovered my heart on the floor, I picked up its pieces. They glowed, and I realized if I harbored the desire for the love they still held—if I decided I needed love back in my life—I could have divined a potion or elixir to allow my heart to rejoin my body. But I wanted nothing to do with love. Its power nearly killed me; I no longer wanted the pain it brought.

"After making arrangements for my father's body to be brought back to the wood, I left with my heart in my hands and not a clue where to go. I knew my free time was short— I would need to return to the wood to begin the ministrations required to become the Keeper—but I didn't know how to navigate the world without my heart as my guide. I decided to keep one of the heart stones, as I call them, and discard the rest. I went to the eastern border of Linden to the village of Cicero and found a wishing well there."

"I know the place you mean," the king said. "I visited it once years ago."

"I threw one of the heart stones into it. From there I traveled to a village in the west and offered the second heart stone to a mason preparing to insert the cornerstone of a building. I told him the stone would bring the proprietor good luck.

"I couldn't decide what to do with the third piece. On my journey home, I entered a garden where the stone pricked my hand as if I held hot needles. I was overwhelmed with loss and pain, which scared me. I picked up a large rock and beat the heart stone with it. It refused to yield at first, but eventually it broke. I kept striking the heart stone until dust remained.

"The smallest heart stone was left. I felt lighter, freer. I decided I could survive the rest of my days with the one stone and came back. I took the oaths to bind me to the wood as its new Keeper and thought all was well. My father possessed a powerful magic, your majesty, and my grandmother before him. That magic goes back generations and has sunk into the roots of the trees. I thought I could rely on that magic to continue, to spend the rest of my days with only one piece of my heart, but I was mistaken.

"The power of the wood is tied to the Keeper's ability to love it. Wholeheartedly. My father told me this once or twice in passing, but I didn't understand until I started living life with just a part of my heart. It was then I discovered the truth."

"What truth?" the king said.

"The one remaining heart stone is failing because it's incomplete. It needs the other stones to thrive. The failing of the wood is tied to all of this. I'm dying, your majesty. I'm dying, and with me, bit by bit, the wood as well."

CHAPTER 12

Christopher drew in a sharp breath. The Keeper was dying? The *wood* was dying?

Martin's eyes flitted to him before going elsewhere. The healer covered her cheeks. Her gaze refused to settle on any one thing.

Can she help the Keeper? he wondered. *Perhaps there is some tonic she could give or a poultice she could apply to the Keeper's scar... But if magic harmed her, it is possible only magic can heal her.*

"Why has the wood only started failing now?" Martin asked. "You say your heart broke after your father's death, when the king's father was himself still a prince. Decades have passed since all you described has transpired."

The orb changed to a lighter color, shading from a lilac to a blush rose.

"When my father was alive, he encouraged Lindeners to visit the forest. They would come to observe birds or bring a meal to enjoy with loved ones. They studied the trees, even claimed spaces for themselves, and visited often. Their affection for the wood, combined with the love my father possessed for the land and the magic from previous generations, sustained the trees.

"After letting go of my heart, I was content alone. I stopped fostering relationships; I didn't present myself at court. I conjured this mask you see now so I wouldn't have to show my true self to others. No one who meets me in my human form knows me as the Keeper.

"People have come to the wood less and less through the years. In the last decade, people have only used the wood for travel, and the lumberjacks do their work and leave. Alistair is the only one who visits out of his love for the trees. Even you, your majesty, haven't visited in quite some time, despite the responsibility you bear."

Christopher ignored the pinch from the Keeper's truth. "If the wood dies, the livelihood of most Lindeners will suffer. Our trade and commerce depend on the lumber. The kingdom depends on it. There must be a way to restore the wood's magic."

"It doesn't matter, your highness. I'm dying. I accept that fact without passion or prejudice, because once I die I'll have no connection to the trees. Whether they die too has no effect on me."

A muffled sob distracted Christopher. The healer's son sank to his knees, and his shoulders shook as he fought to control his emotions. How could the Keeper bear witness to the grief of the boy and not respond with compassion?

"The forest's fate *does* matter, Keeper, to the entire kingdom," he said. "The forest, the trees, and, yes, even you, Keeper, matter. They all matter to us."

From the corner of his eye, he noticed Martin standing a little taller. Geraldine considered him with a thoughtful gaze. Alistair's sobs slowed.

"My father committed many wrongs," he went on, the words making his mouth twist with anger and regret. "I pledge to you and all present here today to make them right. You deserve to have a whole heart, Keeper. Everyone does. Love often requires great sacrifices of us, but it also gives us life's greatest joys. I know this firsthand."

Christopher paused a moment and thought of Lily. Of the last time he held her hand...and the first. Of visiting the memorial room where she lay in state and the formal parlor where he met her for the first time in her father's castle.

He visited King Malcolm mere weeks after his own father's death, and the king received him with compassion. Lily, too, welcomed him with a cordiality that confounded Christopher. He had wished he and King Vincent had possessed the same ease that King Malcolm shared with his daughter.

With Lily's death, he had endured the worst kind of loss; he refused to lose anything else. Not the wood or the main source of income for his people. Not his crown.

"It's been decades since all this happened, sire," the Keeper replied. "I doubt a few formal words will make the entire kingdom care about me again. No, I'm at peace with what the fates have ordained. I'll meet them soon enough, and what comes after I'm gone is not my responsibility."

Alistair's sobs came back with renewed force; Christopher stopped himself from shaking the boy to his senses.

"You are consigning the entire kingdom to death, Keeper," he said.

"Given Vincent's treachery, I think it's fitting his kingdom is ruined."

Heat flushed Christopher's body. "How do I know your claims are true? You may be inventing this entire tale to hide your own incompetency in keeping the trees alive and safe."

"Your majesty?"

He turned to Martin. "What is it?"

Martin's telling glances at the orb and back at him made the hair stand on Christopher's neck.

"What?" he asked again.

"A moment, your majesty," Martin said, tilting his head

away from everyone.

Christopher followed him several paces down the path and stopped when Alistair's crying became a distant murmur.

He crossed his arms, wincing at the pain. "She cannot invent tales to suit herself, Martin. I know my father's faults, but it is unjust to hold him responsible for everything gone wrong."

"Sire, I do not know whether the Keeper speaks the truth, but I do remember my father recounting the former Keeper's trial."

Christopher's mouth went dry. "What did your father tell you?"

"He said the entire affair moved at a brisk pace; much faster than usual. Lindeners were not even provided notice. It was all handled at the castle. My father and another soldier stood guard as the Keeper's body was pulled off the gallows. He did not forget the moment until his dying day."

Christopher's gaze went to the forest floor. His rational sense urged him to seek further confirmation of the Keeper's account. After all, the Keeper alone accused King Vincent of this heinous act. She could have devised the whole anecdote, spinning fanciful notions for sympathy.

Except; except.

A memory returned to Christopher about his former tutor. When the king would ride off with a battalion of royals on his hunting expeditions, Master Gareth soothed Christopher's loneliness with stories from history or experiments in science. The man spent hours writing out mathematical equations and challenging Christopher's debating skills. From Christopher's earliest memories of books and paper, Master Gareth knew the answers to every question he ever asked.

The one question he could not answer for King Vincent, however, was why Christopher's scores dipped so low at the end of the school term the year he turned twelve. King Vincent summoned Master Gareth to the throne room for an inquiry and demanded Christopher attend. Christopher could still hear how the voices rang, how he believed his father's rage would shake the tapestries right off the walls.

"It is your job to educate the boy," King Vincent thundered.

"It is his job to learn," Master Gareth said with a pointed look. "These days he is more inclined to climb trees and ride his horses."

King Vincent set his jaw, and Christopher gulped. He recognized that look. It did not bode well for him or his beloved tutor.

He closed his eyes now, although the rest of the scene continued to play through his memory.

The king forbade him to leave his personal apartments for a full month. When he returned to the royal library, a dull woman had replaced Master Gareth. Her ragged sweater let off the closeted scent of mothballs, and when she placed a dusty textbook on his desk he could see the feathery lines of dryness across the backs of her hands.

"We will begin on page 1 of Practical Mathematical Principles,*" the new tutor intoned, standing in front of his desk.*

"But I had progressed to page 97 under Master Gareth." Christopher leafed through the pages. "Why can I not—"

The woman grabbed the book's front cover. Christopher jerked his hand back just in time to protect his fingers from being slammed shut in the book. The tutor leaned in close, her face twisted into a malevolent scowl.

"If you speak that name again, I have instructions from the king himself to reset your education to the primers for

first-year students. You will do as I say or suffer consequences."

He hung his head now, and his throat constricted as he shut his eyes.

Father, why? he thought. *Was the power worth so much heartache? Was it worth* my *heartache?*

In his childhood, he had revered his father. He endured Vincent's cutting remarks, the askance glances, the doubt voiced in open court about whether Christopher would rule Linden with any aptitude, all for the few times Vincent would nod with approval. Later, after the death of his mother, Christopher learned the true meaning of loneliness as his father spent weeks, sometimes months, on his campaigns. When the king disapproved of Christopher's friend—forcing the young prince to engage in long-suffering social events with the vapid children of other royals—Christopher defied his father and continued spending time with Martin. He still maintained appearances, however. As far as Vincent knew, Christopher fulfilled all the duties and obligations a young prince should.

Even as he hated his father's dismissiveness, he still craved that single nod of approval.

After King Vincent's hunting accident, when whispers susurrated through the castle halls about the late monarch's tyranny, Christopher forced himself to stay engaged with the task at hand: preparing to ascend the throne. He ignored the lightness of step in the pages and castle staffers. He turned a blind eye to the smiles that crept across faces when people thought he did not see. Through it all, a part of him clutched at the hope of some sign, some forgotten memory or document, proving Christopher was worthy of the king's love. That deep beneath the self-absorbed exterior beat the heart of a father and a gentleman.

The Keeper had destroyed any last shred of hope he held.

Alistair's tears continued to flow, and his mother came and knelt beside him. She put her arms around him and gave him a tight squeeze. He wanted to turn and let her hold him as he used to do when he was young, but he was sixteen, not a child anymore.

"My dear, sweet boy," Mother murmured. "I know this hurts, but losing loved ones is a fact of life."

He wanted to lie on the ground and wail until his own heart broke apart; instead, he gestured toward the glowing orb.

"Friend. Only friend."

"Alistair," the Keeper said in a gentle voice, "I'll always consider myself fortunate to have known you. This wood is as much yours as mine. You know that."

"Help. King; me. Help."

Mother squeezed his shoulders again but turned toward the orb. "Sometimes it's not that simple, love. The king's father hurt the Keeper very much; she lost something precious because of it. Do you understand?"

Alistair shook his head. People often treated him like a simpleton because he couldn't speak like others. Sometimes Mother, too, assumed he couldn't understand basic thoughts and ideas.

The Keeper had always spoken to him with respect. Her voice never took on that sympathetic, patient tone people used when they discovered his speech impediment. She spoke to him as he'd heard other people speak to one another. Normal tones; normal words. No assumptions.

Now she was dying, and so was the forest.

"Time," he said, exasperated. "No wood; no home."

The orb changed colors again, turning cobalt. Alistair recognized the Keeper's contemplative mood. He pushed himself to his feet and went to the tree. After a moment, he placed his hand on it and closed his eyes.

He pressed into the tree trunk all of his thoughts and feelings: how the forest provided him a refuge. The serenity, the acceptance that descended on him the moment he entered the wood. Mother and Father didn't visit the wood like he did; the trees didn't rebound their screams or the sinister laughter of the bullies. He sent into the tree his memories of spending time with the chopped tree trunks. Some days, in fact, he thought he'd be the happiest boy alive if he could put his own roots into the ground and stay among the trees.

The Keeper, he added, knew he loved the trees. She'd said so herself. If she died, it would devastate him. If the trees died, it would destroy him.

A shuddering breath emanated from the orb, and that shudder traveled through the tree trunk and Alistair's arms.

"Enough, Alistair," the Keeper said. "Enough. I hear you."

"What do you mean?" Mother asked, coming to stand next to him.

"It means the king will get his wish. He can try to save the trees."

Christopher watched from afar as Alistair put a hand on the tree then bowed his head. Several minutes later, the Keeper's orb changed to a light lavender. Geraldine cupped her mouth and called for him to come back.

"Perhaps the boy..." Martin said.

Surely the Keeper would not change her mind because of

a boy, he thought as he and Martin strode back. *I am the king; if she will not concede to my request...*

They approached the tree, and Christopher saw that Alistair's tears had disappeared. In fact, the boy smiled as wide as the outer courtyard in the castle of Rosewood. With a pang, Christopher wondered whether King Malcolm and Queen Celia had come to any harm.

"Very well, your highness," the Keeper said. "You can try to save the heart stones."

Christopher exchanged a glance with Martin. "Thank you, Keep—"

"I have two conditions. The first, that you undertake the quest yourself. You said you wanted to right Vincent's wrongs. This is where you begin to do so."

"Done. And the second condition?"

"Alistair goes with you."

Christopher pursed his lips. "That is not necessary. I do not know what kind of dangers I will encounter on my journey. I would not want the boy to come to any undue harm."

"To save the trees, you must bring the heart stones back here for the necessary incantations to be performed," the Keeper said. "If you don't take Alistair, I won't allow for the stones to be joined again."

"You would dare to set your king with conditions, Keeper?"

"Simply a guarantee, your majesty, that someone who represents the wellbeing of the forest is present."

Her mild tone irritated Christopher, and he narrowed his eyes.

"Very well."

"I will accompany you, your highness," Martin said. Christopher opened his mouth to argue, but Martin shook his head. "No, sire. Safety in numbers. The Keeper may deem

Alistair's presence necessary, but he is, after all, a boy."

Christopher nodded.

"I'll go too," Geraldine said.

"And why would you concern yourself with this matter, Mistress Geraldine?" Christopher asked.

"I...you...your arm," she said. "If Sir Martin dedicates all his time to protecting you, he can't look after your arm. I can make sure no infection invades the healing process and also help in case anyone gets injured in any other way. And I can look after Alistair."

"Old enough," Alistair said in a sullen tone.

"What about the people under your care?" Martin asked.

Geraldine waved the matter away. "I can ask Widow Hannity to take care of them. We won't be gone for long, will we?"

Christopher heaved a sigh. "I hope to return as soon as possible. Every hour and day spent away from Rosewood means the king, queen, and everyone else in the castle are in even greater peril. And we do not know what Lemuel plans for the city afterward."

"We'll need supplies for traveling," Geraldine said.

Christopher realized his shoulders felt warm and looked up. The sun had crept downward in the time they stood in the forest, and judging by its position evening approached. He debated the merits of starting on their journey right away or staying the night in Ingleside.

"If Lemuel has sent men to retrieve us, the cover of darkness may aid our cause," Martin said.

"This evening it is," Geraldine said. "Alistair, come with me. Sir Martin, may I ask you for a favor?"

"Yes?"

"Would you accompany Alistair and me home? I'll have to inform Widow Hannity and Sullivan of my leaving and I may need help. With supplies."

Christopher raised his eyebrows at her cowed words, wondering whether this Sullivan was responsible for her change in tone.

"Of course, Mistress Geraldine," Martin said, surprising Christopher with his response. The soldier turned to him. "Your highness, if I may take your leave?"

Christopher nodded. "I will await you here."

Martin gestured for Geraldine and Alistair to take the lead, and they followed the path back. As he watched them leave, Christopher's confidence lurched. What if they failed? What if they were too late to save the king and queen? What if they could not find all of the heart stones? The Keeper said she ground one stone into dust; how in the entire kingdom would they re-form it?

He scoffed with impatience; they did not possess enough time or resources.

"Is there no magic, Keeper, to transport us quickly across the kingdom?" Christopher asked, turning back to the orb. "My tutor... That is, I seem to remember from a history lesson years ago that at one time the forest contained portals allowing people to go between sections of the wood at a moment's notice."

The orb pulsed before glowing steady again.

"I, too, heard those same tales, your highness, but I never found any of those portals in all the years I spent walking the wood. If they do exist, they must be dormant now. It's possible they require a magic I don't possess or has dissipated."

Christopher's hope faded. Perhaps Master Gareth had invented those tales. The king wished, more than ever, he could consult his tutor on this and so many other matters.

Thinking of Master Gareth made him miss Lily yet again. He wanted so much to talk to her. To see her perched on a stool in her art studio or settled in a chair in his study, eyes bright with fire as she argued her own point. He wanted her approval of him going on this quest without strategizing first how to regain the castle. How would he return to the fates with any peace if he did not save Lily's mother and father? Why was no one left with whom he could discuss these issues?

"It's a lonely world without loved ones close," the Keeper said, almost in a whisper.

Christopher sighed long and deep. "It is. Do you ever feel lonely?"

"Not the way most people do, although I am aware of how alone I am. When your father broke my heart, it changed my life forever."

Christopher could not deny the truth any longer: his father had been wrong. Wholly and without refute. Resignation to the fact made him stare at the ground.

"That applies to both of us, Keeper."

CHAPTER 13

Lemuel opened his eyes to the early morning sun and unfamiliar surroundings. He bolted upright and surveyed the room: the tapestries on the walls; the ornate wooden spindles at each corner of the bed; the soft linens that cradled him like a cloud. His stomach fluttered.

I'm in the castle. I slept in the castle in a royal bed last night.

The momentary thrill dissipated as he remembered his failure to make King Christopher pay the sum he and his family were owed.

Where did he go? When is he going to come back and make this right?

Lemuel pushed back the bedclothes and went to the comfort room. The events from the previous day swirled through his mind as he washed up and spent an extra minute to take a deep inhale of the scent of the silky soap in its delicate porcelain dish on the sink. It made him think of his mother and how much she would have enjoyed washing with the soap. After a moment, he shoved the dish back and found a tiny measure of satisfaction in the *chink* it made when it hit the wall. A surprising pinch of remorse for striking the dish made him shake his head.

What was I thinking, taking over the castle like this? I don't want to be here. I just want what's mine and then to go home.

A pounding on the door of the room drew his attention, and when he answered it Bailey charged in with enough energy for ten men.

"Oh, good, you're awake," he said with a broad grin. "You won't believe what the kitchen is turning out for breakfast. I've always wondered how the royals dined in the morning. At least that chef and the others stopped looking at us like deer behind a crossbow."

Despite his uncertainty, Lemuel couldn't help smiling at his friend's enthusiasm.

"Well, then, what are we waiting for? I am kind of hungry."

Bailey shook his head. "Not yet. Some people are here to see the king."

"So? How is that my problem?"

"Because the king isn't here, but *you* are. I told them you were the king's envoy and that you'd be along soon."

"Who are they?"

"Representatives from Swanwick. Something about returning a consignment of lumber."

"What consignment? Wait, they want to *return* the wood?"

Bailey shrugged. "They were ready to drop it outside the castle and leave. I convinced them to stay and talk to you."

Lemuel rolled his eyes, following him down the corridor. "Bailey..."

"What? Isn't this what we wanted? To be in control? To prove that we can do better than the king?"

"I just want the coin owed to me—to all of us—and then to go home."

Bailey's steps slowed. "So all of that talk yesterday...it was just talk?"

"No, of course not," Lemuel said, the lie coming without

a hitch. "I just haven't sorted out how we should go about it, that's all."

"Well, talk with these Swanwick representatives first, and then we can make a plan."

He nodded and kept moving. After a few wrong turns, they found their way to the carved wooden doors of the receiving hall. Lemuel tried to loosen the muscles in his neck by tilting his head from side to side. Knots of tension pummeled his shoulders.

Why are they bringing lumber back? And where's the king? Why isn't he here to deal with this?

He and Bailey entered the receiving hall. It mirrored the other rooms in the castle open to the public: a rectangle with paintings on either long wall. These paintings depicted scenes from places Lemuel suspected weren't in Linden. One showed mountains that dwarfed the land on a crisp winter day. Another offered a seaside view so realistic Lemuel thought he could feel the heat from the sand on his face. In a third painting, buildings crowded one another until they almost went past the frame. Windows between the paintings let in the light of another pleasant spring morning.

This hall housed several tables and chairs. All remained empty except the one where a man and woman sat. Their crimson and gold uniforms looked like royal colors, and Lemuel assumed they must be the representatives from Swanwick. He'd never traveled as far as Swanwick; in truth, he'd never traveled much at all. Finley's work with the lumber guild had allowed him the luxury of traveling. He wondered whether Fin had seen some of these places.

Brushing away thoughts of his brother, Lemuel attempted a smile he hoped made him look approachable and confident at the same time.

"Welcome to Linden." He sat, and Bailey joined him.

"How can we help?"

The woman reached into a shoulder bag, withdrew an envelope, and placed it on the table. Lemuel eyed the fancy handwriting on the front. Instead of reaching for it—who knew if he'd get into trouble for reading a formal letter to the king?—he looked at the representatives instead.

"The queen of Swanwick is returning a consignment of Linden lumber," the woman said. "Some of the previously purchased lumber began collapsing into heaps of dust. The queen does not wish to take a risk on newer imports."

Lemuel's mouth went dry.

The lumber collapsed? But...how? Is this what the king meant when he said there was an urgent matter?

"Does that mean the logs you brought back are still in good condition?" Bailey asked.

"They are," the man said.

"Then why can't the queen use them?" Lemuel asked.

"Her majesty requested Linden wood for its magical properties," the woman replied. "If the wood is in danger of collapsing, the kingdom of Swanwick cannot use—"

Lemuel held up a hand. "I'm sorry to say we're in the middle of...a challenging situation. The king can't accept any consignments."

The woman nailed him with a look, and Lemuel tried not to squirm. He knew he didn't look or sound like a member of the court, but he hoped his confident attitude would be enough to curb the woman's skepticism. After a moment, she spoke again.

"We are under strict orders to leave the wood here, sir. We serve the queen. She said under no circumstances—none—were we to return with the wood. Given recent events, she will contact King Christopher at a later time regarding the issue of refund."

Without another word, the representatives stood and left the hall. Lemuel opened his mouth to stop them but didn't. What could he say, after all? Instead, he picked up the envelope and examined it.

The fates help me, what have I gotten myself into?

"How can the wood collapse?" Bailey asked, the same uneasiness in his voice that Lemuel felt. "Do we need to worry about this?"

"I don't know."

An urge overtook him: to run after the representatives and beg for a ride in their carriage to his parents' home and back to his normal life.

That life where you don't have enough to eat and the castle ignores your petitions? a voice in his head taunted. *Are you just going to back down and let someone else fix your problem?*

"Lemuel?"

"I think...I think I'll ask King Malcolm—no, I'll *order* King Malcolm to fix this. He's been a king for a long time, right? And now that he's our prisoner, he has to do what we say."

Bailey's grin unfurled again.

"That's the spirit. Just think, kings and queens doing our bidding. Maybe we could even crown ourselves kings. Then we can do what we want. We can take the silvers owed to us, and no one would be the wiser."

"Let's not tempt the fates by doing something rash," Lemuel said as he pocketed the letter from Swanwick. "All we have to do is prove to everyone we can handle the kingdom better than King Christopher ever could. Then no one will doubt our right to those silvers."

Bailey clapped him on the back. "This is why you're the man to lead us. Let's go talk to King Malcolm."

Lemuel sauntered out of the receiving hall, hoping his gait would mask his apprehension.

Within minutes, he and Bailey stood outside the door to King Malcolm's assigned room.

"I hope the men are treating the royals with some respect," Lemuel said.

"I reminded them twice yesterday to guard, not harm, and I watched King Malcolm myself last night with a couple of the city men."

"I don't want King Christopher to come back and charge us with a crime. There's no way we'll get what we deserve if he's able to do that."

Bailey opened his mouth then closed it again. He put his hands on his hips, and his gaze moved to some unseen thought. After a moment, he nodded.

"I'll go remind them again to stay within their limits. You deal with King Malcolm."

A flower of relief bloomed in Lemuel's gut. "Thanks."

His friend went to try to make sense again of the overlapping corridors, and Lemuel turned back toward King Malcolm's door. He knocked and waited for the king to respond. When he didn't, he knocked again. Still nothing.

Those men from the city better not have hurt him, he thought, his doubt making the relief shrink. *I knew it was a mistake to let them stay.*

After a moment of deliberation, Lemuel knocked one last time and pushed the door open. The bed in the oversized royal guest quarters sat empty, although the way the bedclothes were folded made him think the king had woken up not long ago. He shut the door and clasped his hands behind his back.

King Malcolm exited the comfort room and jerked back

in surprise when Lemuel caught his eye.

"Good morning, your highness," he said. "I trust you slept well."

Even without an answer, Lemuel could see he hadn't. The king's face sagged with worry and grief. It reminded Lemuel that the man came to Linden to bury his daughter. Guilt planted a seed in his chest.

"I am well, Master Lemuel. What is the nature of your visit?"

"A problem has come to the castle, and I need you to... that is, you should..."

Talking about ordering around a king and doing it, Lemuel discovered, were two separate things.

It's a good thing Bailey isn't here.

"What may I do, Master Lemuel?"

The king's calmness irritated Lemuel, and he reminded himself that Bailey and the other men were relying on him. He pulled the envelope from his pocket and handed it to the king. As King Malcolm opened the letter, Lemuel crossed his arms.

"Some of the wood sold to the kingdom of Swanwick has collapsed. The queen sent back the rest of the logs she purchased even though they're still in good condition. Do you know anything about this?"

The king's eyebrows pinched as he read the letter, but after a moment his expression became neutral again.

"I came here to attend my daughter's funeral, Master Lemuel. If there are any doubts about the resources Linden provides to other kingdoms, it is best to speak to King Christopher on the matter. I am but a guest."

"Well, King Christopher isn't here, is he? You'll have to take his place for now and deal with these concerns."

The king studied him, and Lemuel fought the urge to

fidget. Instead he looked King Malcolm in the eye. After a long time, the king nodded once.

"I will assist you on the condition that you allow me to see the queen first. I have not seen her since yesterday."

Lemuel tugged on his ear then forced his hand back to his side. He hadn't expected the king to agree so quickly, and he certainly hadn't thought about what it might mean to separate the king and queen. Now he wondered whether doing so was a mistake.

Still, he didn't want to give King Malcolm the idea that he could be manipulated. He tilted his head as if in thought then nodded. The hope in the king's face made Lemuel suppress a wince.

"All right, your highness, I'm a reasonable man. You can see the queen for five minutes."

"Thirty."

"Ten, and not a minute more."

Malcolm gave him another single nod. "Ten minutes it is."

"We go now."

He turned and walked out of the room.

It's because I'm a kind person that I'm letting the king see the queen, he told himself. *I take other people's thoughts and feelings into consideration. King Malcolm wants to see his wife; he can see his wife. I'm not cruel.*

He nodded to himself, pleased with his benevolence, and led the king to Councilor Ariana's apartment in the councilors' corridor.

Ariana fought a yawn as she brewed her morning tea and set two cups on a tray.

"Sugar, your majesty?" she called.

The queen exited the bedroom where she spent the night and nodded. "Please."

Ariana set the sugar bowl on the tray and was grateful that Lemuel had left them, more or less, to their own devices. After seeing Bonnie and the kitchen staff the previous day, Ariana returned to her apartment and found the queen unharmed if a little bored. Ariana updated Queen Celia on her conversation with the others. For the rest of the evening, they discussed one plan of escape after another. None of them made sense or else required too much risk, and none of Lemuel's men returned for them although they continued to remain locked in.

As she carried the tray to the table in the sitting area, keys jingled outside her door and it swung open. Lemuel himself strode in, puffed up like one of those ridiculous pink birds Ariana had read about years earlier. Behind him came King Malcolm, and Ariana curtsied even as she balanced the tray.

"Your majesty," Queen Celia exclaimed, jumping to her feet.

"Are you well, my queen?"

She nodded. "And you, your highness?"

"As well as can be expected in these times."

Ariana sensed their longing as if a rope tied the two royals to one another.

"Ariana," the king said, "have you endured any hardships since yesterday?"

"No, sire," Ariana said. "Master Lemuel has been courteous."

"You see, your majesty?" Lemuel asked. "I'm a man of honor. I'm here to take what's rightfully mine, not hurt anyone else."

"And for that we thank you," Queen Celia said drily.

She turned her attention back to the king. Ariana's gaze drifted. She did not know why Lemuel had come, but could she turn the situation to their advantage?

"Master Lemuel," she said, brightening with an idea, "I just remembered an important matter I must discuss with Councilor Duncan. It is of an urgent nature, but in all the commotion yesterday, it slipped my mind. Would it be all right for me to see him now? If you approve, of course."

Lemuel looked at her as if she were a puzzle to solve. She offered a gentle smile, hoping he would not see the intent in her eyes. Just as she gave up hope, he nodded.

"All right, but you get the ten minutes I'm allowing the king and queen. And those ten minutes start the minute we leave this room."

Her heartbeat accelerated as she placed the tray on the table in front of the settee.

"Your majesties," she said, curtsying toward them, "I will return shortly."

The king and queen glanced at her and murmured their dismissal, but Ariana knew their thoughts focused on one another.

"Ten minutes, your highness," Lemuel said. He waved toward the corridor. "After you, Councilor."

Ariana scurried out the door before he could change his mind.

A precious two minutes later, she stopped outside Councilor Duncan's apartment and the fates-forsaken guard outside it. After a brief conversation, the guard unlocked the door. Only the greatest force of will stopped Ariana from hopping in place or snatching the keys from the guard.

Lemuel went inside first. "Councilor Duncan?"

When no reply came, Ariana could no longer resist. She charged ahead, pushing the door open all the way. Despite calling for the head councilor, no response came.

Ariana whirled around. "What have you done with him?"

Lemuel looked around the room. "I didn't do anything. Max?"

The guard came inside. "What?"

"Where's the councilor?"

Max scrubbed his hair. "He couldn't have escaped. We locked the door from the outside, and there's been a guard out here."

A soft groan from down the hall drew Ariana's attention. She followed the noise to a bedroom on the left. The sound held the timbre of Councilor Duncan's voice, yet Ariana had never heard him make that noise before. She moved two steps into the room and stopped short.

The councilor lay on top of the bed, still dressed from the previous day but with blood stains on his shirt. His nose had swollen to almost twice its size, and he struggled to open one of his eyes ringed in dark colors. Ariana gasped.

"Head Councilor?" she whispered.

She hurried across the study, pulled open the curtains, and rotated the lever on the sill. The fresh air brought the scent of the flowers planted below the window. The councilor groaned again, clenching his teeth as he put the heel of his hand to his head.

"Wha...Ariana?" Councilor Duncan asked.

She stomped back to where Lemuel stood with his mouth hanging open.

"You said you would not hurt anyone; is this what you

meant? Does your word have no honor?"

He averted his gaze from the head councilor. "I didn't give anyone permission to do this."

"Well, someone clearly ignored you. Councilor Duncan needs help. Bandages, water, some cooling salves. You will find all of these things and bring them back, and take that guard with you. I will have no more threats hanging over the head councilor."

Lemuel muttered under his breath as he closed the door. Moments later, Ariana heard the lock of the apartment's main door slide back into place. She hurried into the kitchen for a glass of water and brought it back just as the head councilor pushed himself to a seated position. He sucked in a few shallow breaths before accepting the water with gratitude.

"Have Lemuel and his men treated you badly?" he asked, squeezing his eyes shut in pain.

Ariana shook her head. "No, Councilor, but that does not change the fact that these tree stumps have no honor."

Councilor Duncan panted for a moment. "How did you convince that boar to let you out?"

She explained the conversation with Lemuel but stopped halfway when it was clear the councilor suffered another wave of pain. After his breathing returned to normal, she pulled a chair next to the bed. Ariana took in the sight of him again and shook her head in anger.

"How did you come to be in this condition?"

The head councilor rolled his eyes. "The men who marched me here insisted on entering the apartment and tried to set orders for how I should behave in my own home. I...disagreed."

Ariana tucked her chin in amazement. "You fought, Head Councilor?"

He grinned, and Ariana recalled one of her first meetings

with the man who led the royal advisory panel. In those early days, as they spent time getting to know one another, they shared bits of their childhoods and experiences. Ariana remembered the head councilor offering a rueful smile when he said he had spent his youth in much rowdiness. Had anyone told his mother he would hold an esteemed position in court, she would have returned to the fates from shock.

In his grin now, she saw that young boy who must have engaged in his fair share of scrapes.

"It does not matter," he said, his amusement fading. "I admit I am at a loss at how in all of Linden we will work this out. The king is missing. King Malcolm and Queen Celia—any word of them? Did they manage to escape?"

Ariana's face fell. "No, Head Councilor. The queen was imprisoned with me last night in my own apartment. I do not know where they kept the king, but he was allowed to visit just now. Lemuel gave us all a ten-minute time limit, which is not much, but I knew if I could devise a way to visit you then we might, perhaps, work together toward a plan. The queen and I spent hours last night plotting ways to escape, but the risk of exposure prevented us from finding a viable solution."

Councilor Duncan pushed a fist into a yawn, and Ariana picked at a thread on the cuff of her sleeve. Her ears remained alert, praying that the fates would keep Lemuel away as long as possible. The head councilor's forehead furrowed for a few minutes; then his face relaxed.

"I believe I may help," he said. "When King Christopher first ascended the throne, he and I discussed security measures around the castle. At that time, he mentioned something from his childhood to me that might prove useful. I cannot think of a plan in this moment, but the queen may be able to offer her thoughts."

Ariana bobbed her head. "Anything, Councilor."

As he shared what the king told him years earlier, Ariana's limbs tingled with anticipation.

CHAPTER 14

Within a quarter hour, Lemuel returned carrying a tray with all the things Ariana demanded. He set the tray on the low dresser in Councilor Duncan's room. Ariana noted how Lemuel could not meet the head councilor's eyes.

Maybe the horrible man has a thimbleful of integrity yet.

"Your time's ended," he said to Ariana.

Ariana bit her lip as she followed Lemuel down the corridor again. They found their way back to her apartment. Lemuel gestured to the guard outside her door who unlocked it.

I hope we will not interrupt a private moment, she thought.

The king and queen sat on the settee holding hands. When the door swung open, the king pulled away and stood. Regret flit across Queen Celia's face as she smoothed back her skirts and stood as well.

"Your time's done, your majesty," Lemuel said.

Ariana expected a crass remark, but Lemuel's expression remained troubled. She curtsied to the king and murmured a goodbye. To Lemuel she offered a cold, hard stare. He returned it and left.

"Did your 'urgent matter' with Councilor Duncan yield any useful information?" Queen Celia asked. Ariana noticed her smile came with ease now.

"It did, your majesty," she said, sitting in the chair across from the queen. "The head councilor shared with me a unique feature of the castle that may help us. We were able to formulate a plan, but it will require a measure of conviction."

"How can I contribute, Ariana?"

Ariana went into her kitchen and withdrew the sharpest knife she could find from a drawer.

"It is time for the captives to turn on one another."

She handed the knife to the queen and folded her arms with satisfaction.

Arthur's head jerked back as he awoke with a start, and he shifted his body on the chair outside Councilor Ariana's apartment. He'd guarded her the previous day too, and it was turning out to be one of the most boring jobs he'd ever had. When Lemuel and Bailey approached him and the others about coming to the castle, Arthur imagined a battle like the ones the artisans' guild performed onstage. After a long, drawn-out fight, King Christopher would apologize for his shortsightedness and reward all of them for their bravery. He would give Arthur, Lemuel, and the others the funds they deserved; maybe even hold a parade in their honor.

Instead, the fight with the king and the others lasted mere minutes. Then Lemuel shouted at him in front of everyone for not watching King Christopher in the petitioners' hall. It was his fault, Lemuel screamed, that the ruler slipped away.

He'd been stuck on this ridiculous chair ever since, studying the lines in his hands and falling asleep.

He rolled his shoulders and slumped down, his chin

almost touching his chest. It could've been worse. He could still have been working with his mother, punching dough and carrying trays of bread from the oven to the glass case in the front of the bakery. At least here the smell of yeast didn't coat his body, embedding into his skin. Of course, he did miss his mother's savory tarts, but the royal kitchen staff turned out to be talented. Almost as good as his mama.

Just then, a scream came from Councilor Ariana's apartment.

Arthur shot straight up, his eyes getting wider as he heard another scream. He stood and fished the keys out of his pocket, dropping them once, then twice as a third scream came. His hands shook as he tried the keys, forgetting the symbol on the door that matched the corresponding key on the ring.

Finally, finally, he fit the correct key to the lock and opened the door to yet another scream. The queen held a knife to the councilor's throat, her eyes darting from side to side, her other hand twisting one of the councilor's arms behind her back. Arthur froze.

Queen Celia may have been his prisoner, but she was still a queen.

"Please help me," the councilor whimpered. "Please. The queen says she—"

"I came here to participate in the last rites for my daughter," Queen Celia said, eyes wild, her breathing heavy. "All of Linden is responsible for her death, and it is only fair the kingdom trade a life for hers."

Arthur held up his hands in a placating manner, noting the queen's rumpled clothing and messy hair.

"Your majesty, I'm sure you're in pain after losing your daughter, but that's no reason to—"

"You know nothing," she exclaimed, pushing the knife

closer to the councilor's neck. "You have not suffered the pain of the death of a child and the betrayal of a man you once considered a son!"

"Queen Celia, please, I'm sure we—"

The queen pushed the councilor forward; as they came closer, Arthur saw sweat beading on the councilor's upper lip.

"Your majesty," he said, failing to keep the panic from his voice, "think of King Malcolm. He wouldn't—"

"I will take this woman to the center of the castle so all may witness her execution and then turn this knife on myself!" the queen screamed. "I have no purpose left anymore."

The last words came in a wail, and Arthur took a few deep breaths.

"I'll get Lemuel," he said, following them into the corridor. "I'm sure he can help you with...with...all this."

The queen thrust the knife in his direction. "Do you presume to tell me your spineless leader knows how I feel?"

His legs trembled beneath him; without another word, he turned and ran down the hall.

As the guard's footsteps receded in the distance, the queen let Ariana go.

The councilor took several deep breaths to slow her heart rate. Even as she knew the entire scene was a ruse, she had felt Queen Celia's body trembling with despair. She resisted the urge to touch her throat. Instead, she reminded herself of the window of time the guard had just given them.

She ducked her head back through her door and grabbed the travel pack hidden in the kitchen.

"This way, your majesty," Ariana said, rushing down the corridor in the direction opposite from the guard. "Councilor Duncan said to look for the fourth tapestry on the right after my door."

She took several more steps then realized the queen had not followed. Turning back, she returned and saw tears in the monarch's eyes. Ariana glanced down the corridor behind her then looked back.

"Every word I uttered was the truth, Ariana," Queen Celia said. She let the knife drop to the floor; the metal rang with the finality of death. "I have lost my child and have never known an anguish as great as this."

The queen began to cry in soft, quiet tones.

Ariana's sense of protocol told her she should wait for the queen to stop; at the very least, she should have turned around so Queen Celia did not have to suffer the embarrassment of anyone witnessing her tears. Her sense as a woman, however, made her embrace the queen.

"She was loved by all and will be missed," Ariana said into the queen's hair. "I vow to you that when all is right again, we will grieve her. She deserves it, as do you and King Malcolm."

"Where has Christopher gone?" the queen murmured, and Ariana pushed down her shock at hearing the king's name without the title.

"I do not know, your majesty. Perhaps he is procuring help. We must be sure you can do the same."

After another minute of shedding tears, the queen nodded against Ariana's shoulder and cleared her throat. She pulled away, smoothed her hair, and cleared her throat a second time. Kneeling, she grabbed the knife and held it out for Ariana. The councilor shook her head.

"You have a long journey ahead of you and may need to defend yourself."

The queen nodded and tucked the knife into one of the hidden pockets in her skirts. Ariana headed down the corridor again; this time, the queen followed. They found the fourth tapestry on the right, pulled it back, and saw the faint outline of a door. Ariana ran her fingers around the outline and found the coin-sized knob. She pressed it, and the door swung inwards.

"Councilor Duncan said ten paces down from any of the hidden doors, you will find a shelf built into the wall." Ariana glanced over the queen's shoulder again; satisfied no one came for them, she gave the queen the travel pack and continued. "A box of matches will be on that shelf and a torch on the wall next to it. Continue for another hundred paces, and you will find a door on your right that should lead to one of the gardens outside."

Queen Celia nodded, the determination of a ruler back in place, and stepped into the passage. Before Ariana could close the door, the queen stretched a hand in her direction. Ariana took it, squeezed it as she would a friend's palm, and nodded her on. Without another word, the queen went down the secret corridor. Ariana pulled the door shut and eased the tapestry back into place.

A clattering of footsteps came toward her. Indecision rooted her to the floor when every instinct screamed she should run. A moment later, she turned in the direction of the footsteps. As she did so, she let all of her frustration at being held captive, her fear of what would happen next, and her grief for Queen Lily come to the fore of her mind.

Her tears started flowing within five paces.

The guard returned, followed by Lemuel, and they all met close to the door of Ariana's apartment. The young leader seized her arm and jerked it to get her attention. Ariana bent almost in half, her sobs echoing against the walls.

"Where's the queen? Where did she go?"

"Please...do not hurt us," Ariana said between shudders. "I am...frightened for my life. Please...I beg of you."

Lemuel thrust her arm away, a gesture almost as painful as when he held it. The guard who had watched her door ran into her apartment and came out moments later, confusion on his face.

"She's gone, Lemuel."

"What do you mean she's gone?"

"The queen was right here holding the knife, but she's not there anymore."

Lemuel narrowed his eyes at Ariana. "Where. Is. She?"

She continued to sob, hoping he would take that as a sign that she was too inconsolable to offer any coherent answers. Her heart thundered in her ears as she put increased effort into her wailing. For added effect, she covered her face with her hands.

"Tell the men to go to the dungeons and find every chain with a lock they can carry back," Lemuel said, "then bring everyone to the petitioners' hall. It's time we stop minding our manners and remind these castle dwellers they're people too. Let's be on our way, *Councilor*."

He forced her forward with a rough gesture, and his tone made gooseflesh appear on Ariana's arms. She thought for a moment about the worst that might befall her and all those left in the royal residence. Her stomach hardened around a stone of fear.

Then she remembered the queen's quest. Provided she found her way out of the castle's secret passageways, Queen Celia would return to Wyndemere and bring back help. Ariana willed herself to believe it, envisioned it happening, and focused all her energy on asking the fates to make it so as Lemuel pushed her toward the petitioners' hall.

By the time they arrived, a chip had broken off the fear in her stomach and began to glow. With faith.

"This is to remind all of you that we're not here to waste our time," Lemuel called to the entire hall.

He crossed his arms. The sight of every courtier in wrist and ankle shackles gave him some confidence that he was back in control, but the feeling didn't last. He'd waded into the situation thinking it was a manageable brook; now he found himself in a roaring rapid with no bank of safety ahead.

The royal councilors stood with heads held high, and Lemuel tried to ignore Councilor Duncan's face. Even with the bandages and salves, the man's bruises looked worse in the full light of the hall. The reassurance he'd just found slipped again.

After questioning the pages in the castle the previous day, Lemuel discovered that in the days after the queen's death many of the courtiers and staff had been sent home. Some archaic law dictated that when a member of the royal family died, only the most necessary help stayed to facilitate the day-to-day workings of castle life. At the time, he'd pounded his fist into his hand, cursing the fact that he didn't have a larger audience for his takeover of the castle. Now he was grateful he wouldn't have to keep track of so many prisoners. It had already become a cumbersome job dealing with the ones he had.

He let his eyes move to King Malcolm and registered the triumph in the king's face. Even with the heavy metal restricting his movements, the blasted man looked regal. Some people had the sense to express their fear. Most of them were kitchen staff and laundry workers, but the tremor in their voices as they talked amongst themselves comforted Lemuel—a little—that he still held the upper hand.

"If King Christopher can't control his people, I will," he went on, locking his knees to keep them from shaking. "From now on, you'll all remain in shackles day and night."

"You are complicating matters for yourself, Master Lemuel," Councilor Duncan said, his words careful and enunciated through the bandage on his upper lip. "When the king returns, he will see to it you are punished beyond any—"

"Well, the king isn't here, so I'm not going to waste my time talking about him. Men, escort everyone back to their quarters."

Bailey and his other friends started herding pages and castle staffers toward the doors of the hall, arms sweeping back and forth. Instead of following, one of the men who had joined them on the spur of the moment the previous day came to Lemuel. The burly man stood at least a head above him, and his bulky muscles told of hard labor.

He watched Bailey, Oliver, Ernest, and the others. After a long look at the back of the crowd dispersing, he turned his gaze back to Lemuel. The leader of the insurrection tried not to squirm.

"You're making a mistake," the man said, his baritone lower than the floor.

Lemuel narrowed his eyes. "Who are you?"

"Name's Rupert, and I'm telling you, you're making a mistake."

"And you say this because..."

"Because the queen's escaped," Rupert said, cocking his head. "She'll hitch a carriage back to Wyndemere and bring an army down on our heads within two days. I came here to make the king hear my complaints, not to get carted off to prison."

"Get to the point."

"My friends and I have decided to leave."

Lemuel noticed several men coming to stand behind Rupert.

"Are you giving up?" Lemuel asked. "You don't want to hold the king accountable for all the hardships he's let us endure?"

Rupert scoffed. "It's hard to hold him accountable when he's not here, isn't it?"

"For all we know, he ran straight to Wyndemere himself," one of the men behind Rupert called. "If the queen meets him halfway, I don't want to be here when they all come back."

"And they *will* come back," Rupert added. "No, we're leaving. You can carry on the fight, can't you, Lemuel? After all, this was your idea."

"It was my idea, but I'm doing this for all of us," Lemuel shot back. "Or did you forget about all the times you and your family have gone to bed with half-empty bellies?"

Rupert shook his head. "I haven't forgotten, Lemuel, but I also know a hopeless situation when I see one. You have nothing left here to fight with."

"I have the castle, Rupert. I think that's a good place to start."

The burly man glanced over his shoulder. At first Lemuel thought he was reconsidering. When one of the men smirked and Rupert grinned back, Lemuel knew it was a lost cause.

He wished he could punch the man. He'd seen it happen many times in the common room of the inn he and his friends liked to visit. The trouble, of course, was Rupert's size and the crowd of men that now surrounded them. None of the faces looked familiar, and Lemuel didn't want to test his chances.

If Rupert was by himself I could have, but there's no sense in upsetting this many people.

"Fine," he said, "go. But when the storytellers share this tale in the future, everyone will hear how you and the others ran at the first challenge."

Rupert rolled his eyes. "Running isn't always a bad thing, Lemuel."

He called for the others to follow, and they made their way out of the hall. A few of the men gave Lemuel dirty looks, and he shrugged. As they walked past, he counted heads to see how many he was losing: eight men in all.

The sight of them leaving brought him a little relief, which he would never have admitted to anyone else. He'd worried since seeing Councilor Duncan's state about what these men could do. He didn't want to be the next to find out.

Oliver came back into the hall and turned to watch Rupert and the others. "Where are they going?"

"They're leaving. They didn't want to take any more risks. Cowards."

The word seemed to fall the wrong way to the ground, floating with uncertainty instead of landing with the weight of how right he was to stay. How right he and the *others* were to stay, he reminded himself. If Rupert and his men didn't have the courage to see this through, it made sense for them to go.

Of course; that was it. They didn't have the courage Lemuel did. He wasn't just trying to convince himself.

"They're axe grinders, Lemuel." Oliver clapped him on his back. "Come on, let's go see the horses. I bet we can pick out which ones we want to take home with us."

"Horses. Right."

Lemuel allowed himself to be led away, wondering for a moment what might have happened if he had followed Rupert out of the castle walls.

You would have gone home empty-handed and listened to Mother and Father spend the rest of their days telling you how right they were. How Fin would have made the king listen to reason and made sure they got what they're owed.

Fin.

Well, Fin's not here now, is he? I'm here, and I'm going to make sure the king listens. I'm going to make sure the king gives me what we're owed. Not Fin.

"Let's tell the kitchen staff to make something extra special for dinner tonight," he said. "We've earned it."

Oliver laughed in agreement, and the men swaggered down the hall.

CHAPTER 15

In a village that was two days' ride away from the castle, Martin sat on the driver's box of the carriage and glowered at the backs of the horses.

As they had ridden east from Ingleside, Martin and the others saw firsthand the evidence of the trees' demise. Mounds of white ash stood alongside the path like markers in a graveyard. Scorch marks in the ground in the shapes of trunks showed where the trees once stood.

A sickly sweet scent pervaded the air, making Martin's nose tighten in disgust. Ever since the queen's return to the fates, nothing had gone right. First Martin watched his friend drown himself in his pain; then came word of the trees. Martin believed the news would offer King Christopher a rope with which he could climb out of the well of his sorrow. Hearing of the trees dying and seeing the reality now for the two days they had traveled made Martin wonder if, instead, the king would find himself gasping for breath.

In a way, allowing the healer and her son to travel with them had provided some measure of relief, if only from the emotions that threatened to engulf him and the king. Martin knew his relationship with Queen Lily differed greatly from that with King Christopher, but they had shared a comradery nonetheless. For that, if nothing else, the guardsmaster would miss her.

At the moment, however, the only emotion that coursed

through him was irritation and regret. Irritation that the healer seemed to be spending an inordinate amount of time in the comfort room before they left. Regret that she and Alistair had joined them at all.

We would have traveled a greater distance had that woman not endeavored to stop here, he thought. *Thank the fates Alistair is no trouble.*

The soldier had never met someone as quiet as Alistair. The boy did not talk about friends or athletic games or notice the young girls who walked some of the paths they traveled. Either he stared at the trees while the carriage moved, or he murmured short answers to his mother's questions. Any attempts to engage him in conversation resulted in a shrug or a look of apprehension.

None of that bothered Martin, however. Not much, anyway. Many people had quirks; some just hid those quirks better than others. If the boy had no will to talk to anyone other than his mother, so be it.

It was his mother talking that led to the argument this morning, causing Geraldine to run from the carriage just before leaving and back into the inn. She had slowed only long enough to tell them over her shoulder that she needed to visit the comfort room one more time. The king and Alistair had long since settled themselves in the carriage and waited without complaint. Martin, however, could not find the same level of patience.

What could she possibly be doing for this long?

After what felt like a year, Geraldine emerged from the inn and hurried to the carriage. She avoided Martin's eye, despite his best efforts to stare her down. He watched for her foot to clear the ground then gave the reins a flick, ignoring the exclamation that came from the carriage and the jerking motion behind him that said the healer had most likely lost her balance while sitting down.

I told her. I told *her that staying in an inn would slow our progress. Yet she insisted, and, like a fool, I agreed. What is wrong with me? That is it. No more inns until we find all the heart stones and can return to the castle.*

He pushed the horses to a well-paced trot and continued on the path to Cicero. While it would have been impossible to engage in any conversation with those inside the carriage, he knew he would have chosen not to that morning. All their efforts at anonymity could have been undone if Geraldine had not watched her tongue at the last moment.

Maybe the king was right in dismissing her in the first place. The woman has no sense of discretion. Telling the innkeeper we came from Ingleside! What if Lemuel sent men after us? We have no way of knowing what path they are using or how large their search party is. Has the woman no brains?

After they made good time and distance away from their starting point that morning, he slowed the horses to a walk and let them cool off before pulling on the reins to direct them to stop. He jumped down from the driver's box and went to the low door of the carriage, opening it and looking only at the king.

"An opportunity to stretch your legs, your highness, if you need one," he said.

King Christopher nodded, avoiding looking at Geraldine. "Thank you, Martin."

"We can afford only a half hour, nothing more," Martin said, still ignoring his other two passengers.

He offered the king a hand and helped him hop out of the carriage. Next came Alistair, and he offered the boy a hand as well. After a moment, Alistair just shook his head and jumped down. The boy rushed into the forest and slipped from sight within seconds.

Martin turned to face Geraldine and saw anger flashing in her eyes.

"I don't need any help, Sir Martin, thank you," she said, batting away his outstretched hand.

He shrugged and turned away. "As you wish, Mistress Geraldine."

The grunt behind him, followed by a wordless exclaim, told him that Geraldine had more or less fallen out of the carriage. He debated for a moment about whether he should ask after her. His chivalry won the argument.

"Are you all right, Healer?"

She scowled. "I'm fine, Guardsmaster. No need to worry. Not that you ever would."

Martin crossed his arms. "And what do you mean by that?"

"Just that you're more concerned about the king than anyone else," she said, mimicking his posture. "Alistair and I didn't have to come on this quest, but here we are."

"Yes, here you are," Martin said, his teeth clenched, "leaving a trail like breadcrumbs for Lemuel if he chooses to look for it."

"All I did was strike up a friendly conversation."

"No, a friendly conversation concerns the weather or the quality of the innkeeper's ale, maybe a compliment on the food and the service," Martin replied, his tone increasing in volume. "It does not mean telling the innkeeper where we came from. Why not leave a personal message for Lemuel so that he may find us that much sooner?"

At least the healer had the grace to blush. "I am...I could have thought that through, I guess. But you didn't have to act like a boor and march us out of there like prisoners. Didn't anyone teach you how to behave in public? This isn't the soldiers' barracks, you know!"

Martin breathed hard through his nose but did not respond. How could he, when all this woman saw was an uneducated lout?

"Besides, I learned more talking to those people than stomping around like a bully."

"Such as?" Martin asked, putting his hands on his hips.

Geraldine took a deep breath and looked around at the forest. When she spoke again, her voice had returned to a more normal tone. The troubled look on her face said there was still much to worry over, however.

"People were talking about the trees and the way they're collapsing," she said. "They were also talking about how King Christopher didn't ride in the procession for the queen. A few were arguing about whether that meant he was sick or too deep in his grief to leave the castle. They're starting to question what that means for the future."

"Given the state of affairs, they have a right to do so."

Martin whirled around at the voice. The king strode from between the trees, his hands dripping with water. Geraldine hurried into the forest in the same direction Alistair had gone.

"Your highness," Martin said, "the healer was merely reporting what she had heard. We cannot assume everyone in the kingdom feels the same way as a roomful of visitors to an inn."

The king checked the wound on his arm, which Martin was pleased to see he had kept dry as Geraldine had instructed.

"I also cannot escape the possibility that, had I ridden in Lily's processional, we might not have been forced to run like criminals," King Christopher said. "I did not bring Lemuel to the castle, but I had a hand in putting King Malcolm and Queen Celia in danger."

Martin fidgeted, unsure of how to answer his friend's charge. After a few moments of staring at the ground, he followed Geraldine to call her back. They needed to resume their journey as quickly as possible so everyone could be safe once again.

On the afternoon of the fourth day of travel, the group reached the village of Cicero.

It was not truly a village, Christopher noted. A collection of houses sat on either side of the path. As they rode past, they saw one shop marked by the sign hanging outside it. The homes looked well-kept but old, and one or two residents came out to watch the carriage. The residents looked even older than the cottages.

Martin parked the carriage at the end of the lane and advised them to wait while he gathered information. On instinct, Christopher opened and closed his left fist. The two previous evenings, Geraldine had examined his arm to make sure no infection set in and changed his dressings with supplies from her compact bag that seemed to contain every necessity possible. The previous night she told him his recovery meant the stitches could come out soon.

Her compassion reminded him of Lily. He had embarked on this journey because he no longer had her, and every passing day made her absence more pronounced. In the castle, he fooled himself more than once by pretending she had just gone down the hall to paint or to consult with a lady-in-waiting on one of her many charitable efforts. Here, in this plain carriage, with no royal colors or standard to announce his arrival, the difference between his life before losing her and after came into stark relief.

The healer could have saved her, he thought again, although the words lacked conviction now.

Martin came back with a frown. "These people are wary of newcomers and with good reason. The old gentleman there told me travelers do not venture this way."

"But don't people come to make wishes?" Geraldine asked. "This place should be teeming with visitors."

"The man said since the magic of the well was reversed, people have stopped coming. The last visitor arrived about fifteen years ago, maybe more."

Christopher's heart beat harder. "The magic was reversed? What does that mean?"

"I do not know, your highness. He did not seem eager to talk, and I did not want to rouse suspicion, so I asked him where I could find the well and thanked him for his time."

"Perhaps his mind has become muddled with age. Did you ask where we could find clean water?"

"Close to the well. He said it was in a shady area, a good place to make camp. I suggest we go there, let the horses off their leads, and rest. Perhaps we may also have something to eat."

Christopher nodded his assent. Martin climbed back up to the driver's seat and clucked at the horses to begin moving. Alistair's gaze remained fixed on the trees.

A scant half hour later, the carriage tugged to a gentle stop. The old man had spoken true. Tall trees provided ample shade. Slivers of sunlight slipped through the gaps in the canopy of the dark, glossy leaves above them. Alistair ducked his head out the window and pulled back.

"Trees healthy," he said, the sparkle in his eyes a sharp contrast to his sallow complexion.

The boy has begun to look ill since leaving Ingleside, Christopher thought.

The door to the carriage opened, and Christopher clasped Martin's hand to disembark the carriage then turned and offered his hand to Geraldine. Surprised, she accepted it and let him hand her down. Alistair, too, gave the king an outstretched hand and a grateful smile, which made Christopher smile back. He tried to ignore the weakness of the boy's grip.

"Do you think the well will be hard to find, Martin?" he called as he rounded the horses at the front of the carriage.

"I think we have reached it, your highness."

Christopher stopped short at the sight before him.

A cylinder of stone stood three feet high, but gouges and dents plagued the rocks forming the well. A sheet of algae in a putrid green color lay on the surface. Leaves sat on top of the algae, making the king wonder whether it had solidified.

"Can this truly be it?" Christopher asked.

He approached the well. Within several paces, he stopped. The stench of decay made him press his hand to his nose and mouth.

Martin came to stand beside him and covered his own nose with a handkerchief. "The man said there was no other well for nearly three hundred miles."

Geraldine joined them with hands on hips, her mouth twisting. "This is a mistake. The Keeper couldn't have meant this well."

"There is only one wishing well in all of Linden, Healer," Martin said.

"Could she have visited another wishing well somewhere else?"

How did one approach a wishing well? Christopher wondered. Was a formal greeting required? Some sort of offering?

He forced himself to ignore the odor and moved closer to the stone facade. Letting his gaze go over every bit of it, he noticed a plaque on the side facing them. Christopher kneeled and tried to read the words, but they were nothing more than bumps against his fingertips.

"Wishing Well," he said as he rose, using the tone for formal pronouncements, "we have come to you with a request. Will you hear us?"

No reply.

"The king of Linden requests your attention, Wishing Well, and I do so with humility," he tried again. "Will you entertain our question?"

Alistair stepped forward and raised a hand. "Try?"

Christopher gestured him forward and moved half a pace to give him room. Alistair reached into his pocket and pulled out a stone, which he tossed into the water. Geraldine and Martin stepped forward to see what happened.

The stone landed on a leaf; it floated for a moment, then sunk as if in a funnel, taking the algae and the leaf down with it.

Christopher gave Alistair an indulgent nod. They would wait for a few moments so Alistair would not feel bad that nothing happened, and then...and then what? What if the well had lost its magic? What if the heart stone in it had dissolved years ago?

Every day at some point, the group discussed what to do about the stone the Keeper said she had ground into dust. It seemed a lost cause, although Christopher refused to admit that aloud. Would they be unable to retrieve this stone as well?

Just then the sludgy water started rippling outward from the place where the boy's stone struck it. The surface became the deep yellow of a ripe lemon and shimmered as if Alistair had tossed a handful of stardust across it. The ripples changed shades to the color of corn silk.

Then they heard a long yawn.

"Oh, my," a voice murmured, "such a delightful nap. Who comes to fulfill a wish made?"

Christopher exchanged looks with Martin, Geraldine, and Alistair.

"I, Christopher, king of Linden, come to you, Wishing Well."

The well yawned again; this one lasted longer than the first. "Welcome, your highness. Excuse me. It's been quite some time since anyone's come here."

Christopher nodded. "We bring a specific wish to you, Well, and hope to see it granted."

"I am happy to make a wish for you," the well said. Its stretched words made Christopher think of a cat arching in the sun. "You must concentrate on what you want most."

The air around Christopher became still. From the corner of his eye, he saw Martin turn to him with expectation. He thought Martin might have even spoken, but his thoughts clouded his hearing.

What I most want? I want for Lily to return to me. Can the well...could the well bring her back?

"Your highness?" the well asked, more alert now. "Have you focused your concentration? May I make the wish?"

"I..." He smoothed the front of his tunic to hide how his hands fluttered. "You said you would make a wish. Are we not responsible for making the wish and you for granting it?"

The rippling in the water increased for a moment.

"My magic was reversed many years ago," the well replied. "A woman made a wish that changed my purpose. Now I make the wishes, and the wish seekers become compelled to fulfill them. Well, they did. No one's visited me in almost...fifteen years? Twenty? I've slept so long I don't remember."

"That woman is the Keeper of the Linden Wood," Christopher said. "She is dying and the forest with her. She made a wish and left with you one piece of her heart solidified in stone. We are here to wish for her heart stone back. It is the only way to restore the wood and its magic."

The well stayed silent for several long seconds.

"It seems like a big task. I don't know if I can make a wish of that magnitude."

"You keep saying you're the one that makes the wishes," Geraldine said. "What do you mean?"

"Before the woman reversed my magic, people would make wishes and I'd grant them," the well said. "Often they made wishes on an impulse. They wanted to be someone's true love or go on an adventure. They didn't understand that they weren't suited to the object of their affections or that their families needed them.

"When the woman—the Keeper, you say?—made her wish, it changed me. Instead of people making wishes and me granting them, the magic from the Keeper's wish and the stone compelled people to fulfill the wishes *I* made. Except after some time"—the well yawned yet again—"when word spread of how I made the wishes instead of the other way around, the wishmakers stopped coming."

Those people did not lose what I lost, else they would have not left the well to its own devices, Christopher thought.

"To be perfectly honest, I miss the wishmakers. When I granted wishes, people would stop by so often. They didn't mind that they had to see the full outcome of their first wish before making a second one. Really, some of them came to talk more than anything else. Once a woman visited every day for a year. Her husband was unkind to her, you see, and she was lonely. She told me—"

"Can you help us?" Geraldine interrupted.

"I suppose so," the well said. "If you desire the heart stone more than anything, I could make a wish for you to retrieve it. In fact, if you did get it back, I would be able to grant wishes again. Oh, yes, I like this idea."

"People do not change, Wishing Well," Martin said. "They will return, yes, but they will make wishes designed by their folly. Rare will be the person who considers the consequences of a wish before making it."

"True," the well replied, "and if I went back to granting wishes, I'd have to give up these leisurely naps. But I would definitely welcome the company. The Keeper may have wished to spare others from heartbreak, but how can people appreciate the joys of life without a little sadness?"

Even if heartbreak threatens to undo a person? Christopher thought.

"You speak the truth, Wishing Well," Martin said. "Your highness, are you prepared to proceed?"

Perhaps, after the well restores the heart stone, I may ask for Lily to come back to me. Could *she come back? Can the well defy death itself?*

"Whatever you decide," the well said, "I wish you would do it soon. Oh, I made a joke."

The well chuckled, and its surface rippled with merriment.

"Yes, please decide soon. I might slip into another little slumber any minute now. I must say, it's so peaceful and quiet under the surface of the water. No loud sounds; the elements of the weather don't even touch me. I feel as if I could just drift away..."

The voice faded a bit, and Christopher could feel the eyes of the others on him.

"But I must warn you," the well said. "You must concentrate on your heart's truest desire. If you don't, the magic could be forced to change course and require a sacrifice for me to make the wish."

"Our greatest need in this moment is the heart stone," Martin asked. "I daresay a sacrifice would not be necessary."

"I don't know," the well said. "A wish this big might require it. It might even ask of that sacrifice from everyone."

My heart's truest desire is nothing more than Lily, Christopher thought. *How can I...the Keeper is dying but Lily...*

"Again, a nonessential matter," Martin said. "Your majesty, should we proceed?"

Christopher looked at each of them in turn.

"I... I believe I... I am not ready to move forward just yet. I must contemplate this further."

He ignored the astonishment on the others' faces as he hurried past them and climbed back into the carriage.

Alistair folded one arm against his stomach and squeezed his eyes shut against the ache that had traveled to Cicero with him. His greatest worry all the way from Ingleside had been that he'd turn around and see Father chasing them on a horse, demanding that Mother go home to her patients. That Alistair go back to work in the inn. That one of them explain the note Mother had left, stating they were leaving.

He didn't know he had to worry about the king.

"What's wrong?" Mother asked the guardsmaster. "We're here to get the heart stone. What is there to think about?"

Sir Martin looked just as mystified as her. "Perhaps he needs a moment to consider the wording of his request."

Alistair rolled his eyes. Adults often didn't want to see what was right in front of them. If they did see it, they didn't want to name it for what it was. From the moment the well began talking, Alistair had watched the king.

The king didn't want to wish for the heart stone; he wanted to wish for something else.

Alistair's face got hot, and he stomped to the carriage. Throwing the door open, he climbed inside and dropped into a seat. The king opened his mouth, but Alistair held up a hand to stop him.

"Trees dying. Wish, now."

The king crossed his arms. "These matters must be studied with a great deal of—"

"Trees. Dying."

"I do not appreciate your insolence nor your disrespect for—"

"Trees. Keeper. Dying. Wish."

Alistair grimaced as a spasm made his stomach clench into a tight ball.

The king leaned forward on the carriage bench, his eyebrows tilting downward. "Alistair, are you all right?"

He didn't bother to answer the king. Instead, he stood, his body surging with energy, and jumped out of the carriage. A moment later, he heard the king's footsteps behind him.

"Alistair, stop!"

He whirled around, his breathing shallow. His body heaved with anxiety, disappointment, and injustice. Why couldn't adults do the right thing the first time?

King Christopher came closer, clutching his arm. "Alistair, I understand your concern for the wood and the Keeper, but the dilemmas in question must be taken in turn."

Alistair flung a finger in the direction of the well. "You wish? I wish?"

The king's jaw tightened.

"Geraldine, if you cannot control your son's temper, we will need to reconsider this entire—"

"You. Wish? I. Wish?" Alistair yelled.

King Christopher's mouth dropped open. He snapped it shut a moment later and licked his lips.

"Wishing Well," he said, "my truest desire is to retrieve the heart stone of the Keeper of the Linden Wood."

The water in the well fluttered, and Christopher got the absurd notion that it was thinking. He bit back a curse as they waited. How dare a child challenge his authority? What could he know of the predicaments before the kingdom?

We cannot proceed as a group if the boy shows such disrespect. I am the king.

He opened his mouth to speak to the healer, but just then the water in the well began rippling so fast it lapped against the stone edge. As it rippled, it shimmered. Christopher squinted against the light, and the well's voice echoed around them and throughout the trees.

"I see your heart's deepest want, King Christopher of Linden," the well announced. "You have not asked for it."

Christopher's breath ceased for a moment.

"In exchange for your half-truth, each of you will make a sacrifice. The magic demands, King Christopher, that you give up your first love to save your kingdom. Guardsmaster Martin, you will forsake all to trust only one. Healer Geraldine, you will forfeit one of your greatest gifts. Alistair, you will leave behind your former life. These sacrifices will fulfill my wish for you: to retrieve the heart stone of the Keeper of the Wood."

"But—"

The yellow light rose as a beam from the water and fanned toward all of them. The light's brilliance increased as if they stood inside a diamond, and around them sparkles whirled. The trees did not move, but the light whipped in circles and created a funnel. Through the slits of his eyes, Christopher could just make out shorter funnels breaking away from the largest one and encircling each of them.

A window opened in the light to a scene: Lily sitting at an easel. Her back faced him, but he knew that posture, the considering angle of the head, the way she raised her brush before using the paint to caress the flat surface and turn it into a work of art. Then he heard his own voice call her name, and Christopher realized the wishing well had taken him inside a memory.

"Do you plan to paint all night, my love?"

Lily beamed at him over her shoulder. She turned all the way around, and his lips twitched at how sweet she looked with her swollen belly. He came to her and clasped her arm.

"I thought I would add a few more touches before I retired for the night. Do you think the baby will like it?"

He let his hand graze her cheek. She leaned into his palm and closed her eyes. Christopher managed to stop himself from kissing her in full view of the lady-in-waiting who stood by the door and tried to fade into the wall.

The window snapped shut; the funnel whipped around him twice more and disappeared.

"Wait!"

Christopher swiped at the air in front of him, adding a wordless yell when the muscles in his arm protested. The pain brought him back to the clearing and his traveling companions. The others stood as if the four of them formed the corners of a square. They panted from exertion, and Christopher noticed his own heavy breathing.

Geraldine's face looked ashen. Martin refused to meet his gaze, shame rolling off him in waves. Alistair jerked his head from side to side, searching for some unseen threat.

Comprehension dawned on the boy. Wherever the wishing well's memory took Alistair, bit by bit he returned. Recognition made the wildness in his eyes dissipate, and he exhaled a sharp breath as if a great force had released him.

Both healer and soldier hung their heads. Martin's face filled with surrender.

Geraldine clasped her middle as if she might be sick, although her normal color returned.

Christopher turned toward the well. The cracks and dents had become whole again. The stone, a dull dishwater gray before, gleamed in the same cream color that formed the walls bordering the castle of Rosewood. Seeing the stones made Christopher long for home in a way that drove straight to his soul.

The well stood taller too. Now two stone steps led to its lip. On the top of the steps sat an orchid-colored stone in a rough teardrop shape. The stone pulsed from light inside it. The plaque, once unreadable with dulled letters, now gleamed. Had Christopher had the fortitude, he would have stepped forward to read it.

"Thank you, your majesty," the well intoned in a richer, fuller voice. "You have restored me."

He stepped forward and picked up the pulsing rock. This had to be the Keeper's heart stone. The others came forward as well and stood around him.

"We've done it," Geraldine said, her voice scratchy as if she had screamed herself hoarse. "We've gotten the first heart stone."

She reached for the stone, and Christopher let her take

it. Geraldine turned toward the carriage then stopped. She turned away from the carriage, her gaze intent on the stone, then turned back to the carriage again.

"What is it, Mistress Geraldine?" Martin asked.

"When I move with the heart stone, the light gets dimmer, as if it's going to go out, but when I turn in this one particular direction, it starts to pulse again. Almost like it's... like it's beating."

"Could it be a signal, I wonder?" Martin said. "Perhaps it could lead us to the other stones."

Geraldine pulled a compass out of her skirt pocket and consulted it. "It's telling us...northwest."

Christopher turned back to the well.

"Our deepest gratitude, Well," he said. "Your contribution to the restoration of the Keeper's health will not be forgotten."

He looked at the others, expecting them to offer their own thanks. Instead, all three stared back with inscrutable looks. He cleared his throat and offered the well a short bow.

"We will take your leave."

Geraldine, Martin, and Alistair moved toward the carriage without a word. He frowned at their backs. What made them behave this way? They had accomplished the first task in their journey.

"I thank you as well, your highness," the well replied. "If you'd like, you can be the first to make a wish to mark the occasion."

Christopher's companions all halted mid-step then turned around as if one.

Does that mean I may still make my wish for Lily? he thought. *But not where others could hear it.*

"We are pressed for time, Wishing Well," he said, "but I thank you for the offer and will return to avail you of it."

"Actually, I have a wish," Geraldine said, charging forward. "I wish for us to arrive within a half-day's ride of our next location."

"And I grant it with pleasure, Healer," the well replied. "To success on your quest."

The light on the surface of the water glimmered once again. Christopher braced himself for another memory, but the yellow light zipped around their entire party and the carriage in large circles. Geraldine's mouth opened in a wide O, and she tightened her grip on the heart stone. Alistair stood a little straighter. Martin folded his arms and grimaced.

Minutes later the whirling yellow light slowed down and stopped. They had not moved an inch, had not walked a pace, but the woods around them looked different. The sun slanted at them from a different angle, and the color of the bark on the trees had changed to a soft gray. Martin huffed and went to the carriage to check the horses who raised their heads as if to ask where they were.

"I am prepared to return to Linden this instant," he said. "It is clear I am not needed."

Geraldine rolled her eyes. "No one said that, Sir Martin. The wishing well just gave us the first stone. I don't think it would send us into danger. This helps us move faster in looking for the heart stones. Isn't that what you want?"

"A soldier's duty is to assess threats before anyone else. We cannot pursue our larger goal by forgetting our safety in the interim."

"I certainly didn't mean for us to forget our safety, and I don't appreciate you implying that I'm so irresponsible as to—"

"Enough," Christopher said. He glanced at the way Alistair sidled to one of the trees and leaned hard against it. "What does the heart stone say now, Geraldine?"

Her eyes burned with unshed tears. She stared at Martin for several seconds before turning her gaze back to the stone in her hands. Stepping back from the group, she turned in a slow circle and stopped when the light in the stone pulsed again.

"That way," she announced, pointing. "The stone wants us to go down that path."

CHAPTER 16

Geraldine handed Sir Martin the heart stone to use as a guide, then climbed into the carriage.

It had all happened so fast. The well's awakening; the king's hesitation; Alistair's challenge. They succeeded in getting the heart stone, but Geraldine was without words.

What has the king done to us? she thought again since hearing the well's pronouncement. *What gift will I have to give up? King Christopher said I could officially go back to caring for my patients* and *that he'd pay me the amount owed for the queen's treatment. Will he try to go back on his word?*

She glanced at Alistair.

Will I have to give up something else?

Tears welled in her eyes; she turned toward the window so the king and her beautiful son couldn't see her cry.

No one spoke for the five hours it took them to ride through the wood. The trees thinned, and a few homes replaced the foliage. The carriage came to a stop, and after a moment Martin opened the door.

"The heart stone still beats a steady pulse," he said in a gruff voice, "and the signs name this as the village of Ellery."

"Very well," the king said. "Continue driving until the heart stone indicates otherwise."

The soldier shut the door with a hard swing and clucked at the horses to begin moving.

Geraldine glowered at the king, and he frowned back at her.

I'm not giving up anything. I'll get my wages and start my new life and keep Alistair safe no matter what.

A half hour later, the carriage stopped.

Geraldine climbed out first and stretched her arms overhead, then closed the carriage door and went to the horses. She gave one a soft pat and turned to the guardsmaster who held the heart stone cupped in both hands. Geraldine noticed the pulsing had stopped; instead, the heart stone now shone a steady beam of light.

"Where are we?"

"The Keeper said she gave one of the stones to a mason near a building," Sir Martin said. "This must be it."

She shaded her eyes against the sun and stared at the solid three-story structure. The practical gray concrete blocks couldn't keep back a sense of welcome. Boxes attached to the windows on the first floor held sprays of spring color, and a tall white picket fence bordered the ample green yard in front of the building. Above the front door, a sign announced it to be the home for the Left Ones of Ellery; beneath that another sign stated the home also functioned as the Ellery learning institution.

On the second floor, a curtain moved and a girl stared at them; after a moment, the curtain dropped back into place.

"It may be best for you to keep this," Sir Martin said, handing her the heart stone.

She nodded and tucked it into the wide pocket of her skirt next to the compass. Despite the temperate weather, her parched throat left her thirsty. They hadn't filled their water skins from the brook close to the well.

We didn't have a chance to think back there, she thought.

Just then, a plump woman in a form-fitting blue dress exited the building. She smiled at them both and clasped her hands in front of her. Dimples punctuated a smile that also held curiosity, and when the woman came within speaking distance the scent of baked goods wafted toward them. Geraldine's stomach growled.

"I'm Madam Clarice, proprietor of the Ellery Home for Left Ones," the woman said.

Sir Martin's mouth fell open. "Clarice?"

Madam Clarice nodded. "Do I know you, Sir...?"

"Martin," the soldier replied, his face breaking into the widest smile Geraldine had seen. "If I am not mistaken, you lived in a home for Left Ones in Long Creek, correct?"

The woman's eyes lost their sparkle for a moment. "Yes, but I left it after a while."

"I well remember, Clarice, but I missed your presence after you were gone."

Missed her presence? Does that mean Sir Martin...?

Recognition unfurled in Clarice's face, and her eyes brightened to full joy. "Martin? Are you the same Martin of the Long Creek home?"

Sir Martin dipped his chin in a single nod. "Yes. Oh, Clarice, it is wonderful to see you."

Their hands found one another, and they began talking at the same time. Laughter punctuated their reunion as Geraldine tried to absorb the information she'd just learned. She put her hands in her pockets; her fingers brushed against the heart stone, and she cleared her throat.

"My name is Geraldine, and I'm the healer of Ingleside."

Clarice offered her a bow.

"Welcome, Mistress Geraldine, to our home. To what do I owe the honor of an old friend and a skilled healer?"

Sir Martin extracted one hand from Clarice's and took a step back. "We have urgent business, Clarice, but it is better conducted in private."

She nodded and opened an arm toward the entrance of the home. "Please, come in."

The soldier made a move as if to follow Madam Clarice, but Geraldine caught his sleeve.

"Sir Martin? What about our fellow travelers? In the carriage?"

The soldier scoffed at his own forgetfulness. "Yes, of course. One moment, Clarice."

He opened the door to the carriage. Alistair alighted first, and Geraldine's heart flipped. Had his face gotten even more pale in the past few minutes? Did she need to skirr him again?

"And who is this handsome young man?" Madam Clarice asked.

Alistair blushed and looked at his shoes as he gave his name.

The king alighted next, and Madam Clarice's mouth dropped open. She looked back at Sir Martin. Then her gaze found Geraldine, and she dropped into a hasty curtsy.

"Your majesty, welcome."

"Thank you, Madam Clarice. We appreciate your hospitality."

Sir Martin's delight faded; Geraldine knew how he felt.

Nothing now but to move forward.

"Shall we go inside?" she said.

Christopher followed the group into the home. To their left, desks filled a long space in a simple room with a large blackboard at one end. Books with navy blue covers sat on top of desks in rows. It looked as though Clarice had concluded lessons for the day. He lingered, wondering how his life might have differed had he attended school instead of receiving private tutoring.

"Your majesty?"

Nodding at the proprietress, he entered a study facing the school room. Clarice allowed him to cross the threshold and pushed the study door shut. She smiled at him.

"Once again, welcome, your highness. It is an honor to have you in our home."

Christopher offered her a small bow in return, although her station did not require it. Lily used to say giving a person more respect would often garner better results. Her advice proved effective when he met a visitor in a casual setting such as this one.

Lily.

He forced his thoughts back to Clarice's repeated offer for a drink with a genial nod; she leaned out the door and called for one of the girls to bring in a tray.

"Thank you," Christopher said. "I am indebted to you for your hospitality in welcoming us."

"Please, your highness," Clarice said, gesturing to the table, "make yourself comfortable. And call me Clarice. How may the Ellery home of Left Ones serve you today?"

Christopher settled into one of the chairs. "We have come on a matter requiring us to make an unusual request of you, Clarice. It is not a request we make lightly."

Clarice clasped her hands in front of her generous girth as she stood across the table. "I will do my best, your majesty, but I won't do anything to hurt the girls or Ellery."

"This goes beyond Ellery." Christopher opened his mouth to continue, but just then the door opened. A young woman came in with a tray. She set it down with a shy smile then offered the room a curtsy and scurried out.

"Your highness, may I?" Clarice asked, gesturing toward the pitcher.

He nodded, and she took the jug beading with condensation and poured a glass of lemonade. Christopher took a long sip, welcoming the soothing liquid. The head of the home continued pouring glasses for everyone else, and the woman gave Martin an affectionate smile. Why had Martin never confided in him about his origins? A flicker of emotion he did not want to name came and went.

"Your highness?"

The king shook himself out of his thoughts. "Our request has to do with the kingdom at large. Has any news from the castle traveled this far west yet?"

"Well, your highness, I've never been one to put stock in rumors. No messengers wearing castle livery have come by, only the odd peddler or young man wanting to stir up excitement, and I don't think we should waste any—"

"What have you heard, Clarice?"

She looked at Martin, then Geraldine and Alistair. "That you've become a recluse, which, clearly is wrong."

"What else?"

"That you didn't ride in the queen's funeral procession."

Christopher glanced at the table then back. "Anything else?"

"Is it true, sire? Did you miss the procession?"

The king sat a little straighter. "It has no bearing on the matter at hand, but, yes, I chose to abstain."

"Why?"

Her curiosity irritated Christopher; he did not come to entertain idle speculation.

"If you have received any other information from Rosewood,

I ask you to share it. Otherwise, our time is better spent on more urgent issues."

Clarice blushed. Biting her lip, she let her gaze drop to the floor. Christopher took a gulp of his lemonade and cleared his throat.

"Geraldine, show Clarice the heart stone."

The healer pulled the stone out of her pocket. A long rectangular window high up on the wall streamed sunlight into the room, but the heart stone's brilliance filled the space. Clarice took a step away from the stone, her eyebrows drawn.

"It's pulsing again," Geraldine said. "Outside it was a steady beam."

"What is that?" Clarice asked.

Christopher told her an abbreviated version of the story: the failing of the wood and the Keeper's heart breaking, the custody to him and the others to find the heart stones before she died, and the way the stone led them to the home for Left Ones. He did not mention Lemuel's charge on the castle, nor did he talk about his father's role in the Keeper's state. He did not know whether Clarice or any of those close to her had ever supported Vincent, and he did not want to lose any more time in debates about policies and rulers.

"You believe the Keeper's heart stone is inside our building?"

"Yes."

"And you want to dig out the stone and take it back to Rosewood? You might have to destroy the building, which would mean uprooting all of my girls."

Christopher placed his palms on the table and spread his fingers wide. "On behalf of the throne of Linden, I vow no harm will come to the girls under your care."

The proprietress tilted her head in thought. She opened

her mouth to speak but closed it. After a moment, she repeated the gesture.

"You may speak freely, Clarice. I trust everyone here, and we are long past the time to employ formalities. Speed is of the essence, not ceremony."

"I can't allow you to destroy this building, your highness," she said. "It's the only place any of these children have known as a home."

"I can understand your apprehension, Clarice—"

"I don't believe you could, your highness. You've grown up in a privileged life with luxuries beyond any of our imaginations. These girls were cast out from their homes. They're often told no one wants them or loves them; they make do with garments handed down and simple food. This home provides them with the only stability most of them have ever known. So, no, you can't possibly understand, and I won't allow you to retrieve the heart stone if it means destroying the building."

Christopher pressed the table with his palms. Geraldine gripped her glass in both hands. Alistair let out a soft moan.

"Clarice, I do not believe you have considered what this would mean to the kingdom, to the livelihoods of all those in the lumber guild," Christopher said. "Lives are at stake. You are concerned for the girls, as you should be, but if the wood continues to fail and we lose that essential part of our trade, Linden may not survive."

And I would lose my throne.

The woman shrugged. "My apologies for my impudence, your highness, but I've run this home longer than you've ruled. In terms of experience, I outbid yours by years. Struggles work themselves out eventually. I can't allow you to take away the one thing that doesn't go away, which is this home."

"Clarice," Martin chided.

"No, Martin. I'm not blind to the challenge this poses, but my responsibility is to my girls. The king wants to demolish the home so he can retrieve the heart stone, take it back to the Keeper, and save the wood. In the meantime, we'll be left without a place to stay. Where do the girls go while we're waiting for the home to be rebuilt?"

"I pledge you my full support," Christopher said. "The home will be rebuilt without interruption of task or timeline."

"And you've come here with a detailed plan of where we'd live in the meantime and how we'll move everyone from one place to another with minimal disruption to our lives, yes?"

He had no plan, of course, and he would not fumble his way through a vague explanation. From the corner of his eye, Christopher saw Geraldine shift her weight. Her expression changed too. If he did not know better, he would have said Geraldine was annoyed.

"Martin, perhaps you can offer Clarice an explanation."

He turned to his guardsmaster, his oldest friend, expecting his steadfast support. Instead of Martin's confident nod, however, the soldier met his gaze with an unreadable expression. Christopher clenched and unclenched his fists.

"Martin?"

"I agree with Clarice."

"*What*?"

"We should not destroy the home just for the sake of the heart stone."

Dizziness made Christopher's head spin. After several seconds of silence, he inhaled a deep breath. Heaviness settled into his abdomen.

"What about the Keeper? What about saving her and the wood? Have you stopped caring about all that is important to the kingdom?"

For the first time he could ever remember in their many years as friends, Martin looked unsure of himself.

"I wish the Keeper of the Wood nothing but the best of health, but Clarice makes a valid point, your highness. The homes for Left Ones are all they have. The world has cast these children aside, leaving them with no family. When even that bit of comfort is snatched from them, they begin to believe they cannot trust anything or anyone."

"Does my word count for nothing?" Christopher argued. His left arm ached. "You, Martin, of all people should know I keep my vows."

"No one is doubting your sincerity, your highness, only your methods. Surely, if we spend time in discussion, we can formulate a plan to—"

"There is no other way," Christopher thundered. "We must extract the heart stone. The heart stone is in the cornerstone of this building. If we do not bring the stone back to the Keeper, she will die and the wood as well. Life in Linden will change forever."

Martin's face folded in anguish. "I understand, your majesty, but—"

"The solution is within reach, here, in this building, Martin. Why do you not trust me enough to make the best decision for everyone involved? Why are you ready to trust someone from your past who you have not met for years? Were you two sweethearts in Long Creek? Did you wile away your afternoons with whispers and promises?"

"You have no idea what you're talking about," Clarice exclaimed, eyes blazing. "That home was terrible. The children couldn't count on anyone, especially the adults who claimed they would protect us. If I had not run away, I would have been beaten like Martin, or worse. You will *not* belittle me for trying to build a better life for the girls who live here."

Christopher flinched. Every word struck him harder than the previous one. He found his breath ragged.

Beaten? Martin was...beaten? But...but he never...

The soldier hung his head, came to the table, and sank into a chair. His shoulders rounded so far forward it looked like he would fall onto the tabletop. Christopher's back stiffened.

"Martin, were you... Is what Clarice says..."

His guardsmaster nodded as he sighed long and slow.

"The home for Left Ones in Long Creek was not a happy place," Martin said in a tone Christopher had never heard before. "The proprietors treated the children like slaves. The boys were forced into manual labor from the early morning hours until late at night. The girls were given all the household chores. If we did not obey fast enough, walk fast enough, carry the wood fast enough, anything the master and madam demanded, the boys were beaten. The girls too, when the master did not..."

Martin's eyes slid to Clarice; she tilted her head in sympathy and shook it. Martin dropped his gaze and relief flowed from him, but it did not seem to ease his fatigue. The others remained still.

"Clarice treated me as she would a younger brother," Martin went on. "She taught me and some of the other boys how to use our knives for carving and how to identify berries safe to eat. I realized years later she was preparing us for a time when we might have the opportunity to escape. Whenever one of us would get into trouble, she would comfort us with stories and songs and silly games. She kept telling us she would run away and then send for us when she could support us."

"And I did send for you," Clarice said, grasping the back

of a chair, "but by then you were all gone."

"Gone?" Geraldine asked.

"One day one of Vincent's soldiers was traveling through Long Creek," Martin said. "He stopped for a meal at the inn, which stood right next door to the home. I...encountered some trouble earlier, and the master of the home, Master—"

"Don't, Martin," Clarice interrupted. "He can't hurt us anymore. Don't give him the respect of his name."

The soldier nodded again. "The master pulled me outside by my ear. He carried one of his heaviest switches with him and beat me. The soldier saw us from the inn and came running outside."

"He saved your life," Geraldine said.

"He saved my life," Martin repeated, "and after he rescued me, I took note of his uniform. I thought, 'I can be brave too. I can help others, like this soldier.' When he questioned me about what else took place in the home, I told him everything. Eventually, he brought back a contingent, and the home was shut down. The soldier asked if anyone could take me in—distant relatives, perhaps—but I had no one, so he brought me to Rosewood and adopted me. Then he brought me to the castle."

Christopher remembered Martin's father, a young soldier. Too young, he realized now, to have a son that age. At the time, he never paid attention to those sorts of things; the lonely child he was, his one care was for the pleasure of having a playmate, someone who would climb trees and ride horses with him.

His mother, Queen Dahlia, encouraged the friendship, and even though a young Christopher found it odd that Martin slept in the barn in those first few years, he knew not to question it. He did everything within his princely power and his short time as king thus far to protect and help Martin, even arguing for his promotion to guardsmaster after Vincent's death.

"You offered me, and continue to offer me, a life of dignity, your highness," Martin said, "but Clarice was the one who taught me I deserved such a life. I cannot betray her friendship when she is doing the work that brought us together and will, no doubt, bring together so many other Left Ones. They only have one another."

"That is why you instituted the work program for them," Christopher said, recalling how hard Martin fought with the council about the program's necessity.

"I wanted to give those children a sense of purpose, a sense of the same dignity you afforded me. They have been taught from birth that society does not want them. I want to prove that not all of society holds those views, that they can join that very society and become productive, respected citizens of our kingdom."

Christopher pushed back from the table and stood. Martin stood as well, but Christopher turned to Clarice instead. The heaviness in his abdomen hardened into a lead fist. How would he save the trees now? How would he fulfill his promise to the Keeper?

"And what," Christopher said, "if there is no kingdom left for them? What then, Martin?"

"Surely we can find another way, your highness," Martin said. "There are many men and women, like Clarice, who run the homes for the Left Ones. Think of how these homes benefit the villages. Not only do they care for the unwanted children, but also many of the homes are the sole learning institutions in those areas. Would you also take the opportunity of learning away from the other children?"

"I am the king; my word is law," Christopher said, his tone increasing in volume. "Clarice, if you do not deem it your duty to follow a direct order from your king, then I will see to it you must be punished."

"You may threaten me, your highness, but it won't do you any good," Clarice said. "I'll fight until my dying day to protect my girls and their home."

The king's entire body shook with fury.

"And what of the kingdom? Do you not care for it?"

"Do you?" Clarice countered. "Or are you more worried about how not retrieving the heart stones will make *you* look?"

"I will not stand here for your impudence," Christopher said. "You will be punished as soon as I return to the castle. We will go on, find the other heart stone, and continue on our way. Our business here is done."

CHAPTER 17

Anxiety roiled in Alistair's stomach. Did Madam Clarice understand—really understand—what would happen if they didn't retrieve the stones? And why was the king giving up? Why did adults always let their anger jump ahead of their common sense?

He opened his mouth to beg Madam Clarice to reconsider, but the edges of his vision grew dark. Alistair blinked several times to clear his eyes, but black spots appeared. He put a hand to his forehead but dropped it right away; his entire body burned.

"Mother…" he said, his voice sounding like a croak.

She turned to him and Alistair thought she said his name, but his ears couldn't catch the sounds and he slumped to the floor.

"Alistair!"

Geraldine ran to her son and dropped to her knees. She cradled him and looked to the king, Sir Martin, and Madam Clarice. All three stood frozen in shock.

"Help me, please," she said, her voice cracking. "Oh, Alistair!"

Sir Martin crossed the room in three strides and managed

to pick Alistair up, despite the boy's height. "Clarice, a room."

"Of course."

Madam Clarice darted out of the room ahead of him, and Sir Martin exited next. Geraldine followed them past the lesson room and a long dining room to a bedroom in the back of the house. Along the way, girls stopped and stared at them. One hefted a basket of laundry on her hip. Another dropped the rag she held. The healer's panic dimmed for a moment at the sight of other children.

"He'll be comfortable here," Madam Clarice said, pushing open a door. "This is where the girls stay when they're ill."

Sir Martin took Alistair to the bed and then stepped back, and Geraldine noted the cleanliness of the room. The bed shouldered one corner. A narrow table sat next to the bed, its length running along the wall for about three feet. Another table opposite the bed held stoppered vials and boxes marked in a neat hand with the names of common remedies in tablet or liquid form.

"You're welcome to anything on the table, Mistress Geraldine. I'm sure you know better than anyone what might help Alistair."

I don't, Geraldine wanted to scream. *I don't know what might help him, because I don't know what's wrong with him.*

Instead, she turned and tried to smile in gratitude.

"Could you bring me a few clean towels and a pail?" she asked. "If he gets sick, I don't want to dirty the floor."

"Of course," Madam Clarice said without hesitation and left. Geraldine appreciated that the woman didn't flinch when she asked for the pail. She would have taken care of her fair share of sick girls through the years. It made sense she would fight so hard to keep her home.

"Do you suspect any particular ailment, Healer?" Sir Martin asked, his brow furrowed.

Geraldine's hands fluttered with worry as she sat next to Alistair. His face lacked almost any color and it looked thinner, as if he hadn't eaten in days. It frightened Geraldine almost as much as the possibility of losing her healer's badge. As much as facing the reality of Queen Lily's death.

As much as the well's pronouncement that she would lose one of her greatest gifts.

She shot to her feet and whirled to face the soldier.

"How much more will the king take from all of us? He revoked my healer's badge, he forced us to make sacrifices at the wishing well, he wants to take away this home from these girls. How much will be enough? When will he realize that at some point he has to give back to the kingdom and his people as much as he's asking from us? What does he want out of all this?"

The trembling from her hands traveled to her entire body. She dropped back onto the bed and looked at Alistair. He remained still, eyes closed. She bowed her head, begging the fates with a silent prayer to restore Alistair's health.

"I wanted to do what was best for everyone. To be a king for the people."

Her head whipped up, and on instinct she stood.

The king stepped through the doorway. His shoulders drooped as he caught sight of Alistair. It reminded Geraldine of how he looked when she saw him after Lily's death, and her memories of that morning fought to come back. Once again, she blocked them. The king turned his gaze to his guardsmaster who crossed his arms and went to stare out of the window above the long nightstand.

Geraldine burst into tears and sank back onto the bed.

She cried for them all: for her son and her frustration in her inability to treat him. For Sir Martin and the other children in the Long Creek home and what they suffered from malicious adults with selfish, evil intentions. For the king's plaintive response and how she knew, in her heart, he believed what he said.

"I will ask Clarice to come," Sir Martin said after a few minutes.

He brushed past the king without looking at him. As she cried, Geraldine saw the king open his mouth. She buried her face in her hands. A moment later, she heard the soft click of the door closing.

Not knowing where else to go, Christopher returned to the study. He fell hard into one of the chairs and pressed the heels of his palms to his eyes. Geraldine's question tumbled like the large laundry drums in the castle, in reverberating circles.

What do I want from everyone?

The study door opened, prompting Christopher to sit up; Martin entered and shut the door behind him.

"Clarice offered us refuge for the night. Considering evening is upon us, I accepted on your behalf. We all need some rest and a hot meal. I hope I did not overstep my authority, your highness."

"Not at all."

Monarch and soldier maintained eye contact for several moments.

"Why did you never share any of your former life with me, Martin?"

Martin exhaled a long sigh. "When I came to the castle, I wanted nothing more than to forget the past, your highness. And, in truth, I never imagined we would become friends. I always assumed I would work in the castle until I came of age and then go on my way."

"Your bond with Clarice is much older and stronger," Christopher said.

"Clarice was my family, sire. She taught me what the word meant. I have no memories of the parents who left me at the home. I do not even know if I have any siblings. Clarice was my mother and my sister. Her presence taught me to trust others."

"Trust," Christopher repeated.

"Yes, I trust her."

"More than anything or anyone?" Christopher said. "More than me?"

Martin did not answer, and, in truth, Christopher did not have the heart to hear the reply. He thought about all the years Martin had served the castle, the life they shared, their journey thus far. Could they have stood before the wishing well mere hours earlier?

Guardsmaster Martin, you will forsake all to trust only one.

The well's words echoed in his mind so loudly Christopher thought they came from the walls. The well had charged each of them with a sacrifice in exchange for the first heart stone. For the first time, he realized the sacrifices tied them to one another.

"The well's demands. You have forfeited our years of friendship, of brotherhood, for Clarice."

Martin tightened his hands into fists. His gaze traveled around the room as if searching for an explanation. Christopher's heart frittered with disappointment.

Another emotion wormed its way through his midsection: fear. If the wishing well's demands extracted this of Martin, what could it want from him? Or Geraldine? Or even Alistair?

"Your majesty, I—I never meant—"

Christopher held up a hand to stop him.

Geraldine turned Alistair's hands so she could place her own palms on top of his. With another prayer to the fates, she closed her eyes. For the third time in the last thirty minutes, she skirred her son.

"Any change?" Madam Clarice asked.

The tingling in her palms meant she'd succeeded in initiating the skirring, but the energy she sent met a wall.

What's wrong with my abilities now?

After one last attempt, she pulled back her hands and opened her eyes. "I don't know. The skirring seemed to begin, but then...I don't know."

Madam Clarice came from the doorway and placed a hand on Geraldine's shoulder.

"He might just need some rest. Have you been traveling for a long time?"

"A few days," Geraldine said, her attention on Alistair, "but we've slept on the forest ground and eaten cold meals. Alistair didn't mind; he loves the wood and would live there if I let him. But it's been challenging. I think I've missed a comfort room and the opportunity of a real bath the most."

She tried to smile; Madam Clarice put an arm around her shoulders and squeezed.

"He's not the only one who could use some rest. Would you like me to take you to a room upstairs?"

Geraldine turned back to Alistair.

"You could just lie down," Madam Clarice went on, "and I'll check on him as I prepare dinner. If there's any change in his condition, I'll send one of the girls to you immediately."

A real bed, she thought. *Just for an hour. I'll rest and then come down in one hour.*

"Thank you, Madam Clarice. That would help."

"Clarice, please. I only ask the girls to call me by a title."

"Then call me Geraldine. Titles always put distance between new friends."

Clarice nodded. "Yes, they do. Should we go?"

Geraldine bit her lip and turned back to Alistair. He stayed in the same position, not even murmuring in his sleep. If his chest didn't rise and fall in a regular rhythm, Geraldine would have wondered if—

No. I won't think the worst.

To distract herself from darker thoughts, she stood and gestured for Clarice to lead the way.

Several more silent minutes passed in the study.

"The castle changed my life," Martin said finally. "I am indebted to Clarice, but I am also deeply grateful to you, sire."

Christopher's hands remained folded on top of the table. He thought of when Martin had come to the castle, how excited—how *relieved*—he was to find a friend. Never mind that Martin spent most of his day mucking stalls in the royal stables to earn his keep. Young Prince Christopher had learned his father's indifference as a parent contained a hidden gift: so long as he completed his schooling lessons and the lessons required of him to learn the ways of the court, King Vincent did not inquire about the prince's daily activities.

After the dismissal of his beloved tutor, Christopher knew to provide the king with the answers he wanted to hear. When he stood in the royal study every night for the ten minutes his father afforded him, he talked about learning to wield a quarterstaff or studying Linden's history. He never mentioned the stable boy who held a staff next to him in the practice yards.

"If your gratitude runs so deep, then help me understand, Martin. I endeavor to make the right decision to protect the livelihoods of Lindeners, yet you tell me it is wrong."

"I did not say your decision to save the Keeper or the wood was the wrong one, your highness. I merely support Clarice's desire to protect the home."

"And the two are not at odds?"

"I do not believe so, your majesty; if you allowed yourself a moment of composure, you would agree."

Christopher pushed back from the table to pace.

"You desire to be a better king than your father," Martin said. "If I may be so bold, your highness, King Vincent's singular characteristic was to think of himself and his own opinions. If you deem yourself a king of the people, you must consider the demands and concerns of the people before proclaiming your will."

Christopher rolled his eyes and kept pacing.

"Do you consider Left Ones your subjects, your highness? Lindeners as all others in the kingdom?"

"Of course; what sort of question is that?"

"Then why do you purport to tell your subjects they have no right to their own home? They did nothing wrong; *we* brought this dilemma here. It is imperative, then, that *we* find a solution for it."

Christopher stopped mid-pace to consider Martin's words.

All I ever wanted was to distinguish myself from Father's methods, his reputation, he thought. *Have I become as narrowminded as he in my own goals?*

He wished he could escape the solidity of Martin's assertion, but he realized he agreed with his head off guard. The girls in the home did not have parents, but they had one another and Clarice. He rested his hands on the back of a chair at the end of the table and squeezed the top rung.

He realized then that, like the Left Ones, he possessed no connection to his own parents. From his earliest memories, Queen Dahlia had fought a variety of illnesses and succumbed to them before he could comprehend how much he needed her. On some days, when they crossed paths in the castle or the stables, King Vincent would catch sight of him and jerk back in surprise. As if he had forgotten he had a son.

Like the Left Ones, he, too, had been left behind, and now—now when he had a choice in the matter—could he destroy one of the few sources of happiness and stability belonging to the girls in Clarice's home?

"Clarice and an entire home full of children knew you, Martin," he said in a low voice. "Until you came to the castle, no one in my life... When Lily... Lemuel holds King Malcolm and Queen Celia, and I fear I will continue to lose those who I hold in greatest esteem until I find myself alone. Again."

"We all mourn the death of the queen, and, by the fates, we will regain the castle and see the king and queen safe again. Lemuel is a threat, yes, but one we face together."

"And the wood? The Keeper?" Christopher asked, hanging his head.

"We will find a resolution. I swore an oath to serve you, sire, and I will uphold that oath. You are not alone."

Christopher released a breath he did not know he held and stared at the table. It gleamed, but the patterns in the wood did not match those of the wood from Linden. An import, then, but solid still. He ran his fingers over the table, tracing the whorls of the tree's life.

His fingertips bumped against an aberration. As he leaned closer, he saw someone had carved her initials into the table. Small and clean, but strong and assertive. It reminded him of Clarice, and he knew she infused each of her girls with the same characteristics.

He looked back at Martin with a greater clarity than he had possessed in a long time.

"We will find a solution then. Together."

Alistair opened his eyes and stared at the ceiling. Why did his room look different? His bed had been on the other side; why was it here? And where were all his things?

He reached for his blanket and realized it wasn't on the bed either. As he pushed himself to a sitting position, his head began to pound. The temperature of the room increased as he sat on the edge of the bed and waited for the headache to go away. Where was he?

The pain in his head rolled forward, and with it came memories of the day. The wishing well; arriving in Ellery and the home for Left Ones; Madam Clarice's refusal to retrieve the heart stone. The Keeper's sickness.

He moaned but forced himself to stand. Mother always recommended fresh air when his head hurt. Where was she?

Summoning the little energy he had left, Alistair shuffled to the door. He opened it and leaned out, using the doorknob to steady himself. Girlish voices in the distance told him he, Mother, and the king and guardsmaster were still in the Ellery home, but Alistair didn't care. He needed to get outside and, if possible, to the trees.

He took a moment to get his bearings and kept listening.

A gush of water and the clattering of dishes told him people were in the kitchen. Even better. He wouldn't have to struggle to explain himself to any of them.

Going down a short hall, he turned right and saw all the way to the back of the home. A door with a window in it showed him glimpses of outside. He went closer and saw what must have been the back yard. Pushing the door open, he crossed the large garden behind the building that held pockets of flowerbeds. Alistair wondered if the girls took turns weeding.

Ten paces past the edge of the garden, he spotted a bench just big enough for two. He gasped with delight when he saw the path from the house running so close to the wood. The sight of the bench and the trees made him move a little faster. He tried to ignore the mounds of white ash in the distance as well as the peculiar odor wafting in his direction. Instead, he put all of his energy toward increasing his pace to get to the bench.

As he took a seat, he put a hand against the tree. It sent back a soft greeting: gentle pinpricks in his palm, like a bird's beak plucking seed right from his hand. Tears burned at the corners of his eyes, and he used his free hand to swipe them away. He wasn't a baby. He might have been ill, but he could still be brave.

Bit by bit, moment by moment, the tree infused him with hints of energy. The tree wanted to give him more, he knew, but his body refused. Like a bucket with a hole in it, Alistair could sense the tree's offering of its life source wouldn't last long. That thought scared him almost as much as losing the trees themselves.

"Alistair?"

He turned toward Madame Clarice's voice and couldn't stop a scowl. He hadn't forgotten that she'd refused them the heart stone. Still, Mother taught him to be polite, even if it was the last thing he wanted to do. He started to stand, but Madame Clarice waved him to sit back down. She put a tray with cold cheeses, fruit, and some bread next to him.

"May I?" she asked, gesturing to the empty space next to the tray.

He shrugged.

"How are you feeling?"

He gave her a side glance. "Tired."

"Your mother is worried about you," Madam Clarice said, folding her hands in her lap. "I sent her upstairs to rest. She looks..."

"Traveling. Days."

"I know, she told me. Everyone is having dinner inside, but I figured you'd like to eat in the fresh air."

Alistair looked at the tray for a moment. He should have been hungry. It had been quite a while since he'd last eaten. Yet even though his stomach growled a little, he didn't have much of an appetite. He leaned his head against the trunk next to him.

"Trees. Dying."

Madam Clarice let her gaze travel upward.

"You know, when I was young, back in the home in Long Creek, some of the trees there were wide enough for two or three of us to hide behind. We spent so many hours playing around them. They made me happy."

Of course they made her happy. Alistair didn't know anything else that made him happier. Why did she have to grow up and forget? Didn't adults understand *anything*?

A pain shot across his head, and he screwed his eyes tight.

"Alistair, are you all right? I can call your mother. She may have some tablets or, or...I don't know, some kind of tea or medicine to help."

He shook his head. "No tea. Trees."

He shuddered then. When had it gotten so cold? Wasn't he feeling too hot inside? He slumped against the tree and wrapped one arm around it. A tear threatened to run down his cheek, and he thought of Father to make himself stop crying. It worked; it always did. Thoughts of Father only made him angry these days.

"Trees dying. Heart stone."

Madam Clarice sighed. "It's not that simple, Alistair. The girls..."

"No trees, sad."

"Do you mean...do you mean the girls would enjoy the trees like I did?"

He nodded, but his brain felt like it was rolling around inside his skull again. The pinpricks in his hand became sharper and traveled down his arm. Alistair tried to pull away.

The tree wouldn't let go.

His shoulders got tight, and he tried again to pull back.

"Trees dying," he whispered. "Keeper. Worried."

"The trees are special to you, aren't they?" Madam Clarice asked. She placed a hand on his shoulder but jerked it away.

"Alistair, your body is on fire," she said, her panic scaring him. "We need to get you to your mother *now*."

"Can't," he said, a sob breaking his voice. "Tree."

Madam Clarice shot to her feet and came to the other side of him. She reached for Alistair's hand on the tree. The pinpricks dug deeper...almost as if the tree didn't want him to leave.

"Mother," he whispered.

The proprietress nodded and ran back to the house.

CHAPTER 18

Geraldine licked her lips, but she ignored her parched throat. Her attention remained on Alistair as she tried to reassure him and skirr him at the same time. She held his free hand in both of hers and alternated between screwing her eyes shut and opening them as wide as they'd go.

"Don't worry, sweetheart," she murmured yet again, "you'll be fine. I won't let anything happen to you."

"Mother." His body slumped forward.

"You have to keep asking the tree to let you go. Say we'll help it and the others, but you can't do that if it...if it..."

Her lower lip trembled, and once again she closed her eyes tight.

"Steady, Healer," Sir Martin said. "Courage."

She wanted to take heart. She wanted to believe she could do this. Even if she could skirr him and find the source of the tree's power, though, she didn't know if she'd be able to offer Alistair any advice to overpower the tree.

The familiar tingle from the skirring reassured her a little, and she drew in a deep breath.

"You have to stay calm, Alistair, and remind the tree of how much you love it. Remind it why we came to Ellery."

"Try." Did he sound less stressed now? She couldn't tell.

"Geraldine," the king said, "Geraldine, do not worry. Your son will be fine. He is a strong, brave boy, and he will be fine."

She opened her eyes. King Christopher frowned with worry but nodded in encouragement at her. The creases in his clothing, dingy after him wearing them for so many days, seemed to dissipate. With squared shoulders and a confident stance, she saw a man who ruled his people. A man who led them.

The burning in her throat became less fiery, and she nodded back.

"Alistair," she said, "tell this tree to let go of you. Don't ask it; tell it."

His head bobbed, and the skirring continued. Once again her searching energy met resistance, but she kept trying. Alistair's hand became tense in hers; after a moment, he clasped her palm so hard she bit back a cry.

He sat up, moving as if he were underwater, and pulled his arm away from the tree.

"Tired, Mother. So tired."

Her heart pounded as she took his other hand. "It's all right, Alistair, at least now—"

The back of his right hand was covered in a strange mossy substance. She tried to brush it away, but the moss tightened. She brought his hand closer to her face, but the deepening twilight made it hard to see.

"We should go inside," Clarice said, a blanket in her hands.

Geraldine turned back to Alistair. "Do you think you can stand?"

He tried to push off the bench but lost his balance. Sir Martin darted forward and caught him before Alistair fell to the ground. He put Alistair's arm around his own shoulders.

"Are you able to walk?"

Alistair bobbed his head in a languid sort of way, and it rolled from side to side.

"Mother?" he called, the word almost slurred.

"Here, love. I'm right here."

Sir Martin stepped forward and waited for Alistair to move. Alistair let his body fall forward a few paces, and the soldier matched his stride. They continued across the garden toward the home.

Geraldine shivered. Clarice put the blanket around her and draped it over her arms. The king clasped his hands behind him and fell into step with them.

"What happened?" Geraldine asked.

"We were talking about the trees," Clarice said, "and Alistair had his arm around the tree as if he were hugging it. Then he told me he couldn't pull away. It was almost as if the tree..."

She let the rest of the sentence drift into the evening. Twilight had faded into the early night, and stars fanned across the sky. Crickets chirped nearby. Despite the reassuring sights and sounds of spring, Geraldine's gut twisted with panic. What was on Alistair's hand? Why had the tree latched onto him?

As she, the king, and Clarice entered the house, several girls with open mouths faced them. Some watched Sir Martin as he led Alistair back to the sick room. Others turned their attention to her. When they saw the king, they dropped into awkward curtsies. A few nudged the girls gawking in the direction the soldier went or tugged on their skirts. Within moments all of them were showing obeisance to the king.

"Your majesty," they murmured.

"Good evening, girls of the Ellery home for Left Ones," King Christopher said, his tone more formal. It reminded Geraldine of how he'd addressed the wishing well. "I am honored to visit you. Madam Clarice has offered us a few corners of your home this evening, and I hope we are not disturbing your routine."

The ones who weren't gaping as the king spoke shook their heads. One child who couldn't have been more than four years old held her arms out to him. He glanced at Clarice, and she nodded. The king picked up the child, and despite her worry Geraldine almost laughed at the stiff way he held her. She could see he had had no practice with children.

The reminder of why made her smile disappear.

"Thank you for coming," the child said in a sweet voice. "We hope you like it here."

"With your unmatched hospitality, I have no doubt I will," the king said. As he set her down with care, grins spread among the other residents. Clarice clapped twice, and the grins faded.

"All right, girls," Clarice said, "off to bed with you. Lagging behind tonight means..."

"Extra chores tomorrow," the girls intoned. "Good night, Madam Clarice."

"Good night. I'll be up soon."

Several of the girls stopped for hugs from Clarice, and a few added a kiss on the cheek. She gave almost every single girl a reminder about lessons or chores assigned. A few needed to complete applications to local guilds for apprenticeships, and Clarice chided them with affection like a mother would.

Within minutes, the common room stood empty save for the adults, and the walls rang with silence. Geraldine wished for a moment she was one of the girls going upstairs instead of staying down here to face the frightening possibilities of Alistair's condition.

"Let us see to Alistair," the king said, waving for Geraldine and Clarice to lead.

Geraldine returned to the sick room. When she entered,

she saw several lit candles. Despite the severity of the situation, their light filled her with a wick's worth of hope.

She went straight to Alistair, and Sir Martin vacated his chair. As she sat, she asked Alistair to show her the moss. He offered the back of his hand, and she examined the strange plant-like structure embedded in his skin.

"I don't know what this is," Geraldine said to the others. "I've never seen any kind of infection or illness like it on a patient. It's some sort of growth, but I'm sure Alistair didn't have it before we left Ingleside. I skirred him before we left. Right, Alistair? I skirred you, and you were fine then."

"No one doubts you, Healer," Sir Martin said, coming to stand next to her. "May I see his hand?"

She left the chair, and he sat again and took Alistair's hand.

"Your highness," Sir Martin said after a moment, "when Councilor Ariana received the letter from Severson Dells, did the lumberjack not report this type of plant on the trees there?"

Geraldine's eyes became wide, and she jerked around to look at the king. His face confirmed her worst suspicion. She didn't want to believe this could happen to Alistair, but her instincts told her it couldn't be anything else.

"No," Geraldine said, blinking fast and hard, "no, that can't be. I won't let it. Clarice…"

She went to the proprietress and pressed her palms as if in prayer.

"Clarice, please, you have to let us take the heart stone. I can't lose my boy; I can't! He's the only precious thing I have left, Clarice, please."

She dissolved into tears and kept repeating the words over and over as Clarice enfolded her in an embrace and patted Geraldine on the back.

"All right, Geraldine, all right. Shh. Hush now."

"I fear we have no choice, Clarice," the king said. "I understand your predicament, but if we do not find the pieces of the Keeper's heart and reunite them, Alistair may be in grave danger."

Clarice didn't respond and Geraldine drew a ragged breath and forced herself to stop crying, despite the effort it took.

"I do not know what the extraction of the heart stone might entail," the king went on, "but might I suggest alternative living quarters if they are needed?"

"What alternative?" Clarice asked.

"If retrieving the heart stone destroys the home, the girls may go to Wyndemere and take up residence in the castle there," King Christopher said. "I will fund any necessities and expenses you all might incur."

Clarice exchanged a long look with him.

"I'll need to think about it."

The fist in Geraldine's gut unclenched, and she threw her arms around the proprietress. Clarice hugged her back and suggested a meal, but Geraldine shook her head as did the king and Sir Martin. Within minutes, they bid Alistair good night. Geraldine pulled the blanket close to his chin.

"Did you hear that, Alistair?" she whispered. "I think Clarice will let us have the heart stone after all."

He murmured a response she couldn't understand, but she took it as a positive sign. She took his hand again and forced herself to examine the moss as a healer and not a mother. As she followed its textures, one part of her mind cataloged the color of the moss, the way it implanted itself into Alistair's skin, and its resistance to being removed. Another part of her mind wandered to Ingleside and the children she'd treated through the years.

Could the moss attack other children? she thought. *Could it attack* anyone*?*

A scenario, unbidden, came to her in which she tried to explain to parents why their children suffered from the disease attacking the trees and then every healer's worst nightmare: admitting there was nothing she could do about it

She put Alistair's hand down and smoothed back his hair. She didn't know how to fight the illness, but she had to make sure Clarice kept her word. The Keeper was already dying. Now Alistair was infected. How many more people would be hurt before all this ended?

No. We can't let this happen to Alistair, and we won't let it happen to anyone else.

She could have sat in the chair all night, but she knew going to bed was the better decision. If they did, indeed, retrieve the heart stone the next day, they would be traveling again soon. She needed to be rested and ready for both.

After another moment, she blew out all the candles and went upstairs.

Sleep eluded Christopher after he bid everyone else good night. The most immediate intrusion came from the sounds of the girls settling into their rooms. As he listened to the calls to one another to sleep well, Christopher realized how subdued the castle became after he retired for the evening. Did the staff quarters sound this lively at the end of each day? The question left him, by equal turns, relieved for the quiet he enjoyed every night and envious of the companionship he did not.

When the light underneath the door darkened, he considered

the solution he offered Clarice. King Malcolm or Queen Celia alone had the right to make it; he spoke as a family member and, now, an honorary one. How could he presume to make such a pledge when his father-in-law and mother-in-law lay imprisoned themselves?

I will free them and set all this right, Christopher thought. *I must. I owe Lily that much.*

The next morning, just after the sun broke over the tops of the homes in Ellery, the traveling group sat to a subdued breakfast. Other than requests to pass a dish, no one spoke. Christopher offered a genial smile to both Geraldine and Alistair when he saw the boy trudge into the study with the healer hovering close by. Alistair did not eat much, but any sustenance would help. Clarice, it seemed, noticed Alistair's minimal appetite as well and encouraged Geraldine to wrap the cold items for him for later.

"I've thought a great deal about your offer, your majesty," Clarice said at the end of the meal, "and even though I'm scared, yes, you can try to extract the heart stone."

Christopher offered a single nod to mask his relief.

"I know your concerns in making this decision were valid and deep, Clarice, and I am aware of the potential cost. You have my word, as your king and fellow Lindener, I will do what I can to protect the girls."

"Thank you."

Martin frowned. "Clarice, are you certain?"

She nodded. "Yes, Martin. I want to protect my girls, but I can't put Alistair's life in danger. Or anyone else's. What if other children suffer from this too? If finding the heart stones and reconstructing the Keeper's heart can keep Alistair and maybe others from harm, that's as important as making sure the girls have a stable home life."

Martin smiled at her, and Christopher read in that smile the familiarity of friendship. Of love. Of trust.

"Should we contact a stone mason?" she asked.

"Perhaps we should ascertain where the heart stone lies first," Christopher said. "Geraldine, would you bring the stone from the well?"

"Yes, your majesty." She patted Alistair's hand and left, returning within minutes with the stone still wrapped in a handkerchief.

"If we take the stone outside, it may lead us to its companion," the king said.

Geraldine helped Alistair stand, and they made their way out of the study and the front door. Once Clarice closed it behind her, Geraldine unwrapped the stone. It pulsed with the purple light that led them the previous day to Clarice's doorstep. Geraldine cradled the stone in both palms and held out her arms as if in offering.

The pulsing continued, and Geraldine walked to one side of the home. Christopher narrowed his eyes to focus. As Geraldine reached the corner, the pulsing became slower. Just before she turned to follow the wall to the back, the pulsing dissipated into a steady beam of amethyst-colored light.

What to do now?

Before anyone could make a suggestion, a light matching the heart stone appeared inside one of the cement blocks at the edge of the wall. Christopher came closer to confirm the light came from inside the cement and was not reflecting somehow from the stone in Geraldine's hand. He kneeled as he ran his fingers over the block. It sat on top of the block that met the ground.

"This must be the cornerstone," he said, rising.

"I have an idea," Martin said as he and the others came forward. "Clarice, do you have a hammer and chisel?"

"Martin, if the heart stone is in the cornerstone of the building, the entire building would need to come down. I have to tell the girls, we'd need to move our belongings—the process of just *leaving* the home would take a week."

"I ask for a chance, Clarice," Martin replied. "Please, trust me; I will not cause any permanent damage."

Her nose and lips compressed into a line, but she did not argue. Instead, she went back into the home. A few minutes later, she returned with a hammer and chisel.

"One of the girls had a grand idea once of sculpting rock," she said to Christopher's questioning look. "It took three tries for her to decide she was bored. I don't let the girls dispose of any usable tools, so..."

She held out the instruments to Martin. A few calls from the direction of the street made Christopher turn around. A man and woman craned their necks from the other side of the white picket fence to spy on their venture.

"Madam Clarice," the man called. "What's going on?"

Clarice waved, despite the tension around her eyes. "Nothing to worry about, I assure you."

The Ellery residents waved back and went on their way.

"You should hurry before more people become curious," she said.

Martin nodded and kneeled just as Christopher had moments earlier. He took a deep breath then angled the chisel against one edge of the block and knocked on it with the hammer. After several taps, he moved the chisel a few inches down the edge and kept knocking. Martin made his way around the cement block once, then twice. As he angled the chisel for a third turn around, one of the short sides of the block came free from the mortar.

"Your majesty," Martin said, "I believe this is a false front. I do not think this block is solid after all."

Christopher shifted his weight to his toes. "The fates are with us."

Martin grabbed the edge of the false front. Instead of breaking free at the other edges from the mortar, it moved as if on hinges. A steady amethyst-colored light with sparkles like dust motes beamed outward. Geraldine stepped forward and reached into the cornerstone. When she retrieved the second heart stone, she held both pieces together. They fit into one another and formed a seam; seconds later the seam and the light both disappeared, and the larger heart stone became dull again.

Christopher coughed, unable to believe what he had just witnessed. When he exchanged glances with the others, he saw what he felt himself. Relief; wonder; awe.

Hope.

"We should resume our journey right away," he said, "as much for Alistair's sake as the Keeper's health."

Martin swung the face of the cornerstone back into place and urged Clarice to contact a mason in her first spare moment to refill the mortar. Geraldine rewrapped the larger heart stone and placed it inside a leather pouch from the carriage. Everyone went into the home to retrieve what few belongings they took inside the previous evening, and within the half hour their party stood by the carriage, ready to climb in again.

The soldier scrambled onto the driver's box, and Geraldine handed him the leather pouch so the joined heart stones could guide them. Christopher allowed her to get into the carriage first then helped Alistair mount the few steps. The boy lay on the bench on one side of the carriage, taking care not to compress the hand the moss had claimed. As Alistair stretched his arm, Christopher saw the moss had extended further.

He ignored his trepidation as he turned to Clarice.

"You gave us an invaluable gift, Clarice."

"Well, your highness, I believe anyone would've—"

"I do not mean just the heart stone. You reminded me of why I have embarked on this journey: to be the kind of king I vowed on my coronation day."

Clarice blushed and murmured a few words about trying to fulfill her duty then held out the basket in her hands.

"I packed some morning bread, a jar of our home's jam, and a few boiled eggs for your journey."

He smiled as he took the basket. "You have an open invitation to the castle, Clarice. Should the girls ever need an outing or want to see the court as it performs, the gates are open to you."

Her face broke into a smile so wide he could see the happiness of an entire kingdom in it.

"Thank you again, Clarice, for the recollection of memories," Martin said.

"Please come back to see me, Martin. It would be so nice to spend more time with my younger brother."

Geraldine climbed back out of the carriage for one last hug with Clarice and murmured in her ear. Clarice whispered a reply, and Geraldine tightened her arms around the woman. Then she ascended the steps into the carriage, and Christopher followed.

The horses jerked forward, and they resumed their journey.

Celia concentrated on guiding her horse through the forest. Despite the comfortable climate, the sun baked her head. It had been five days since she had left the home of a trusted Lindener friend on a borrowed horse with saddlebags full of food; now she craved something to drink. For the last hour, she had thought of nothing else. It made her rethink her strategy. Had she actually believed she could accomplish this absurd plan to continue to Wyndemere all alone?

The sound of bubbling water nearby encouraged her. After letting the horse walk a dozen steps, she spotted the brook and brought the horse to a stop. Slipping down from the saddle, she moved as fast as she could and dropped to her knees at the edge of the brook, not caring how her formal skirts sank into the moist ground.

After cupping her hand and bringing the liquid to her lips several times, she took in a sharp breath of satisfaction and pushed herself to her feet to survey the woods. These trees did not seem to suffer the same fate as so many others she saw on her journey.

The sight of a well encouraged her to grab her horse's reins and begin walking again; as she approached the well, the water glistened like thousands of tiny jewels.

"Welcome," a voice said. "I am the Wishing Well. State your wish, and I will grant it."

"Any wish I desire?"

"Any wish." The well remained quiet then spoke again. "Oh, your majesty, my apologies. I didn't recognize you."

A short laugh fell from Celia's lips. "In truth, Wishing Well, I have trouble recognizing myself in this attire."

"If I could offer you a bow, I would. Tell me, how may I be of service? What would you wish for?"

Celia knew she needed to make her request with care. Once, when Vincent visited the court of Wyndemere, he boasted of the wishing well's existence and how sensibly it behaved as a purveyor of magic to grant wishes and yet only do so one at a time. The well, he said, took into account what a person wished but also what the person intended. Such an intelligent being, he went on, that matched Linden's other superior qualities.

Here, in the privacy of the forest, she rolled her eyes at Vincent's pride. His intentions had hurt so many. They were, in fact, responsible for her present condition. Her hair hung limply, her clothes were travel-stained, and, oh, how Celia missed the luxury of a deep bath. What she would have given to wish herself right back to her comfort room in the royal quarters in Wyndemere now.

The thought of Vincent made her consider Christopher and the pain he had endured in the years as the former monarch's son. The grief of losing her younger child still lodged in her chest like a deep cough that would not leave; Celia knew it would diminish with time, but it had become a permanent part of her body. Still, Celia and Malcolm had given Lily and her brother all the love in the world they held inside them. Christopher had no one to do so anymore.

After several quiet moments, she nodded to herself. "I am ready to make a wish, Well."

The surface of the water rippled with anticipation and, she thought, a touch of pride.

"And I'm ready to grant it, your majesty."

CHAPTER 19

For the tenth time since leaving Ellery, Christopher craned his neck around Martin's back and focused on the pulsing light from the enlarged heart stone. Alistair's health wobbled and rocked like the carriage itself. Once the journey came to an end, Christopher vowed not to travel by carriage for at least a year.

He smiled wryly, but as his gaze went to Alistair lying in Geraldine's lap his smile faded.

"How fares Alistair?" Martin asked above the sound of the carriage wheels creaking.

Geraldine leaned toward the window. "No change."

"Take heart, Geraldine," Christopher said, speaking over the clop-clop-clop of the horses' hooves. "We have acquired two of the three stones. We will succeed yet."

Geraldine gave him a wan smile.

"Martin, I feel the need to straighten my back," he called out the window. "Please stop."

"Yes, your majesty."

Soon the horses slowed, and the carriage did as well. Not for the first time, Christopher wished the carriage had window coverings to protect them from the sun's harsh angles. He brushed his sleeves, and dust powdered the air. Christopher ignored the grimy condition of his clothes as he descended the carriage steps.

The road lay flat and long in both directions; for the

moment, no one else appeared on it. The light from the combined heart stones pulsed, and even though they sat half-covered in the leather pouch Christopher could see an increase in the intensity of the pulses. He gestured for Martin to follow him down the road out of earshot of Geraldine and Alistair. As they walked, the soldier scanned the fields around them.

"We need to travel faster," Christopher said. "The moss is working its way up the sides of Alistair's throat."

"I cannot push the horses any harder, your highness. Without a confirmed destination, it would be unwise to force them to strain themselves. Although..."

He let his gaze wander down the road.

"I may be speaking prematurely, sire, but it seems as though we are headed back to Rosewood. Most travelers use this road for the fastest route back to the capital."

The king stared at the ground. "Do you think the Keeper left her third heart stone there?"

"It is possible. She told us she discarded it in a garden; she never revealed how far she traveled after Ellery. Perhaps she was tired from the burden of her father's death and King Vincent's betrayal. When one is weary, one craves the comforts of home."

"And it was imperative she return to take her oaths as Keeper," Christopher mused. He glanced back at the carriage. "If you are right, we will arrive at our final destination soon. Although I worry about how we are to piece together the final stone if the Keeper ground it into the dust. Have we embarked on a hopeless quest, Martin?"

The soldier shook his head. "The magic in these two stones has shown us unbelievable things, your highness. We must trust, for the boy's sake, that the third stone will do the same."

They returned to the carriage without another word. As

Christopher ascended the steps, Alistair drew a ragged breath. Geraldine glanced at him, her eyes tight.

Please, Christopher thought, invoking the fates, *please let us make it back to the Keeper with all the stones.*

Geraldine leaned her head back then tipped it forward to stretch her neck. Her muscles twinged as she looked down at Alistair. The previous morning he lay down in her lap and had stayed ever since, even when she eased his head to the bench to stretch her legs when they stopped.

If only Widow Hannity were here. How do I treat something I don't know? Could she have seen something like this? Why was the tree trying to hurt Alistair?

The carriage bumped, and Alistair jerked awake with a relentless cough. King Christopher scrambled for a water skin and shoved it in Geraldine's hands. She fumbled with the opening, and the king helped her as Alistair pushed himself to a sitting position.

"Alistair?" She tried to put the water skin to his lips, but he pushed it away. "Son, please, drink something. You need fluids to keep you refreshed."

He stared at her with glassy eyes.

"Sweetheart?"

He didn't respond; instead, he turned his attention to the window and stared at the landscape, his expression vacant.

The water skin slipped from her hands.

King Christopher caught it just before it hit the floor of the carriage. He took Alistair's hands and closed them around the neck of the vessel. Alistair looked at the water skin, and his eyebrows tilted downward.

"Alistair, drink."

Her son—her dear, sweet, talented, quiet boy—turned to the king and blinked. After a moment, he shook his head as if to clear it and she saw recognition return. Alistair took the water skin and gulped several large sips before handing it back to her.

"Sorry, Mother," he whispered. "Troubling you."

She shook her head hard, fighting a sob. "Never, my darling. Never."

The carriage slowed. Geraldine ducked her head through the window to ask Sir Martin if they could stop so she could have a private moment to relieve herself. At the sight of the trees, the words crumbled in her mouth.

Mounds of white ash piled high at random intervals in the wood around them. Some stood taller than others, in relation, no doubt, to the sizes of the trees that once stood in those places. The odor of decay wafted toward Geraldine, and she buried her face in the crook of her elbow. King Christopher mirrored her movements. Alistair sank back into her lap. The moss now covered both arms and crept up the sides of his neck where it met the hairline.

Fatigue burrowed into her bones, and for a moment her vision swam as she fought a bout of dizziness. She recognized the feeling from staying up late several nights with a sick patient. Would they find the third heart stone? How could they even do so when the Keeper said she'd ground it into dust? Would they return to the Keeper in time?

Could she save Alistair?

In the afternoon of the fifth day, they reached the outskirts of Rosewood. The growth of the villages that buttressed the capital city on this side encouraged Christopher. The majority of their residents benefited from the lumber trade.

And if I do not complete this task, their growth will be for naught, he thought with a grimace.

Even inside the pouch, Martin said the heart stone pulsed without interruption. He guided the carriage through smaller lanes and larger ones. The afternoon waned as they rode toward the city. After a few hours, Christopher realized they moved in the direction of the castle itself. During a quick stop at an inn for their evening meal, which Christopher ate in the carriage, he and Martin did not discuss their apparent direction.

The heart stones had not failed them before; they would not do so now.

Malcolm sat at the center table of a hall in the castle and studied a list of numbers.

"And you are certain there is no more space in the fourth storage house?"

An attendant shook his head. "No, your majesty. And considering the speed at which the lumber is being returned…"

Malcolm nodded. "We must anticipate what might be required in the coming days. Very well. Open the fifth storage house and prepare it for shipments. I will research other storage possibilities."

The attendant bowed in acquiescence but did not leave.

"Was there anything else?"

The man tightened his fingers on his reports; the chains linking the shackles on his wrists rang.

"Your majesty, while the castle staff and I find ourselves full of gratitude for your role in managing this growing problem, we... That is to say, do you think..."

Malcolm sat back, his own shackle chains sliding to his lap, and the man flinched.

"Out with it, man. I must review the latest consignments returned so I may prepare for what tomorrow brings."

"Do you know when the wood might return to its natural state?"

The king glanced at the voluminous reports on the table. "I am confident King Christopher is searching for a solution at this very moment. As we await his return, know he and I both appreciate your service and the service of the other attendants and castle staff."

He smiled with confidence; the attendant answered with a relieved smile of his own and a deep bow and left. The sounds of the chains on his hands and feet echoed back as he made his way down the corridor. Malcolm dropped the latest reports on top of the pages on the table and sighed.

Which begs the question, of course: when *will Christopher return?*

In the week since Lemuel's occupation of the castle began, Malcolm spent every waking moment performing two tasks: dealing with the returns of lumber consignments and reassuring those still in the castle that Christopher would come home. Both tasks competed for his time, energy, and optimism. Both left him with more questions than answers.

The failure of the Linden wood baffled him as it did everyone else, and in that regard he found it easier to comfort people. No one could remember the magic of the Linden wood failing, so no one knew quite how to react. He convinced the councilors, the castle staffers, and the messengers bringing back the wood that all would be well in the end. By hiding his own misgivings, it gave others the confidence to return to their tasks.

Christopher's disappearance became harder to defend as the days passed. Everyone in the castle still remembered Vincent's self-centered approach during his years on the throne. Christopher had taken every opportunity since being crowned to show he differed from his father, but Lemuel's defiance, coupled with the failing of the wood, constituted the biggest challenge of Christopher's reign thus far. Had he decided, in the end, to follow in his father's footsteps after all?

Just then Lemuel entered the hall, followed by two of his men.

"Well, your highness, what's the latest about the wood?"

It made Malcolm want to grind his teeth, but he stood in acknowledgment of the imbecile. The shackles on his legs clanked as they struck the floor. He tried to tamp down the shame crawling along his skin from being bound like a common prisoner.

"The fourth storage house is full," he replied. "I have instructed the attendants to prepare the fifth storage house to accept deliveries."

"And when is all this going to stop? When will people stop sending the wood back?"

Malcolm spread his hands, but the shackles stopped the movement short. "I do not know. We do not know why the wood is failing at all."

"And just how do you suppose we'll find out?"

"I am confident King Christopher is pursuing the best course of action for the people of Linden. His leave-taking must be connected to the situation. There is no other explanation for his disappearance."

"There is, your highness," Lemuel said, stepping forward. "He wants to avoid my men and me, because the castle has kept the funds owed to us. He's run away so he doesn't have to face his responsibility. The wood's just a convenient excuse, and by supporting him it's obvious you're capable of the same thing."

The two sidekicks Lemuel brought with him smiled with satisfaction. One folded his arms as if to challenge Malcolm to find an answer. The king had none, but he did possess a trait Lemuel did not.

For all his grandiosity, Lemuel's eyes crinkled with trepidation. Malcolm heard whispers from pages and others that Lemuel's men found guarding castle staff and councilors increasingly tedious. Some had even been heard debating whether they should just leave without informing Lemuel. After all, his aim was to keep the castle dwellers and members of Christopher's court, not them, from escaping.

Celia...

"If you propose I would do anything to keep my people safe, then, yes, I am capable of the same as King Christopher."

Lemuel narrowed his eyes. "That's not what I meant."

"Then what do you mean, Lemuel? You have occupied the castle for the better part of a week, you have bound us like common prisoners, and yet you do not seem closer to your goal. Do you even remember it?"

"Of course I remember it. I've been searching through the castle records. I know the king is hiding what's owed to me."

Malcolm tilted his head in consideration. "And? What have you found thus far?"

"That's not important. What *is* important—"

"Oh, but the question begs the utmost of importance," Malcolm said, crossing his arms as much as the shackles would allow. "You claim my son-in-law stole coin from your family. That he harbors some secret desire to keep the funds for his own gain that you and your loved ones and others have earned. Tell me, why would he commit such a crime when he possesses an entire treasury full of riches?"

"I don't know, but—"

"Especially considering the legacy his father left. Have you found the king lacking in any other facet? Has he not brokered agreements benefiting the lumber guild?"

"Yes, but—"

"Did he not undo years of resentment by calling for the building of the bridge over the river between Briarwood and Linden?"

"The people of Briarwood are the ones who benefit—"

"Has he not shown his commitment to peace between the kingdoms?"

"I think—"

"I *know*," Malcolm said. "When the former king left him a kingdom where uncertainty and unrest reigned, King Christopher met the challenge and transformed relationships. He reassured envoys and ambassadors from surrounding kingdoms that his intentions, while naïve at times, remained pure. I know, because I entrusted to him the most precious thing in my life: my daughter."

His heart despaired for Lily. His sweet girl who debated his decisions instead of accepting them at face value and who imbibed diplomacy with her mother's milk. Oh, how he missed her and her impish smile.

Come back, Celia, he thought. *I do not know how much longer I can sustain myself through this grief without you.*

Lemuel pursed his lips. "If King Christopher is so wonderful, why did he leave? Who's going to take care of Lindeners?"

"He will return, and he will show himself to be a true

leader. I am confident he is out searching for a solution, even as we stand here."

The door opened, and one of the castle pages brought in a sheaf of papers. Malcolm knew, even without examining them, that they contained more messages about the wood. The page stared at Lemuel wide-eyed, her shackles chattering as her hands shook, and she thrust the messages at Malcolm before darting out of the room.

"A ruler is one who leads by example," Malcolm said, "not one who waits for circumstances to favor him."

"And you believe that's what I'm doing? Just waiting for my fortune to turn?"

"I believe," Malcolm said, taking a step closer, "you are out of your depth, Lemuel. You have thought about what you demand, yes, but you do not know how this might affect anyone else. Tell me, this father on whose behalf you fight, does he endorse your presence here?"

Lemuel met him stare for stare. After a moment, he looked away. The correct guess emboldened Malcolm.

"If your father did not ask you to fight on his behalf, then why do you insist on trying to start a revolution?"

"I'm not trying to start a revolution." Lemuel lifted his gaze to meet Malcolm's once again. "I'm trying to prove the king can't take advantage of anyone and get away with it."

He turned and stomped out of the hall. The two men followed Lemuel without bothering to bow. It still irritated Malcolm that Lemuel and his men had forgotten the proper protocol around royals.

He sat again and leafed through the messages. More notes asking for explanations for the failure of the wood. News of seven more buildings collapsing; dozens of pieces of furniture. An entire wagon carrying crates of berries for sale. Kings and queens and ambassadors pleading or demanding responses. No one had proposed military action yet, but Malcolm's experience taught him to look for it every day. Generic responses from him and Linden's councilors promising vague resolutions would only take Linden so far.

After a moment, he pinched the bridge of his nose with his finger and thumb. The chains of the shackles brushed against his face, the cold metal reminding him much of the battle still remained unfought. He pleaded with the fates to bring Christopher back soon then allowed his thoughts to return to the one constant that stayed with him every hour of every day.

Celia, my love, he thought, *return soon. I am in need of reinforcements. And courage.*

Lemuel stalked to the castle records room.

"Tell Bailey to come," he barked over his shoulder at his men.

"Do you think we should go looking for the king, Lemuel?"

"I think, Ernest," he said, stopping short and turning around, "you should go get Bailey before I send you to work as a maid in the kitchens."

"All right." Ernest held up his hands in surrender. "Looks like someone didn't have breakfast."

Lemuel wanted to retort but couldn't come up with one fast enough. He kept going down the oversized corridor toward the records room. When he reached the door, he turned to Ernest's partner who still followed.

"Don't you have tasks, Oliver?"

Oliver shrugged. "I was guarding Councilor Caleb this

morning, but then Arthur came for his shift."

"I'm working my way through the ledgers of the castle. They show all of the accounts of all the kings who've ruled Linden. Do you want to help?"

Oliver's eyes widened. "You know, I just remembered, Arthur asked me a question and I never answered it. I'll go make sure Councilor Caleb isn't causing trouble."

As Oliver trotted away, Lemuel pushed in the tall door to the records room and stopped to survey the mess he'd left for himself on the expansive table. At least a dozen ledgers lay there, some opened, some closed. The oversized record books fought for space, sitting on top of one another at haphazard angles.

Lemuel let his fingers trail over the faded leather cover of one of the ledgers, soft and pliable after dozens of hands opening and closing it through the generations. Hundreds more ledgers lined the bookshelves in the walls with the shelves going high enough to need a rolling ladder to reach them. Careful hands had labeled the ledger spines. The various types of handwriting from all the accountants that had served Linden almost told their own tale of the kingdom's history.

When he'd first discovered the records room, he thought the fates had sent him the answers to all his problems. The excitement of capturing the castle in those first few days had worn off, leaving him empty. Without King Christopher present, his reason for remaining in the castle seemed paper-thin at best.

On the third day, trailing through the large corridors and wondering why a castle needed so many rooms, he had opened the door to the records room. All at once, a plan fell into place. King Christopher would return eventually. When he did, Lemuel would have all the evidence he needed to prove the king cheated him and his family. The proof lay somewhere in the scores of files he saw.

In those first hours, he read the most recent ledgers and found reports of the honey the kingdom exported, as well as the crops, few but bountiful. The royal accountant made careful notations about less prolific exports: bolts of fabric or pottery by the artisans or glass beads fired in kilns. And, of course, there were the ledgers about the wood itself, or the lumber rather. Ledgers and ledgers about lumber. If discrepancies existed, Lemuel thought they'd be here where it would be much easier to hide missing coin.

As he worked through the patient handwriting of the royal accountant, though, Lemuel's eagerness dimmed. Lines in the ledgers suggesting dishonesty led him to cross reference older, dustier ledgers where he found reasonable explanations for it all. His own note taking revealed to Lemuel a pattern. All of the questionable accounts led back to the state of the treasury from King Vincent's time and even earlier. Nothing pointed to new instances of corruption. Yet.

He leafed through a few pages now as the door opened and Bailey entered.

"Ernest said you wanted to see me. Wait, are you still reading these accounts?"

"There has to be proof here somewhere. Either the king's lying or the councilors are, and I'm going to find out who."

"Well, the king isn't here to defend himself."

Lemuel turned to his best friend. "And how am I responsible for that?"

"You're not, Lemuel, but you have to admit, we're not making much progress. Some of the men are asking about the future. How long do you plan to occupy the castle?"

"I can't do anything about the fact that the king ran like a weakling," Lemuel snapped. "Have you been looking into the wood like I asked?"

Bailey nodded. "Some of the men are making progress, but it's slow going."

"Tell them to work faster. We need more than just accounts to make our case. I want the king to know that if he can't make the most of his resources, we'll find a way to do so."

Lemuel dropped into a chair. One of the ledgers teetered on the edge of the table and flipped onto the floor with a loud slam. He flinched and reached down for it.

"You didn't answer my question," Bailey said.

"What question?"

"How long do you plan to occupy the castle?"

"As long as it takes to find proof of the king's deception."

"And if he comes back before you find it?"

Lemuel glared at Bailey. "You just tell the men to get moving on the wood."

Bailey raised his eyebrows then heaved a huge sigh and left the room. Lemuel yanked the nearest ledger toward him, although the pulsing in his temple wouldn't let him concentrate.

King Malcolm has no right to question my motives. He doesn't know anything about my life and what Father and Mother have been through. Easy for a royal to pass judgment when he's never had to struggle for a meal.

It didn't help that Bailey voiced the doubts floating through Lemuel's own mind. When would all this end? *How* would it end?

He tried to squash the answer from his conscience as he had done so many times. His hand went to his pocket with the note his father had sent three days earlier. In a short letter full of brash words, Lemuel had written home to tell his mother and father where he was. When the response came the same day by speed courier, Lemuel tore into the envelope expecting praise.

Instead, his father admonished him. Told him to stop "all this nonsense." He warned that King Christopher wouldn't hesitate to punish a commoner playing at king, and he had written how disappointed he was that Lemuel would stoop to such a childish gesture.

"If you don't come home soon, I'll come to the castle and drag you out myself. Start behaving like an adult, and help your mother and me by being a responsible son," the letter ended.

Lemuel's fingers crushed the envelope.

Father doesn't know what he's talking about. If Fin had been in my place, Father would have been hefting a quarterstaff right next to him. I didn't make a mistake taking over the castle, and if King Christopher does come back... well, I'm the one here right now, not him.

He pushed aside the ledger in the same way he forced his doubt to the edge of his mind. The answers lay in this room. He just had to find them.

CHAPTER 20

By nightfall, the travelers reached the edge of the castle grounds. As Martin brought the carriage to a stop, the sight of the castle renewed Christopher's worry about King Malcolm and Queen Celia. Had Lemuel crossed lines of social protocol? Would their majesties think Christopher a coward for going on this journey instead of staying to fight? Were the councilors safe? Would anyone respect him after all this?

Christopher considered for a moment what it meant that the answer to the last question carried the most weight.

He heard the horses stomp their hooves and snort, and he tugged at his collar. The carriage rocked for a moment as Martin climbed down from the driver's box. Christopher heard a wordless exclamation from his oldest friend, quiet but full of surprise.

"Your highness," Martin said, holding the joined heart stones. "The private gardens."

Christopher climbed down from the carriage, groaning as a cramp in his left leg threatened to make his knee buckle. He hobbled a few steps to work it out. The orchid light from the joined stone in the pouch pulsed sharper and with more clarity at night, and Martin affixed the pouch to his waistband and held the stone in his bare hands. Christopher heard Geraldine and Alistair descend from the carriage behind him, but all of his attention was on the gardens kept for the royal family's pleasure.

The grounds sparkled with thousands of purple pin-pricks, as if the fates had tossed the stars across the earth. Martin held the heart stone toward the garden. It pulsed with a luminosity matching a bright torch and in time to the lights in the garden.

"What is that?" Geraldine asked as she came to stand next to him.

"I believe...but, no," Christopher interrupted himself. "We must get closer."

Alistair joined him on the other side, and they all made their way down the stone steps built into the side of the gentle slope. They followed Martin who held out the heart stone like an homage to the night. The pulse of light glowed brighter as they got closer until Christopher worried it would betray them to someone inside the castle. He glanced between the light and the castle windows, holding his breath.

"I do not want us to be caught unawares by any of Lemuel's men," Martin whispered to the group. "We are approaching the castle with no information on hand. He may have set up a night watch of some sort. We must avoid detection."

Christopher nodded. "Lead the way."

The soldier pulled open the wrought iron gate in the wall on the perimeter of the grounds and pulled it shut behind them. Alistair's gait slowed until he lumbered several paces behind. Christopher reached for one of Alistair's arms and looped it behind his neck. Alistair murmured a protest.

"Speed, my boy," he whispered. "We must accomplish our task soon if you are to recover."

Alistair did not respond, but he relaxed into Christopher. With another whisper to Geraldine to hasten her step, he turned his attention back to Martin. The soldier moved ahead several paces and stopped.

"Hurry," he urged them in a loud whisper.

They followed the pulsing light, and Christopher's heart started thumping. Was the joined stone leading them to Lily's garden?

They came to the edge of the lights blanketing the ground. Christopher looked up at the castle and the windows on the second story. He remembered the first time Lily saw the view from those windows. On the third day after their wedding, she entered the room and inhaled in surprise and delight.

"This room will make a perfect art studio," she announced.

Christopher watched her hurry to the window. She exclaimed at the gardens below then turned back to him. Her smile dimmed.

"If your highness has no objection, that is."

He shook his head. "The castle is your home, your majesty. You have full reign over it as you do over Linden."

Her smile returned and wider this time. "I shall ask the gardeners to use that plot for the plants needed to make my paints. Then I may look down at this beautiful space for inspiration, should I need it."

A profound loneliness settled in his soul.

"The Keeper must have come back here out of spite," Geraldine whispered. "What better place to take her revenge than on the grounds of the castle itself? But what do we do? She said she ground the heart stone into the dirt. How do we put it back together again?"

Christopher could not help himself; he looked up at Lily's windows again. A faint hue clouded the glass, and he realized the orchid light reached the windows. They pulsed in time to the heart stone and the lights on the ground.

"Martin."

The soldier followed his outstretched arm. As soon as

Martin pointed the heart stone in the direction of the windows, the light became a steady beam. The stone sent light like thick ribbons from them to the castle.

"Is that room...?" Geraldine asked.

Christopher could not answer. He had often visited Lily's space, but the beauty it held intimidated him. Through the years, he developed many skills but not the ability to create in such a fashion.

"It is the queen's painting studio," Martin whispered. "The heart stone wants us to go there."

"Lemuel," Alistair said, his whisper softer than everyone else's. "How?"

Christopher's stomach clenched as he remembered the way he and the king and queen mourned Lily together in the studio. Why would the stone want him to go there now? What connection did it have to Lily? To the Keeper?

What if he did not have the heart to face whatever the stones required of him?

Martin put the joined stone in the pouch at his waist. The sudden disappearance of light shocked all of them. Christopher rounded on his guardsmaster.

"What are you doing?"

In the light of the full moon, he saw Martin hold up his hands in a placating gesture.

"Your majesty, we must consider the state of those left inside. Are we prepared to face them?"

"Shouldn't we worry first about how we'll get in?" Geraldine said.

Martin shook his head. "The castle contains secret passages, and some are accessible to us here. We can enter the castle on this side, but we must make the decision to do so."

Christopher took a moment to look at each of them. Their company on this journey had offered a constant reminder of why he endeavored the venture in the first place. They reminded him, he realized suddenly, of Lily. Of the way she would place a hand on his shoulder when he worked in his study late into the night on a peace negotiation. Of the way she clasped his hand as they rode through the streets of Rosewood on festival days.

Of the absolute faith she had in him to accomplish whatever he set out to do.

"We have no choice, Martin," he replied. "We must see where the stone leads us and, if we are able, to reassemble the final heart stone. The Keeper's life depends on it."

Martin nodded once, straightened his shoulders, then gestured for them to follow him to the castle wall below the windows of the queen's art studio. He found a section of wall covered by a tree and counted the number of blocks from the ground up. When he came to the one he wanted, he pressed his fingertips into the lower right-hand corner of the block, and a hidden door swung open on silent hinges.

Christopher watched as Martin stepped to the iron door and twisted the dials next to the doorknob to open the lock. When it gave a soft click of release, Christopher let go of a breath he did not realize he had held. Martin tipped his head toward the door.

From his years playing the hiding game with Martin, Christopher remembered the passage wrapping around the castle in a rough oval. The soldier ushered them through the doorway and pointed to the right. After Alistair crossed the threshold, Martin pulled the door shut.

The soldier's boots echoed on the cobblestone floor. After several moments, light flared and Martin unhooked a torch from a wall sconce. He held the lit torch aloft and gestured to the path.

For several minutes they all shuffled behind Martin in

silence. Twice Geraldine whispered a request to stop so Alistair could rest. Christopher tapped on Martin's shoulder, and they stood and listened to the boy's hoarse gasps. When Alistair said he could continue, they did.

During the second wait, Christopher leaned toward the guardsmaster.

"I thought you had given up the hiding game years ago."

Martin chuckled. "Every year I select a handful of soldiers to reaffirm the safety and usability of the passages. We inspect the torches as well as the matches. I want the soldiers to remain ready should we ever need the passages in an emergency. It is one of the few practices of the former king I supported."

He pressed once again on a particular place in the wall, and a panel clicked open. Muted light crept into the passage. Placing the torch in an empty sconce, Martin moved aside the tapestry hanging in front of the secret door. Christopher held his breath as Martin poked his head around the tapestry. After several moments, the soldier drew back.

"I think we may be able to use the corridor instead of continuing through the walls. It will be much faster, and—"

A strident set of footsteps cut off the rest of his words, and Christopher clenched his fists at the sound. Martin pulled the door closed so the tapestry did not jut into the corridor and alert anyone to their position. Geraldine's eyes widened with fear. Alistair slumped against a wall.

After several minutes, the footsteps receded.

"We must move now," Martin whispered. "We cannot risk discovery."

He checked the corridor once more before gesturing the healer to push past the tapestry. Christopher turned to Alistair and put the boy's arm around his neck again. This time Alistair did not protest. As the boy leaned on him, the intense heat from his body startled Christopher.

How much longer can the child sustain himself? he wondered.

Ignoring his alarm, Christopher and Alistair followed Geraldine into the corridor. Martin doused the torch and made sure the secret door closed behind them. After the darkness of the interior passage, the light from the fat candles along the corridor walls made them all squint as their eyes adjusted. Martin did not wait, rushing down the corridor in the opposite direction of the footsteps.

As they did their best to stay quiet but also hurry, Christopher tried to catch glimpses of the castle he knew so well. An oversized portrait on a wall; an offshoot leading to the petitioners' court. He heard snatches of himself as a child racing through the corridors chasing Martin. Turning to the right would take him on the path of the funeral processional in the days after King Vincent's death. Straight ahead and to the left, he could picture the first pages of his regime gawking at the castle as he tried not to do the same in awe that he now ruled the building, the city, and the kingdom.

"Here we are," Martin whispered as they approached the back stairwell closest to the royal apartments.

They climbed the steps, stopping more than once for Alistair to rest. During each stop, Christopher concentrated his hearing for more footsteps. He refused to allow Lemuel's men to waylay them so close to their goal.

Several minutes later, they alighted on the floor of the private apartments of the royal family. Christopher took the lead in guiding them to Lily's art studio, but as he approached the door his feet slowed. He hesitated, not wanting to face what lay inside.

A tug on his arm made him turn toward Geraldine.

"Your highness, if we're going to do this, now is the time

for it," she whispered.

Christopher inhaled a hard, deep breath and nodded. Waiting for everyone to collect behind him, he pushed the door open and winced at the loud creak it made. He waved everyone in and peered down both sides of the corridor then eased the door shut.

Martin helped Alistair into a chair and lit a single candle on the table. Geraldine stood close to her son with her hands pressed to her stomach. She attempted a smile as Martin reached into his pouch for the heart stone.

"We've made it this far, your highness," she said. "Now all we need—"

The paintings on the wall blazed with a brilliant light that made Christopher throw his hand in front of his face. He screwed his eyes tight, leaving mere slits, then forced them open all the way. The heart stone in Martin's hands glowed with a steady beam as well.

"What's happening?" Geraldine asked.

"I do not know," Christopher said. "The garden below was for the plants Lily would have dried and used in her paint pigments. The Keeper said she spread the heart stone dust over a garden, but...but why would the paintings glow?"

"Paints," Alistair said. "Earth. Plants."

Christopher pondered the boy's words, and his eyes widened as he realized what Alistair meant. The plants had grown in the very earth where the Keeper spread the dust from her heart stone. Those plants formed the basis for Lily's paints, which she used to create the incredible works of art hanging on the walls and sitting on half-finished canvases all around.

Just then, the paintings glowed with thousands of orchid sparkles. All of the pieces Lily toiled over became illuminated, as if candles lit them from behind. The flowers in one scene almost fluttered in an imaginary wind; a waterfall seemed to pitch over a cliff as a bird soared over it. A portrait of King Malcolm and Queen Celia glowed as their smiles brightened the entire room.

Then the paints in each piece began to disintegrate.

The purple points rushed toward the joined heart stone in Martin's hands. Canvases full of color and movement moments earlier now stood devoid of both. Lily's paintings were being destroyed.

"No!" Christopher roared.

He charged into the fray and waved his arms around at the minuscule points of light, trying to catch them, trying to push them back into the paintings. For a moment, he managed to capture a handful of sparkling dust, but it whipped out of his cupped palms and flew straight to the heart stone in Martin's grasp.

Christopher stormed toward his guardsmaster. He swiped the joined stone from the soldier's hands. It clattered to the floor, but the dust continued to fly toward the heart stone. It coalesced into a solid form. Christopher snatched up the heart stones and tried to pry them apart.

"No! I will not lose her again! You...cannot...take... her!"

With his full effort expended, he dropped the heart stones on the floor and fell to his knees. A wailing sound filled his head, his heart, the room, the world...and Christopher realized the wail came from him. He drew a ragged breath and howled again.

Centuries passed in the gaps between his laments.

From the moment the paintings started to glow, the hairs on the back of Geraldine's neck stood.

"Mother?"

"I don't know why, Alistair," she answered his unspoken question.

As the grains of paint flew from the paintings, Geraldine threw her arms around Alistair. She closed her eyes tight but then realized the paints weren't striking her. She forced herself to open her eyes.

The sight of the paint grains flying to the heart stones made Geraldine suck in a sharp breath. Then she heard the king's screams, the torment in his voice, and her own heart contracted until she squinted in pain. Within moments, the canvases on the wall emptied themselves of all the queen's labors.

Now she wanted to comfort the king as she had so many people after they'd lost sweethearts and spouses. He bent over so far that she worried his head would hit the ground. His keening slowed, and his shoulders hitched at his efforts to control his breathing.

"It was my duty to protect and cherish her," he whimpered. "I broke my vow, and now...now I have nothing left of her. I have lost everything."

Geraldine's memory sparked then, and she heard the words of the wishing well as if they stood before it.

"The magic demands, King Christopher, that you give up your first love to save your kingdom..."

Her breath became shaky. Sir Martin's sacrifice of the well came true. Now the king's sacrifice was complete. What would the well demand from her?

"Your majesty," Martin said, his voice hollow. "Your majesty, we must go. The heart stones have joined together again. We must return them to the Keeper."

The king drew himself to his knees and shook his head.

"I have nothing left to give, Martin," he said, his voice

smaller than Geraldine had ever heard it. "I could not keep the queen safe. I could not make my father see me. Perhaps... perhaps Lemuel was right to question my ability as king."

The full meaning of his words sunk in. The severity of their situation—the danger to Alistair—swarmed Geraldine's as the heart stone dust had swarmed the room moments ago, making her ears buzz. She went to the king and dropped to one knee then grabbed his arm.

"King Christopher. Listen. You must listen to me."

He turned to her, and the shadows created by the candle sharpened the agony on his face. He'd lost the love of his life twice. How could she censure him for a moment of grief?

"Your majesty," she said in a kinder tone, "you can only claim responsibility for what's under your control. The queen's death was beyond any of us. The fates deemed it her time to go. That doesn't mean you failed as king."

"She was the one person who believed I *could* be king, Geraldine, the one who believed I could accomplish all the things my father could not. The only thing I had left of her, of her love, was..."

Remembrance bloomed in his eyes.

"The wishing well."

Geraldine nodded. "The wishing well said it would require a sacrifice from each of us. Maybe you needed to sacrifice what you had left from the queen so you could see who you are without her."

"I am a man carrying the burden of my father's faults. Lemuel suspects I am stealing from my own people. I am not my father. I refuse to be known as his son."

"Then you have to prove to Lemuel and all the other doubters how wrong they are," Geraldine said. "You're still a king, your majesty, even if Queen Lily's no longer with you."

He started to shake his head, and Geraldine held up her

hands to stop him.

"You came on this quest to rescue the Keeper's heart stones. You allowed Alistair and me to come, even though you had every reason to leave us behind."

"The Keeper said I—"

"The Keeper's still a subject of the Linden throne. If you'd wanted, you could have left us behind. You and Sir Martin could have continued on the journey. But you gave us—me— a chance. You worked with Clarice; you slept on the ground, for fates' sake. You did what needed to be done, because a true leader doesn't look at the personal indignities he might suffer as long as it benefits his kingdom. You behaved as a king, your highness, because that's what you are, and right now you have the fate of the entire kingdom in your hands."

King Christopher let his head drop for a moment. The heart stones pulsed, a larger object than before, and she could see the place where the last heart stone would fit.

We're so close to helping the Keeper. To saving the trees. To making sure Alistair is well again.

The king lifted his head and drew a ragged breath. The shadows almost hid the expression on his face. After several quiet moments, he nodded.

"I do not know whether I am worthy of all the grandiosity you claim, Geraldine, but I do know I will not let Linden fall. I am not willing to let our journey go in vain."

He pushed himself to a standing position and heaved another deep breath. This one seemed smoother than the first. His hand wandered to the healing cut on his left arm.

"I must seek out Lemuel and lay his accusations to rest."

Geraldine exchanged a look with Sir Martin. "Your highness, the heart stones..."

He encouraged her with a gesture to stand.

"You, Martin, and Alistair must return to the wood and

deliver the heart stones to the Keeper. I will deal with Lemuel and his men."

Sir Martin stepped forward. "Absolutely not, sire. I cannot let you take an undue risk to yourself."

"The healer just affirmed I am the king, did she not, Martin?"

"Yes, your highness, but—"

"And all residents in Linden are subject to my authority, are they not, Guardsmaster?"

Martin pursed his lips. "They are, sire, but Linden law also stipulates you not put yourself in any unnecessary danger."

The king's expression softened as he tilted his head. "I know your concern for me is valid and true, old friend, but if I am to live up to the people's expectations, I must do so in the open, where they can see I have met the challenges set before me. I escaped once before, but I will run no longer."

Without waiting for Sir Martin to respond, King Christopher went and helped Alistair stand.

"We will meet with Lemuel and his men." He draped Alistair's arm over his shoulders. "His dispute is with me, so I will resolve it. Come."

Before Geraldine knew what to say, she found herself following the king and Alistair back into the large corridor. Sir Martin doused the candle and shut the door to the queen's art studio behind them. The scowl on his face mirrored her own dissatisfaction with the king's assertiveness.

Well, you wanted him to start moving again.

Instead of returning to the side staircase, the king led them down a different corridor. Sir Martin muttered behind her, and Geraldine heard snatches like "leaving ourselves open to attack" and "letting folly leap ahead of sound judgment." His grousing sounded how one brother would complain about another. Despite the way her heart fluttered, she couldn't help smiling.

Footsteps echoed ahead of them, but these sounded lighter. Mingling with the footsteps, though, was a clinking sound Geraldine couldn't place. She'd heard it before, but where?

They rounded a corner, and a woman wearing a formal brown gown edged with a wide white border almost ran into King Christopher. She jumped back, murmuring apologies. The circle brooch just below her left shoulder marked her as a royal councilor. Her dark hair trembled in wisps around her head, almost like a halo, and her eyes became large. Her wrists and feet were in shackles, and as the woman covered her mouth Geraldine realized the clinking sound came from the chains.

"Your highness," the woman exclaimed. She dropped into a deep curtsy.

"Ariana? What is the meaning of all this?"

Councilor Ariana averted her gaze. "Lemuel's men shackled all of us six days ago, your majesty. He…"

King Christopher asked Martin to take Alistair then stepped forward.

"Has he injured anyone? How fare the king and queen?"

Councilor Ariana's face relaxed a little. "King Malcolm is well, although Lemuel put him in shackles as well."

"Bloody axe grinder," the king muttered.

Geraldine's face flushed with heat. "Your majesty, please. My son."

King Christopher's cheeks reddened. "Forgive me, Geraldine. Ariana, what of the queen?"

A look of deep satisfaction crossed her face. "The queen escaped the day after you did, your highness. That is precisely why Lemuel shackled everyone, as punishment."

"Has he doled out other punishments?"

Geraldine had never heard the king speak in such a menacing tone. Goosebumps pebbled her skin, and she rubbed her arms. She opened her mouth to ask a question, but the sound of boots on the smooth floor cut off her words.

Her first instinct told her to run away. Sir Martin balled his free hand into a fist. The king squared his shoulders just in time for two brawny men to round the corner of the hallway.

"Councilor Ariana," one man called, "what are you doing?"

The councilor crossed her arms as best she could, despite the shackles. "The king has returned."

The second man scoffed. "Well, it's about time. I'm sick of waiting for what's owed to us."

"I have returned to right the wrongs committed against my people," the king said. "Lead me to Lemuel. We will settle this once and for all."

The two men exchanged confused looks but recovered within moments.

"This way, your highness," the first man said with a mock bow. "I'm sure Lemuel will be thrilled to see all of you."

"No. I will meet Lemuel alone. Guardsmaster Martin, Mistress Geraldine, and her son, Alistair, will leave."

The men laughed in scorn, but King Christopher didn't react to their laughter. After several seconds, their mirth stuttered then became quiet. The king tipped his head to the side, waiting for them to collect themselves.

"All of you go to Lemuel first," the second man said. "He decides what happens."

A muscle in King Christopher's cheek twitched, but he nodded. "Lead the way."

Councilor Ariana's eyebrows folded, and Geraldine felt

every ounce of her concern if for a different reason. They all fell in step behind the men. Geraldine forced herself to follow, despite every instinct to bolt in the other direction.

We need to get back to the wood now. *Alistair may not have much...much energy left.*

As if he heard her thoughts, the king glanced over his shoulder and reassured her with a look.

Hold on, Alistair, she thought, wringing her hands at the way he dragged his feet despite Sir Martin's help. *Hold on.*

CHAPTER 21

As Ariana followed Lemuel's men down the corridor, her spirit became light. All the tension she had carried with her since the previous week disappeared. The king had returned after all.

Tears burned the corners of her eyes. She raised a hand to wipe them away, for once not caring about the shackles. The king glared at the manacles on her wrists.

"Did Lemuel forget all semblance of decency, or were the shackles the only injustice you suffered?"

"He did not cross the lines of social graces in any other—"

"He *shackled* you, Councilor. When he made that decision, he also shackled any leniency I might have offered. Have we received any more news of the wood?"

She glanced ahead to gauge whether the rogue guards could hear them.

"Other kingdoms have sent back lumber shipments in exceeding quantities, and members from our own guild chapters arrive daily in Rosewood," she said in a quieter tone. "King Malcolm has dealt with the outside correspondence and returned shipments, but he tasked me to speak to the Lindeners. I have spent every day, hours at a time, trying to reassure guild members the wood will be restored, but I repeat the words with no confidence myself."

The king pressed his lips into a hard line. "You and the rest of the court have lost confidence in my abilities."

"No, your majesty, but we do not know what ails the wood."

Just then, Lemuel's men stopped outside the records room. Oliver entered while Ernest stayed behind and kept watch. Ariana wanted to beat her fists against the door. How long did Lemuel intend to search for proof that did not exist?

The king turned toward the guardsmaster. "Martin, take Geraldine and Alistair to the Keeper. We cannot afford to lose more time."

"Your majesty..."

King Christopher dipped his chin to level a look at the soldier. "You must trust me, Martin. There is no other way."

Ariana exchanged a worried glance with Mistress Geraldine. The healer drew her son's arm over her own shoulders, and a coughing fit overtook him. He bent half over with the effort, and Ariana noticed a bizarre white growth covering his arms and neck. A quick glance at his legs showed the same growth covering the right leg from the knee down.

Her mind brought forth the possibility that the growth was connected in some way to the trees, and Ariana swallowed hard.

"Alistair and the Keeper cannot wait any longer," King Christopher said.

Ernest eyed them with suspicion. "Wait a minute, no one's going anywhere—"

Sir Martin bowed. "Yes, your majesty. Healer, Alistair, follow me."

"You can't leave," Ernest went on, putting up his hands. Sir Martin brushed right past the man. With a furtive look at all of them, Mistress Geraldine followed Sir Martin. Her son hobbled as best he could in between coughs.

The door swung open, and Lemuel came out with a smirk. "So the king has returned."

"Lemuel, the guardsmaster," Ernest said, glancing down the corridor.

"What about him?"

"He just left with the healer and a boy."

"For fates' sake, follow them, you idiot!"

Ernest hurried down the corridor, pausing at the split of corridors at the far end. Ariana allowed herself a self-satisfied smile. The guardsmaster would be long gone before Ernest found them.

"You have defied the sanctity of my home and made my people your servants when all you deserve is to be one yourself," King Christopher said. "You will take your men and leave the castle. Now."

Lemuel crossed his arms. "And what if I don't?"

"Then you will pay a greater price than what you claim for your family's comfort."

"Are you threatening me, your highness?"

Ernest came running back. "They're leaving the castle! I tried to stop them, but the guardsmaster shook me off. I think they're going to get help."

Lemuel bolted after Sir Martin and the others, and Ernest followed. Oliver came out of the records room and took in the situation, stepping forward to block Ariana's way. King Christopher blinked in surprise then ran after Lemuel and Ernest. Ariana took two steps toward them, but Oliver held his arms wide.

"Now, now, Councilor," he leered, "you wouldn't want a punishment worse than the shackles, would you? Unless you bargain with *me*. Then I might take them off."

He let a suggestive gaze travel up and down her frame, and suddenly Ariana could not tolerate any of it. She let out a wordless yell and kicked Oliver as hard as she could in the shin. He dropped to his knee with a yelp, and Ariana kicked him again in the side. Oliver roared, and she dashed after the rest. Before she made it halfway down the corridor, though, Oliver yanked her back.

"See?" he said with a malicious smile. "You've just made things worse for yourself."

Christopher reached Lemuel and Ernest as they reached a place in the corridor that branched into three.

"Which way did they go?" Lemuel demanded.

Ernest shook his head, panting. "I don't know."

Lemuel grit his teeth and turned to Christopher. "Where did you send them?"

The absurdity of their circumstances—Lemuel overtaking the castle yet still looking to him for answers—made Christopher snigger. The entire situation struck him as absurd, in fact: wearing the same clothes for days on end; a wishing well that discerned his selfish thoughts; discovering the loyalties of his dearest friend lay elsewhere. Losing the love of his life.

All of it, so profoundly absurd, made Christopher shake with laughter.

"You won't think it's so funny when your precious court sees you in shackles. Ernest?"

Ernest grabbed Christopher's left arm, sending daggers into his shoulder, and pulled both arms behind him. Christopher tried to blink away the stars he saw from the pain.

"Take him to the petitioners' hall, and tell the others to bring everyone else," Lemuel said. "It's time to end this."

Geraldine gulped huge breaths as she settled in the carriage from the royal stables. Alistair slid onto the cushioned bench opposite her and lay down, panting in shorter gasps. The carriage jolted forward, and she squeaked in surprise. A muffled apology floated from the driver's box.

The run through the castle had taken much longer than she'd expected or even wanted, and the sights she witnessed seemed to whir in her memory now. Dozens of people with mouths dropped open, some in castle livery and shackled like Councilor Ariana; others, Lemuel's men she thought, in plain clothes. Glimpses of rooms with fine furniture and rugs; wall sconces with intricate metalwork designs; cavernous spaces that could have swallowed her cottage. She wished she could've taken a moment to enjoy them once again as she had during her months by the queen's side.

"The horses are much fresher than the ones that pulled our other carriage," she said in a voice pitched too high.

Alistair didn't respond.

"Sweetheart?"

Still no answer.

Please let us not be too late for Alistair or the Keeper.

She pushed aside the curtain at the window. Her own carriage had simple wooden benches and an open-air top. This carriage provided a roof and curtains to block the sun. Geraldine fingered the fine fabric at the windows, which, she realized, also contained square panes of glass one could roll open and shut.

The evening hour offered paths almost empty of traffic. Geraldine craned her neck out the window and saw the pulsing of the joined heart stones from where they sat next to Sir Martin. The beating orchid light acted like a beacon, reminding her of what she'd heard about lighthouses on the edge of the sea. The carriage, too, rocked less and almost glided, much like a ship.

"Can you believe that man at the castle?" Geraldine said. "I hope the king makes things right. After all..." A yawn interrupted her words. "After all he's endured, he deserves some rest. In fact, we could all use a good night's sleep. But don't worry, we'll reach the Keeper soon, and then after that..."

Despite her intention to keep Alistair company, Geraldine's eyes fluttered shut.

Hours later, the carriage jolted to a stop and woke Geraldine. She was unsure for a moment of where she was. The moon shone through three windows to her left onto Alistair, and she scrambled to sit up.

"Mistress Geraldine."

The door to the carriage opened, and Geraldine rubbed her eyes. Sir Martin waited for them to descend the steps of the carriage. She leaned forward and shook Alistair.

"Alistair? Alistair, darling, wake up."

He sighed in his sleep but didn't move.

"We're back in Ingleside. We need to take the heart stones to the Keeper."

"Perhaps I may wake him," Sir Martin suggested.

She nodded, her hands clammy as she took the pouch with the heart stones. The pulsing became more rapid, reminding her of how her patients behaved when their breathing became shallow. They often reacted that way when they were scared...or close to the end.

The thought distracted her, and Geraldine missed a step as she left the carriage. Instead of a graceful drop to the ground, she half tumbled and landed hard on her right foot. A sharp pain made her gasp, and she took a moment to test her weight on the ankle.

A twist, she thought, shaking her head. *I have to be more careful.*

"Mother?"

"Here, Alistair." Her heartbeat matched the pace of the light from the stones.

"Hurt?" he asked as Sir Martin helped him out of the carriage.

"No, my sweet, but we must hurry. I think the Keeper needs us urgently."

His head bobbed in agreement, but in the pulsing light Geraldine could see how his eyes became unfocused as Sir Martin put Alistair's arm around his neck.

"Guide us on our way, Alistair," the soldier said. "We cannot accomplish this task without you."

Alistair's attention returned, and he nodded. Geraldine held out the heart stones to him. He put his hand on the joined pieces and shuddered.

"What's wrong?"

"Not wrong," he whispered, his eyes closed. "Better."

She handed him the pouch, and he clutched the heart stones to his chest. The light stretched to form a beam of orchid sparkles pointing toward the woods. Geraldine waved Alistair and Sir Martin ahead, hobbling after them and ignoring the pain of every step.

They retraced the path they used more than a week earlier. After several minutes, the pulsing beam took a sharp turn to the right and lit the top of a pile of white ash taller and wider than any other they'd seen on the journey. Geraldine's heart lurched at the sight of the former tree, and Sir Martin grunted. Alistair sucked in a sharp breath and coughed again.

Just then the heart stone light traced the pile down to the ground, turning the ash a brilliant violet color that made it glow from within.

"Keeper," Alistair said in Geraldine's ear, startling her.

"What do you mean?" she asked, her heart beating even harder.

"Keeper's tree." His voice broke. "Gone."

Christopher held his head high as he followed Lemuel to the petitioners' hall. The axe grinder had found a pair of shackles, and now Ernest walked next to Christopher with the chain of the shackles in his hand as if Christopher were a mere pet. Lemuel's other comrade, Oliver, held the chain of Ariana's shackles, dragging her along.

"You will suffer consequences for handling members of the court in this manner," Christopher said to Lemuel's back.

"You're not my king anymore."

"Saying so does not exempt you from the laws of the land, Lemuel."

"You're not in a position at the moment to dictate anything."

Insolent child, Christopher thought. *This will end tonight, come what may.*

People trickled down the corridors, everyone going toward the petitioners' hall, and Christopher knew those who worked in the castle by the shackles on their wrists and their livery. Their reactions to his return seemed mixed. While all of them shared the same shock, some smiled in relief. Others grimaced. A few studied him with expressions he could not read. His cheeks burned as their eyes traveled to the shackles on his wrists.

Ernest led Christopher down the aisle of the hall toward the head of the room. Lemuel quickened his pace and went to the dais, watching the progress of all those who came. His men swaggered into the hall behind their charges, and the sight of them revitalized Christopher's anger. These men did not possess the wherewithal to lead a train of mules, never mind a kingdom.

He saw King Malcolm enter, two men following him. The sight of him in shackles made Christopher's heart clench. The king's face showed a mix of relief and apprehension.

King Malcolm stopped in front of Christopher and offered him a hand. Christopher took his father-in-law's hand in both his own. He squeezed hard and received an answering squeeze.

"The fates smile upon Linden," King Malcolm said. "It is good to see you in the castle once again."

Christopher bowed over their hands. "I am indebted to you, your highness. Ariana told me of your tireless efforts to maintain Linden's diplomatic relations."

"Anything to protect the kingdom's interests from this cretin," King Malcolm said with a glance over Christopher's shoulder.

"As you can see," Lemuel announced, "the king has returned. He believes he can still rule, even though he ran at the first sight of a challenge. It's time we find a new ruler. Better yet, we should rule ourselves."

"Here, here," called several of his men.

"And you believe you will lead Linden and all its residents in this new life?" Christopher asked.

"At least I stayed, your highness," Lemuel said. "I saw the injustice happening to my family, and I took a stand. Where were you? Oh, I forgot: running."

"I left to search for answers, Lemuel, to root out the source of the threat to our kingdom's greatest resource. You have spent the week hiding from your family's challenges, sulking because the answers do not suit your current state of life."

Lemuel rolled his eyes. "You've only been king for seven years and brought this terrible disease to our trees. Who knows what else might happen if you continue to rule? I say we need a new system in place, and we don't need the likes of *you* at the head of it all."

"I take it you have formulated a grand plan to rule then?"

"I know when to take the worst of a situation and turn it into an opportunity. Bailey, bring in our newest contribution to Linden's exports."

Bailey smirked and left the hall. Several moments later, he returned carrying two quarterstaffs. As he came closer, Christopher's skin prickled without knowing why.

"You see, your highness," Lemuel said as Bailey came down the aisle and handed him the weapons, "it occurred to me we have all this wood coming back to Linden and nothing to do with it. The other kingdoms don't want it anymore, but it's still good lumber. So I asked a few of my comrades to experiment with the wood, and they made these."

Christopher recognized the color and grain pattern in the wood of the quarterstaffs, and the full meaning of Lemuel's words doused his confidence in cold shock.

"You...you created weapons out of Linden wood? But that is impossible. It cannot yield to evil intentions."

"If the wood is losing its magic, it'll yield to any intentions we have," Lemuel said, that ridiculous smirk still on his face, "and the intention I have is to turn whatever is usable into a new resource for the kingdom. After all, if we're taking the kingdom in a new direction, then it's time we offer the best of Linden to the rest of the land."

His men cheered, and a snake of fear slithered up Christopher's spine.

"What happened to the Keeper?" Geraldine asked. "What do we do now?"

Alistair tightened his grip on the heart stones and closed his eyes; Geraldine prayed to the fates for guidance.

The beam of light from the heart stones inched from the pile of ash and down a hard-packed lane back into Ingleside. Geraldine shifted her weight, wincing at the pain still in her ankle as the beam settled in its new location.

"We must seek answers elsewhere, Healer," Sir Martin said in a gruff voice, holding out his hand for the heart stones. "It will do neither you nor Alistair any good to strain yourselves further."

Geraldine nodded, unable to respond with words.

They climbed back into the carriage, and Sir Martin directed the horses to turn around and follow the lane into the village. As they traveled, the stench of the decay around them pressed into the carriage. Geraldine could almost taste it, as if she'd bitten into a moldy piece of bread. She shook her head to rid herself of the horrible sensation in her mouth, but it didn't go away.

"Keeper," Alistair said with a moan.

"We can't lose heart, Alistair," Geraldine said, trying to believe her own words. "She must have found a safe place to hide; that tree was just a tree."

"Just a..."

Tears rolled down his cheeks, and Geraldine chided

herself for her choice of words.

Within minutes, the woods thinned and gave way to the homes and businesses of the village. The moon stood high overhead, lighting everything in a pearlescent glow. Geraldine cursed the night, wishing it didn't look so beautiful.

Terrible things should happen on terrible nights, she thought, the words sour in her mind.

The carriage rocked to a stop.

"We have arrived, Healer," Sir Martin said through the carriage door. He opened it and offered her a hand. Grateful, she took it and leaned on him as she climbed out.

"Do you recognize this home?" he asked, reaching into the carriage for Alistair.

She stopped short, her gaze going from the heart stones to the cottage they illuminated.

"Widow?" Alistair asked behind Geraldine.

"Yes," she said. "This is Widow Hannity's home, but... why?"

Sir Martin tethered the horses to the fence.

"There is only one way to answer your questions, Healer."

The heart stones directed their beam at the house, and the pulsing became so rapid it almost looked like a steady ray. Geraldine put a trembling hand to her throat. She pushed open the gate in the fence and walked the short path to the front door she'd entered countless times before.

In those dozen steps, she thought of the first time she'd visited the healer who became her mentor. New to Ingleside, she didn't know anyone other than Sullivan and, later, the new life she carried inside her. Widow Hannity took care of her and her child, and she taught Geraldine how to take care of others. How to heal.

How to live.

Christopher's mind raced. How could the wood consent to being fashioned into weapons? Would the weapons become affected by the failing magic?

The fates help me, what do I do now?

"Your silence tells us as much as your escape," Lemuel said, satisfaction radiating from him. "It's obvious you shouldn't rule. Many of us have felt that way since you ascended the throne. After all, a son of Vincent is bound to continue his father's mistakes. It's time you let Lindeners rule themselves."

"Linden for Lindeners," someone called.

Others took up the cheer, and soon their voices rang to the ceiling.

"Christopher."

He turned to his father-in-law.

"They are challenging your right to be king, my son," King Malcolm said, taking in the men cheering and pumping their fists. "You must show them you alone deserve the right."

Christopher looked around at the people Lemuel had brought with him. He saw, too, those who worked in the castle under his rule and guidance. Their faces urged him to take action. His gaze came to rest on the quarterstaffs. He called to Lemuel then, and the head of the resistance raised his hands to make his people quiet.

It galled Christopher, how they listened to Lemuel.

"A leader leads with words and example," he said. "You have shown you are capable of both, but the crown of Linden is my birthright. I will not yield it."

Lemuel snickered. "How do you propose to settle this

then, your majesty?"

"With a duel of quarterstaffs. The winner will lead Linden."

Cheers and groans alike rose, and Christopher's heart began to pound.

Geraldine knocked on Widow Hannity's door for the third time. "Widow Hannity? We need to speak to you."

Her mentor didn't answer. Alistair shuffled to the door and knocked. Nothing.

"What now?" Geraldine said.

"Could she have gone to visit someone?" Sir Martin asked.

"There's no one for her to visit," Geraldine said. "She has no family. She's a widow, for fates' sake. No children; no siblings. Her parents are long dead."

Alistair cupped his hands around his eyes as he looked through one of the windows.

"Is it possible she is attending to a patient?"

"I don't know. But that doesn't explain the heart stones."

"Inside," Alistair said. "Answers."

"I agree," Sir Martin said. "If Widow Hannity cannot open the door, it is possible she may be in danger."

He went back to the front door and tried the doorknob. To everyone's surprise, it wasn't locked. Sir Martin put a finger to his lips and gestured for Geraldine and Alistair to follow him. Geraldine helped Alistair move back to the porch as the soldier opened the door and peered inside. After a moment, they entered the cottage. Sir Martin shut the door and took a moment to survey their surroundings in the semi-darkness.

"Alistair, the stones," Geraldine said.

He took them out, and the stones beamed a steady light toward the hallway leading off the living room. Geraldine's heart pounded as she recalled their meeting with the Keeper. A thought unfurled in her mind.

She remembered all the times she watched Widow Hannity deal with patients in a kind but detached manner. The unfazed way she approached life. When Geraldine puddled on her doorstep into loud wails about the horrible words she and Sullivan exchanged, Widow Hannity took Geraldine inside. She sat with Geraldine, rubbed her back, listened to the incoherence bubbling with Geraldine's tears.

But she never shed a single tear in solidarity. Didn't rage in commiseration. Not once did she even raise her voice on Geraldine's behalf in a rant against Sullivan. Afterward, whenever Geraldine thought about that midday visit and remembered the widow's reaction, she wondered whether the woman endured something much worse that taught her to remain stoic.

Now as she, Alistair, and Sir Martin followed the heart stones, Geraldine knew what it was, which made her question every memory of her mentor and friend.

The light of the stones beamed brighter the farther down the hall they went. Geraldine had traveled down this same hallway dozens of times as she assisted in caring for patients too sick or contagious to return to their own homes. What would they find now?

A blast of glittering purple light poured from the last doorway on the right. Geraldine's hand fluttered to her mouth, and Alistair hesitated. The soldier pushed ahead, and they turned into the bedroom.

The widow lay on her bed, and a keepsake box on the top of the dresser beamed back the purple light. Alistair hurried to the box; Geraldine went to Widow Hannity. Sir Martin stopped at a respectful distance just inside the doorway.

Her years of experience treating patients told her the widow was dead even before Geraldine put two fingers to her neck where her pulse should have thrummed. Her training—the training this very woman gave her—forbade her from making a formal pronouncement until she confirmed the worst. As her fingertips rested on the widow's skin, Geraldine prayed to the fates she would find some hint of life.

She didn't.

"Mother," Alistair called. He handed her a piece of paper and fell into the lone chair in the corner of the room. Without another word, he dropped his head into his hands.

The light from the heart stones allowed Geraldine to read the paper with ease.

> My dearest Geraldine,
>
> I know that you and the king had good intentions to rejoin the pieces of my heart. As I write this now, I realize I won't live to see you again.
>
> You may wonder about the "widow" title ahead of my name. Vincent and I never married, but I wanted to ward myself from other young men. In some ways, I was a widow of my own love when it died. If not a widow in truth, I felt one in fact.
>
> I have no regrets about my life. You cannot imagine how freeing it is not to get entangled in matters of the heart. When Vincent promised me the world, I should have known then that no one has the right to make that promise. No one has the right to offer every single happiness available to us. The fates and our own stupid choices keep us from accomplishing it.
>
> I always did my duty as Keeper of the Wood, but I found my truest contentment in taking care of the

people of Ingleside. Helping to heal their cuts and bruises, the wounds of their hearts, and the gashes across their souls. I counted myself lucky every single day to live here and help them.

When you came to me all those years ago, so young, I debated about warning you not to trust your heart too much. We don't listen to reason when our hearts overflow; we get swept away with emotions and forget to keep our sights on the horizon ahead.

I learned that early on and know true heartbreak. It's horrible, and now I'm tired. I just want to rest.

I realize this isn't the answer you sought, that by the time you read this you've traveled all over Linden to search for the heart stones. I know I said it doesn't matter to me whether you find them, but now, at the end of my life, I hope you do. My heart, when complete, might still do some good.

Take care, my dear girl. Even if I could no longer feel love, I considered you a close friend, and I knew, even with my head, that my life was richer for having you in it.

Much love to Alistair.
Gail Hannity
Keeper of the Linden Wood

The last few lines blurred on the page as tears filled Geraldine's eyes. She sank to her knees, and the pain from losing her mentor and her friend pressed her down until she found herself curled around her own heart on the floor. Her sobs grew loud, and for a few minutes she cried as she had never cried before to mourn one of the dearest people she knew.

CHAPTER 22

Geraldine wanted to spend the rest of her days on the floor sobbing. For the first time since hearing the Keeper's story, she could see the value of not possessing a heart. No heart meant she wouldn't have to spend her life experiencing this pain.

She didn't spend days keening, however. Even there, in her deepest grief, a pinprick of conscience reminded her why they followed the heart stones in the first place. She sat up, her sobs slowing until only her breath hitched.

Could the completed heart still help the wood? The Keeper had seemed to say so in her letter. Geraldine scrubbed her face with the heels of her hands.

"Alistair," she said. A hitch cut the word in half; she tried again. "Alistair. The...the heart...stones. We need to rejoin them."

Alistair stared into empty space, but he held the stones out to her. Their comfortable weight settled into her palms. Pushing herself off the floor, she went to the box on the dresser where Alistair found the letter. In it sat the fourth heart stone, this time pulsing the familiar purple light. Geraldine gulped as she placed the joined heart stones, now pulsing in time to her heartbeats, next to the fourth piece. Would something terrible happen when the four came together?

Please, she urged the fates, *don't let all this be for nothing. The widow's sacrifice, Queen Lily's death, the failing of the trees...please, let this work.*

She pushed the pieces together, cupping her hands around them to make sure they would touch. They fit into one another without hesitation. When Geraldine pulled away, though, the pieces didn't stay joined. They separated and continued pulsing.

Why didn't they... How do we make them...

She tried pushing the pieces together again, and once again they fell apart.

Geraldine's hands got clammy. Didn't the stones need to become one heart? Didn't the magic of the wood depend on the heart being whole and well? How could they get the heart stones to fuse into a single living entity?

What would happen if they didn't?

Christopher waited for Lemuel to consider his challenge.

"A duel?" Lemuel scoffed. "You're willing to settle the fate of the kingdom with a duel?"

"I tried reason, and you refused it," Christopher said. "Perhaps you will understand the language of a tavern common room."

"It always comes down to violence, doesn't it, your highness? King Vincent used it to solve everything."

Christopher's cheeks burned. "I am not my father, but every monarch understands when force is the one viable option left."

Lemuel rubbed the back of his neck. Christopher wondered whether the man would allow common sense to prevail and step back from the ridiculous mess he created, or whether he would insist on following along. Weariness pressed on Christopher's shoulders then. Since entering the castle, he wanted nothing more than to retreat to his private apartment and sleep.

"All right," Lemuel said, "we'll duel. Maybe, by fighting me, you'll understand that the common man of Linden has more strength than you're willing to admit."

And perhaps dueling with you will allow Martin and Geraldine time to accomplish the deed Linden sorely needs.

He held up his shackled wrists. "Remove these, and let us commence. I need to return to my duties."

A cruel smile unfurled across Lemuel's face. "If you're prepared to do anything for Linden, then you can fight with those on."

Christopher examined the manacles and counted the inch-long links on the chain. Twelve links offered just enough slack to give him comfort of some movement. Not enough to wield a quarterstaff with ease, but, then, he did not need to display fighting forms of the staff. He simply needed to keep Lemuel engaged long enough for Martin and Geraldine to reach the Keeper so they could save the wood and he could reclaim the castle as king.

"Agreed."

Geraldine's mind raced as she tried, again and again, to push the stones together. She refused to accept they might not form a full heart again. She owed it to Widow Hannity to continue her legacy.

I won't let Widow Hannity die for nothing.

The heart stones still refused to join to one another; after several attempts, Geraldine dropped her hands in frustration.

Think, Geraldine!

She turned to the box that had held the final heart stone and found nothing. The widow's letter remained where she'd dropped it. Geraldine read it again as if it would yield additional information. On instinct she flipped the paper over.

For the next Keeper of the Linden Wood. To be spoken with clarity of heart and mind.

Widow Hannity had left a spell to make the heart stones fuse to one another.

"Alistair, look!"

She thrust the paper at Alistair, showing him the spell, and a smile grew on his face.

"Save trees," he said in a soft voice.

"Yes, we can..."

She thought of her son's love for the wood. The serenity that enveloped him whenever he spent time in the forest. The inexplicable way the moss attacked him.

Could saving the stones be tied to Alistair because the trees want to claim him?

"*You* can save the heart stones, Alistair," she said. "You can save the trees. You can be the next Keeper of the Wood."

His head jerked up from the paper, and his eyes grew big around. Despite the pale color of his face, Geraldine could see it get a shade lighter. She knelt next to him where he still sat in the chair and took his hands in hers.

"Don't you see, Alistair? You're fated to do this. You love the wood more than anyone I've ever known. Maybe even more than the widow herself. She's given you a way to tie yourself to the forest, and I know she meant for you to take this responsibility. You'll never have to worry about anyone thinking less of you ever again."

Alistair frowned, and Geraldine got the sense that he was trying to gather his strength.

"Father. You..."

She squeezed his hands. "Don't worry about me, my sweet boy. I can take care of myself. I've done so thus far, haven't I?"

Sir Martin came and knelt next to her. "Your mother's reasoning makes sense, Alistair. If Linden loses her wood, people will suffer, but you..."

"Won't leave Mother," Alistair said, defiance in his eyes.

Her eyes filled with tears again. "You wouldn't be leaving me. You'd be right here, in the wood, and people would listen to you and respect you. It would be like starting a whole new..."

I wish from all of you a sacrifice. Healer Geraldine, you will forfeit one of your greatest gifts. Alistair, you will leave behind your former life.

The wishing well. The time for its demands had come. Geraldine realized the well had demanded the widow's friendship from her. It required now that Alistair step into a whole new life with this role.

"Don't you see, Alistair? We have to do these things. This is what the wishing well meant. If we don't, Linden and the wood and you..."

He dropped the letter and clasped her hands, shaking his head.

"Not Keeper. Not strong. Not brave."

Geraldine's mouth dropped open. Not strong? Not brave?

"You *are* brave," she said, her tears disappearing. "I know how you've suffered because of the boys who tease you for the way you talk. Yet you don't stop trying to reach people. You don't let them keep you from your lessons. You left the Keeper even though you wanted to stay with her. You've been fighting this horrible illness the tree gave you. You made the king address the wishing well, even though he didn't want the heart stone more than anything else. Not brave? Why, Alistair, that's *all* you are."

"Alistair," Sir Martin said, "if you were a soldier, I would be proud to serve in a regiment with you."

Alistair barked a laugh. "Not strong."

"Strength comes in many forms, my boy," Sir Martin said. "There is strength of body, but over time that diminishes. Strength of heart never does."

"Sweetheart," Geraldine said, "you have to stop expecting that you'll be just like everyone else, because you will never be like them. You'll always be you, and right now the kingdom needs you. If you don't take on this role, then someone else will become Keeper and won't love the wood and the trees the same way you do. You have to stop being disappointed in yourself, because I never was. In fact, I always believed it was the other way around."

Her tears spilled once again as she dropped his hands. Alistair threw his arms around her and murmured words she couldn't make out. It didn't matter; she understood their intent.

After several more minutes in her arms, he pushed himself away from her and stood.

As soon as Christopher agreed to the duel while shackled, the hall exploded in exclamations. King Malcolm stepped toward him, lifting both hands so he could clap Christopher's shoulder. Christopher set his mouth in a straight line.

"You do not have to undergo this humiliation, Christopher. He can be dealt with."

"If I am to earn his trust and ensure he does not rise

against me again, your highness, I must give him some semblance of dignity," Christopher murmured back.

King Malcolm looked at him as if anew then stepped back and bowed.

"The fates favored my daughter when she married you. I am proud of the way you have conducted yourself, my son."

In that moment, Christopher knew everything would be well again.

"All right, your majesty," Lemuel called over the din of voices, "time to fulfill your bargain."

Bailey handed the king one of the quarterstaffs. Christopher tested its weight as well as his range of motion. His heart folded in anxiety at the heady scent and the familiar grain patterns of the Linden wood swirling down the edge of the weapon. If the wood yielded to this atrocity, what else might people do with it?

"Shall we begin?"

Christopher looked up in time to see Lemuel stomp toward him, quarterstaff in an attack position.

Geraldine and Sir Martin scrambled to their feet.

"Alistair?" she asked.

He clenched his hands into fists. A coughing fit took him, and he fought to stop. Geraldine put out her arms in case he fell or fainted, but he shook his head.

"No disappointment," he whispered. "No more."

"No more," Geraldine said.

He drew in a huge breath and held it for a moment then exhaled long and slow. "Mother."

The pounding inside her echoed in her ears as she went

to the chest of drawers for the heart stones. They warmed her hands as she scooped them up. After making sure Alistair held them tight, she went back for the letter and brought it to him.

"Now, just take your time, sweetheart."

He nodded and recited the spell, enunciating every syllable, tripping over words once or twice. As he spoke, the heart stones quivered then pulsed in time with one another. Geraldine blinked; their pulsing matched the rhythm of a heartbeat.

With the final words, Alistair cupped the stones together. The seams between them glowed like a full moon on a clear night, and Geraldine squinted as she shielded her eyes with one hand while still trying to watch. The heart stones fused together and stopped pulsing; instead they glowed a strong, steady violet light so bright that Geraldine looked away.

Alistair shrieked and dropped the heart; its glow filled the entire room, and it radiated the heat of a roaring fire. Alistair dashed out of the room. Geraldine followed him down the hallway and outside of the house.

They ran across the path and she turned back, expecting Sir Martin right behind her, but the soldier was nowhere in sight.

"Sir Martin!"

The violet glow shot through the windows and the chimney of the widow's home. The roof and the outside walls glowed the same color, and the glass in the windows exploded. Geraldine screamed.

"Sir Martin!"

The soldier ran out and across the path. He joined them, panting as if he'd run for miles.

"I thought...I might...save...your friend," he said, bent over and in between breaths, "but I could not...lift her... The magic refused...to let her...go, but...I...rescued...her heart."

He held up the leather pouch they all knew so well, and Geraldine threw her arms around the soldier.

"Thank you for trying." She gulped back the tears in her throat.

A roar from the house drew her attention, and she turned around just in time to see it explode into millions of violet and gold sparkles.

Alistair dropped to his knees with a cry, but Geraldine stood transfixed. The widow's home—the place she had run to in times of anguish and joy, to discuss a new recipe or a patient's prognosis—her refuge was gone. Her *friend* was gone.

Lemuel spun the staff with both hands over his head as his men cheered him on. The king raised his own staff, preparing to parry Lemuel's first strike. After two more spins, Lemuel swung the staff behind his back and around his side, then stepped forward with it like a javelin and jabbed it at Christopher.

Christopher blocked the jab and stepped back two paces. Lemuel shifted the staff and tried to knock it into Christopher's face. The king whipped his staff against Lemuel's then dropped to his knees and rolled away. In the middle of his roll, a lash of pain landed on his back. Boos made Christopher lose heart for a moment.

"Defeat him, your majesty!"

He found himself on his feet again and tried to swing the quarterstaff in a large circle. The staff entangled with the shackle chain, and Lemuel rushed at Christopher and swung at his head. Christopher ducked, then kicked Lemuel to throw off his balance. The move caused him to stumble and land on his back. He saw a quarterstaff coming straight to his face, and jeers from the crowd brought everything into clear focus.

His thoughts went to the wood in his hands. How had he allowed himself to use it to fight? Where were Martin, Geraldine, and Alistair? What happened to them?

The wide column of sparkles flew through the air and into the forest. As Geraldine gaped, the glowing motes infused the trees. The trees still standing began to glow, and she could see the light restoring cracks in trucks and enlivening the branches that drooped. The leaves became taut, spreading as if cheering in victory.

By the light of the magical dust, she could see the piles of ash from the destroyed trees. The glowing dust infused the piles one by one and caused the ash to swirl upward. Within moments, the sky was full of white ash floating as if winter's harshest snow had decided to rise to meet the sky instead of descend from it. Shoots of new growth broke the earth where the old trees had stood and reached for the sky.

Voices came to her; people ran out of their homes and exclaimed how the light from the trees lit up the lanes of Ingleside. She didn't pay attention to them; instead, she focused on what Alistair did.

The Linden wood had been restored.

Christopher blocked the blow from Lemuel and scrambled to his feet. He thrust his staff into the man's stomach. Lemuel grunted in pain but did not stop. He thrust his own staff into Christopher's left arm.

The king of Linden howled and dropped to his knees; Lemuel's men cheered again.

"You can't even sustain minor pains," Lemuel said, panting from his efforts. "How are you fit to rule?"

Christopher cradled his arm and looked up to see Lemuel raise his staff over his head. He tried to lift his own weapon to block the blow, but he knew he would not be able to do so in time. He tightened his grip anyway as Lemuel's staff came down toward him.

The quarterstaff burst into thousands of sparkles.

The snarl on Lemuel's face morphed into angry confusion as he stared at his empty hands. Christopher brought up his own staff, and it also burst into motes of light. His heart lurched as the motes floated toward the windows.

The wood!

The doors to the petitioners' hall burst open, and Queen Celia strode in with a regiment of soldiers. The castle staffers and councilors cheered, mimicking the fireworks bursting inside Christopher's chest. The queen made her way down the center aisle of the hall. She caught Christopher's eye, and her expression went from determination to concern.

Queen Celia stopped when she came to King Malcolm and offered him a deep curtsy. The king, in turn, offered her his most formal bow. The queen turned to the two guards nearest her, and they helped Christopher to his feet. Two more soldiers grabbed Lemuel by the arms, and men continued marching in until they filled the entire aisle between the pews. More soldiers entered the doors and spread throughout the hall until they stood behind Lemuel's men.

"For Linden and the king," King Malcolm called.

The Wyndemere guards took up the cry.

"For Linden and the king!"

Others chanted the words until the entire hall rang. Christopher turned to look at all of them and then faced Lemuel. The man's anger made his lips curl.

"What does all this mean? What did you do to the quarterstaffs?"

Christopher drew himself to his full height, despite the way his body ached.

"My people and I restored the wood," he said, "and the magic of the trees does not allow them to be used as weapons. You have lost your bid for my kingdom, Lemuel."

As the trees in Ingleside continued to glow, a young woman in a nightdress rushed to Geraldine's side and tugged on her arm.

"Mistress Geraldine, what's the meaning of all this?" she asked, her face lit with wonderment.

"The wood's been saved," Geraldine said. "Alistair..."

A dart of realization shot through her. She turned and saw Alistair still on the ground. As she dropped to her knees and put her arms around him, she thought he felt colder than before. But that didn't make any sense. Wouldn't the restoration of the magic make him stronger?

"Alistair?" she said, shaking him. "Alistair."

The boy didn't respond. Instead his head fell forward, and Geraldine, caught off guard by his weight, half slipped as he fell. She did her best to ease him down, but he landed hard on his left side.

"Alistair!" she screamed. "Sir Martin, help!"

Sir Martin picked up Alistair. He searched their surroundings and found a wheelbarrow someone had left in a garden. Cradling the boy in his arms, he lay Alistair in the wheelbarrow then grabbed its handles, grunting with effort.

"Where should we take him, Healer?"

Geraldine tried to draw a deep breath but found she couldn't.

"Perhaps your clinic," Sir Martin said in a gentler tone, "I believe it might be of use to us in this instance. You may find what you need there."

She bobbed her head as if it were one of those silly toys with springs. "Yes, the clinic. Please hurry, Sir Martin."

She ran ahead of him as fast as she dared, clutching the widow's heart and pleading with the fates for her son.

CHAPTER 23

"As king of Linden, I declare the wood restored," Christopher announced.

Several court members cheered.

"And how do we know you're telling the truth?" Lemuel sneered. "Maybe you've learned some peddler's magic while on your travels and just performed a trick to distract us."

Christopher turned to King Malcolm. "Sire, with your permission, I would like to command your soldiers."

"They are yours," King Malcolm said with a courteous nod.

"Wyndemere soldiers," Christopher called, "I ask you to open the window coverings."

Murmurs rose in the hall as the soldiers complied with Christopher's order. Within minutes, the elaborate wood shutters swung open to reveal the grove of trees outside. The trees glowed in the same sparkles as the quarterstaffs just before they disappeared.

Lemuel's face became red, but Christopher could not tell whether from anger, fear, or embarrassment. The man struggled against the hold of the guards to no avail. After several moments, he consented to being held but glared at Christopher.

The king fought the urge to squirm at the tight pain in his arm. It reminded him of the fight in the same hall more than a week earlier, of the way Lemuel threatened the sanctity of the castle with his selfishness. Anger flickered then disappeared. He did not have time to waste on frivolous men.

"I suppose you'll order my execution next," Lemuel said.

"I do not believe in violence for the sake of violence," Christopher said. "I prefer diplomacy."

He waited for Lemuel to relax before finishing his thought.

"However, there are times for diplomacy, and there are times for more forceful measures. Wyndemere soldiers, confiscate the keys to the shackles, then lead Lemuel and his followers to the dungeons."

Lemuel protested loudly, but Christopher eyed him without a word. The soldiers in the hall moved with speed to gather the rogue guards into tight knots and retrieve the keys to the chains of Linden's loyal subjects. Within minutes, castle staffers and Christopher's councilors were free. As they rubbed their wrists and the hall filled with exclamations and conversation, a guard came to Christopher.

"Sire, with your permission."

He gestured to the shackles Christopher wore, and the king extended his wrists to the guard. The soldier unlocked the shackles and hung them over one shoulder then bowed and moved back to join the group of guards around Lemuel. Christopher called out short directions to the dungeons, and the guards marched out of the petitioners' hall with the prisoners. As some of Lemuel's men passed him, they gave Christopher looks of contempt.

Ariana stepped forward and offered him a deep curtsy. "Welcome back, your highness."

The other councilors mirrored Ariana's actions. "Welcome back, your highness."

Christopher acknowledged their obeisance with a short bow of his own then went to the nearest pew and collapsed into it.

The violet haze from the trees lingered like smoke after a bonfire. Geraldine kept moving, blinking against the haze, the late hour, and her own fatigue. A slight breeze brushed her arms, and she shivered as much from exhaustion as from the coolness of the late hour. The light around them transformed to a muted gray.

Is the Keeper's magic changing the way the entire world looks now? Oh, my poor Alistair. What else will this spell take from him?

Shame flashed then disappeared. Alistair had restored the wood. She could put all of her attention on him and on restoring his health. She didn't need to spend time worrying about anything else.

A chittering nearby caught her attention, and she realized the muted gray wasn't connected to the trees; it came from the start of a new day.

In the soft gray, her arms seemed to shimmer. Her breath caught. What did this mean? Had the magic touched her in some way?

I don't need any more complications in my life. Alistair needs me.

As she approached the clinic, she realized the front door stood ajar.

"Sir Martin?" she said over her shoulder. "I don't... Could you..."

"Wait here, Healer," he said, setting the wheelbarrow down. Without another word, he charged forward, a drawn dagger in his hand as he pushed through the door. Where in all the wood had he found a weapon?

She went back to the wheelbarrow and smoothed Alistair's

hair back. Moments later, Sir Martin returned to her with a frown.

"It is your husband, although I do not know why he would... What he..."

The air around his words grew wary. "What?"

Sir Martin opened his mouth then closed it again. She waited for him to continue his thought. He didn't.

"I don't have time for guessing games," she said, striding forward. She pushed through the clinic door and stopped short. Sullivan was bent over her money box. Her gaze went to the ring of keys in his hand, poised to insert one into the lock.

"Well, well," Sullivan said, straightening, "if the wayward wife hasn't returned home. Had your fill of adventure?"

"What are you doing?"

"I needed funds for new flatware."

"So you're just taking what I earned?"

"How was I supposed to know you'd come back?" he snarled. "You ran off, leaving me with nothing but a note and a lot of nosy neighbors asking too many questions. For a while, Widow Hannity made excuses for you, but then she stopped seeing me too. Did you expect me to sit around and pine after you?"

"I don't have time for this, Sullivan. I—"

"Of course not. You never have time for what's important to me. It's just your son and your patients and this *sap-sucking* clinic."

"How am I supposed to make time when you practically live at the inn?"

"If I stay there, it's because people appreciate what I do, and I'm working hard to earn a living for our family."

"Not hard enough if you have to steal from your own wife."

Sullivan jerked back as if struck. His expression wavered between embarrassment and malice. For a moment, Geraldine thought he would apologize and ask something, *anything,* about why she was coming home in the middle of the night like this.

Boots behind her announced Sir Martin's return; she opened her mouth to ask about Alistair, and he placated her with a gesture.

"Did you run off with the guardsmaster?" Sullivan said, his chin trembling. "Is an innkeeper from a village no longer good enough for you? Or do you like being someone's night visitor?"

She charged forward, but a force pinned her back. Sir Martin. She balled her hands into fists, struggling against him.

"He betrayed your trust, Healer," Sir Martin said. "Do not betray your dignity for him."

Anger burned white hot at what Sullivan called her, but she knew Sir Martin was right. Alistair needed her right now. She stopped fighting against the soldier's strong grip. He gave her shoulders one last squeeze, as if to remind her to behave, and let go. She let her gaze drop to the money box for a moment then marched forward and slapped Sullivan as hard as she could.

"You tree-burning maggot," she spat. "You have no idea what I've been through to come home."

"What *you've* been through?" Sullivan said. "What *you've* been through? What about what *I've* been through? Living with a wife who's shut me out all these years, who's always behaved like I was the villain in a story. Everything was to take care of you, of *us,* but you've only seen where you've been wronged. What about the times I tried to make things right? Have you ever thought about that?"

Memories and assumptions warred inside her. She recalled how she and Sullivan had left their little village with promises to take care of one another no matter what. She thought of all the times, after Alistair's birth, that they'd fought and how easily Sullivan rebuffed her. The way he turned away in the dark or yelled at her to leave him alone or simply left the room.

All this time, she'd convinced herself Sullivan hadn't cared. That he turned away because he didn't love her or yelled to drown out the way she second-guessed him. Not once, she was ashamed to admit, did she stop to consider that she'd hurt him just as deeply. That he would have complaints, valid ones, against her. Never, though, had she stolen money from the inn. Even in the moments when her anger roared inside of her, she'd never considered stooping so low.

Any shred of love they'd had blew away in the whirlwind of discovering his theft.

"Get out," Geraldine said, narrowing her eyes at Sullivan. "I need to take care of my son."

She expected him to fight back. If she were honest with herself, a part of her hoped he would. Instead, after glaring at her one last time, he marched out the door. Her one consolation came in the way his palm slid to his cheek and stayed there. A sob clawed at the back of her throat, but she wouldn't—couldn't—give in to it now.

"Sir Martin, please bring Alistair in here. I need to skirr him to see if I can determine what might be wrong."

The soldier carried Alistair into the clinic, grunting under the boy's weight. She directed him to the back room where he transferred Alistair to the narrow bed. After taking the wheelbarrow outside, Sir Martin came back and stood in the doorway. Geraldine realized she still held the heart stones and handed the pouch to him.

"Can you take care of this for Alistair?"

Sir Martin bowed his head in a single nod. Geraldine turned her son's palms over and placed her hands on top. Her arms shimmered even more by the candle she'd lit, and she wondered what it meant before closing her eyes and asking the fates for allowing her skirring to work this time.

Her palms tingled within seconds, making her eyes pop open. The skirring came so easily; how? What did it mean?

Later, Geraldine, she chided herself.

She allowed her energy to search him. Her forehead furrowed as she examined each part of him in her mind. All his main organs, his limbs, his blood flow, all of the primary functioning features of Alistair's body throbbed with signs of good health.

The energy she sent shifted, and she flinched.

What is this?

She realized her attention had wandered and pressed her hands against Alistair's hands again. For the first time, her energy did more than skirr a patient. It flowed into Alistair with the intention to heal and sent images like the shards of light a diamond made in the sun. She wondered if the Keeper's health would have looked this way.

A jagged longing for her friend engulfed her for a moment, and Geraldine fought for control of her attention again. She could feel Alistair getting stronger. His heart beat so loudly and clearly that she opened her eyes.

"What is it, Healer?" Sir Martin asked.

A whimper escaped her throat.

"Geraldine, what is it? How fares Alistair?"

Tears streamed down her face as she withdrew her hands.

"He's all right," she whispered. "He's going to be all right."

The tension seeped out of Sir Martin's body. He hung his head for a moment then smiled a full smile that crossed his face the way they'd crossed Linden. She'd never seen him so relaxed. He looked younger. Less militaristic.

"Thank you," she whispered. "I couldn't have brought him here without your help."

He shook off her thanks, tucked the pouch with the heart stones into the crook of Alistair's arm, and gestured for her to follow him out of the room. She kissed Alistair on the head and pulled the summer-weight blanket up to his shoulders. Picking up the candle, she followed Sir Martin and closed the door behind her.

They made their way to the sitting area in the front of the clinic. Geraldine remembered the light meal they'd all sat for there, what seemed an age ago now, before the table collapsed and they'd embarked on the journey for the heart stones. With a sigh, she settled into a chair and made a mental note to commission a new table soon.

"I owe you an apology," Sir Martin said, easing into the chair across from her.

"For what?"

"I have been harsh with you, Mistress Geraldine," he said, "unnecessarily so, I know now. I suspected your intentions at the start of our quest. When the queen returned to the fates..."

He stopped then, and his gaze fell to his hands.

"You loved her."

"As a loyal subject. As a friend. When the king ascended the throne, he honored me with the role of guardsmaster. Our responsibilities grew, and we could not devote as much time to the friendship we enjoyed when he was crown prince. Queen Lily honored and encouraged our friendship and became a friend in her own right, especially when I shared my desire for the Left Ones. When we saw you here in Ingleside afterward, it brought the loss of her—and my deep dislike for you—to the fore. But I was wrong about you."

A short laugh escaped Geraldine's lips. "If it's any consolation, I wasn't fond of you in the beginning either."

The soldier chuckled, but after a few moments his mirth faded.

"Thank you for your part in saving the wood. Your contribution was invaluable and irreplaceable."

Geraldine's cheeks got warm.

"I'm sorry you lost such a dear friend. Maybe...maybe we could become friends one day."

The soldier's lips twitched, and another smile appeared. "Perhaps."

Two days later, Christopher winced as a gentleman-in-waiting helped him dress after bathing. All the days of travel had left him sore, and the fight with Lemuel had exacerbated his aches and pains. The bath helped, but now, as he tightened his left hand into a fist and opened it again, fatigue washed over him.

After Lemuel's arrest, Christopher had returned to his private apartments with trepidation. The fear of losing Linden dwarfed in comparison to the dread of knowing Lily was gone. His victory at the restoration of the wood seemed incomplete without her shining eyes to tell him he had done well.

He had pushed in the door and waited for the heavy mantle of grief to return to his shoulders. Instead, a memory came of the first time he brought Lily to the bedchamber.

With amusement making her lips curl, she asked whether she could change a few of the furnishings.

He chuckled now as he sat on a wide stool with a leather seat and planted his feet into a pair of fine boots. Lily allowed him to keep the stool, but most everything else disappeared within her first year as queen. When he asked her why she allowed the stool to remain, she quipped she wanted him to feel at home. It was, after all, as much his bedchamber as hers.

A knock at the door brought his thoughts back to the present. A present that he lived without her. At one time, that thought threatened to shred his day in tatters. Now he accepted it. Could the quest to find the heart stones have changed him so much?

His gentleman-in-waiting answered the knock. "Sire, Guardsmaster Martin."

Christopher nodded. "He may enter."

The man pulled the door open, and Martin crossed the threshold. Christopher dismissed the gentleman-in-waiting. The man bowed to both him and Martin and left.

"Your Majesty," Martin said with a bow, "I have received news from the outer villages."

"And?"

"The white ash has disappeared completely. On the sites of the lost trees, new saplings have begun to grow and the brush surrounding the saplings has been restored to full health. The lumber guild reports we may see restoration of the trees within the year, provided no other harm befalls them."

Christopher exhaled a short breath as his shoulders rounded. "Thank the fates."

"We have sent runners on all major thoroughfares to Linden to intercept caravans carrying lumber from other kingdoms," Martin went on. "As ordered, the runners carry promissory notes to compensate the kingdoms for the lost logs."

"I will also need to speak to the councilors regarding the structures and tools that dissipated before the restoration. We must find a way to reimburse those involved."

"As you wish, sire."

"And the new Kee... Alistair? How fares Alistair?"

"Mistress Geraldine sent word his health is the best she has ever known, and his new role suits him as if he were born to it."

"The fates chose well, then."

"They did, your majesty."

While Lily's death no longer weighed on him, Christopher carried a pocket of disappointment in his chest since receiving word of the Keeper's demise. He never met Widow Hannity, but Geraldine had spoken of her often during their journey. The healer held her mentor in the highest esteem. The fact that Widow Hannity and the Keeper of the Wood, the woman who loved his father and made such an immense sacrifice for him, were one and the same still confounded Christopher. Saving the wood seemed less triumphant without the return of the Keeper's good health to her.

"Have Lemuel and the others troubled the guards?"

Martin's countenance darkened. "Lemuel tried to protest their conditions when I made my rounds, but I informed him protests would not be entertained. I also told him I would personally address any further complaints. He appeared much more amenable."

Christopher inhaled, bracing himself. "Next week I will announce their release from the dungeons."

"They do not deserve to be released, your majesty."

"They are residents of Linden, Martin."

Martin's scowl became deeper. "They held members of court hostage. The king and queen of one of Linden's closest allies, your highness."

Christopher acknowledged Martin's words with a nod. "If I am to encourage a rehabilitation of their mindset, they must trust I will treat them fairly."

"They committed treason."

"They made grave errors," Christopher said in a gentle voice. "They wished to better the lives of their families and themselves. To claim what is their right. If their methods were extreme, their ideas were not. I must remind them, even in the heat of their tempers, that they are my subjects. I will not abandon them to their wiles as my father would have."

Martin crossed his arms, his stormy gaze directed to a corner of the room.

"Release from the dungeons does not mean absolution, however. I do not want them to reach the incorrect conclusion that they can behave as they did and not suffer any consequences."

"Releasing them from the dungeons will give them and anyone else with such ideas of insurrection that very idea."

"They will be released from the dungeons, not their punishment," Christopher said. "They will not return to their homes for a full year. Instead, they will reside in the castle's outer apartments with the rest of the servants. Hard labor should temper their anger and teach them the castle is not a figurehead. We do, in fact, care for our people. With the opportunity to witness the castle's workings firsthand, I hope their opinions of me and the throne will change."

"And the funds they demanded?" Martin asked. "You say what they claimed was their right. Does it remain their right even now?"

"I have spoken to the council and the royal accountant, and we will allow the families to come to the castle during this year and receive foodstuffs and other necessities in an amount equivalent to the silvers and coppers owed them. We will not reward the insurgents with coin, but we will not punish their families for their foolishness."

Martin's expression remained unchanged.

"Lily would have treated hot-headedness with kindness, Martin. We must continue the work she began. She would have had it no other way."

His guardsmaster's body relaxed.

"Now, on to other matters. Are all members in place for the procession this afternoon?"

They discussed the details of the event: a memorial procession through the city in Lily's honor. A scant hour later, Christopher sat in his first meeting with his councilors since returning to the castle. There he reviewed the details again.

"It was my duty to ride in the funeral procession after Linden's queen returned to the fates," Christopher said. "I did not fulfill that obligation, and I do not want to give the residents of Rosewood and the kingdom at large a chance to accuse me of shirking my duties ever again."

At the mention of the queen, the councilors bowed their heads.

"After the release of Lemuel and the others, I will announce a special commendation for you, Ariana, for helping Queen Celia escape. Your contribution to keeping the members of the court safe was invaluable, and the kingdom should know of it."

"I did what any of the councilors would have done, your highness," Ariana said, her cheeks flushing.

"All of you proved your loyalty and bravery as well as your integrity," Christopher said, letting his gaze sweep over his councilors. "I will be forever indebted to your faith in me and your willingness to risk yourselves for the sanctity of the kingdom. I may hold the throne, but the wellbeing of this kingdom is maintained by all here."

Soft murmurs of appreciation went around the room, and Christopher's gaze stopped on Head Councilor Duncan. His bruises had begun to fade, but Christopher knew all of his councilors had suffered in ways not visible to the eye. He concluded the meeting and encouraged the councilors to take the day to rest. Everyone deserved some peace and quiet after the harrowing events of the past two weeks.

"Martin," he said as he exited the meeting hall, "I wish to meet with Lemuel."

Martin's eyes tightened, but he bowed. "As you wish, your highness."

A quarter of an hour later, Christopher stood in front of Lemuel's cell.

With a reassuring glance at Martin and the other soldiers who accompanied him, Christopher turned and met Lemuel's gaze. The dozen oversized candles on the wall behind him lit the dungeon cell so he could see its every part.

Lemuel glared at him from the narrow bed on the right tucked into the back corner. To the man's left sat a wooden desk and chair. The desk, Christopher knew, was bolted into the wall. Made of the hardiest Linden wood, it could not be ripped from the dull gray stone and used in a harmful method. Neither could the chair, no matter how much the simple four legs invited rage to break them.

Unlike other monarchs, Christopher allowed prisoners to

leave their cells one at a time under supervision to visit the basic comfort room at the end of the corridor. Prisoners could call for a guard four times a day to relieve themselves. In the spring, summer, and more pleasant days of fall, the guards shackled the prisoners twice a day and escorted them to the large yard in the back of the castle for fresh air and exercise.

"What do you want?" Lemuel asked.

"I came to see how you fare."

"How do you think? You've imprisoned me. Five days ago I was sleeping in a bed in the castle, and now I'm stuck on this."

He banged his fist against the thin mattress and winced.

"You are responsible for your state," Christopher said. "Had you and your friends used more amiable measures, you would have returned to your family."

"Empty-handed? That would have defeated the purpose of my coming here at all, wouldn't it?"

"What was your purpose in coming to the castle that day, Lemuel?"

"To take care of my family," the man said, springing to his feet and coming to the bars of the cell. "I was supposed to save them. But you wouldn't know anything about saving others, would you, your highness? You've never worried about where your meals came from or whether you could afford candles or oil to burn your lamps all month. You don't have to hang your head when you stand in front of your neighbor *yet again* because your larder is so empty even mice leave it alone. You've never lived in another person's shadow."

Christopher did not reply. He would not share his personal challenges with Lemuel, and he would not change the man's mind even if he did. His only recourse was to try to be a good ruler and hope that, in time, Lemuel would understand.

"You know what the worst part of all this is?" Lemuel went on in a bitter tone. "You know I was right. King Vincent wasn't giving Lindeners—us, his people—what we deserved."

Christopher sighed. "You are correct on that point, Lemuel. My father exhibited the worst kind of greed, and I am committed to making it right."

"Meaning what?"

"Meaning, in a week, you and your friends will be released. At that time, I will reveal to you how I plan to restore to the people what is rightfully theirs."

Lemuel grabbed the bars and squeezed them. "How?"

Christopher shook his head. "I understand my predecessor made mistakes, Lemuel, but so did you. It would serve you well to spend this week thinking on the serious errors you committed. We will speak again when your imprisonment has ended."

Lemuel slammed an open palm against the bars and this time barked in pain. Christopher turned from the man's taunts to return and finish the conversation. A few of Lemuel's friends called to the king from adjoining cells, but Christopher did not stop for them either.

As he made his way to the steps that led to the main level of the castle, he considered Lemuel's charge of living in another person's shadow.

If you had made different choices, Lemuel, he thought, *you would have discovered what I did: eventually those choices allow you to move out of the shadows so that light surrounds you.*

That afternoon the sun shone bright and hot overhead in the outer courtyard. Christopher could not stop a sigh as he climbed into the carriage for the procession. Geraldine and Alistair settled themselves on the cushioned bench across from him. Alistair's skin glowed with good health; the moss had disappeared, and he looked like any youth in the city.

He gave the king a broad grin. "Carriage. Again."

Christopher fought a smile. "Yes, Alistair, once again we travel by carriage. I had hoped to avoid it for some time."

"And how would you have managed your diplomatic relations, your highness?" Geraldine asked with a chuckle. "By carrier pigeon?"

"I could have attempted it, Healer," he said, feigning a frown.

They shared a quiet laugh; it felt good to enjoy a joke with friends once again.

I am beginning to understand why Lily engaged Geraldine's services, he thought.

The thought of his first love brought a peculiar sensation to Christopher: happiness. In returning to the castle, he discovered his grief no longer sidled up to him. The happiness bewildered him and left him relieved by the same token.

"I will be forever indebted to you, Geraldine. To you and Alistair both."

As the carriage jerked forward, the healer shook her head but smiled at the same time. "I should be saying that to you, your majesty. Going on this journey gave me the courage to make a decision for a better life for Alistair and me. And Alistair's found his true calling. I only wish we hadn't lost the queen."

Christopher's smile dimmed. "The event has changed my life."

"And mine, your highness."

"And you, Alistair?" he said. "How do you find your new responsibilities?"

Alistair ducked his head. "Trees, home. Mother, happy."

The carriage pulled through the streets at the pace of a garden snail, and Christopher resisted the urge to tell the driver to increase their speed. He tried to distract himself by waving at the people who lined the streets to watch the process of the three carriages in the caravan—two full of guards in front and behind the king with his carriage in the middle—but even the smiles of his subjects could not keep his mind off the heat.

Unlike the covered carriages he used in other travels, this carriage did not include a full roof. Instead, a canopy above their heads purported to protect them from the sun. Still, perspiration ran down Christopher's back, and he wondered whether he could ask the driver to stop for a few moments at an inn for a cool drink.

This day is as much for Linden as it is for Lily, he chided himself. *Small discomforts can be tolerated for both.*

Geraldine and Alistair continued a steady stream of conversation. With the repayment of her income, Geraldine bought a cottage at the edge of the city. When Christopher asked, as delicately as possible, about Sullivan, she simply shook her head.

"We've agreed that some time and space may be good right now," she said. "The new cottage gives us both, but it's close enough to Ingleside that I can still take care of my people there. I can also come into the city to see Sir Mar—the friends I made in the castle while caring for the queen."

"It is good to foster new friendships," Christopher said, trying not to react to her slip. "I hope, in time, you will consider me a friend as well."

Geraldine offered him a sweet smile, the most relaxed, sincere one he had seen from her in all the days they were acquainted; it made him think of Lily and how happy she would have been to know he was mending wrongs he committed.

They returned to the castle later in the afternoon tired, hot, and thirsty. Geraldine declined Christopher's offer to come inside for refreshment but promised to return soon. With a warm goodbye, she and Alistair climbed into a city carriage bound for their corner of homes in Rosewood.

Christopher returned to his apartments for a quick bath. Just as he finished dressing, in less formal garb this time, a knock sounded at the door. His gentleman-in-waiting answered it.

"Your highness, his highness, King Malcolm, and her highness, Queen Celia, have just arrived."

Christopher frowned. When the king and queen left, they made no mention of a return this soon. His heart fluttered with the possibility that something untoward had happened on their journey home, yet the gentleman-in-waiting did not look ill at ease.

"Have their belongings sent to the royal guest apartments," he said, "and ask the kitchen to prepare cooling refreshments."

The man hurried away, and within minutes Christopher made his way to the private receiving hall for royal guests. Two of the soldiers who followed him stationed themselves on either side of the doors, and a third soldier entered the hall. A few moments later, he announced it was safe to enter and the king did so.

"You may wait outside," Christopher told the king and queen's attendants as they bowed to him. "Ask for a page to send for refreshment for all of you."

They bowed again and left; Christopher turned to his father-in-law and mother-in-law.

"Your highnesses," he said, placing a hand on his heart.

"I welcome you to Linden once again. Is all well? I did not receive word of your travel."

"All is well," King Malcolm reassured him as they sat. "We returned, in part, because we made a discovery and could not wait until the next festival season to share it with you."

"We believe the fates and a certain wishing well brought it to our attention," the queen said with a kind smile.

The king tilted his head. "Wishing well...?"

Queen Celia exchanged a look with King Malcolm.

"When I escaped the castle," she said, "my travels took me to Ellery. I found the wishing well, and I made a wish for you."

Christopher sat up in surprise. "For me?"

"The king and I have one another," she explained, "but you are alone, my son. I did not want you to carry that burden for the rest of your life, so I wished the grief of losing Lily would dissipate and that you would remember her in your happiest moments together. And then I discovered something in the castle in Wyndemere that convinced me the wish would be fulfilled."

"What?"

"One of Lily's paintings."

Christopher's heart clenched but not, he realized, with pain. It clenched with excitement. Anticipation.

Confusion.

"But...the former Keeper's heart stones destroyed... How..."

"In the first year of your marriage," Queen Celia said, "when she returned to us for the festival season, Lily spent her time talking of you and painting. She complained the paints in Wyndemere could not compare to her paints here. Too ordinary, she said, but she would give it her best."

"She completed a portrait of the two of you," King Malcolm said.

"Of us?"

"Yes," Queen Celia said, "and we brought the painting with us. In fact, we took the liberty of instructing your staff to hang it in your study. I hope we did not overstep, but in the circumstances we believe we erred on the correct side."

"A portrait of Lily and me," Christopher repeated.

"Yes, my son. A portrait so you may spend your days with the best of her and so it will inspire you to become the best of yourself."

He bolted to his feet. "Forgive me, your highnesses, but I must—"

King Malcolm stood but waved him on. "Please, go."

Christopher raced through the doors of the receiving hall, stopping just long enough to instruct the startled attendants and soldiers they should help the king and queen settle in the guest apartment. Without another word, he dashed down the corridor to his study. Footsteps behind him told him the soldiers followed, but the sounds became distant as he threw open the doors of the study and ran inside. A ladder still leaned against the far wall, and Christopher jerked his head from side to side looking for the portrait. He turned and saw it hanging above the doors.

Lily had painted a garden scene—the same garden, he realized, where the plants for her paint pigments used to grow—and flowers bloomed all around them on a glorious spring day. In the portrait, his face remained in profile as he put his concentration on her. His arms enclosed her at the waist.

The portrait Lily did not look at the portrait version of him, however. She looked straight at the real him, and for one moment Christopher wondered whether she would speak. Would the wishing well grant him the luxury of hearing her voice again?

After staring at the painting for several moments, he realized how foolish he was. The love of his life had been a talented painter, no doubt, but she had created this portrait with ordinary paints from Wyndemere. Not the magic paints of Linden.

He let go of the breath he only now realized he held and hung his head for a moment. Should he leave the painting on the wall? Could he come and work, day in and day out, knowing that he would never see the love of his life again?

What should I do, my queen?

No answer came from the portrait, but as his eyes searched every bit of her face and the way the two of them held one another, it brought her to life in his mind and heart. Once again, he could hear the sound of Lily's voice. The way she laughed when she beat him in a game of chess. The hard edge when they argued about a trade treaty. The quiet whispers in his ear as they came so close in the bedchamber that a single garment could not find space between them.

King Malcolm and Queen Celia said Lily had painted this in their first year of marriage, and memories of that year tumbled through his mind. He thought of Queen Celia's words—that she had the king, but Christopher had no one. Did the wishing well really deem him worthy of enjoying Lily's company like this then?

She will always be this young and framed in this era of our lives together. She will never be the queen who lost the baby or returned to the fates.

Happiness made his heart feel as though it would burst.

She has left me this valuable gift. I may not be able to hold her hand again, but she will be my Lily forever.

Everything he had endured since losing Lily had brought him to this realization: the Keeper may have allowed her own heart to splinter to avoid lifelong pain, but she also lost the possibility of immense joy. Lily may have returned to the fates, but he alone could treasure the gift of loving her.

Losing Lily meant his own heart had broken, but knowing he had her love forever had also healed it.

THE KEEPER'S ANSWER

I took the heart stones of the former Keeper and planted them where her old tree used to stand. Within weeks, a new tree took root in that place. When I'm not traveling to different parts of the kingdom to check on the forest, I come back to the tree and place my hand on it to feel the depth of the Keeper's friendship.

I've thought a lot about what the Keeper—Widow Hannity—said about hearts and how living without one allowed her a lifetime of peace. In some ways, I understand what she means. My own heart screamed when the boys in Ingleside would bully and tease me. But it's like Sir Martin said: physical strength can get weaker over time. The strength of a heart doesn't have limits.

Mother and Father have spent the last few years working out their differences, but I don't think they'll share a home again. They're both healing from the hurts they've caused each other, but that healing is leaving scars that are still visible. Whatever else happens in the future, I want both of them to be at peace.

Sir Martin and King Christopher come to visit often, Sir Martin more than the king. I see the way he looks at Mother, and I wonder how their friendship might change in the future. If it did, I would be happy for both of them.

The king, too, is happy again, and everyone can see it. I hear Lindeners talking about it as they come through the wood to visit one another or to play. One of the things that has made my heart happy is to encourage the people of the kingdom to spend time in the forest again. They're rediscovering its beauty and that it can offer them more than a resource for money. Some still don't understand that last part—Lemuel, for one—but we can't change everyone's hearts.

The former Keeper may have given hers up willingly, but I don't think I can ever do the same. It's tied too closely to the trees, their majesty, and their friendship. It's an incredible, precious gift. For the rest of my days, no matter what else may happen or what challenges befall the kingdom, I will always find my true calling—my life's greatest accomplishments—in the heart of the Linden Wood.

ACKNOWLEDGMENTS

There's a reason why writers often compare their books to having babies. The first one is utterly terrifying and absolutely magical all at the same time. The second one is both the same and completely different—all at the same time. The magic happens during the writing process; the terror has diminished, but it's still there. Yet there's also a sense of accomplishment on a different level than the first book. The first will always be your first; the second is your reassurance that, yes, you actually can do this thing, do it (mostly) well, and do it more than once.

All that to say that I have to thank mostly the same people but also all new ones this time around.

First, a big thank you to author Erin Morgenstern. Without her ethereal novel *The Night Circus,* I would never have written this book. I finished Erin's book for the first time several years ago and, along with wishing I could actually go to the circus myself, thought, "That felt like a fairy tale. I wonder if *I* could write a fairy tale."

Just like with *The Truth About Elves*, I set out with *Linden* with the express intention of turning conventions upside down. Most modern-day fairy tales end the same way: "...and they lived happily ever after." As I started brainstorming ideas for this novel, I thought, "But what happens after the 'ever after'? What happens if the king loses his queen—what then?"

Christopher's story came fairly easily after that, and so many people made it shine.

Peggy Williams, mentor extraordinaire! I'm so grateful that I got to be a part of the Pathway to Publication program (and still utterly heartbroken—the same way the Keeper was—that the program has since been disbanded.) Your thoughtful questions made me dig deeper into these characters and this story. It's because of you that it found its way as it did, and if I achieve any level of success with this book a big part of that belongs to you. Thank you, Peggy!

A huge thank you, as always, to Jennie, my first reader on so many important manuscripts through the years. Only a true friend like you wouldn't bat an eye when I sent final chapters at 11:45 p.m. on New Year's Eve so that I could meet my own deadlines. Big hug!

I also want to thank my beta readers. These six brave souls didn't hesitate when I asked them to read the book and give me their honest feedback. They even had to fill out a questionnaire and everything! (Hey, I wasn't about to let them off the hook with a simple, "Yeah, it was good" or "Nope, not for me.") Bette, Cari, Heather, Jeanne, Natasha, and Suzanna: your feedback helped me make this book even better. Thank you!

To my family:

Nat, I know I thanked you in the list of beta readers, but you are, after all, my sister. Thank you for your unending support, for sharing my posts on social media, for getting people excited about my books. It really means more than I could express.

To Di-Di, Jijaji, and Jaytin: Thank you for giving people copies of *Elves* and talking about it to so many others. It's bewildering and heartwarming that you have so much faith in my work. I hope you feel the same way about this book as well.

Thank you to my father-in-law for the gift of this gorgeous desk where I sit every day and pound on the keys to make these writing dreams come true.

To my husband who went to every single book event with me when *Elves* released: thank you for making the rounds and chatting people up, for texting everyone repeatedly about *Elves*, and for reminding me how important it is to put myself first sometimes.

To my children, Sixteen and Fourteen, who heard the first version of this story on that birthday trip to Niagara Falls and kept asking when I was going to get it published already. Here you go! I hope I've made you both proud.

To my parents who taught me the art of storytelling in the first place: I love you, Mom and Dad. All of my stories have some connection to you, because I am first and foremost your child. I hope I've made you proud as well.

A huge thank you to the entire team at Atmosphere Press! Several times a week, I find myself thinking about how blessed I am to have you on my side.

Nick, your fast response when I sent you this manuscript was the best start any girl could get to summer vacation. I'm looking forward to working together on many books to come!

Asata, when I think about the fact that this is only the second book we've worked on together, I find myself a little mystified. How is that possible when I feel like I've known you for so long? Thank you for your insights in making this the best it could possibly be.

Kevin, my dream cover designer: I swear you have Linden magic in your hands. My deepest apologies for the number of times we went back and forth to get this one right, but it was so worth it in the end. Once again I've fallen in love with your work. Thank you!

Cam and everyone in marketing: I find myself invigorated

every time I talk to all of you. Thank you for literally spreading the word everywhere about *Linden*!

Lastly, this is for you, my wonderful readers. I'm starting to find my space and voice as an author. Thank you for being willing to come on the ride with me and for your encouraging words in person, via email, and in your reviews.

If you liked this book, please leave a review on your favorite online retailer. Even a couple of sentences helps independent authors like me continue doing what we do: bring the stories of our whole hearts to you.

ABOUT ATMOSPHERE PRESS

Atmosphere Press is an independent, full-service publisher for excellent books in all genres and for all audiences. Learn more about what we do at atmospherepress.com.

We encourage you to check out some of Atmosphere's latest releases, which are available at Amazon.com and via order from your local bookstore:

Icarus Never Flew 'Round Here, by Matt Edwards

COMFREY, WYOMING: Maiden Voyage, by Daphne Birkmeyer

The Chimera Wolf, by P.A. Power

Umbilical, by Jane Kay

The Two-Blood Lion, by Nick Westfield

Shogun of the Heavens: The Fall of Immortals, by I.D.G. Curry

Hot Air Rising, by Matthew Taylor

30 Summers, by A.S. Randall

Delilah Recovered, by Amelia Estelle Dellos

A Prophecy in Ash, by Julie Zantopoulos

The Killer Half, by JB Blake

Ocean Lessons, by Karen Lethlean

Unrealized Fantasies, by Marilyn Whitehorse

The Mayari Chronicles: Initium, by Karen McClain

Squeeze Plays, by Jeffrey Marshall

JADA: Just Another Dead Animal, by James Morris

Hart Street and Main: Metamorphosis, by Tabitha Sprunger

Karma One, by Colleen Hollis

ABOUT THE AUTHOR

Since her start in niche publishing in 2005, Ekta has written and edited about everything from healthcare to home improvement to Hindi films. She became a freelance editor in 2011 and is currently the managing editor of a community magazine. A writing contest judge and frequent writing workshop presenter at her local library, Ekta also hosts Biblio Breakdown on her author website. In this writing podcast, she offers exercises so writers can improve their craft and hear about great books all at the same time (visit https://ektargarg.com and click on Biblio Breakdown).

Ekta devours books like a kid on Halloween. She also manages The Write Edge (http://thewriteedge.wordpress.com) and its extension blogs of original fiction, book reviews, and parenting adventures. Outside of reading, writing, and editing, Ekta follows the latest gossip out of Bollywood, dances in the kitchen while she's making dinner, and tries to keep her compulsion to reorganize everything in check. She lives in Central Illinois with her husband and family.

In the Heart of the Linden Wood is her second book and first full-length novel to be published.

CPSIA information can be obtained
at www.ICGtesting.com
Printed in the USA
BVHW042003230723
667554BV00002B/9